Watchers

Watchers

S T Boston

Fourth Edition
Published 2013 by Creativia
Paperback design by Creativia (www.creativia.org)
ISBN: 978-1482514858
Edited by D.S. Williams

For Finley

Contents

Chapter 1

Pins and needles were the first thing Euri Peterson felt as he began to ease back toward consciousness from his drug-induced sleep. Pins and needles in his hands, similar to when he woke in the night having slept on his arm – only this was different. Somewhere far off in the real world, away from the dark spinning pool in his semi-conscious mind, he could feel sharp pain, pain in his wrists and pain in his ankles. As the seconds ticked by, the drug began to wear off, allowing him brief, fleeting snippets of reality: pins and needles and pain, the hum of an air-conditioning unit, the chill on his sweaty brow. Then he slipped back, reeling and falling into the depths of his cloudy mind. The unconsciousness was far more tempting than reality. Desperately, Peterson tried to hold on to it as he felt himself spinning once again – he wasn't ready to wake yet and face whatever it was that awaited him, but it was too late! The spinning pool released him, and he opened his eyes. If it hadn't been for the hammering pain raging through his head, Peterson wouldn't have even known he was conscious, as the room was completely dark. Blinking with slow, deliberate actions, he tried to clear the pounding, woolly fuzz in his head. Attempts to move his wrists and feet only caused the chair to which he was bound to scrape and skip across the floor, emitting a sound like nails scraping down a blackboard. As his eyes adjusted to the darkness, a thin bead of light on the far side of the room gradually revealed itself, followed by the dim, faint outline of a door. A chill ran through his body. Whoever was in charge of the air-conditioning had it cranked up high, and the cool air hit his brow, chilling the sweaty sheen which matted his greying hair to his head.

What can I remember, Peterson asked himself. *I remember the meeting, and giving the speech. I remember leaving the Convention Centre, the rush hour traffic of Kuala Lumpur and almost being late for the Presidential dinner at the JW Marriott. After dinner and a few drinks, I went to my room and showered before heading straight to bed.* The memories flooded back, one after another, each encouraging the next. *So, I remember going to bed,* he confirmed. *But then?* That's where the memories stopped and gave way to confusion. *Then I woke up here, bound to a chair in a dark room.* Peterson's heart hammered in his chest like a drum; the sound of it flowed through his body and filled his ears with a rhythmic throbbing.

He cleared his throat and forced back the dry, parched sensation on his tongue. "Hello, anyone? Hey?" he cried in a cracked and broken voice, the effort causing sharp pain to flare up in his throat. In almost immediate response to his plea, heavy footsteps emanated from the other side of the door, followed by the click of a latch and a blast of light which forced him to lower his head and close his eyes to protect them. Someone flicked a switch and more light flooded the room when an array of fluorescent bulbs buzzed and pinged reluctantly into life.

Small, deliberate blinks allowed his vision to adjust to the bright, light which filled the room. Lifting his gaze and ignoring the searing pain in his head, Peterson took a moment to take in his surroundings; the room was small, no more that fifteen feet square. Bright white walls were complimented by matching tiles on the floor. There were no windows and only one large, strong-looking metal door. The footsteps belonged to a tall, thick-set male with dark brown, swept back-hair. His jet black suit looked fresh from the dry cleaners and the shirt underneath was as dazzling as the walls. Reaching behind him, the stranger pushed the door closed with a heavy metallic clunk.

"Mr. Peterson," the man began, fixing him with chilling ice-blue eyes and the type of smile usually associated with overly-keen used car salesmen. "Firstly, let me apologise for the way we had to meet. It was believed that this was the only way possible for you to listen to what I have to say. What happens after that is entirely down to you." Something about his whole demeanour gave Peterson the chills, and as the stranger spoke, the false, crazed smile never once left his lips.

"Judging by my position," Peterson croaked, "I find it hard to believe I have any control over what happens next." Speaking was getting easier with each moment, but it was hard to hide the panic that was setting in. Whatever drug they had used on him was slowly wearing off, but not fast enough for him to figure out a way out of the situation.

"On the contrary, your destiny is entirely in your hands," the stranger contradicted. "You see, Mr. Peterson, we know who you are." Peterson watched him cross the room, the heels of his well-polished black shoes clicking on the white tiles like the ticking of a clock.

"Of course you know who I am," Peterson snapped. "I've been at the World Summit for the past week! I addressed almost every head of state in the world this afternoon!"

The suited stranger beamed at him, presenting a row of perfectly white, unnatural-looking teeth, "Oh I think you underestimate what I know," he sneered. "I saw your speech by the way. It was excellent!" His heels continued to click rhythmically on the spotless floor, the sound almost falling into rhythm with Peterson's heartbeat, which still pounded in his ears. Circling around behind Peterson, he slid his jacket off. "It's rather warm in here don't you think?"

"I hadn't noticed," Peterson replied. "Mr.— I don't think I got your name."

"My name is not important," the stranger answered curtly, then seemed to reconsider. "But I am a firm believer in good manners." The man approached Peterson's chair, "Robert Finch," he said, extending his hand. "Oh, excuse me, I forgot, your hands are otherwise indisposed at present." Finch treated him to a mocking smile before turning. His shoes clicked their way to the back of the room. Bound and helpless, Peterson watched as he neatly folded the jacket and placed it in the corner. The removal of the blazer made Peterson very uneasy; in truth, it wasn't that warm, in fact it was positively chilly. The monotone drone of the air-conditioner continued to hum away above the door, pumping more frigid air into the small room. Peterson suspected Finch had removed the jacket to prevent his blood from soiling it, and the thought terrified him.

"Enough games!" Peterson snapped. "If it's a ransom you're after, I'm sure you have the details for my people. They will pay. You must know both my company and I are good for millions of whatever currency you desire."

"Oh, you misunderstand the situation, Euri," sighed Finch, shaking his head. The use of his first name took Peterson off guard. Obviously the time for formalities was gone. "Euri Peterson, the Swedish businessman and director of Zeon Developments, the man who rose to fame two years ago with patents for hydro powered engines, as well as a host of other ingenious ideas to rid the world of its dependence on fossil fuels. Those very ideas secured you a scientific Nobel Prize last year. I'm guessing after today's keynote speech, there are a whole load of oil companies baying for your head on a stick." Finch walked behind him and clamped both his hands down on Peterson's shoulders, like an overzealous masseuse. The physical contact made Peterson want to retch. Finch brought his face down level with his ear, so close Peterson could smell the warm, garlic-scented breath on his cheek. "That is who you are, is it not?"

"Yes, of course!" Peterson's mind was reeling. Could this really be about his patents? And would the big oil companies sink this low? "I know my products are going to hit some businesses hard," he admitted in a shaky voice, "but really, kidnapping! People like me don't just disappear, you know."

Finch ignored the statement. "But that's not who you really are, is it, Euri?" he continued, whispering as if he were about to tell a secret no one else should hear. His hands were still clamped tightly around Peterson's shoulder blades, doing nothing to improve the restricted circulation caused by the restraints. "You see, Euri, we know who you really are!" Finch let the words hang in the air. Peterson froze. Finch must have felt every muscle in his body tense, the grip of those strong, vice-like hands not relenting for a second. "And the reason you are here, Euri, is because of who you really are." Finch finally released his hands and threw them up in the air like a manic preacher. "We're not interested in your inventions, or the fact that you might have pissed off a few fat-cat oil barons, Euri, it's much bigger than that! We not only figured out your true identity, but also the identity of the other three." Finch was standing in front of him now, that smile back and his eyes full of loathing. He resembled a venomous snake about to strike.

"Impossible!" Peterson spat, shaking his head.

"Entirely possible," replied Finch, obviously pleased with the impact his revelations were having. "It's taken us almost nine years to get to where we are today!" he shouted with glee, his words bouncing off the bare white walls. "Nine years to figure out who the four of you are. You were the last piece of the puzzle. Once we had you all figured out, it was just a matter of time. So just in case you are in any doubt, let's see who else makes the list. We have Jaques Guillard the EU politician, saviour of the Euro, the man who helped avert a pending economic crash." Finch counted them out on his fingers, "That makes two. Then we have Archbishop Francis Tillard, the holy man, head of the Catholic Church in France." Finch laughed. "A holy man, I mean come on, what a ruse. Even you must appreciate the irony in that one. Personally, I find it disgusting." Finch regarded him for a few seconds – the way a person might look at dog mess on his shoe – before continuing his rant.

"Last, but by no means least, and coming in at number four, we have none other than John Remy, President of the United States of America." Finch grinned, his smile as wide as that of a Cheshire Cat.

Peterson's insides turned to ice. For this Finch character to know so much, there was only one thing he could be, one place he could be from, and the thought terrified Peterson more than anything else had in his life. This moment, here and now, was his very reason for being, the one thing he was supposed to prevent. He had failed, they'd all failed!

"Well, you seem to have this all figured out, Mr. Finch." Peterson couldn't hide the anger brewing in his voice. "But as you said, I'm only one of four. What about the others? Just killing me will get you nowhere!"

"Oh I wouldn't worry about them." Finch grinned. "They're dead already; well, two of them are, anyway."

The statement hit Peterson like a train and he stared up at Finch in disbelief.

"You're the next on my agenda! The other one requires a more, shall we say, gentle approach." Finch paused, mulling over his own words, running a hand over his cleanly-shaven chin. "We have people in places and roles you can't imagine, places and roles you all missed!" He let the words hang once again, allowing Peterson to soak them in. "But I'm sure you can appreciate," he continued, "even we can't just whisk away the President of the United States in the middle of the night. No! As I said, that requires a more delicate approach. Unfortunately for him, he won't get the option you have; the chance to choose, the chance to live." Finch was pacing around the room again, seemingly enjoying every moment, knowing the torment it was causing. "You see; this World Summit was just what we needed: all four of you in one city at the same time. It gave us the chance to take you all out, in one fell swoop."

"Kill me," Peterson exclaimed in a shrill, panic-ridden voice. "Do it, because I won't accept any bargain you offer, any more than the other two would!" At least for the moment, Remy was still alive, and that afforded Peterson a spoonful of hope in this fast-developing ocean of doubt.

Finch chuckled and nodded in understanding, "Euri, I'm impressed; your courage is admirable, just as I would have expected, and while I knew all along none of you would choose to side with us, I'm going to lay out the offer, nonetheless."

Peterson tugged at the hand restraints, making the chair rock dangerously. "Why? What's the point?" he snarled through gritted teeth. "You've killed them, and I want no part in any deal. Just get it done."

Finch stopped pacing and spun around to face him. "Because I want to! Because I can, and because I know how much it will eat you up, in the brief moments you have left, before I have the pleasure of ending your long, worthless life! It's not every day I get to have a Watcher as a captive audience, let alone three of you! And to have the pleasure of killing you, –one by one, repaying some of the suffering and anguish you've caused to my people over the long years! When I watch you die, I'll enjoy the defeat on your face, knowing you've failed. Then, once I'm done with you, I will personally be attending to President Remy."

"How the hell do you intend to get to the US President?" cried Peterson. "Not even I can just walk up and speak to him, despite our role behind the scenes." His tongue scraped over his mouth like sandpaper. He desperately needed water, but he very much doubted he was going to get it.

"Like I said, Euri, we have people everywhere, infiltrated into places which are key to tonight's plan, as well as the bigger picture. Trust me when I say I will have no issue at all getting to President Remy; in fact, I'll just walk right into his personal quarters. He's staying not far from here; you know?"

"Aghhhh!" cried Peterson in a mixture of frustration and anger. He was tugging so hard at his restraints, the skin on his wrists felt as if it was being shredded away from the muscle beneath. "Do you really think that just killing the four of us will solve all your problems? These deaths won't go unnoticed, and the repercussions for you and your people will be massive. Do you have any idea what you're starting here?"

Finch smiled mockingly at the outburst. "What we're starting?" he sneered. "What we are *ending* is a more apt description. We know everything about you, Euri – you and the other three. We know how you operate. It's thought by my superiors that if just one of you chooses to help us, it will buy us time to complete our plans unobstructed. That said, we're not overly concerned. You see, what we have in store will only take a few weeks, before it becomes irreversible. Of course, we're not naive enough to think it will never go unnoticed, but when your people do eventually realise what's happened, we'll be more than ready." Finch paused and allowed himself a smug grin. "So, you will appreciate why I'm more than happy to kill you right now. It's your choice." Finch held his hands up like a set of scales. "Live?" he raised the left, "or die?" He pointed his right hand at Peterson's head and formed his fingers into the shape of a gun.

"What could you possibly hope to accomplish in just a few weeks?" Peterson's fear had turned to anger and it boiled in his gut.

"More than you could ever imagine! It's really quite beautiful, how we plan to put an end to this charade and claim what's rightfully ours. You really should join us and see."

"And in return for being a traitor, I get… what?"

"A place on the council, a position high in the new order which will arise. You'll retain your status as an Elder, but within our society. It's more than I personally would have offered, but I don't call the shots."

"You really are deluded," Peterson laughed. "Why did you bother to put this to any of us? Why risk the exposure of kidnapping us? You knew none of us would ever take the offer, you knew we would rather die, than help you achieve what we've been preventing for thousands of years."

Finch bent down and fished in the pocket of his suit jacket; Peterson caught sight of something metallic clutched in his hand when he straightened. A gun!

"There's one other piece of information we hoped one of you might help us with – the location of the Tabut." Finch eyed him, testing the weight of the gun in his hand.

"Not even I know that, none of us do," Peterson lied, managing a slight chuckle. "Even if I was privy to such information, why should I share it with you? I'm dead anyway!"

Finch raised his eyebrows in suspicion. "Really? Not one of the four Watchers knows where the Tabut is kept? I find that very hard to believe."

"Even if I knew, the information would be of no use to you. The Key Tablet hasn't been held here for more than three millennia."

"Oh, we don't mean to use it," Finch snapped. "We mean to destroy it!" Finch waved the gun, emphasising each word, stabbing the muzzle toward Peterson. "I could torture you. That might loosen you up a little."

"Do what you must," Peterson sighed. "We both know that torture is of no use, when it comes to extracting accurate information. A man will tell you anything, if you inflict enough pain." He could see the frustration on Finch's face and knew that though he might be a dead man, he had his captor on this one.

"Very well. We have other lines of enquiry to follow up, ones that will hopefully prove fruitful. It's a loose end my superiors would like to tie up." Finch waved the gun nonchalantly in the air, hiding the frustration caused by Peterson's accurate analysis of the situation. Even if he extracted a location from him, it would no doubt prove to be a lie. Besides, his orders were to make sure none of them were left alive by the end of the night. Peterson would be dead before they could figure out whether he'd sent them on a wild goose chase. With the Tabut dormant for thousands of years and no Key Tablet to activate it, it provided no risk as far as he was concerned. Trying to find it was a waste of resources.

"Well, Euri, we'd hoped that you might have seen sense, might have wanted to live and help us shape our new future, the one you and your people robbed us of. But as I suspected, it was a waste of time." Finch raised the gun and levelled it squarely at Peterson's head. "One good head shot for an instant death," he announced, as though considering his options, "or destroy your heart and let you slip away slowly over the next hour?" He waved the gun between Peterson's head and his heart and back again in a taunting fashion. "Even I'm not devoid of mercy, despite what your kind has put my people through." He swung the gun back to Peterson's head and Peterson closed his eyes. He would never open them again.

Finch fired a single shot, and the bullet passed cleanly through Peterson's skull, lodging itself securely into the plastered wall behind him, splattering the tiles with blood and tissue. The force of the blast knocked his chair over, and his limp body fell backwards. Peterson's shattered skull hit the tiled floor with a soggy *thwaaaack*. Blood poured from the wound and trickled along the grouting in small, geometric rivers of red.

Finch retrieved his jacket and brushed a few specks of dust from the sleeve, concealing the pistol at the same time. As he left the room, he removed a small radio from his trouser pocket. "It's Finch. Can you get a clean-up crew to room four? Needless to say, he never took the deal!" He didn't wait for a reply before placing the small handset back in his pocket.

Time was short and he had an appointment with the President.

Chapter 2

President John Remy began to feel the stress of the day slowly ebbing from his tired, aching body. Unscrewing the cap from a shot-sized bottle of bourbon, he poured the contents into an ornately decorated crystal glass. As he shook the last drops out, the ice cracked in protest as the warmer liquid swirled around it. Placing the empty bottle to one side, he added a measure of tonic water and gave the drink a gentle swirl before taking a sip. The taste of the warm, sour mixture against his tongue instantly relieved a little more stress from his tense muscles. Drink in hand, he padded across the presidential suite of the JW Marriott and eased himself onto the plush sofa before taking another generous mouthful. Savouring the icy burn, he turned on the television and put his feet up on the coffee table. Scouting through the vast array of programs available, he selected BBC News 24 and was met with a potted review of the last day of the World Summit. A middle-aged female reporter, who in Remy's opinion had more of a face for radio, was in the middle of a live broadcast covering the day's events. A brief montage of the speech given by Euri Peterson cut in and out of her report as she highlighted the important parts.

"*Euri Peterson claims that by using the technologies developed by his company, we can expect to see the production of oil-fuelled combustion engines cease inside the next ten years,*" she began. "*He followed this up with the bold claim that we can expect to see the world free of fossil fuel dependency by 2080. His claims were met by a wave of applause, but I'm sure there are those in the oil industry who won't be so pleased by these developments, despite the ever dwindling oil supplies. As you know if there were ever any future issues between Russia and the west, they could literally put a stranglehold on the world. A situation that everyone is keen to avoid"* The reporter's face on the screen was replaced by the studio anchor.

Remy was certain there was a significant amount of grief heading his and Euri's way from the oil firms – not to mention the loss in tax revenue worldwide. The American oil fields had all but run dry, and despite repeated surveys in the North Sea, the same could be said for Europe. The Siberian fields, now under Russian control, were the main ones left and it was down to them to see the world through to a time when hydro power could take over. *You can't make an omelette without breaking a few eggs*, he thought to himself, remembering the old cliché. Governments would have to adapt. The bigger picture was what mattered here, not bottom line profits, and the price of oil per barrel was creeping ever upward.

"And what of the keynote speech by President Remy?" asked the anchor in his pristine British accent.

The camera switched back to the reporter. *"More landmark moments, Mike. President Remy is claiming that all peacekeeping activities and the military presence throughout the Middle East will cease in the next six months. We've seen an unprecedented period of peace in the region, seven months have passed since the last suicide bombing, which claimed the lives of fifteen civilians in the Helmand Province of Afghanistan. I'm sure the American people must be wondering who is going to fill such big shoes, when President Remy's second term in office comes to an end next year."*

The footage cut back to the summit and Remy watched a similar montage of himself, which covered the juicier parts of his speech. Even after all these years in the public eye, he still found it uncomfortable to watch himself. Reaching for the remote, he switched the set off and drained the last of the bourbon and tonic from the glass, before placing it on the perfectly polished table. Standing up, he made his way through to the bathroom to prepare for bed. It was set to be another long day tomorrow, with an early departure on Air Force One, followed by more meetings and conference calls on the flight back to Washington.

Remy brushed his teeth before making his way back to the lounge to tidy a few things away. He definitely needed sleep, but with so much to do tomorrow, he doubted it would come easily. As he shut and latched his briefcase, a knock came from the door.

"Come in," he called, placing the briefcase on a luxurious oriental-styled chair. The head of his Secret Service task force made his way into the room, clutching a chilled bottle of mineral water. "Ah, Agent Finch," Remy exclaimed.

"Mr. President," Special Agent Robert Finch replied with a nod. "As requested, sir, one mineral water. I'll make sure room service is informed that the mini bar wasn't stocked."

"I wouldn't worry too much," Remy replied, "just set it down on the table."

Finch made his way across the room and placed the bottle on an ornate metal coaster. "Good speech today, sir," he commented. "I think your hard work has finally paid off."

"Well, I've never been one to count my chickens, as you know," he replied, "but I think we might finally be seeing an end to the years of war and unrest in the region." Remy walked over and took the bottle of water. "Are you the late shift tonight?" he asked, cracking the screw cap and tipping the contents of the bottle into a fresh glass. Finch eyed him as he gulped half the chilled liquid in one long swallow, before wiping his mouth on his sleeve.

"Yes sir, on the red eye shift tonight. I'm on post right outside your door." Finch edged a step or two back, waiting to be dismissed.

13

"Excellent, I'll sleep soundly tonight then," Remy commented, still holding the half-full glass.

Special Agent Robert Finch had joined his security detail in the week Remy took office. He'd been one of the youngest Secret Service Agents ever tasked with Presidential protection, taking up the role at the age of twenty-two, after graduating from West Point at the top of his class, with a bachelor's degree in Military Sciences. Over the past nine years, he'd worked his way through the ranks. Now, as Remy's second and final term in office was reaching its conclusion, Finch was head of the Presidential security detail, at the tender age of thirty-one. Remy hoped Finch would choose to stay on for the ten years of Secret Service protection afforded to former Presidents', but he suspected such a young high flyer would be tasked back to Washington, to rise further through the ranks.

"I've prepared the security detail for the morning, Mr. President," he stated. "The car will be picking you up at eight am sharp, the local police and our agents will have the route secured, and we should be wheels up and heading home by nine thirty."

"Thank you, Robert," Remy replied, opting to use the agent's first name, as he often did when they were alone. After all, he'd known the man for nine years and in that time, he'd come to like him. He respected both his drive and his ambition. "That will be all for now. I'd better try and get some sleep," he concluded, turning and carrying his glass through to the bedroom.

"Very good, Mr. President. Sleep well," Finch replied, before leaving the room and closing the door quietly behind him.

Remy changed into his pyjamas. The sight of the Presidential Seal on the breast of the shirt always made him smile. Almost everything was personalised and offered a constant reminder of his position – as if he could ever forget. The freshly laundered linen was cool and crisp against his skin, a stark contrast to the humid and draining weather outside; even at night the heat seemed relentless. Draining the last of his water, he touched the base of the bedside lamp, plunging the room into darkness. The thick, tailor-made blackout curtains ensured none of the bright city lights filtered into the lavish suite.

Lying in the dark, Remy closed his eyes and tried hard not to think of the conference call meetings he would need to make on Air Force One in the morning; however, the more he tried to avoid thinking about it, the more it crept into his mind. Sleep or not, it would be nice to be back in the cooler, crisper air of DC tomorrow. The humidity and heat of Kuala Lumpur were draining. Even though he spent so much of the time in air-conditioned buildings, it was like opening an oven door every time he stepped outside. The pungent heat helped retain the fumes and pollution from the countless motor vehicles that seemed to clog the streets, twenty-four hours a day. The smog hung constantly in the air, fouling every breath. He wondered how long it would take the air quality to improve in these Asian cities. once the world's de- pendence on fossil fuels was finally at an end. Thankfully, such a day would soon be a reality.

As the random thoughts filled his brain, the first waves of sleep crept up on him. Not something he was used to, sleep had never come easily, even before he'd held the most powerful job on the planet. The drowsi- ness increased, but with it, Remy started to experience a deep burning sensation in his chest. *Something's wrong,* he thought, a slight vein of panic running through his body. Propping himself up in bed, he tried to force back the sleep that was suddenly so desperate to claim him. The burning in his chest grew, spreading to his throat and mouth. His hands were shaking; something was definitely wrong, very wrong! He reached out with a clammy hand and located the lamp. Just brushing its cool metallic base brought the light back to life cast the darkness back to the very edges of the large bedroom. forced himself to sit up, swinging his legs out of the bed. He struggled to fill his lungs with air; sharp pains stabbed through his chest like a hundred daggers. His mind raced, trying to figure out what was happening. The room around him began to multiply. First, he could see two doors and then three, before they started to spin. He closed his eyes and shook his head, hoping to cast the sensation off. For a few short seconds, it helped to steady his sight and he searched the bedside unit to locate the Presidential Panic Button. Reaching for it, he froze as realization hit. Someone had gotten to him; he was in no doubt that a deadly poison was coursing through his veins – but how? Surely no normal poisons could touch him, they would just flush straight through his system without leaving him with so much as a headache. The gravity of what this meant was more than he could comprehend in his worsening state. He needed to get to his briefcase, and fast. Straining to stand and force his legs to take his weight, he placed a steadying hand on the bedside table. His hand slipped, knocking the empty glass to the floor. His legs gave out beneath him and he went down hard. Face down on the carpet, he caught sight of the glass, laying on its side. *The water*, he thought, *Finch brought me the water, it's the last thing I drank*. His brain refused to accept that Finch had any part in this, but reason told him otherwise. Earlier in the day, Finch had commented on the fact there was still no still mineral water in the fridge. He'd personally gone to get a bottle, knowing his Commander in Chief took a glass before bed every night, without fail.

More pain thrashed through his chest, snapping him out of his delirium. *The briefcase*! he thought again, *I need to get to the briefcase*. Summoning all his strength, he crawled across the thick, carpet, digging his fingers into its ample pile. It was a mere six feet to the chair where he'd left his briefcase, but it seemed like six miles. Blindly he reached up, fumbling, before he managed to knock it from the chair. *If they got to me*, he thought, *they must have gotten to the others*. The latches sprang open at his light touch. He blindly spilled the paperwork onto the floor; his heart beating so fast he thought it was trying to break right out of his body. Trying to focus through watering eyes, Remy tore the bottom lining of the briefcase free and reached desperately beneath it. Finding the flat, piano-black disc, he rolled onto his back and let out a shaky sigh of relief before pushing his thumb against the surface. Instantly the disc sprang to life, scanning his print and biometric signature. When the process ended, the surface transformed from black to bright green, releasing the disc into his fingers. "Yes, yes," the President gasped. Gritting his teeth against the pain, Remy clawed his way across the floor to the ensuite bathroom, each movement harder to manage than the last. The bathroom tiles were icy against his skin, sending a wave of uncontrolled shivers through his sweat-drenched body. In a final, desperate movement he threw the disc into the toilet and pulled the chain, activating the flush. Clinging onto the white porcelain rim like a drunken teenager at a keg party, Remy watched the disc spin around the bowl twice before disappearing. Pain exploded through his chest, stronger, more intense, and he released his grip on the toilet and fell to the cold tiles. Lying there in the dimly lit bathroom, Remy's vision blurred and darkened. Pain racked his dying body, and he closed his eyes and watched bright white sparks of light dance in front of his eyelids. With his last coherent thoughts, Remy prayed his message had been received, because if the other three had been compromised, there was only one hope left.

* * *

Finch checked his watch; ten minutes had passed since he'd left the suite. Fishing in his pocket, he removed the Presidential Panic Alarm and eyed it uneasily, expecting it to activate at any second and send a team of his best agents rushing to help the Commander in Chief. As the eleventh minute ticked by he relaxed a little. Surely by now, Remy was dead. Finch checked his watch again. Though only thirty seconds had passed, to him it seemed to have ticked away as slowly as an hour. Even though he'd clocked three deaths in a single night, this one had his nerves on edge. This was the final stage; his last nine years of service had all been leading to this one moment. The rewards for the completion of his mission would be great. He was to be given The Gift; it would push him through the ranks to the same social status as the few Elders who remained. He wondered what his new orders would be, no doubt something grand for the next stage of the plan. Once he possessed The Gift, no one could deny him a role in shaping the great future that was to come. Gazing down the hall he eyed Tom Richards, the agent in his line of sight. Richards was just another sheep, like the billions of others crawling all over the planet, ignorant to what was happening right under their noses.

Twenty minutes. Finch allowed himself to relax fully. He'd seen Remy drink half the water; just a sip was enough to kill him. By the time they found the President's body, there would be no trace of the poison left in his system. Even if they tested any water left in the glass, no trace of the substance would be found. No, it would appear to all that the great Jonathan Remy had died tragically of a heart attack during the night.

The nation would mourn his loss. No other president had been loved the way the American people loved Remy. In his nine years of office, he'd managed to repair the struggling Obama Care health scheme left by the previous administration. Now, thanks to Remy, good, fair healthcare was accessible no matter what the patient's social status. His peace-keeping work had seen the end of all conflict in the Middle East and doors had been opened for negotiations with countries such as North Korea. There had even been talk of changing the constitution to allow him to run for a third term. Remy had put a stop to it, claiming the constitution was sacred and should be adhered to. In truth, he'd been ready to take a step back. But the president had not been truthful to his people, they didn't know who he really was. Finch did. Finch had always known. After nine years of working next to his enemy, it was a relief to have finished the job.

Twenty-five minutes. Finch slipped the Presidential Alarm Fob back into his pocket. It wouldn't sound now. "Richards!" he called.

"Yes, sir?" The agent turned to face him from the other end of the hall.

"I'm needed down in ops, something about changes to the security detail for the morning. I'll send Agent Blake up to cover my post."

Richards nodded, he was a typical ex jar-head. Stern features and a square jaw was complimented by a buzz cut, so short it made it hard to tell if his hair was truly brown or a little mousier. "Sure, no problem, sir. I can cover the hallway. Nothing would get past the elevator anyway," he said confidently, adjusting his post so he could see both the door to the President's suite and the agent standing by the elevator.

Leaving his post, Finch made his way past Richards, patting him on the shoulder in appreciation. The agent by the elevator had the door open, the lift waiting and ready. Stepping in, Finch was whisked swiftly to the ground floor; a tinny, panpipe version of 'Greensleeves' keeping him entertained for the short ride before the doors slid open, depositing him into the lobby. Despite it being two am, the hotel was still a hive of activity. Many of the delegates from the summit were staying at The Marriott, and piano music and laughter emanated from one of the high-class lounge bars. It was obvious many of the visiting dignitaries were making the most of the free drinks on this last night. Finch flashed his all areas access pass at the armed police guard at the door and exited into the rear courtyard of the hotel. A wall of humid night air hit him, along with the noise of the city that filled the background. A siren was sounding somewhere in the distance, accompanied by the various beeps and blasts of car horns. Like all big cities, Kuala Lumpur never really slept. There was always someone going somewhere, no matter what the hour. Cutting across the courtyard, Finch entered the temporary ops centre. Usually housing the hotel's staff, the inside of this room was far less grand than the rooms provided to paying customers. The live-in employees had been shipped out for the full seven days of the summit and moved to less desirable hotels in the vicinity, all at the expense of the visiting countries. Various security teams had been assigned parts of the staff building; the lion's share, though, belonged to his Secret Service Team.

The agent at the door greeted Finch with a very formal, "Sir!" and a nod of the head as he stepped into the hub, a place where his tech team monitored not only the hotel's CCTV system, but all the city cameras for a two block radius. All incoming and outgoing calls were also screened. There was no privacy for anyone within a mile of the hotel. Teams of technicians stared at screens, flicking between cameras whilst others were seated at listening stations, no doubt relishing the ability to eavesdrop on every call, be it landline or cell phone. A few of the staff noticed Finch and offered up nods in greeting, all too busy to stop and chat, which was fine by him. Passing through the room and down a small corridor, he entered the break room designated only for the President's close protection team. Four agents were inside enjoying their break, as a live football game between the Washington Red Skins and the Denver Broncos played on the small TV in the corner of the room.

"Sir!" Agent Michael Blake noticed his boss first, prompting the other three agents to react in a flurry of taking feet off tables and trying to look as if they hadn't been caught off guard.

"Gentlemen," said Finch, inwardly smiling at their reaction. "Agent Blake," he continued, "sorry for disturbing your rest, but I've been called away to revise some of the security detail with the local authorities for our morning trip to the airport. I need you to cover my post outside the President's suite." The disappointment on Blake's face was apparent. No doubt the football game was heating up and he didn't want to miss the end.

"Of course, sir, no problem, I'll just get my gear," he replied, looking rather dejected. It was likely that Blake would be the one to discover his Commander in Chief in the morning when Remy failed to rise with the six thirty wake-up call. Blake was in for a long night, and an even longer day.

Finch gave the other agents a curt nod and left the room. Pacing down the long, drab and slightly musty-smelling corridor, he stopped by the communal bathroom, unclipped his tie pin and threw it into the hand towel bin. The pin contained a small tracking device which allowed the hub to monitor every Secret Service Agent. If he left the complex wearing it, they would know immediately that he was off plot. At least now if they checked on him, it would appear he was taking a quick bathroom break. He only needed five minutes to get clear; after that he didn't care.

Slipping out the back of the staff quarters, he made his way to the rear gate. Pausing for a few moments Finch watched as the guard went to the back of the hut and lit a cigarette, before fiddling with his mobile. Satisfied that his attentions were elsewhere Finch slipped by, completely unseen. Had he actually cared about the security of his president, a gaping hole in the site integrity such as this would have been inexcusable. As it was, the lacklustre attention to detail found in many of the local police and security firms suited him just fine.

Pacing quietly down the back of the hotel, Finch followed an alley that ran behind the Starhill Gallery. The upper market shopping centre was in darkness; Finch had studied the camera layout in depth and knew exactly how to leave the site without being detected. As he followed the tree line, the looming towers of the Ritz Carlton came into view. More sirens and horns sounded far off in the city, almost lost in the constant drone of traffic. Jumping a small wire fence, Finch landed in the car park of the Bintang Garden Hotel. Even their cameras were being fed back to the Ops Centre at The Marriott. Finch knew every system well; he'd studied the angles and view of each camera in detail for weeks before even arriving at the summit.

Striding across the grass verge and out of camera view, he watched as a pair of car headlights lit up in the far corner of the small parking lot. Sticking strictly to his pre-planned route, he walked briskly to the rather battered-looking Toyota Avensis. The car sported a dull red metallic paint job on the sides and trunk; the bonnet and roof were a pearlescent white. It looked exactly like the thousands of other tired taxis crawling around the city. Opening the back door, Finch slid onto the cool faux leather seat. The air-conditioning causing the sweat to chill instantly on his face.

"You're late," the driver commented in an annoyed voice.

Finch checked his watch, "Yes, ten minutes. My apologies."

"The pickup time was two am," the driver protested, "not ten past two."

"Listen," Finch snapped, "it took me longer to get away than I would have liked. It had to look natural."

"Is it done?" asked the driver, turning his bulky body in the seat. Finch knew him well. The man behind the wheel was Roddick Laney, an overweight grunt in his forties, with scruffy, unkempt, greying brown hair. It looked as if his hair hadn't seen a comb or barber's shop in a good while. The smell of BO poured from his body, despite the vehicle's air-conditioning; the putrid stench caught the back of Finch's throat, making him want to gag.

"Yes, it's done; now let's get out of here." Laney's attitude was enraging him. The driver was far below Finch on the food chain. How dare he question him for being late to the RV point? Roddick put the Toyota into gear and guided it out of the hotel parking lot. Almost immediately, they melded into the countless other dirty and battered cabs packing the city streets.

"How far out are we?" Finch asked after almost fifteen minutes of stop-and-go traffic. So far, they had barely managed to achieve more than fifteen miles an hour.

"Two miles," came the curt reply from the front.

Satisfied, Finch pulled his phone from his pocket. Despite it being secure, he hadn't trusted that the monitoring station wouldn't be able to decrypt it within close proximity of the hotel. He had the number ready to go; it was answered in less than one full ring. "It's Finch," he began, "the matter has been dealt with as planned. I'm on my way back now."

"Very good, Mr. Finch." The man at the other end spoke in a flat and emotionless tone. The voice belonged to Buer, the head of the whole operation. Finch both feared and envied Buer simultaneously; if he'd failed in his task, Buer would have seen to it that he was disposed of, no questions asked, despite his long years of faithful service. "You've done well," Buer continued. "It's time to leave your old life behind now – Agent Robert Finch is no more."

"Yes, sir, I understand," replied Finch, his heart pounding so hard, he could feel it pulsing in his throat.

"On your return to the States, we'll see to it that your appearance is changed and your new identity issued. It's all waiting for you. Even though it will appear to all that President Remy died of a heart attack, there will be questions asked about the sudden disappearance of his top Secret Service Agent. You'll no doubt be hunted."

"I understand. And what of The Gift?" Finch heard his own voice grow a little shaky.

Buer laughed. The sound boomed down the phone and Finch held the echoing device away from his ear until the noise subsided. "You never take your eye off the prize, do you, Mr. Finch?"

"I just want what was promised to me!" he interjected, wondering if he was pushing too far.

"You will receive all that has been promised to you – you have my word. In a few weeks' time, the world is going to be a very different place. Your success is merely the start, there is still much for you to do."

Before Finch could reply, the line went dead.

Chapter 3

Adam Fisher turned uneasily in his sleep, caught in one of those strange dreams where he knew he was dreaming, but couldn't seem to wake up. He was in the passenger seat of the RV; trees lined each side of the road, the dark foreboding pines briefly illuminated by the headlights that sliced through the darkness like twin daggers. Rain was pouring down, smacking the window with rhythmic thuds accompanied by the mechanical whine of the wipers as they struggled to keep up with the deluge. Sam was driving; he could see his best friend talking, but no sounds came from his lips. It was like watching TV with the volume down. For some reason he could hear the radio. 'Annie's Song' by John Denver was gently drifting through the cab.

Adam became aware of the RV slowing down, the indicator light blinking bright orange against the night as plump raindrops reflected back, giving a strobe-like effect against the dirty, wet darkness.

Sam swung the lumbering vehicle onto a gravel track. A rest area sign lit up briefly as the headlights cut to the left. Dread swept through his body as the front tyres found the rough surface of the unkempt road. Back in his bedroom he fidgeted uneasily, clutching the covers, small murmurs and whimpering sounds coming from his lips. He wanted to wake up, but the dream held him like a prisoner.

The RV bounced its way slowly down the track, wallowing on soft suspension as the wheels seemed to find every pothole. Without warning, a large stag darted from the bushes. Sam jammed on the brakes and the pressure of the seatbelt bit into his shoulder as it locked, preventing his body from lunging forward. Glancing at Sam, he saw him speaking more words noiselessly, his face fixed with a concerned expression.

The stag, who'd spent a few seconds transfixed by the headlights darted off into the trees, claimed by the forest. The RV started to move again, creeping forward. The lane opened out into a large turning area, a giant redwood standing proud in the middle of the makeshift roundabout.

The melodic and soothing sound of John Denver's voice, and the sweet tune of his acoustic guitar did nothing but fill Adam with dread.

Just as the first chorus ended Adam saw her, and from the depths of his uneasy sleep, he stopped breathing for a few long moments, as if an unseen entity had covered his mouth and nose. Her white clothing juxtaposed against the blackness of the night, and drew his attention completely, as if she were a beacon standing out against the storm. Sam had seen her; he hit the brakes hard for the second time in quick succession. The RV skidded to an abrupt halt, the tyres grinding in protest against the gravel, Sam already reaching for the door.

At the far end of the gravel car park the river rushed by, bubbling and angry from the deluge. She was lying on the bank, on a small gravel beach no doubt popular in the warmer weather with bathers and children. Her legs swept back and forth in the current of the raging water, her tangled blonde hair obstructing her face. Blood flowed freely from a wound in her thigh. The dark red liquid contrasted brightly against the whiteness of her clothes, which despite being wet and dirty, seemed to glow brightly in the headlights.

The scene changed, like a poorly edited movie. They were both out of the RV now; Sam looking back and shouting more silent words urgently. Rushing across the rain-soaked gravel, Sam reached the body first.

Back in the safety of his room, Adam groaned and twisted beneath the covers. "No, no," he whispered.

Sam's hands were pulling at the girl, dragging her away from the river bank. Adam watched as Sam turned her over. His sandy blond hair was plastered to his face, his clothes soaked with water. When her limp body turned, Adam saw her face, pale, almost lifeless, but so beautiful his heart ached and his head spun. Transfixed, he watched her face start to distort, transform, the skin growing darker, younger. Her whole appearance was changing, right before his eyes. His horror was complete when a bullet hole appeared on her forehead, accompanied by a trickle of blood that seemed to defy the pouring rain. He found himself staring at the young girl he'd seen executed during his time with Sam in Afghanistan, six years ago.

At the time, he'd been following Sam's squad, covering the war for an article he was writing when they'd come under heavy fire from insurgents. Adam got separated from the squad during the attack and ducked into a house. Shaking with fear, he'd managed to hide in a wardrobe. Outside, the sound of the battle raged for what seemed like an eternity, until eventually the soldiers had needed to pull back, leaving Adam stranded. Through a gap in the wardrobe door he watched the rebels drag a family into the house. Forcing them to their knees, with hands tied behind their backs, the insurgents proceeded to execute them, one by one.

Crack! The father's body slumped to the floor.

Crack! The mother followed suit.

Last was the daughter, who couldn't have been more than twelve. Her eyes filled with panic, she spotted Adam in the brief moments before her death. Those eyes, resembling a rabbit caught in the headlights of a fast-approaching car, had pleaded for him to do something. In all his life, Adam had never felt so helpless.

Crack!

Three hours passed, before the allied troops regained the village and rescued him. For three hours he'd been unable to draw his gaze from the girl; her lifeless eyes staring at him the whole time. She'd often haunted his dreams in the years since, but this time, it felt different.

The scream started deep in his body, building like a steam train charging through a tunnel. His eyes snapped open, a scream sounding from between his clenched teeth. His hands gripped the covers like a vice, his whole body paralysed, as if unseen hands held him on the cold, clammy, sweat-drenched bed.

Adam lay motionless for long moments, taking short, sharp breaths, allowing his body to relax. He was back in his bedroom; the house silent apart from the rhythmic ticking of the large clock which had hung on his bedroom wall for more years than he cared to remember. Steeling himself against the residual terror of the nightmare, he rolled to his side and brushed his hand across the screen of the iPhone Mini. 04:45 blinked back at him, the screen light illuminating the room for a second, casting shadows against the walls.

Drawing a deep breath, Adam forced himself out of bed and made his way to the bathroom. In the darkness, he easily found the cord to the small mirror light and clicked it on, bathing the room in a dim, phosphorus-yellow glow. Greeted by his own tired reflection, he ran a hand through his hair, trying to ignore the dark shadows framing his green eyes. He turned on the cold tap and splashed water over his face, the freezing liquid instantly casting out the last vestiges of sleep.

"Oh well," he muttered, "it was almost time to get up anyway." Turning off the tap, Adam dried his face on a towel which smelt sweetly of fabric softener, before padding quietly downstairs and into the kitchen.

"Don't you ever sleep?" The groggy voice came from the lounge, as Adam filled the kettle and clicked it on. "What the hell kind of time is this anyway?" added Sam Becker, sitting up on the sofa and peeling back his green, army issue sleeping bag.

"About ten to five, mate," replied Adam, grabbing two cups from a mug tree on the bench.

Sam had been his best friend since they were six, though after school, they'd taken very different routes in life. Adam had gone off to study media at the local college, then followed on through university before working as a freelance writer, selling his stories and articles to a variety of newspapers and magazines all over the world. Sam had fulfilled his childhood ambition by enlisting in the army. Sometimes, six or seven months would pass before they managed to catch up, but they always came back together, one way or another.

Six years ago, Sam had secured Adam a position as a war reporter, following his squad on manoeuvres in Afghanistan during the second uprising. This had led to the incident in the village, the same incident which had ended Sam's military career.

While Adam had been frozen with fear in that wardrobe, with only the dead family for company, Sam had been shot twice during the push to regain the village; once in the leg and once in the shoulder. The leg wound, unfortunately, had hit an artery, nearly costing Sam his life. He'd been lucky to survive. They had both been just twenty-six then... and it seemed a lifetime ago.

Old habits die hard, and after returning to the UK and spending six months lodging with Adam, Sam had secured a close protection job with a private firm and found himself back in the Middle East, babysitting rich businessmen and construction teams. Sam often joked that his new line of work was a walk in the park compared to army life – not to mention the fact that the money was a damn sight better than the British Government offered for putting your life on the line on a daily basis.

Five more years passed with only fleeting visits home, and Sam always stayed with Adam, since he had no family to speak of. As a child, he'd been taken into care and spent most of his childhood days being passed from pillar to post, living in a variety of foster and care homes.

The well paid, close protection work meant he had more than enough cash to buy a small house outright, but Sam refused, saying it was pointless owning a property he wouldn't be living in. Besides, he had good lodgings for free whenever he was back in the UK.

Eventually, as peace began to sweep all the regions of the Middle East, the work had dried up. Sam found himself back in London with no job and no real qualifications he could use on Civvy Street. He eventually got around to buying himself a small flat, but he was rarely there, opting to bunk down at Adam's whenever possible. Adam was fine with the arrangement and enjoyed the company. Following the death of his own parents in a car accident ten years earlier, he'd taken on the family home in Eltham, London, on the promise that he would buy out his younger sister, Lucie's, share of the legacy as soon as he was working and able to obtain a mortgage. She had been just eleven at the time of their parents' death, and while Adam attended university, Lucie had lived with their aunt and uncle in Brighton. In truth, she'd come out of the deal pretty well. At twenty-one, she not only had a tidy sum of money from her share of the house, but she'd moved back in with Adam and lived rent free. Of course, no amount of money or wealth could replace what they'd both lost on that terrible night.

Neither Sam nor Adam had married; Sam's long periods away from home meant he was never around long enough to meet someone and settle down, and Adam had travelled the world for his work. A relationship wasn't something he had the time for; he knew his line of employment was best suited to someone without any emotional ties.

"Shit!" Sam grumbled, rubbing his eyes and stretching. "Ten to five! My alarm doesn't go off until half five! You know I hate getting up before the alarm. It's like cheating yourself."

"Sorry, bud, bad dream," Adam said, staring blankly at the kettle as it began to boil.

"Was it the village again?" asked Sam, reaching for a tee-shirt that had been folded with military precision and left on the pine coffee table.

"Kind of," Adam replied. "It was different though, we were— Never mind." He decided to drop the subject; the dream still had him shaken and in truth, he didn't want to talk about it.

"I told ya, mate, you need to learn to block that shit out, it will eat you up." Sam pulled on his shirt, sliding it over the scar on his shoulder.

"Yeah, well that's easy for you to say, that kind of thing was your life for over ten years!" Adam grumbled, picking up the kettle. "Tea or coffee?"

"It would still be my life," Sam began. "Don't get me wrong, all this peace in the area is great – it's just bad for business." He shook out the sleeping bag and began to roll it back into its pack. "Tea please."

Adam dropped a teabag into each of the mugs and filled them with boiling water.

"Make that a third," came a voice from the hall. Lucie staggered into the lounge still half asleep, closely followed by Jinx, her well-groomed and slightly overfed tabby cat. She flopped into one of the large leather chairs as Jinx busied himself, weaving in and out of her legs, no doubt sensing the opportunity for an earlier than normal breakfast. "You guys really need to keep it down. I never even knew this time existed," she groaned, sliding a scrunchie off her wrist and pulling her shoulder length brown hair expertly into a ponytail. "I didn't think your taxi was coming until seven? I know you kids must be excited, you've had this trip planned for ages, but I thought you'd be past waking up at silly o'clock." She grinned at them as Adam passed her a steaming mug of tea. Taking the hot beverage, she tucked her legs up under herself. Jinx stared up at her disapprovingly, clearly annoyed by the lack of attention.

"Well, Sam needed to do his makeup and straighten his hair. You know how long he takes to get ready," joked Adam. The company of his friend and his sister was a welcome distraction from the nightmare.

He had to admit, the early start meant it was going to be a long day; they had two hours still until the taxi was due to pick them up. The trip to Heathrow should only take an hour this early on a Sunday morning, but it was the flight to Denver Adam wasn't looking forward to. Despite the fact the trip across North America to take in the Rockies had been in the planning for the past two years, Adam felt drained. He'd only been back in the country for twelve days, after being hired by the Financial Times to cover the World Summit in Malaysia, and what an event that had turned out to be. The day after the summit, President John Remy had been found dead in the bathroom of his suite at the Marriott. The press was reporting that he'd suffered a massive coronary. The strangest thing, was the disappearance of the head of his security detail the night he'd died, not to mention the fact that during the same night, three of the delegates had also vanished without a trace. The American government was holding their cards close to the chest in regard to President Remy and the Secret Service Agent, some guy named Finch. The conspiracy theorists were already having a field day. Many people strongly believed the President had been assassinated, but over the last week or so, it became clear that no toxins had been found in his system. As usual, it had done nothing to silence the suspicions. Whatever had happened that night had caused a hell of a stir. Kuala Lumpur International had been on its highest level of security. Notices had been sent to all press travelling home in the days after the summit, warning that check-in times were as much as six hours before flights. Unfortunately for Adam, he'd been booked to fly back to London on the morning the whole mess started. He'd spent twenty hours at the airport, before finally getting airborne. Many of the media workers had opted to stay on and cover the story as it developed, but the Financial Times had no interest in conspiracies and manhunts and consequently, Adam had no reason to stay. He was sure there was a good story to be had out of the whole situation, but he'd missed out. Besides, with the passing of almost two weeks, there had been no further developments and no one seemed to know anything. From Adam's perspective, the press was just scratching about, reporting the same old stories repeatedly.

Whatever the truth, it probably wasn't going to be the happiest time to be in the States. The country had been in a state of official mourning for the past twelve days. The memorial for President Remy was due to be held later that day. By the time they landed it would just about be finished, no doubt leaving the entire country in a sombre mood.

"Well, I'm heading back to bed!" Lucie announced, draining the last of her tea before placing the empty mug on the table. "You guys have fun; don't do anything I wouldn't do." She giggled. "See you in three weeks." She got up and crossed the room, stopping to give her brother a farewell peck on the cheek.

"Hey where's my kiss?" called Sam as she left the room. Lucie slipped her hand around the door frame and flipped him the bird.

"Yeah, love you too, Luce," he laughed.

Adam watched her disappear up the stairs, leaving a rather frustrated-looking Jinx to wonder where his breakfast was coming from.

Chapter 4

The mirror reflected back an image that was not his own. Finch stared for a few long moments and allowed the differences to sink in. Gone was his dark, swept back hair, replaced with a much lighter shade of brown, cut short on top and cropped neatly around the neck. Matching his new hair colour was a well-trimmed goatee beard. The transformation didn't stop there; his chin seemed sharper, more defined. The small prominent bridge of his nose had also been altered. The thing he found the hardest to get over was the change in eye colour. The once arresting ice-blue eyes he'd sported for the past thirty-one years were no more. The ones staring back at him were brown; they matched his new features well. Finch was confident he could pass any one of his old Secret Service team in the street and they wouldn't look at him twice. This was the new him, it would take some getting used to, but so far he liked what he saw.

Tearing his attention away from the mirror, he made his way back into his room and removed the hospital gown he'd been wearing for the past few days, changing into a suit. Not the bland, Secret Service issued one he'd worn for the last nine years, but a smart grey Armani number. Tying his shoes, Finch stole one last glance in the mirror, allowing himself a wry smile. *Yes, that will do nicely*, he thought. He was a new man; the old Robert Finch was gone, as good as dead. The new Finch was destined for bigger and better things. Slipping out the door, he made his way down the long, sterile corridor and out of the medical wing.

Following the most memorable night of his life, he'd been smuggled out of the country and back to the United States. It was amazing the things that could be done with a nearly limitless supply of money and the right connections. *The rules are the same the planet over,* he'd thought, *everyone has a price and everything is for sale.* Moving him across the globe had proved no issue, thanks to the materialistic, weak-willed nature of humanity.

For the two days following Remy's death, prior to attending the headquarters medical wing, he'd kept himself appraised of developments in Kuala Lumpur – not from the news, but from sources inside many of the government organisations. Top investigators from each country who had mysteriously lost their high profile delegates, had been sent out to the city. Police and government officials from Sweden, Germany and France, all worked alongside the Malaysian Police, who were notoriously inept and not capable of handling such a protracted enquiry. They'd been joined by the special investigators sent by the Gendarmes Corps, the Vatican's very own police force. Fruitlessly, they'd searched for some clue about what had happened to Archbishop Tillard. If only the church knew who he really was, and what he knew, Finch suspected they wouldn't be so keen to locate him.

Regardless of the investigators' skills or experience, they'd all been left scratching around in the sand. The US Government was still on the fence in regard to President Remy's death. All toxicology and autopsy reports pointed to the fact that he'd suffered a massive heart attack. His room at the Marriott had literally been pulled apart, from the ground up. Everything was examined, but as Finch already knew, they would turn up nothing of evidentiary value. They were equally confused about Finch's own disappearance. Had he had something to do with Remy's death? Or was he just another unfortunate soul who had vanished into thin air that night? The only trace of Finch to be found had been his personal tracker, left in the toilet of the staff block. Every piece of CCTV had been examined and re-examined, every call had been combed through – the reviewers searching for any key words or clues as to what had occurred. In truth, they didn't know if Finch was linked to the death or not. Regardless, he was still a wanted man. The FBI was certain Finch held some knowledge regarding Remy's demise, and they desperately wanted to speak to him. It was one of the only things they were right about.

The knowledge that President Remy had failed to see those hiding in plain sight gave Finch a warm glow. They'd been as skillful – if not more so – than the Watchers, at covertly installing their people in some very high level places. Finch's former role was no exception; he'd been right under Remy's nose for nine years. During his time studying Military Science, he'd learned that often the best place to hide from the enemy was in plain sight. It's the place they least expect to find you. Of course, this tactic only worked for those working covertly, spending years as a sleeper before striking a deadly blow, like the faithful dog which one day turns on its owner.

Once safely back in the States, he'd been taken to the headquarters of the operation. Situated in Allentown, it was less than a two-hour drive to New York, where the official business face of the operation was located. The town's small airport housed their four Gulfstream jets and afforded them the luxury of being able to reach any part of the country by air, without the hassle of having to use one of New York's major hubs. With a quick fuel stop, the fleet of jets could spread their reach worldwide.

Following Finch's arrival, he'd been taken into the medical suite, where he'd remained for the next eleven days. Not only had they masterfully changed his appearance, but on Buer's authority, The Gift had been bestowed upon him. There was no doubting his ranking within their society had been bumped up a great deal. He'd been the first in close to a millennium who'd been granted the honour, not only that, but the very first of his kind to receive it – but it had been well earned. It would still be many years before the other Elders truly accepted him.

Stepping out of the building and into the parking lot, he noted the April air was pleasantly warm and smelled of opportunity. He wasn't relishing the thought of the two-hour journey to the city, but Buer needed to see him and he wasn't the kind of person Finch could ask to come to him.

Pressing the vehicle's remote key fob, his eyes searched the lot, scanning the variety of cars all neatly lined up. A shrill chirp followed by the brief flash of both indicators caught his eye. At least he had a nice car to endure the drive in. The shiny new, top of the range BMW 5 Series was definitely one of the better vehicles. Such luxuries were saved for those in the higher-ranking positions. Luxuries were definitely something Finch could get used to. Rolling out of the parking lot he took a right, cruised out of town and picked up State Highway 2055.

Finch emerged from the Holland Tunnel in a little under two hours, swinging the car onto Canal Street and heading for New York's financial district. After another twenty minutes of negotiating the city traffic, he drove the BMW down the ramp and into the underground car park of an office building on Liberty Street. Using the elevator's large mirror, he took a few moments to straighten his tie and dust himself off as he was whisked to the top floor. It was done out of nervous energy more than a need to tidy himself – Buer always made him uncomfortable. Head of the whole operation and currently the only Elder here, he'd seen and experienced things Finch had only read about in their history books. Buer had been waiting many lifetimes, for the chance to strike the blow that was about to be dealt.

The lift deposited Finch on the top floor. Stepping out of the sliding doors, his feet were met by thick, plush red carpet. The sign in front of him proclaimed he'd entered the offices of Integra Investments . The large brass plaque was as lavish as the carpet, around four feet high and seven feet long. There was no doubt someone spent a fair bit of time each day polishing it, as Finch's reflection bounced off the surface, slightly distorted by the large black, highly glossed letters.

The company had been set up over eighty years ago, and to those who visited and dealt with them in the business world, they were just another highly successful investment firm. Behind the scenes, it was the bank account for their whole operation. Over the years, they had slowly accrued enough wealth and assets to finally put things into action. Buer had been there from the start, although never as the official face of the business, because he couldn't risk being in the public eye. Even a newspaper article showing his name or face would have spelled the end of their operation. Finch was part of a new generation; born specifically to infiltrate key areas advantageous to them. They possessed normal everyday names, they worked in high profile, yet ordinary jobs, and each of them was completely unknown to the Watchers. Like a game of chess, they had slowly positioned their pieces. It was almost time for the final move and... check mate!

Navigating his way through the top floor corridors, Finch arrived at a large, opaque glass door. Clearing his throat, he knocked twice.

"Enter!" The voice seemed to boom through him, despite the thick glass.

Finch unlatched the door. A grand office lay before him, one which appeared to have a similar square footage to a small family home. The glass walls of the office building provided an awe-inspiring view over the southern tip of New York. Liberty Island glistened in the water of the Upper Bay. The sun bounced its rays off the gleaming World Trade Centre One building. A variety of decadent sofas and expensive antiques furnished the office. It felt more like an apartment than a work space; all that was missing was a bed. At the very end of the room sat a slightly elevated platform which sported a large black glass desk. Buer stood behind it with his back to Finch, taking in the view.

"Mr. Finch," he began, turning slowly to face him, "please come in and take a seat." Buer gestured to the chair opposite him. He was dressed in a fine black suit, topped off with a slate grey tie and a pair of well-polished, expensive Italian leather slip-on shoes. Buer stood at an impressive six feet six inches, and was as wide as a barn door; his jaw looked as if it had been cut by a skilled stonemason from a block of granite. Finch doubted even a twister would move Buer if he stood in its way. Even though Finch was just over six feet himself, he felt dwarfed by this man, whose very presence seemed to fill the entire office. His jet black hair had the appearance of being freshly cut and his smooth, tanned complexion highlighted his dark features. To anyone else he would look like a fit, muscular forty-something, who obviously spent hours at the gym pumping weights.

It seemed to take an age to cross the office floor, Buer's piercing grey eyes following him with every step. Finally reaching the chair, Finch sat down and tried to make himself comfortable.

Buer took his seat, regarding Finch for a few seconds before he asked, "How did you like the car?"

"Car?" The random question had caught him off guard.

"Yes, the BMW I had sent to Allentown, the car you just drove here in," Buer said coldly. He had a short fuse and this one small moment of stupidity on Finch's behalf had lit it.

"Oh yes, sorry, the BMW," Finch added hastily. "It was very nice, thank you."

Buer stared at him, the way a person might look at a mosquito just before they crushed it. He broke his gaze, swung his chair around and stared out of the window. "During my time here, I've come to realise that there are many fine things, such as your car for example, the buildings of the city, useful things like road networks and ships." He gestured toward the view beyond the window. "Many of these things will be useful to us in the future. It's much more habitable than when we first tried. Back then, it was all shacks, carts, wilderness and shit. Now you could say it will be just like moving into a furnished apartment." A grin spread across his face, his moment of anger gone. "You excelled, Robert, you really did. It was argued that the task of dealing with the four Watchers was too big for one man, especially one who was not even an Elder. I'm glad those who doubted you were proved wrong."

Finch began to relax a little, also glad of the fact the doubters had been proven wrong. He wondered if Buer had been one of those doubters, but he didn't dare ask. Had they been right, there was no way he would be seated here now. No, he would have been the one who disappeared. "It was an honour, sir," he replied truthfully.

"I hear you had no luck discovering the location of the Tabut?" Buer's question was posed in such a way that Finch knew he required more than a straightforward 'no'.

"Unfortunately the three I spoke to all claimed the same thing." Finch watched Buer raise a questioning eyebrow and continued. "They claimed none of them knew the location of the artifact, that even they weren't privy to such information." His mouth was dry and he swallowed deeply. He knew Buer desired the Tabut greatly and would be disappointed that his desire had been thwarted.

"I find that hard to believe!" The scepticism was heavy in Buer's voice. "Did you try other methods to obtain the information?"

"Torturing them would have been a pointless and time consuming exercise. They could have told me anything, and we would have no way of knowing if it was the truth. If I'd had more time to work on them, maybe, but my orders were to ensure they all died that night. I highly doubt they would ever have broken. I was told it wasn't worth the risk of leaving any of them alive, unless they chose to help us." Buer's eyes remained locked on him, taking in every word. "Also, they claim there is no Key Tablet to activate it!"

"We knew that already," Buer commented. "What you say is true, though; they could have spun us any lies they wanted. We could have been racing all over the planet to try and locate it. I had hoped that one of them might choose to live and work with us, and then we could have recovered the Tabut and destroyed it. I don't need to remind you how dangerous it could be, if they were to get to it first."

"Sir, it's been dormant for more than three and a half thousand years. Maybe they didn't know... actually, it's highly likely. I wouldn't put it past them to have entrusted that information to only a few of their highest ranking Elders." Finch wasn't sure he believed his own statement, but he was keen to steer Buer away from the subject.

Buer was nodding his head, mulling it over. "You could be right. At least we know there is no Key Tablet, and also, thanks to you Robert, there are no Elders here to activate it. As you well know, both the biometric signature of an Elder and the Key Tablet are needed for the Tabut to work. If they do come and try to reach it, we'll be ready. We've come too far to fail now."

"Have there been any developments in our own search for it?" Finch enquired.

"Nothing to note. The last lead we had was Canada, but we drew a blank. We're sure that in the early days, it was held in the Great Pyramid – the supposed sarcophagus in the King's Chamber is exactly the right size to hold the device, but we know the King's Chamber has been empty since explorers first opened it up." Buer turned his gaze from Finch for a few seconds, pushing some papers around his desk. "So how do you like your new look?" he asked, taking a sip from the cup of black coffee that was steaming away on his desk. Finch had smelt it on entering the office and thought he could have used a cup himself.

"It's a marvel," Finch enthused. "I don't think any of my old staff would know me, even if we bumped into each other in the street."

"As you know, Robert, that was not the only thing we changed." Leaning forward, Buer raised his eyebrows. "I know how much you hungered for it."

"Yes, it's a true honour, sir," Finch began, "I don't really feel any different though. Is that normal?" Finch regretted the question as soon as it left his lips. He suspected he'd sounded foolish.

Buer erupted into a deep belly laugh, so loud that Finch was sure the floor vibrated. Regaining control, Buer said, "What on earth did you expect? The strength of ten men? The ability to fly?" Finch's stupidity was clearly amusing him no end.

"No! Not at all," Finch protested. "I just didn't know if I should feel, well… different."

"No, I'm sorry," Buer began, the first glint of amused tears gleaming around his eyes, "I guess it can be a little confusing at the start. It's been so long since it was bestowed upon anyone. You were the first, but more will follow. Once all this is over, we'll need good, trustworthy and educated people."

Finch allowed himself a small sigh of relief. Somehow, he'd managed to rescue the situation. "I'm sorry if the question sounded stupid," he said, straightening his tie.

"There are some things you need to remember, Robert. You aren't invincible. If you're wounded, you will still bleed. Granted, your healing time will be greatly increased, and you will have no need for dressings or bandages. No diseases will touch you, just as your organs will never tire and fail. Just make sure you don't get shot in the head or heart, or get yourself blown up!" Buer grinned. "Live by this phrase and you won't go far wrong, *Immortality does not mean invincibility.* I don't need to remind you of that; you killed four Elders yourself." He opened one of the desk draws and removed an envelope. "In here is your new identity. You will only be known as Robert Finch to us and no one else." He pushed the envelope across the table and Finch picked it up.

"May I?" he asked, turning it over in his hands.

"Of course," encouraged Buer, "go right ahead." Finch tore the envelope open and shook the contents out onto the smooth black surface of the desk, so he could begin pawing through the medley of items required for a complete change of identity. Opening the US passport, his new face stared back at him from the rear page. Under the photo was the name 'Isaac Stephens'.

"Isaac?" Finch queried, "Really? I mean isn't that a little..."

"Biblical?" Buer cut in with a laugh. "Yes, my personal choice. I liked the irony, a little like our dear friend Tillard. Besides, you won't have that name for long. As soon as everything is done, you may revert back to your birth name." Buer seemed pleased by the joke. Finch failed to see the funny side, but the knowledge that Buer at least possessed a slight sense of humour, no matter how warped, was settling. Also in the envelope, he found a new driver's licence and birth certificate, as well as a new debit and a credit card.

"There's five hundred thousand US dollars in that account," said Buer, gesturing at the debit card. "The Visa has no limit. I don't expect you to require excessive funds over the coming weeks, but it's there as a precaution. After that, the money in those accounts will be as worthless as the plastic the two cards are made of." Buer leaned back in his chair, which creaked under the bulk of his massive body. "Which brings me neatly to the next subject."

Finch felt his heart rate quicken. This was it, this was the end game. Everything up to this point, including the four deaths, had been mere preparation.

Buer reached under his desk and produced a black leather briefcase. Opening it, he stared at the contents for a few long seconds, as if he were admiring a masterpiece. "We were unsure who to task with the US side of the job. We had many volunteers, but almost all of them are still employed in government or the like, and we can't risk pulling them out yet, since they may still be needed. I know we have asked a lot of you already, but I'm hoping you'll accept this final task." Buer spun the briefcase around. Finch studied the contents; they looked completely normal – diaries, pens and a small document folder. Finch looked across the top of the briefcase and saw Buer grinning at him. "It's good, isn't it?" Buer turned the case back so it faced toward him. Fishing inside, he removed an expensive-looking silver pen and unscrewed the base. Where the ink cartridge should have been, was a small glass vial containing a clear liquid. He carefully unscrewed it and held it between his thumb and forefinger. While it appeared to be water, it was in fact quite the opposite. Water was thought of as the giver and sustainer of life; this was the destroyer. The sunlight streaming in through the windows sparkled off the small vial, giving it a jewel-like appearance. "In this vial is a viral agent, far beyond anything their scientists can engineer, and far beyond anything they can cure. We estimate it to have a communicability rate of over ninety-nine point nine percent. After the virus has raged over the planet for a month, we estimate there will be less than seven million people left alive. We have no way of knowing for sure until it goes live." Buer pushed his chair back and stood up, facing the window. "The clever part of this virus is the incubation period." He glanced over his shoulder to check he still had Finch's attention. "From the time of contraction, it will take a full thirty hours to show any symptoms at all. The virus is an airborne infection, meaning it's highly contagious. For thirty hours, the people who carry the virus are just as infectious as when they start to show symptoms. When they do start to show, it will be in the form of a headache and rash-like sores. Then, over the next ten hours, every cell in the human body gradually attacks itself, causing death approximately eleven to twelve hours after infection. I won't go through all the gory details. Let's just say, it's far from a swift and painless death." Buer picked up his cup and drained the last of the coffee. "It's the first thirty hours that are most important to us, as no one will even know it's spreading like a brushfire. That's when the most damage will be done. Once this starts springing up, there will be quarantines put in place, borders and airports will be closed, but it will already be too late!" Buer screwed the vial back into the pen with slow, deliberate movements. Finch, of course, knew all this already, but he enjoyed hearing it as much as Buer enjoyed the theatre of telling it. "We have chosen the locations for the pathogen to be released into the public. It will be your duty to make sure this batch is deployed." Buer walked around the desk and handed the pen to Finch. "To release the agent, all you need to do is push the base of the pen. Just like you would to extend the nib. The pathogen will be released over a two-minute period. Don't worry; you're quite immune." He smiled. "Be sure to keep hold of the pen and move through your location, mixing among as many people as possible. The virus will survive outside of the vial and the human body for three hours, giving it plenty of time to work its way into air-conditioning systems. I believe a famous English author once wrote that the pen is mightier than the sword. He will never know how right he was!" Buer gazed out of the window at the city. "I almost pity them," he said smugly. "All completely unaware of the fate that's about to strike!"

"What of those who survive?" asked Finch, turning the pen in his hand. "There are bound to be outlying areas and islands that won't be infected. Also, as you say, there will be those who just won't contract the disease at all."

"The numbers will be so small in comparison, we can just mop up those unlucky enough not to die. There may even be some use for them, I don't know. As you're aware, this is by far our best option. When we tried before, they had no technology to strike back at us with. Things are different now. They have the ability to cause us some real damage, if we just confront them." Reaching back into the case, Buer retrieved a small ticket pouch and handed it to Finch. It contained a return, first class ticket to Paris on American Airlines. Looking at the departure date, Finch saw he was leaving tomorrow. "I've arranged for you to stay in the city tonight," Buer said, moving back around the desk and relaxing into his chair. "Tomorrow, four vials of the pathogen will be released. One at Heathrow Airport, in the International Departure Lounge. One at Hong Kong International Airport, again in the International Departure Lounge. The same for LAX, and then yours. It's to be released just before you board your flight from JFK. With the help of air travel, the virus will be spread across the globe in a matter of hours." In truth, Finch didn't need it spelled out. During his time at college they'd covered possible terrorist tactics, looking at the ways a viral agent might be spread into the population. Releasing it at an airport was considered by far the best option. "From there," Buer continued, "the passengers will carry it to their destination airports and the infection will spread. There will be no point in trying to quarantine the sick. Within thirty hours, it will be impossible to contain."

Chapter 5

Sam drained the last dregs of beer from his glass and placed it back on the table. "This American beer is like making love in a canoe," he commented, wiping his mouth on his sleeve.

Adam shot him a slightly confused glance.

"You know – fucking close to water!" Sam chuckled, obviously pleased with his joke.

Adam swilled the remainder of his pint around the glass, staring at the golden liquid. "Very funny," he replied dryly, watching as the rather rotund waitress in an ill-fitting, bright blue pinny arrived at their table with two very large plates of Mac 'n Cheese.

"There you go, gentlemen," she chirped in the same slightly annoying, enthusiastic tone she'd taken their order in. "Will there be anything else?" Her pink and white checked uniform looked as if someone had dragged it straight out of a fifties American diner before she'd started work. The more modern plastic name badge, pinned neatly to the fabric, announced her name as 'Patty'.

"Two more beers please," replied Sam, already drenching the daily special in far more ketchup than was needed, "and can you make them Buds this time?" The waitress nodded and hurried across the bar, her bobbed blonde hair swooshing as she went. They'd received her pretty much undivided attention since their arrival. No one wanted to be out making merry today. The memorial service for President Remy had been held and the whole place had a sullen feel to it. A large projection TV in the corner silently replayed highlights from the service which had taken place in Washington DC earlier in the day, while a jukebox pumped out trashy country music. They'd been in the air during the actual service, landing in Denver just a few hours after it ended.

"It never fails to amaze me, just how many meals you add bloody ketchup to," laughed Adam as he began to tuck into his own dinner.

"Old military habit, mate," said Sam, wiping his mouth. "It was one of the only things that took the taste of the ration packs away." He mixed the sauce in and proceeded to add yet another large dollop to the daily special for good measure.

"And what's with ordering more beer? One of us has to drive after this."

"Stop being such a fusspot," said Sam, shovelling forkfuls of the now red-tinged Mac 'n Cheese into his mouth. "The beer here is so weak, I reckon I could drink five pints and not be over the limit."

They'd arrived in Denver a few hours ago, after a laborious, nine-hour flight. Adam hated flying in what the Americans called 'coach'. Usually when he was contracted by a paper or magazine to do a story that required overseas travel, he at least managed to get business class. When they'd booked the flights six months ago, Sam had refused to pay the extra five hundred Euros to travel on one of the new intercontinental Boeing fast jets that many major airlines now offered, and wouldn't even consider upgrading to business class on the slower flight. Had he not been so tight-fisted, they could have cut the journey time down to just three hours, or at the very least, had a decent-sized seat and a meal. Also, every time the hostess trolley made an appearance, Sam had been keen to make the most of the free alcohol, leaving Adam to remind him they had to pick up the RV as soon as they landed. Then after finally touching down in Denver, they discovered that the rental firm, who had advertised themselves as being right next to the airport, was actually just over five miles away. After a brief taxi ride, they eventually picked up the large camper which was going to be home for the next few weeks. The Ford MTR Freedom was classified as a five berth RV; neither of them was sure how comfortable it would be with five passengers, however for two, it was perfect. The subject of who would be claiming the double bed was yet to be resolved; the smaller singles which needed making up each night looked so narrow, they both feared they might fall right out of bed by rolling over.

The waitress returned with two fresh beers on a tray and deposited them onto the table. Apart from a rather drunk-looking guy in a suit and a few college students, they were the only ones in the bar.

"I was going to suggest staying in Denver for the night," Sam began, washing down a mouthful of food with a swig of beer, and eyeing Patty as she busied herself wiping a few tables down. The cloth she was using looked as if it carried more germs than a public toilet seat. "You know, have a few beers, pull some college chicks, it's not like we have to go far to get to our hotel on wheels. It seems a shame to waste that five berther on just the two of us." He gave Adam a knowing wink.

"Nice idea, but I hardly think anyone is in the mood for partying today. Besides, wasn't it your idea to drive out to the park, so you could wake up in the mountains and sample the air?" Adam swallowed his last mouthful of food and began mopping the sauce up with a piece of slightly stale bread.

Pushing his empty plate away, Sam retrieved a map of the Rockies National Park and began folding it out awkwardly on the table. "I had a look on Google Earth before we left," he began, trying to lay the map flat over the empty dinner plates and various condiments. "I reckon if we head out of the city on I70 and through Idaho Springs, then drop onto Route 40, that will take us up into the mountains; there looked to be a few nice rest areas around, right in the heart of the park. Then in the morning, we can walk a few trail ways before heading on." His finger was pressed on a place that appeared to be in the middle of nowhere, and as he held it there, cheese sauce began to leak through onto the page. "Ah, shit!" he protested, lifting the map off the table and giving it a shake.

Adam experienced an odd feeling about the whole idea. He'd never been to the Rockies in his life, but what he'd seen is the dream certainly looked like it could fit the area. A chill ran down his back. On the flight over, he'd tried to get some sleep, but every time he closed his eyes, all he could see was the strange girl's pale, lifeless face.

The week Adam's parents died, he'd been away at university in Bournemouth studying for his media degree. He'd gone out for a few drinks with some friends in the town that night. Returning home slightly drunk, he'd gone straight to bed. Two hours later, he'd woken up screaming like he had last night. In the dream, he'd seen a tanker veer across the road and plough straight into his parents' car. Even though it was two am, he'd phoned home straight away, but to his dismay, a police officer had answered the call. The next day he was back in London, with Lucie crying on his shoulder. Both their parents were dead. They'd been on their way home from a dinner party at his aunt and uncle's. The police believed the tanker driver had fallen asleep at the wheel, veered across the road and virtually crushed their Audi. Over the years, Adam had pushed the memory of that dream to the back of his mind; however, it had resurfaced earlier on the flight to America. It was hard for him to explain – something about the dream of his parents' crash had felt different, more real. The dream about the girl and the river felt the same. He never bothered mentioning it to Sam – although he loved him like a brother, he knew he'd be in for a piss taking, so he'd kept it to himself. "I'm not sure you're allowed to stay overnight in the park's rest areas," Adam cut in, suddenly searching for a reason to avoid driving up into the mountains for the night and wishing he'd encouraged Sam's idea of staying in Denver to get drunk. "If a ranger finds us, we might get a fine."

"God, when did you become such a square?" Sam laughed, shaking his head. "You worry too much. Just chill and have fun. We've been planning this road trip long enough. Besides, that park is massive, I'm sure no one will care if we park the RV for a night. If they do, just play the dumb tourist, although they might find it hard to believe if you say you couldn't read the signs. I guess you could always put on a ropey French accent." He grinned and folded the food-stained map up, before sliding it back into his bag. Draining the last of the Budweiser from the glass, he stood up and kicked back the chair. "Right, I'm going for a quick piss. Try and finish that beer by the time I get back. If we hit the road now, we stand a chance of seeing some of the approach into the park in daylight. Oh, and for God's sake, relax. You're on holiday now!"

Watching Sam disappear through the swing door to the gents' room, Adam picked up both glasses and returned them to the bar. His was still half full.

He was paying for the meal by the time Sam came out of the toilet, still adjusting his zipper. Collecting his bag from the table, he joined Adam at the counter. "Ready for the off then?" he said, patting Adam on the back encouragingly.

As they stepped out into the car park, they could see it was nearing the end of rush hour. An eclectic mixture of oversized American cars and trucks still jostled along West 44th Street, all trying to reach the interstate. Adam could see storm clouds forming in the west over the distant mountains, which were just visible on the horizon. "I'll drive," he said hastily, as he snapped the keys from Sam's hand.

"Like hell you will!" objected Sam, grabbing them back. "For one, you were never any good at drinking, where as I have army training in it." He shot Adam a smile. "Secondly, we have some pretty hairy roads ahead and as good a driver as you are, I'd rather be in control. Plus, I've spent far more time driving on the left. I handled some big old trucks back in the army, often on dirt tracks and passes, so I am, by far, the most qualified."

Adam could tell his friend was only half joking and half serious. In truth, he didn't care for driving. In the dream, Sam had been behind the wheel, so Adam was desperate to change something, even just a small detail.

"It's over twelve hundred miles to San Francisco. You'll have plenty of time to get a go," Sam called back, making his way to the RV. He tossed the keys triumphantly in the air. As they fell, he tried to catch them but failed. He fumbled desperately for purchase before they slipped through his hand and clattered down a drain, "Shit!" he cried, kneeling down onto the tarmac and peering through the grate.

"Nice work," muttered Adam, as he joined him on the ground. "Do you have any idea how much the rental firm charge for lost keys? They make you pay to replace all the vehicle locks and ignition!"

"Sorry," Sam replied a little sheepishly, "it wasn't like I planned to do it."

Adam peered into the darkness. The keys were only about seven inches below the grate, resting on a pile of leaves. Thankfully, whoever was in charge of maintenance hadn't been too hot at keeping the drain cover unclogged.

"I can't get my hand through!" said Sam, flattening out his palm and trying to squeeze it in. "You try."

Adam leaned over the grate and pushed his hand into the drain, his knuckles striking hard against the metal. He gritted his teeth as he pushed down harder. Suddenly, his bones seemed to move and his hand slipped in far enough for his fingers to hook the large plastic key loop. Gripping the loop tightly, he pulled his hand back before holding them up triumphantly. "Good job I've got girly hands." He smiled, passing the keys over reluctantly, no matter how bad he felt he knew it was pointless trying to persuade his friend that heading into the mountains was a bad idea, Sam was stubborn, once his mind was set that was it.

"No, that was some freaky shit," Sam exclaimed, clasping the keys tightly. "Your hand went all out of shape for a couple of seconds; it looked pretty gross. How did you know you could do that?"

"I didn't. Just luck, that's all," Adam replied truthfully, half wishing he hadn't retrieved the keys. If they'd stayed stuck down the drain, it would have put off the trip into the mountains by a good few hours, if not a whole day.

Sam climbed up into the driver's seat of the RV; the large captain's chair was more akin to something you'd find in a lounge room. It was definitely not the kind of vehicle to drive if you happened to be a little tired, as one could easily fall asleep behind the wheel. Turning the key in the ignition, the massive 6.8ltr engine purred into life. He fiddled with the on-board SatNav for a few moments, and the screen blinked as the device obtained a GPS lock before an overview of their route was displayed. "I've programmed in Trail Ridge Road for now," he began, "it's a long-ass road, but from what I saw on Google Earth it has a few places we can stop, so we'll just play it by ear. Time to turn the first eighty odd miles." He grinned with enthusiasm.

Adam eyed the device; the route took them out of the city and right into the heart of the Rocky Mountains National Park. There was no doubt it was going to be a spectacular drive. He just wished he felt better about the whole situation.

"I hope you brought enough spending money for fuel," laughed Sam, "according to the brochure this baby only does fifteen miles to the gallon." He swung the RV out onto West 44th Street and joined the slow-moving traffic heading for the interstate. "Guess these will be going cheap soon, when they start backing off on the production of petrol and diesel engines. Wasn't the guy who developed the new hydro engines one of those poor bastards who went missing in Malaysia?"

Adam rolled his eyes. It had been all over the news for the past two weeks, repeatedly proclaiming that one of the missing men had indeed been Euri Peterson, developer of the hydro engine. Sam had never been good at current affairs, unless it was a war or conflict he was directly involved in. "Yes, where have you been? Under a rock?"

"That's some strange shit that happened out there, I can't believe there's still no sign of those guys. You were there, what do you think?" Sam guided the RV up the on-ramp and joined I70. They were soon cruising at a steady fifty miles an hour.

"No idea, mate," said Adam, gazing at the distant mountains. The sky was looking more threatening by the minute and he swore he saw the odd flash of lightning in the clouds. A big storm looked to be brewing and they were heading right for it. "I missed out on all the action, I'm kind of glad I flew out straightaway now, despite the stupidly long delay. Lots of reporters wasted their time and money hanging around, waiting for a story to break that never did." He took a pack of gum out of his bag, passed one stick to Sam and popped one in his own mouth. "Looks like it might be a bit of a wild night," he said, changing the subject and gesturing toward the clouds.

"Yeah just spotted that. Hopefully we can find a place to park up before it really sets in." Sam reached over and turned on the radio. News reports were still speaking about the memorial, the three missing delegates and prompting people to go to the FBI website to look at the picture of Robert Finch, the head of President Remy's Secret Service Team who had also vanished like Lord Lucan. After a few minutes Sam clicked the radio off, tired of hearing the same old news.

I70 took them out past the Denver city limits. Gradually, the terrain started to turn more rugged, pine covered hills rising to the side of them. For a few miles the westbound lane rose up above its eastbound partner as it wove through the landscape. As Sam had predicted, they left the interstate just past a small town called Idaho Springs. The majority of the town seemed to exist right by the side of the interstate, nestled between two hills. Now motoring along Route 40. the first small town they came to was Empire. Sam pulled the RV into a small tin-pot petrol station and topped up the fuel.

"I'll grab a few supplies as well," he called after brimming the tank. Adam watched him head across the forecourt and into the wooden shack that served as a shop. Inside Sam grabbed a six pack of beers and a variety of nasty-looking corn snacks, along with a pack of bottled water and a six pack of Pepsi Wild Cherry. Paying at the old wooden counter, the cost of the fuel compared to the UK almost made him smile. Back in the cab, Sam steered the RV out onto Route 40 and continued on through Empire. They both marvelled at how antiquated the place still looked; the town hall and sheriff's station resembled something from a Wild West film. Just on the other side of the small, quaint town, the first large drops of rain began to hit the windscreen, causing the automatic wipers to spring into action. Adam's uneasy feeling grew as the rain picked up pace with each passing mile.

"You feeling okay, mate?" asked Sam, noticing the pallid look on Adam's face. Reaching down, he tore open one of the stupidly large bags of cheese snacks. "Try one of these, it will either kill or cure!" he joked, stuffing a handful into his mouth.

"No thanks," replied Adam, shaking his head. "It's just that beer, I don't think it's sitting too well."

"Ha! See, I said you were no good at drinking." Sam laughed through a mouthful of food. Reaching over he clicked the air-con up a little and cranked one of the outlets toward Adam. "Get a little air, just don't open the window. I have a feeling it's going to be raining cats and dogs in a minute." Adam relaxed into his seat, enjoying the cool air in his face.

Around ten miles outside of Empire, Route 40 began to twist and turn up into the mountains. Adam was actually glad he wasn't driving. Sam was a terrible passenger and would no doubt have been shouting at him to watch out for this and look out for that, whilst continually clutching what he called the *'Fuck me handle'*, above the door. The light was failing fast, but they could both see the ravine to their left. The driving conditions continued to deteriorate as the rain upped its assault on the RV's windscreen. Thankfully, after a few miles the road that seemed to be coiled like a snake straightened out. Adam swore he saw Sam breathe a small sigh of relief as the ravine ended and the trees came back to meet them. Within a few more miles they were on a regular, tree-lined road with no risk of plunging to their deaths. As the miles clicked by the rain stepped it up another gear, slamming into the roof of the RV like ball bearings – even with the wipers on full, they struggled to keep up with the deluge.

The dirty, wet night was suddenly torn away by a blast of white light as two helicopters thundered their way overhead, and Sam swerved momentarily before regaining control of the wheel. The helicopters followed the road for a few hundred yards, their Midnight Sun search-lights snaking along the wet tarmac before banking left, illuminating the trees and river. "Jesus!" cried Sam, struggling with the steering wheel as he worked to prevent the RV from losing its rear end on the saturated road. "Those guys can't have been higher than sixty feet!"

"Are they military?" Adam croaked, watching the spotlights as they slowly disappeared into the distance. The sudden shock had left his mouth dry.

"Hard to tell," Sam replied, slowing the RV . "Could have been. Sounded like Cobras – I know the US Marines use them. Look, there are two more on the right." He gestured out of the side window.

Adam could just make out the searchlights through the trees and rain. "I wonder what the hell they're looking for?"

"Most likely some kind of training exercise," Sam replied. "They do love sending you out on stupid tasks when the weather is bad, tough-ens you up." He paused for a few seconds as the choppers' disappeared behind a large, pine-covered hill. "Maybe they're looking for people illegally camped in the car parks," he grinned, firing Adam a sly wink. Before Adam could issue a comeback, an array of blue lights began closing in on them from behind. Sam slowed the RV to a crawl, shaking his head in annoyance at a second disruption. Flicking on the indicator to let them know he was aware of their approach, Sam pulled as far over as he could and watched as three jet black SUVs tore past, far too fast for the conditions, the blue lights in their grills bouncing off the rain like nightclub strobes. "Well, someone's definitely up to something," Sam pondered, watching the vehicles vanish around a, right-hand bend. "Might be a good time to get off the road and bunk down for the night. The SatNav says we're on Trail Ridge Road, so we should see a few rest areas soon."

"Maybe we should push on," Adam interjected. "Who knows what's going on?" He was feeling so nauseous, the Mac 'n Cheese seemed as if it wanted to make a re-appearance.

"Nah, I'm beat; plus, I want to get in a hike like we planned. I'm sure this weather will clear by morning. The guide books say it's really changeable here." Sam leaned forward and flicked on the stereo before craning his neck over the steering wheel, as if the extra few inches would afford him a clearer view of the road ahead.

Adam knew what song would be playing before it came through the RV's speaker system, it was Annie's Song, just like he'd heard in his dream.

"My God, you look like you're going to throw up! I'm definitely stopping!" said Sam, his voice full of concern. Adam couldn't reply, time had slowed down as the world turned black and white, like a slow-motion video replay. "Seriously, mate, you look rough." Sam had half an eye on the road and half on his friend. He spotted the small wooden 'rest area' sign in the headlights. "I'm pulling in here!"

"I'm fine," managed Adam, breathing hard. "Just keep going." He felt his nails bite painfully into his palms as he clenched his hands tightly into fists. It was too late. Sam flicked on the indicator and swung the RV onto the gravel track. Adam watched the headlights illuminate a sign that read 'STRICTLY NO CAMPING.'

As John Denver launched into the first chorus, Adam spied a stag from the corner of his eyes and cried out to Sam. "Watch out for the—"It was almost too late, the animal had darted from the trees and stood, frozen and doe-eyed in the lights.

"Bloody hell, you've got sharp eyes!" cried Sam. As he jammed on the brakes, the open pack of cheesy snacks slid along the dash and spilt all over the cab in a hail of small orange balls. The stag stared at them for a few seconds before taking flight into the woods. "That was a close one," he chuckled nervously.

Adam's fingers dug harder into his sweaty palms with every second as he fought to keep his dinner down. The urge to vomit was overwhelming. Gradually the RV bumped its way down the long gravel track, and just as it had in his dream, the lane opened out into a car park, a mighty redwood forming a natural roundabout in the centre.

Adam knew she would be there, as sure as night follows day, just as he'd known what song would be playing on the radio when Sam turned it on. When Sam swung the RV around in the car park, he saw her. Adam's heart stopped for a split second. She looked dead, mud was caked through her blonde hair, blood oozed from a wound on her thigh, and yet her dirty white clothing luminesced strangely in the headlights of the RV, just as it had in his dream. There was just enough of her body clear of the raging, angry river to keep it from being swept away. Suddenly, time seemed to catch up in a hurry. Colour flooded back into everything, snapping him from the waking, dream-like state.

"Fuck me, there's a body over there!" cried Sam, jamming on the brakes so hard, all four wheels instantly locked in protest, bringing the RV to a skidding halt on the wet gravel. The vehicle had barely stopped moving before Sam was out of the door and soaked by a torrent of rain that immediately drenched his clothes, plastering his shirt to his skin. "Give me a hand, for fuck sake!" he called back as the door swung shut. Adam felt himself moving. With each passing second, he kept expecting to wake up safe in his bed back home. This time, however, it was even more real. Throwing his door open, he launched out into the rain. The deluge immediately soaked him to the skin as the sound of the thunderous downpour filled his ears. "What the hell is she doing out here?" shouted Sam, racing toward the body. Adam could only just hear him over the rain and the raging torrent of the river. Slipping and sliding on the wet riverbank, they managed to drag the body clear and turned her onto her back. The sight of her face made Adam catch his breath, she was as beautiful as in his dream had suggested, despite her pallid colour.

"Help me get her into the RV!" shouted Sam, picking her up beneath her arms.

As he lifted her body, Adam caught sight of a small, metallic object about the size of a credit card. It fell from the girl's hand and bounced on the wet gravel. Adam eyed it for a split second; it almost seemed to be glowing in the darkness.

"Hey, snap out of it and give me a hand!" yelled Sam, struggling to keep his grip under the girl's arms.

Adam bent down and scooped the object up, stuffing it into his pocket before lifting her legs. For a split second as the object dropped into the depth of his pocket, he'd been certain he felt it vibrate.

Gradually they navigated their way across the waterlogged car park; Sam reached the side door of the RV first and threw it open. He hauled the girl's limp body up and into the living quarters as Adam guided her feet. "Get her up onto the bench seat," Sam instructed, pulling the dining table out of the way in one swift movement. The clean linoleum floor was swiftly covered in a mixture of mud, gravel, water and blood. Sam bent down and supported her under the arms once again. "On three we lift, okay?" he encouraged. "One, two, THREE!" They hauled her up onto the seat and immediately regretted not covering it with something as the clean, fresh velour covers were subjected to the same filth that was all over the floor.

"Is she dead?" whispered Adam, standing back and feeling a bit useless. His mind was spinning. Why had he seen her in his dream? Maybe they were meant to find her all along, rescue her. If that was the case, why had his mind steered him back to Afghanistan with all the death and suffering? He couldn't piece it together. He knew one thing, though. The mother of all headaches was brewing away nicely at the back of his head.

"I need to check her," said Sam, slipping straight into army combat mode. He rolled up her dirty, wet sleeve. The fabric was as light as silk, but felt much stronger. Resting two fingers lightly on the cold skin on her wrist, he tried to locate a pulse, simultaneously dropping his head down to place his ear by her mouth.

"Is she breathing?" Adam whispered, his voice shaking.

"Shhh. I'm trying to see if I can hear her breathing," snapped Sam in a low voice, waving him back with a frustrated movement. Adam watched on as the seconds seemed to tick by like minutes, finally Sam looked up, "Okay, I've got a pulse," he said, sounding relieved. "It's a little weak, but that's to be expected. I don't know how long she was in the water for. Her breathing is shallow but it's there and that's the main thing. Can you pass me some towels and a blanket; we need to keep her warm, she might be in hypothermic shock."

Sidestepping Sam, Adam reached over and whipped the tasteless floral double duvet off the bed, then grabbed a fresh towel from the small rail outside the bathroom. The gloom of the RV was abruptly bathed in light, as the *thwack, thwack* of helicopter blades drowned out the rain. In unison Adam and Sam both stopped breathing, as if the sound of an exhaled breath would give away their position. Adam watched Sam gazing up at the ceiling, as if he could actually see the helicopter above them. The chopper was hovering so low, the noise it created made the cupboard doors vibrate on their hinges. Behind the doors, the mugs rattled and danced on the shelves. After what seemed like an eternity, the light whipped away and the sound of the slamming blades faded out as the helicopter left and banked off over the river.

"What the fuck is going on?" asked Sam, his voice low and quiet. "I mean, she's been shot." He gestured to the gaping hole on the girl's thigh which continued to ooze a steady stream of bright red blood.

"I don't know; do you think those choppers were looking for her?"

"Seems pretty fucking likely. I'm guessing people with gunshot wounds don't wash up here all the time, especially not when there's a squadron of 'copters combing the area. Can you grab me a pair of scissors? I need to get a better look at this wound."

"Do you want my belt, too?" asked Adam, already unclipping it from around his waist, "You can use it as a tourniquet to stem the bleeding."

"Good idea, although I'm not sure how bad it is and the position is not great. Some of the blood flow seems to have eased, which is strange. It might not be as bad as I first thought."

Placing the belt by Sam, Adam knelt on the soaking linoleum floor and watched him work, expertly cutting the white fabric of her clothing from around the wound before dabbing it clean with a towel. "Don't often get to use my skills on day to day – what the...?" He trailed off, his face washed in pale confusion.

"What's wrong?"

"I don't understand," Sam began shakily. "When we got to her, I could see blood pouring from her thigh. Hell, she was still bleeding when I checked her vitals. It's— stopped!" He lifted the towel away and Adam could see skin through the hole in her clothing. But where the blood had been flowing not two minutes ago, that area now just looked red and inflamed. Inexplicably the redness faded as they watched, until there was no trace of any wound at all. Sam stood up and backed off a little, his mouth hanging open. "That's impossible," he whispered, dropping the scissors to the floor.

"Maybe you were wrong," Adam suggested, trying to reason out what he'd just witnessed. "Maybe she just had someone else's blood on her? You never know. It was pretty dark out there, not to mention the rain. It was hard to see properly."

"No, she had a fucking gunshot wound!" Sam cried, pointing to the hole in her clothing. "I don't need to be a doctor to know that. God knows I've seen enough of them! And I don't need to be a doctor to know that gunshot wounds don't just heal themselves in a matter of minutes." Sam's blousy expression was set in stone, deep wrinkles creasing his wet brow. For the first time in the past few minutes, Adam suddenly felt like he was the one more in control. Sam seemed frozen, unable to take his eyes away from the miracle which had just occurred right in front of him.

"Maybe we should just take her to a hospital."

"Where?" barked Sam, snapping back to reality. "I bet the closest one is back in Denver, maybe Boulder. That's over two hours away. More like three in this weather. Not forgetting the fact that she seems to be able to do a pretty good job of fixing herself!"

"We should call 911," Adam suggested. He grabbed a fresh towel, threw it on the floor and started soaking up some of the bloodied water by pushing the towel around with his foot. He thought he should be doing something, no matter how pointless. "What if she's been abducted or something? Maybe those police vehicles we saw and the choppers are looking for her."

Sam glanced down at the unconscious girl; her breathing had improved so much that he could now see the gradual rise and fall of her chest. "Those weren't police, mate. Those SUVs were government, or CIA." He kept glancing at the hole in her clothing, where he'd cut the material away to get at the wound. Why the hell would they have all that manpower out looking for this girl? She couldn't be more than twenty-six – twenty-nine at the most. She had no weapons on her and nothing about her seemed dangerous as far as he could tell. She was odd, there was no denying that, but just being odd didn't get you

61

hunted like a dog through the woods, and it certainly didn't get you shot.

"Is that some kind of military uniform she's wearing?" Adam enquired. Her white clothing was a one-piece affair, figure-hugging, almost like a thin and much more flattering flight suit. Strange gold lettering ran the full length of both arms.

"Not that I've ever seen. Just looks like some kind of jumpsuit, but the material's strange. I don't recognise it and I sure as hell don't know what language that is. Could be Russian or something."

"Why would they be after a Russian? The Americans haven't had issues with them for decades." Adam began gingerly dabbing her skin with a clean, dry towel, mopping some of the water from her face and hair. He found it hard to take his eyes away from her face. Even in her unconscious state he was captivated.

"I didn't say she was Russian," snapped Sam, leaning back against the kitchen sink and watching as Adam fussed over her. "I said she could be. The whole situation beats the shit outta me." Adam placed the duvet over her dirty clothing. "Good work," he commented. "We need to keep her warm. She's got some questions to answer when she comes around."

Stepping away, Adam tucked the towel into his back pocket. His hand brushed the strange metal rectangle. Just as when he first touched it, the whole thing seemed to vibrate when his fingers found it. In all the fuss and panic he'd completely forgotten about picking it up. Adam retrieved the object from his pocket. "This was in her hand when we moved her." He lifted it up for Sam to see. In the dim light of the RV, there was no doubt the object had a mysterious glow to it.

"What the hell is that?" asked Sam, his voice flat and barely more than a whisper. He reached out and took the item. The moment his fingers touched the strange object, it vibrated and hummed slightly. It appeared to be made of a mixture of gold and brass, but it was like no metal he'd ever touched before; it rested with impossible lightness in his hand, and yet it felt as strong as steel. Apart from the vibration coming off the surface, he could barely feel its weight. Sam cast his eye along the strange inscriptions that ran down its length, engraved into the smooth, glowing metal. He leaned forward and peeled back the duvet. The lettering seemed to match the strange language that ran down both arms of the mystery girl's jumpsuit. "This is some proper Twilight Zone shit!" he added, placing the object on the table with a metallic clunk suggestive of something much heavier. As it left his hand it seemed to fade slightly, but still retained a soft glow. "I think it's safe to say that our friends in the SUVs and choppers are definitely after her. It's too much of a coincidence otherwise," he concluded, running the options through his head. It didn't seem right to just hand her over, but on the flip side, he didn't know what they were getting themselves into by providing her refuge.

"We should get moving," said Adam hastily. He felt sure that another chopper would arrive at any moment, or worse, one of the oppressive-looking SUVs which had torn past them earlier.

"And go where?" snapped Sam, frustration brewing in his voice. "The area is crawling with FBI, CIA or whoever the hell they are; this vehicle's not exactly easy to miss; not to mention the fact that this road is pretty much just one long run all the way back to Route 40. And why the hell are we suddenly choosing to aid a fugitive?"

"We don't know she's a fugitive!" protested Adam. "She doesn't look like one."

Sam pondered their options. Adam was right. His eyes fell again on the unconscious girl. There was no denying just how strangely beautiful she was. Colour was returning to her face with every passing second. It wouldn't be long before she was awake; her recovery was nothing short of miraculous. When they'd found her, not ten minutes ago, she'd had all the appearance of a subject in major trauma, in need of urgent professional medical care. Nothing fit and nothing made sense.

"Get her off the bench seat," he instructed, tearing the duvet away from her wet body.

"What the hell are you doing?" cried Adam. "We need to keep her warm."

"The seat has storage space beneath it," replied Sam, gripping her under the arms again, "designed to hold bedding and sheets. It's also big enough to hide little Miss Mystery." Adam helped him by taking hold of her feet. Gently, they lowered her to the floor. "We need to get down out of the mountains," he continued, sliding the cushions off the seat. "I'm going to head back the way we came and try to reach Route 40. If we get stopped and try to bluff our way out of trouble, and they take a look in the back and see her snoozing, it's not going to look good. I still don't know why I'm even doing this. My head is screaming at me to leave the whole situation well alone!" Standing back, Sam examined the small coffin-like space under the bench seat. The girl looked to be about five feet four. She would fit, but only just. Reaching down, he picked up the floral duvet that now looked like it had been dragged behind a car through a muddy field. Bending down, Sam lined the cavity with it. "Help me lower her in," he said, taking hold of her again. Slowly, they placed the girl into the narrow space. Adam folded the sides of the duvet around her like a makeshift sleeping bag before Sam replaced the plywood base and cushions.

"What if she wakes up before we clear the area?" asked Adam, studying the mess on the floor.

"Let's just hope she knows how to keep quiet," said Sam, his face deadly serious.

Adam had only ever seen him like this during their time together in Afghanistan. They both took a couple of extra seconds to mop up the dirt and blood on the floor with the towels. The bench seat they'd laid her on was soaking wet, but there was no time to dry it. Tossing the dirty towels into a bag, Sam headed through to the driver's seat and gunned the engine. As a last thought, Adam reached out and grabbed the strange, metallic object off the table. It hummed welcomingly when he wrapped his hand around it. Tucking it safely into his pocket, he made his way to the front. The RV was moving before he got to the passenger seat.

Chapter 6

The heat retaining cardboard cup and plastic cap made sure the coffee inside stayed at near on nuclear temperature for a good fifteen minutes. Finch blew into the small hole in the cap, his breath forcing a dull note to sound, like blowing over a half-filled milk bottle. Despite the fact the cappuccino remained pretty much undrinkable for the first few minutes, it was better than the soup-sized mugs they also served it in. Those lost the heat so fast, you literally had to gulp it down.

Starbucks was heaving; Finch had been lucky enough to grab a barstool seat and now sat facing out into the departure lounge at JFK. He glanced at his Omega Seamaster; it was the only part of his old life that remained. It had been issued to him after being promoted to the head of President Remy's security detail. There were no engravings or government seals on it which could tie him to his old life. It was such a beautiful watch he hadn't been able to bring himself to just throw it away, and now the perfectly crafted Swiss hands told him it was fast approaching four in the afternoon. Checking the departure board, he saw there were still thirty minutes before his flight would be called. He'd been there for the past hour and a half, watching and waiting for the perfect time to deploy the pathogen. Letting his hand fall to his trouser pocket as he'd done every five minutes since his arrival, he felt the pen there poised and ready. Just resting his hand on it was a comfort. Smiling, he thought of his colleagues who would be doing exactly the same in the other three airports, all spaced out tactically across the globe. No doubt the London and Hong Kong vials had already been deployed, each operative choosing the busiest time at their airport, hoping to make the biggest impact. He was to be the third, with LAX being last.

His new passport and identity had worked wonderfully. On check-in, they'd examined his documents before allowing him through to the departure lounge. He still hated the name Isaac Stephens, it just didn't fit his new face. It would do for now, though. There was no way Robert Finch would have breezed through check-in as he had. No, Robert Finch would now be in FBI custody with some very tough questions to answer.

Running his eyes down the departure board he saw the next four flights were bound for Sydney, Argentina, Bangkok and Madrid. The Sydney and Bangkok flights were both fast jet services, meaning the passengers would be at their destinations in hours, ready to spread the virus on.

Braving a sip, Finch let the cappuccino scald his tongue; he would need to get moving soon. His flight to Paris still had 'Wait in Lounge' flashing on the variety of boards spaced throughout the terminal, but a gate number would no doubt be revealed at any moment. Taking a last mouthful, he left the half full cup on the counter and stepped out into the main shopping and lounge area. A rich tapestry of life hustled and bustled its way through here, twenty-four hours a day. It was truly one of the main hubs and gateways to the world. A mother with a stroller containing a screaming child almost smashed into his ankle, whilst businessmen and women with phones glued to their ears hurried by, all looking to secure that last deal before boarding their flights.

Finch made his way to the end of the main shopping gallery. Here, the shops ended and gave way to long automated walkways that led to the departure gates. People for the next four flights were beginning to pour down them, all eager to hurry up and wait in the next section of the airport. Finch was always amused at how keen people were to stand around. The British, he'd learned, had a particular penchant for it.

None of the passengers looked at him, or took notice as he slid the smart-looking silver pen from his pocket and pushed the nib extender. Finch half expected to hear a slight aerosol style sound as the agent released itself into the air, but there was nothing. It was deadly silent. Walking away from the departure gates, he made his way confidently back to the shopping gallery, the pen clutched tightly in his right hand, thumb on the base. Throngs of people bustled past him; he was the only one walking against the tide of bodies all trying to reach their flights.

He knew the two minutes were up; in truth, he had held that activator down for more like five. He'd walked the entire length of the departure lounge without taking his finger off of it. Now relaxing his hand, he saw a small round imprint on his thumb, created by the pressure he'd applied. Double checking the task had been done, he gently unscrewed the pen at the centre and slid the vial out. It was empty. Right at that point the virus was out there, most likely already in the air-conditioning system and being pumped all over the departure lounge. Those he'd passed heading to their planes would soon be sealed up in their metal coffins, the virus spreading through them unseen, like a silent wildfire. Screwing the now-empty vial back into the pen, he slid it into the pocket of his Armani suit while a monotone female voice sounded over the intercom, snapping him from his thoughts.

"Ladies and gentlemen, American Airlines Fast Jet flight twenty-six to Paris will now begin boarding at gate number nine, all passengers please make your way to gate number *nine*." She seemed to emphasise the second 'nine' as if she were addressing a bunch of idiots.

Satisfied his work was done, Finch collected up his briefcase and patted his pocket one last time, checking for the pen. Losing it would no longer be an issue, but he wanted to keep it as a memento of this great day. Making his way to a slightly quieter area, near one of the toilets, he fished his cell phone out; it was time to call Buer. As usual, the phone hardly made it past the first ring before his supervisor answered.

"Yes?" came the voice, sounding expectant but still somehow annoyed by the intrusion.

"It's Finch," he began. "I'm just about to head down to my gate, the flight's just been called."

"Excellent. I trust everything is in order?" Buer sounded calm and confident.

"Of course!"

"Then enjoy Paris. I shall see you in two days." The line went dead. Buer was never one to say a formal goodbye, he never really said more than he needed to in any situation.

Switching his phone off and placing it back in his pocket, Finch made his way down to the boarding gate. As usual it was a good five-minute walk, unless one was lazy enough to use the endless line of belt-driven walkways. As far as he was concerned, any chance to give the legs a stretch before being crammed onto a plane was a blessing. he never used the walkways.

The sleek silver body of the American Airlines Boeing X54 Fast Jet gleamed in the evening sun, and Finch relished the thought that the near-on carbon neutral jet Peterson had been massively involved in, was his transport for the day. The X54s used a revolutionary hydro-oxygen jet engine that was capable of taking its passengers and crew to an impressive two and a half thousand miles an hour in unrivalled comfort. Tickets on these new super liners were not cheap; most travellers still opted to use the slower, conventional jets. Of course, money was no issue for Finch; as long as society was still functioning, he planned to enjoy the best of everything.

A rather camp-sounding, but strangely muscular-looking steward with a toxic orange tan personally showed him to his seat in first class, where a small chilled bottle of fine champagne was waiting for him.

Yes, this will all do very nicely. Within fifteen minutes the X54 was gaining speed down the runway. Once airborne, it banked east and headed out over the Atlantic. Now over the ocean, its massive hydro-oxygen jets kicked in, and the acceleration was breathtaking. Finch felt a small jolt as the plane broke the sound barrier and continued on up to its maximum speed. Once cruising at near two thousand five hundred miles an hour, the ride smoothed out and he couldn't even distinguish any motion.

Sipping the last of the champagne, Finch took a moment to glance around the first class cabin. He wondered who here had already picked up the virus. He was in no doubt that by the end of the three-hour flight, not one person on board would be free of the infection – not that they would be aware of it.

Soon after take-off, the cabin crew came around with the evening meal. Finch opted for the Beef Wellington with seasonal vegetables and a red wine reduction. The food was excellent and far beyond the slop they served on the conventional airliners. The standard wasn't far off some of the finer restaurants he'd been lucky enough to dine in, during his time on presidential protection duties.

Jetting east at supersonic speeds, the sky soon turned dark. Once the dinner service was finished and tidied away, there was a mere two hours of flying time left. Somewhere out across the vast expanse of the Atlantic, Europe was rushing up to meet them. Finch closed his eyes and drifted off into a deep, satisfied sleep.

The captain's request, for passengers to fasten their seat belts in preparation for landing, brought him around from his slumber. Clicking his belt into place he could feel the jet descending on approach to Charles De Gaulle. Glancing out of the small, circular window, he could see the vast, spider-like web of Paris's street lighting system stretching off into the distance, where it gradually eased off and gave way to countryside. Cars that created no more than pinpricks of light far below, still hurried about the city streets despite the local time being just past three am. The two hours of rest he'd managed to steal during the flight wasn't enough; the past month had been the most stressful of his life and his sleep had suffered for it. Once all this was done, he would take some time to relax, time that was well earned as far as he was concerned.

As the jet touched down, Finch cast his thoughts to the virus. No doubt every vial had now been deployed. He wondered how many countries it had already spread to. The next thirty odd hours would be a waiting game. Where would it show up first? And how widespread would it be? With the thirty-hour incubation period, Buer estimated that even after the first cases began to show it would still take a good twenty-four hours for airports to be closed and quarantines to be set up. The thought of watching the chaos unfold made him smile. In a few weeks, none of these planes would be flying, none of the cars he'd just seen hurrying about the city streets would be moving. It would be interesting to see how the human race handled the complete breakdown in their society. He was in no doubt that to start with, there would be wide-spread lawlessness and looting, but even the opportunists taking advantage of the brief spell of chaos would eventually succumb. Gradually, the unrest would ease, leaving nothing but a massive clean-up operation. Whilst there was no doubting one god-awful mess would be left in the weeks after the virus had done its job, once the bodies had been disposed of, the towns and cities would remain. Just as Buer had said, it would be like moving into a furnished apartment, just one that needed a few small repairs and a little TLC.

The sound of the cabin doors being opened snatched Finch from his daydream. He was finding himself lost in thoughts of things to come more and more often these days. Gathering his possessions, he made his way out of the jet and into the arrivals lounge. It should only take him a half hour or so to get to the hotel, where he planned to get some more sleep and have a day of relaxation. There were no formal business matters to attend to in Paris; the whole trip had merely been a ruse to get him into JFK's International Departure Lounge, so that the pathogen could be released. In just over twenty-four hours he would be at the HQ in Allentown, back on US soil where he would remain while the virus did its work. This would mean more relaxation; his hardest task would be watching from the bunker as the whole situation unfolded.

Waiting for what seemed like an age at the carousel for his small overnight bag, Finch turned his phone on. The screen blinked for a few seconds as the small device figured out where on the planet it was. Eventually it found the Bouygues Network, and a text came through, welcoming him to France and informing him of the 4G network service charges. As he began reading through it, more from boredom than interest, his phone flashed to an incoming call. It was Buer. He answered it in the same prompt manner that Buer always managed – allowing no more than one ring.

"Robert!" Buer's voice thundered from across the Atlantic.

Finch picked up on a note of anger and urgency to his supervisor's tone, and his heart rate immediately picked up. "Yes... sir?" he managed. The sudden call had made him miss his bag. He watched in silent annoyance as it disappeared through the plastic screen and back into the loading area.

"There has been a change of plan. You need to make your way directly around to departures. Go to the Air France desk, there's a ticket waiting for you." Buer spoke quickly and concisely, but there was definitely an underlying tone that warned something was wrong.

"Air France?" It was all Finch managed to say before Buer cut back in.

"Yes, Air France," he snapped. "It's a fast jet service to Denver, Colorado. I'll be meeting you on the ground near the airport. The flight leaves in just under an hour. We took the liberty of checking you in online whilst you were in the air. Make no mistake, Robert. You *must* be on that flight!"

The fact that Buer was leaving the New York area did nothing to calm Finch's growing anxiety. Something had obviously happened whilst he was in the air, something which wasn't good. "Yes sir, I'm on my way now." Finch managed to grab his bag before it commenced another lap. He still had the phone glued to his ear and his hand shook slightly as he followed the signs out of arrivals and through to departures. "May I ask why I'm being flown back straightaway?" His heart was hammering like a drum.

"There's a problem," Buer barked at him. "It could be a very big one. There are events unfolding here as we speak which require you to return immediately. You're needed here. We have men on the ground dealing with the situation, but I can't afford to have you swanning around Paris for a day." Buer paused for a brief second; when he spoke again, Finch could hear the stress in his voice. "I'm afraid, Robert, that as you were the one working so closely on locating the Watchers, there are some questions coming your way. We won't discuss it now. You'll be in Denver in just under four hours, we can talk then." As usual, the line went dead before he even had the chance to say goodbye.

Finch slowly removed the BlackBerry from his ear, and he realised he'd stopped walking and was staring blankly at the handset, as if it would suddenly provide him with the answers as to what the hell was going on. Snapping back into action, he hurried to the departures terminal and collected his ticket.

Just over an hour later, he was back in the air. The French cabin crew busied themselves with serving breakfast. By the time they reached Denver, the local time would be around eleven pm; for now though, they were still operating on French time. A beautifully prepared plate of Eggs Benedict was offered, but Finch was in no mood for eating, he waved the flight attendant off when she offered the meal. His stomach was so sick with worry, he couldn't even handle a coffee, the beverage which was a bit of a French speciality. What the hell was happening in Denver that was so important he was being flown directly there?

A quick glance at his watch told him that in just over two hours he'd know – whether he liked it or not.

Chapter 7

Sam watched the trip counter click past two miles. Neither of them had uttered another word in the few long minutes since leaving the rest area. The rain had eased slightly, but water still flowed down the road like a river, trickling and bubbling over small stones worked loose from the verge. Sam continually scanned the dark brooding skies, any second expecting to see the lights of a helicopter bearing down on them. He watched Adam glancing to the rear of the RV, waiting for any signs that their guest had woken up. He eased his foot off the gas.

"Why are we slowing down?" Adam spoke so quietly, Sam only just heard the question.

"Look, up ahead, around the next bend." He gestured with his head. Through the trees the faint throb of blue lights was just visible. He lifted his foot off the accelerator completely and gently applied the brake. Killing the lights, he brought the RV to a stop. "I think there's some kind of roadblock up there, those lights are stationery."

"Oh shit!" hissed Adam. "What the hell are we going to do now?"

"As I said, this road is pretty much a one-way ticket back to Route 40. I could turn around, but I'd bet my arse there would be another barricade in the other direction." Sam was gripping the steering wheel so tightly; his fingers were turning white. "We have two choices – try and bluff it and hope whoever is up there doesn't pull the RV to pieces and lets us through, or—"

"We can't hand her over," Adam cut in. "We don't know what they might do to her."

"Just think for a minute," snapped Sam. "It's true we don't know that, but on the flip side, we don't know why the hell they want her. What do we really know about her? Nothing!" Sam's head was spinning and he was desperately trying to think rationally. There was no way in the world they should be trying to smuggle this girl off the mountain and back to Denver. If they were discovered, they could be arrested and thrown into jail. It certainly wasn't the way he'd intended to start their trip. They should be parked up by now, enjoying a few beers and planning tomorrow's hike – not be on the run from the law.

"I know, I know," Adam said, so quickly the words all rolled into one. "I don't know, any other day I'd agree with you, no question, it's just…" he paused, searching for the right words. "My gut is telling me we need to do this; we need to help her."

Sam chewed the inside of his bottom lip. It was a habit he'd picked up back in his army days, whenever he was under pressure. He worried the skin continually, until he started to taste blood. "You do realise that if they search the RV and find her, we could end up in jail?" He watched the last drops of colour ebb from Adam's face.

"Yes I know. I'm not stupid – I was trying not to think about that," he groaned, giving his friend a nervous smile.

"Fuck it, if this all goes wrong, just remember not to drop the soap! Oh, and let me do the talking." Sam flashed Adam a quick, sly but nervous smile. Flicking the lights on, he got the RV moving again. As they rounded the corner, the lights ahead of them grew in strength, making it hard to see the road. At no more than walking pace, Sam crept up to the two patrol cars blocking their way. He experienced a little relief to see they were local law enforcement from Empire, and not the black government SUVs which had torn past them less than half an hour ago.

He hoped the local police wouldn't be quite so meticulous, perhaps they didn't know the full story and would be pissed about having to spend the night out in the storm for a bunch on desk-jockeying suits from DC.

Bringing the RV to a stop, he counted three uniformed police officers, all clad in full wet-weather gear, standing unhappily on point by their cars. On seeing the RV, one of the men stepped forward and flagged them down using a torch with an orange baton affixed to the top. It looked like something one might see ground crew at an airport use, for directing aircraft. Sam killed the engine and cranked up the parking brake, watching as the officer walked briskly to the driver's side window, gesturing with his free hand for Sam to wind it down. Sam's heart hammered in his chest; he'd operated under pressure plenty of times, this would be no different. He just needed to stay calm and hope Adam could do the same.

"Good evening, gentlemen," the officer began. His accent sounded more southern than those they'd heard back in Denver. "Would y'all mind if I come aboard? It's not the nicest of evenings out here." His hat sported a full waterproof cover. The rain was pooling on it and running off onto his shoulders.

"No problem," Sam replied, "the door's just on the other side." Adam glanced at him nervously. He looked like a frightened rabbit caught in the headlights of a fast-approaching car.

"Much appreciated." The officer tipped his hat in thanks, and a small torrent of water ran off the brim and down the front of his jacket. Clicking off his baton torch, he made his way past the front of the RV, his fluorescent tabard catching the dimmed headlights. As they both watched the officer through the windscreen, two short sharp thumps came from beneath the bench seat. Sam whipped his head around, just in time to see the cushion ride up as their hidden passenger pushed on the seat's plywood base. After being shot and almost drowned, waking up in a box the size of a coffin was bound to be a cause for concern.

"Shit!" spat Sam, quickly swinging out of the large captain's chair and into the living area. This was possibly the worst time for her to come around. Just one strange noise and the game would be up. The officer was almost at the door, so Sam crouched down by the soaking cushion, "Listen, if you can hear me, I really need you to just shut the hell up for a few minutes." His voice was hushed, but loud enough for Adam to make out. He just hoped the rain still pounding on the roof masked his speech enough. "We're trying to help you, but if you make a sound in the next few minutes we're all fucked!" As he finished the sentence, the door creaked and swung open, Sam stood bolt upright as if he were standing to attention.

The tall, wet, oppressive figure of the officer stepped up into the RV, removed his hat and shook it off. "That's some godawful weather out there tonight!" the officer commented, placing his hat on the draining board, "Sheriff Johnson," he said politely, offering Sam a very wet hand.

"Pleased to meet you, sir," Sam began. The Sheriff had a good, strong grip. His greying hair was matted to his head, a neat line indenting it where his hat had been. "Samuel Becker, and my friend up front is Adam Fisher." Sheriff Johnson kept pumping his hand during the whole introduction. Sam placed him in his early fifties; the deep wrinkles on his brow along with his grey hair led Adam to believe he'd spent much of his working life doing shifts. Aside from that, he looked in pretty good shape for a man of his age.

"You boys British?" he asked, standing back slightly so he could take them both in at once.

"Yep, arrived today, just on a bit of a road trip," said Sam, trying to sound calm. The Sheriff nodded his head slowly. "Is there a problem up ahead? We thought all this rain might have closed the road off." Sheriff Johnson shook a little water off his sleeve; it dripped down onto the floor Adam had recently cleaned.

"Road's fine," he began, "it gets closed plenty in the winter months but never due to a drop of rain. This the RV the chopper saw, parked back up on Trail Ridge?"

"Yep, that was us; we drove up from Denver earlier, hoping to find somewhere to camp up for the night," chirped Sam, as Adam made his way through from the front.

"Yeah, I told him there would be nowhere to camp, but he had to see for himself," Adam confirmed. Sam shot him a look that told him to shut up and let him do all the talking.

Sheriff Johnson eyed them both and nodded suspiciously through narrow, testing eyes. "Yep, you can't camp in any of the picnic or rest areas overnight," he began, flicking his alert eyes back and forth between them. "Unfortunately, folk seem to have a habit of leaving all manner of junk behind when they do. Where are ya'll heading now?" He leaned back, resting some of his weight against the small kitchen unit.

"Just back down to Empire," Sam said, cutting in before Adam got a chance to speak. "Maybe Idaho Springs. Find a parking lot we can get on for a few hours before making a fresh start in the morning. We're both pretty beat. It's been a long day."

The Sheriff took a good look around the RV, soaking in every detail.

"You didn't tell us what the problem was. Are we okay to carry on? If not, we're a bit stuck."

"Sorry, the Fed boys have the whole area on lockdown," the Sheriff replied, snapping his eyes back to Sam. "We don't get many vehicles through here at night, but right now, we have to check anyone passing through." He paused for a second and wiped a drop of water off his nose. "A few hours ago, the FBI received some intel to suggest a small jet they were tracking from Canada contained three domestic terrorists. Our Air Force boys brought it down. They have two dead in the wreckage, but one made it out alive. A female. They pursued her for a mile or so, but lost her down by the river, not far from where you boys were stopped. Chances are she fell in, trying to get away, and drowned. The water gets pretty fierce after a storm, what with all the runoff from the mountains and all, but they don't take any chances with things like this. Those boys won't be happy until they have her body."

"Domestic terrorism?" muttered Sam surreptitiously. "What was their cause?"

"That's all I know. They don't tend to tell us more than they need to with things like this. Guess it's a good day for scum like that to hit the country, while it's down 'n all." Sheriff Johnson shook his head sadly, obviously fully suckered in by what Sam suspected was a blatant and rather poor cover story. Sam had worked in military and government circles long enough to know when people lower down the food chain were being kept in the dark like a mushroom and fed shit; this was one of those occasions. There was no way that girl was a terrorist of any description, terrorists didn't possess magical healing powers, for one thing, at least the ones Sam had had the misfortune of dealing with in the past didn't.

"Wow!" he exclaimed, letting a long breath out through his teeth, still trying to play the dumb tourist, "That's some scary stuff; you said it was a female they were looking for?"

"Yes, sir. We don't have a good description, but they believe she's white, about five feet five, blonde hair, in her mid-to-late twenties."

"Well, we certainly haven't seen any blonde, twenty-something females up here," Sam laughed. "I'm sure we would have remembered!"

The sheriff fired him a disapproving look, obviously not amused by the joke. "You boys been outside?" He pointed to Sam's jeans and tee-shirt. "You're both soaking wet." Despite the cold wet shirt clinging to his body, Sam had completely forgotten they were both still drenched. His mouth went dry – the Sheriff was obviously pretty wily. What reason could he give for them venturing out in this storm, without first donning some kind of wet weather gear? He was certain the sheriff would call the other two officers over to start pulling apart the RV at any moment.

"Yep, that was my fault," chipped in Adam. "Musta eaten some dodgy food back in Denver earlier. When we stopped back up in that rest area, I was pretty sick. I didn't want to risk blocking the chemical toilet." He clutched his stomach and tried his best to look a little nauseous.

"Okay, okay, you can spare me the gory details," laughed the Sheriff, holding both of his palms up. "You do look a little green, son. Anyway, if it's alright with you I just need a few details." He removed a small notebook from his waterproofs and took their names, as well as the licence plate number for the RV, which Adam provided from the rental agreement. "I'll take a quick look around, boys, if that's okay. And then I'll be out of your way. Sorry for the hold up." The Sheriff tucked his notebook back in his jacket.

"Sure, knock yourself out," sighed Sam. He had the feeling that saying no to Sheriff Johnson searching the RV wasn't an option anyway. "We'll just go wait up front and get out of your way." Nudging Adam into action, they both climbed back into the cab, turning in their seats to keep an eye on the unwelcome visitor.

"Nice RV," the Sheriff commented as he opened the toilet door, looking inside for far longer than was needed to establish that the small cubicle was empty. "What's she setting you back a night?"

"Sixty-five dollars," Sam replied.

"Not cheap, not cheap at all," the Sheriff said, letting out a small, surprised whistle. He was standing right by the bench seat, his left leg brushing on the wet cushion. "You dropping her back to Denver when you're done?" His search seemed to have been confined to the toilet cubicle. After all, on first appearances it looked to be the only place a person could reasonably hide.

"No, sir. Ultimately we're heading on to San Francisco." Sam was starting to see the light at the end of the tunnel, but they weren't quite out of the woods yet. It felt like an age since the Sheriff had come aboard. Thankfully, there had been no further sounds from under the bench seat.

"Well, I've kept you boys long enough," he concluded, collecting his hat up off the drainer and affixing it to his head. "I think the rain's starting to ease, but you take it careful. I've seen far too many folks killed on these mountain roads."

Sam felt as if he could have kissed the old fool – they were actually going to pull this off. "No problem, Sheriff. Have a good night," he said, getting up from the driver's seat to see him out.

"Thanks for your time. I'll get my boys to let y'all on through. You have yourselves a nice vacation." The Sheriff tipped his hat and shook Sam's hand one last time, before disappearing through the door and out into the ever-easing rain. They both watched him signal for the cars to be drawn back. The two officers who looked pig-sick of being kept out in the filthy weather jumped into action, obviously more than happy to have a few seconds in one of the dry patrol cars. As the road opened out before them, Sam fired the engine and got the RV moving. He treated Sheriff Johnson to a polite wave of thanks as they drove past.

Watching the flashing lights vanish behind them and into the night, Adam let out a massive sigh of relief, actually feeling the stress drain from his shoulders as the air escaped his lungs, "Shit, that was tense," he laughed; the elation at having pulled off the scam giving him a fit of uncontrollable giggles, like a child who'd just gotten away with something naughty.

"Domestic terrorism, I mean what kind of shithouse cover story is that?" added Sam, also trying to suppress a relieved laugh. "Do you want to get back there and see how she is? I need to know what's really going on."

In the relief of getting through the road block, Adam had actually forgotten that their hidden passenger had woken up, just as Sheriff Johnson stopped them. The fact that she hadn't made a sound after Sam told her to keep quiet meant she must at least understand or speak some English. The RV had reached the twisty section of Route 40. The ravine was now right by the side of the camper, dark and brooding. It looked hungry to claim any motorist who was foolhardy enough to test the crash barrier.

Struggling for balance, Adam realised it wasn't the easiest of times to be standing in the back taking apart the bench seat, but with his legs spread far enough apart and using the table as support, he removed the long cushion and opened the plywood top. It creaked slightly on its hinges. In the gloom, he saw her lying there, perfectly still, her large eyes wide open and as blue as an ocean. "It's— it's— o— okay," he mumbled, tripping over his words. Adam held his hand out. Gingerly, the girl slid her arm from her side and took hold of it. The instant his skin touched hers, a wave of emotion flooded his body, like electricity running down a wire. Fear drenched every part of him. He was experiencing her fear, he realized. She was scared for him, for everyone. In an instant it passed, replaced by her vulnerability, and then something else swept that aside. Power. For a brief moment, her very presence seemed to fill every inch of the vehicle as if nothing else existed. Her haunting eyes appeared to hold knowledge and experience far beyond her years. Adam's head swam, as every ounce of strength drained from his muscles. His legs started giving way. Gradually, a warm soft smile crept over her lips; a smile which made him want to melt right into the linoleum.

"You dreamed about me," she purred in a soft, musical tone. Unconsciousness took him and he hit the floor with a thump.

"Adam, what the fuck's going on back there? *Adam!*" As he came around, he could hear Sam shouting. It took a few second for the fuzziness in his mind to clear, and when it did, the past few minutes events rushed back into his head. What had she done to him?

"It's all okay," he managed to say, his tone slightly groggy. The girl was sitting up, still inside the storage area of the seat, looking quizzically at him. "I just slipped, that's all." He could see Sam craning his neck and trying to use the rear view mirror to get a look at what was happening.

"How is the girl? Is she awake? What was that thump?" Sam fired the questions off in quick succession, not waiting for answers. Adam shot her a quick glance. The sight of her face made his heart skip a beat, just as it had in the dream, the very first time he'd laid his eyes on her.

"Yes she's fine, just keep your eyes on the road and I'll be up with you soon." He wasn't sure how long he'd been out, it could only have been seconds. The camper still pitched left and right as Sam navigated the twisty sections of the treacherous road. Reaching into his back pocket, Adam took out the small metallic rectangle. Once again, it greeted him with a welcoming hum. "I… think… this belongs… to…you," he stammered, holding it out to her. The relief on her face was blatant. Whatever the mysterious object was, it was important.

"Thank you," she replied. Adam couldn't place her accent, it sounded like a mixture of Eastern European and French, all rolled into one, the words sliding off her tongue like silk. Reaching up, she took the object. It glowed brighter still at her touch. Drawing it close to her body, she clasped it tightly as if it were the most precious thing in the world.

"It fell from your hand when we rescued you," he managed to say. "It's beautiful; I've never seen anything like it."

"I thought I'd lost it," she whispered. "You have no idea how many lives may hinge on it being kept safe. Thank you." She turned it over in her hand, examining the strange writing on its glowing surface. Before Adam could ask what it was, Sam's voice broke through from the front, cutting him off.

"What the hell is going on back there? A little info would be good!" he called.

"We're fine, mate," Adam snapped, a little more aggressively than he meant. "Just give me a few minutes." He turned back to the strange girl. "Who are you?" The awkward question left his lips before he had time to rephrase it.

84

"Oriyanna," she replied, smiling warmly. "Thank you once again. I think you and your friend just saved my life. It was very brave what you did back there, hiding me away. You don't even know me." Adam felt the RV slowing; it bumped over some gravel before coming to a stop.

Sam climbed out of the captain's seat and joined them in the back. "Right, could someone please tell me what the..." his voice trailed off at the sight of her, sitting upright in the seat cavity, clutching the strange object which glowed brighter than ever.

"Sam, this is Oriyanna," Adam said, suddenly feeling awkward. Everything seemed a little disjointed and strange.

"It's good to see you're awake," Sam replied. The girl's ocean blue eyes were fixed on him; it seemed as if she was looking right into his soul. "My name is Sam, and this is Adam," he said slowly. There was something haunting about her that caught him off guard.

"Samuel," she began, "I was just thanking Adam for what you've done. You risked a lot to help me."

"It's no problem, and you can call me Sam. Only my foster mother ever called me Samuel, and I hated that bitch," he said, managing a small smile, but his words seemed to have no effect on her. "Do you want to come out of the seat cavity? I think we need to have a chat and get a few answers."

Adam took hold of her arm and helped her to her feet. Thankfully this time, there was no reaction to her touch, other than a little giddiness on his part, like a teenager on a first date who'd just stolen a kiss. There was something intoxicating about Oriyanna; he'd never been so drawn to a woman before. Sam bent down and removed the filthy wet duvet from the cavity. Shaking his head at the state of it, he shook it out and placed it back on the bed. It would need a good wash before they returned the rental, or the company would no doubt take a chunk of their security deposit. Finished with the duvet, he brushed the cushion off and replaced it while Adam fixed the small table back in place. Once everything was straight, Sam gestured for Oriyanna to sit down. "Can I get you a drink?" he asked.

"Just some water, please," she purred, sliding in behind the table, not letting the strange metallic object out of her grasp. Turning to the fridge, Sam removed a bottle of water. Removing the lid, he slid the bottle across the table to her before removing another two bottles. Adam broke the seal off his own and took a swig. The cool liquid instantly made him realise how thirsty he was.

"Thought you might have wanted a beer after that," he said, watching Sam take a drink.

"Yeah very funny, I need to keep a steady head, we might not be in the clear just yet. I haven't seen a helicopter for a while, but I bet they're still out there. I just want to get a few answers from Oriyanna before we push on."

"How far past the road block are we?" asked Adam, sitting down next to Oriyanna and setting his bottle on the table. Droplets of condensation ran down the clear plastic and pooled on the wood veneer.

"About six miles. We're just in a small side road. We should be okay for now." Sam glanced at Oriyanna as she drank the last of her water in two long swallows. "Back there, at the road block," he began, "the Sheriff said you were in a plane crash after being shot down by the military. Something about domestic terrorism. Now, I know a cover story when I hear one. I don't think for a second that you're a threat in that way. If I did, you wouldn't be here now. I've been unfortunate enough to deal with domestic terrorists many times before now, and I've never seen a single one heal themselves from a gunshot wound the way you did after we pulled you from the river." Sam paused searching for the right words. Despite the water, his tongue felt parched, like old, dried-out leather. "How did you do that?" He looked up and caught her gaze as she shifted awkwardly on the seat.

"I did wonder if you'd seen that," she began, sounding uneasy about the question. "The process is usually much faster, but being in the water slows it down." She paused and glanced at them both anxiously. "Have you heard of nanorobotics?"

"I've read a little about them," said Adam, caught a little off guard by the directness of her answer. "The theory is that microscopic robotic particles could one day be produced and used in medical research, for rebuilding damaged cells and organs, but as I said, as far as I know, it's just theory that borders on science fiction."

"Is this something the US government is testing?" Sam asked, running a hand over his face. "Were they carrying out trials on you? Is that what you were trying to escape?" During his military days, Sam had heard of some pretty underhanded stuff being carried out by both the British and American governments. If they had somehow developed a way for serious injuries to heal in minutes, he was in no doubt it would be a closely guarded secret, one worth killing for. Not to mention the financial worth of such a product.

"No, Samuel, I wasn't a test subject," she replied, smiling nervously. Sam cast his gaze over the strange object still clutched tightly in her hand. He couldn't even bring himself to approach that subject quite yet. "Though what Adam said is right," she added. "There was no magical trickery to what you saw. I have millions of tiny, nanorobotic particles in my body. My people call it 'The Gift', but it's nothing more than modern medical science. It means I can heal most wounds very quickly."

"Okay," said Sam suspiciously, letting her words sink in. "Now let's have an answer that doesn't sound like it's come from a crazy person." There was something about her deadly serious tone which told him she wasn't joking, but his sceptical mind just couldn't accept it, despite having seen it first-hand.

"It's the truth," she said bluntly. "I can't expect you to understand it, but as well as being able to heal, the nanobots also ensure I never get sick, nor do I age. They keep my body in peak physical condition.

Believe what you want. If you think you can explain what you saw, then that's fine."

I'll make us all a coffee," said Adam, standing up and removing three mugs from the cupboard. "I know I could use one right now." He had a strong urge to do something normal, despite how unreal the situation was. Somewhere deep in his gut, a small portion of the fear he'd felt from Oriyanna still lurked, fluttering around like a demon butterfly. He had no idea how she'd made him feel those things. He knew one thing though. As improbable as her story sounded, and as hard as it was for him to grasp, he didn't doubt it for a second. He put a heaped teaspoon of the rich-smelling powdered drink into each mug and added hot water from the small, instant boil water heater before following it up with a splash of milk. Sam was sitting in silence, thinking through what Oriyanna had told them as Adam placed a steaming mug of coffee in front of her. She eyed it with a slightly puzzled expression. "I wasn't sure if you took sugar," Adam said in a slightly awkward tone, setting a small plastic container and spoon by her mug. He watched her raise the mug to her face and take a sniff, followed by a very tentative sip. Her facial expression changed when she realised she liked the drink.

"This is okay," she said, lifting the mug up for another mouthful. "What did you say it was called again?"

"It's just coffee," replied Adam, frowning. "Where the hell have you been to have never had coffee?"

"It's a long story," said Oriyanna, staring into the dark hot liquid.

"Okay that's enough of the bullshit!" spat Sam, standing up and digging a hand into the pocket of his wet jeans to remove his iPhone.

"What are you doing?" gasped Adam, horrified.

"What we should have done back at that road block – handing her over. I don't know how you seem so calm about it. It's like she's put some kind of spell on you! You don't believe any of this crap, do you? I mean, I could have bought a story about her being a test subject and escaping, hell I know what I saw her do with that bullet wound." He pointed angrily at the place on Oriyanna's thigh; the only trace of the injury now was the hole in her suit which sported a light blood stain around the edges. "I think I know where this is going." His voice grew louder with each word. "We helped you, we risked getting arrested and all you can do is spin us tales about how you can't get sick, or even age, and then pretending you've never had or seen coffee! I mean, please!" He slid his thumb over the screen and selected the call menu. "I'm going to call the Sheriff and get him down here. He can make what he wants of the situation. Personally, I've had enough." He sat back down on the wet seat and began to dial 911.

In a flash, Oriyanna shot her hand across the table and grasped his wrist, slopping some of the coffee from her mug. She moved so fast, Sam didn't even have time to react. His thumb froze over the call button. "Samuel, please!" she pleaded, her eyes locked onto his. The sensation of her touch was electric. Instantly, his body went weak as the iPhone fell from his hand and clattered to the table. "I'm sorry I have to do this, but you have no idea what's at stake." Her voice was hushed and low, as calm as the flattest of oceans. Suddenly he felt it, fear washed over him like the breaking of a wave on a rocky shore. It was her fear though, not his – her fear for him, for Adam and for every living person. It was too much for him to take. Somewhere back in the real world, he felt bile rise in his throat as an icy hand wrapped itself around his heart. As fast as it came, the fear was gone, but he would never forget that feeling. Even the day he'd almost died, rescuing Adam from the village, had nothing on what she had shown him. Oriyanna's grasp was unrelenting. He was seeing through her now, her memories playing back like a movie in his mind's eye. He could see the rising crescent of the Earth, the northern hemisphere gradually slipping into darkness as daylight gave way to night. The beauty of it was undeniable. Sam suspected he could gaze at the scene forever. In a flash, it all changed as the sound of an explosion filled his ears. The Earth was spinning now, becoming bigger. Sounds of alarms and people shouting in panic filled the air. He couldn't place the language, but there was no mistaking their desperate cries. Intense heat seared his flesh as his stomach plunged. Sam felt as if he was falling for an eternity, falling and burning. The Earth was rushing up to meet him, and as he fell, it changed. First he saw entire continents, then mountains and oceans. He levelled out slightly, but the rate of descent was still fast, too fast. Clouds rushed past as the unrelenting heat continued to scorch his skin. Next came the ear-splitting crash of trees as the ground finally claimed him, then nothing but silence. The scene changed as Oriyanna guided him through the memory; he was running now, the scent of the forest filling his nose as pain stabbed every part of his body. Throwing himself left and right he dodged trees and bushes, while the heavy rain slammed into his skin, stinging his eyes. He could hear men shouting, and they were close. Somewhere to his left a dog was barking as it crashed through the undergrowth, gaining ground on him with every step. A bright searchlight sliced through the night, casting hellish shadows as it forced back the darkness. Through the commotion Sam heard the river, the water angry and rabid from the rain. For a brief moment, he felt himself stop at its bank, a moment of indecision brought the crack of gunfire and pain exploded down his leg. For a split second, his own memory overrode hers and he felt the bullet that had almost killed him back in Afghanistan. The force knocked him back and he fell again; this time it was water that greeted him. The thunderous sound of the river was the last thing he heard.

Back in the RV, Oriyanna released his wrist. It fell from her grasp and hit the table with a thump. Like a train emerging from a tunnel, the real world rushed back. Oriyanna's face greeted him, smiling sympathetically. "I'm sorry, Samuel," she said softly, "I didn't want to put you through that, Adam also had a bit of a shock when he helped me up earlier, I was weaker then and couldn't control it. Please understand, it was a last resort."

"You felt it too then?" said Adam quietly. He'd watched Oriyanna grab Sam. Although Sam's eyes had stayed open and locked on hers for the whole time she'd held him, he'd seemed to be in some kind of trance-like state. "At least you didn't pass out," he concluded, taking a small sip from his coffee.

"I had to show Samuel a little more," Oriyanna clarified. "Don't worry, Adam, I will explain everything very soon."

Sam stared blankly at her, his face devoid of expression. "The Sheriff was right," he began, his voice flat, "you were in a crash tonight, back there in the woods." Colour began to fill his cheeks as the effect of the transfer eased off.

"Yes, that's right." Oriyanna reached over and held Sam's hand for support. He flinched at her touch, but relaxed when no further energy passed from her.

"What you showed me," he murmured, "that wasn't a plane crash. I saw the Earth!"

"No, you're right," she agreed. "It wasn't a plane crash, nor were we shot down by your military. They had nothing to do with what happened until after the crash. We were attacked before we even entered your atmosphere."

Although Adam hadn't been privy to whatever Oriyanna had shown Sam, the impossible pieces were beginning to fit together. Her technologically advanced healing, the unusually high military presence in the area, not to mention the way she'd affected him when he'd helped her up. The unbelievable truth of the situation did nothing to halt the headache that was becoming ever more prevalent. Whilst Sam hadn't passed out after she'd taken hold of him, it was clear he was taking a good few minutes to recover.

"I don't understand," began Sam, drawing a few deep breaths as he rubbed his face with his hands, trying to clear his spinning head. "You look human, you sound human, and you even speak English. It's just not possible."

"That's because to all intents and purposes, I am human, Samuel. As for speaking your language, it's not really that hard. I can speak almost every modern Earth language, as well as many of the ancient languages which are long since extinct," she said, eyeing him sincerely.

"How is it possible for you to look exactly like us?" asked Adam, sliding back onto the bench seat beside her. "I'm no scientist, but the chances of two races evolving to look exactly the same must be millions, if not billions to one." His own calm and acceptance of the situation surprised him. He was sure that whatever the girl had done to him, was still affecting him somehow.

"Trillions, actually," replied Oriyanna, turning to face him, "and I think you will find it's more a case of you looking like us, and not the other way around."

"What do you mean?" asked Sam, looking puzzled, "it's more a case of we look like you?"

"Because, Samuel," she let out a long breath, "you were created in our image." Her words fell heavily on both of them. For a few long, drawn-out seconds an awkward silence hung in the air, almost consuming them.

"Impossible," Sam finally muttered, breaking the tension. "I mean there would be some record of it somewhere. Surely we'd know?" Despite all that he'd seen and felt through her touch, he couldn't comprehend the magnitude of what they'd been told.

"It is," cut in Adam a little distantly.

"It is what?"

"Recorded, sort of. It's more theory, really." Adam watched Sam raise his eyes in a fashion that pressed him to continue. "Not long after you went back to the Middle East on close protection work, I went out to Mexico to research a story for Lonely Planet, looking at deforestation on the Yucatan Peninsula. I met a guy there who was doing a dig on one of the Mayan Cities; he was heavily into this stuff. He claimed records had been found at sites of ancient cities all over the globe, which suggested we were visited regularly. I thought it was nonsense, how he believed that thousands of years ago a race that looked like us intermixed their DNA and genetic buildup with those of a native species. It wasn't until we started developing more advanced technology that we could understand exactly what was written." The brief explanation had done nothing to ease the puzzled look on Sam's face. Whilst he was definitely the kind of guy to have around in a scrape, on this occasion – and not surprisingly – he was way out of his comfort zone. Oriyanna, on the other hand, was listening intently. "I honestly thought he was crazy to start with, but when I got home I began looking into it. I guess that's the reporter in me," he smiled weakly. "Anyway, I was shocked to find that a lot of it actually made sense. Plenty of it seemed pretty improbable to tell the truth, but some of the evidence was pretty compelling." Somewhere in the distance a siren pierced through the night, interrupting him. Oriyanna's eyes shot to the side window as if she expected the Sheriff to suddenly appear.

"We need to get moving," she pleaded. "I promise you, I will explain it all fully."

Adam was already in the driver's seat, turning the engine over before she finished speaking; a quick glance at Sam told him his best friend was in no condition to drive right now. He was sitting on the bench seat in a stunned silence. Oriyanna was with him, appearing slightly concerned. Whilst everything he'd seen and heard seemed impossible to him, he was sure of one thing – Oriyanna had told them the truth. The fear he'd experienced when she'd touched him was real. He knew Sam had felt it too. Thinking back to his dream, he remembered how her face had changed to that of the dead girl from the Afghan village. It was clear to him now. Oriyanna posed no threat. The dead girl had represented the fear she'd transferred to him. He had no idea what the fear represented, but nonetheless, it made his hackles rise. When Adam guided the RV over a few potholes and back out onto Route 40, the ride smoothed out as all four wheels mounted the wet tarmac. He allowed himself a brief sigh of relief on seeing the road dark and empty. The rain had all but stopped. A light drizzle still dusted the windscreen, causing the wipers to spring into action every few seconds. Glancing in the rearview mirror he saw Sam making his way to the front to join him. Oriyanna settled herself down in the single seat just behind them.

"Sorry I flipped out a little back there," Sam said vacantly. It was clear he still hadn't quite gotten his head around the situation. Truth be told, neither had Adam. How the hell could you deal with what they had just witnessed and heard?

"Don't be, I'm not sure I believe it myself." Adam shot him an encouraging smile. "So, what the hell do we do now?"

Sam turned slightly in his seat so he could face their passenger. "Oriyanna." It was the first time he'd actually used her name. "The fear I felt when you took my hand, I need to know what it is. Who is it you're afraid of?"

"They are the ones who tried to destroy our craft," she said quietly, a hint of sadness in her voice. "I suspect they also had a hand in the hostile reception I received after the crash."

"How so?" asked Adam. "You said the military were after you?"

"I... don't know – yet," she replied slowly, "I don't know all the details. Things have happened here on Earth in the last few weeks that have caused us to come. We didn't know what we would find when we arrived, and we feared it may already be too late."

"I don't understand," said Sam, running the last few weeks through his head. "Too late for what? Everything is just as it always is, nothing unusual has happened." He paused as the uncommon events in Kuala Lumpur came back to him. "Well, apart from the President of the United States dying a few weeks back, and those guys who disappeared at that summit you were at." He gestured to Adam.

"Their disappearance is the reason I am here," Oriyanna replied matter-of-factly.

"I'm sorry," sighed Sam, his face locked in the confused frown he'd been wearing for a good few minutes. "I have no idea what the hell you're on about. Why would you be here for a dead President and the other three? Who were they? A business man, a politician and some guy who was high up in the church – that just doesn't make sense."

"Things are not always as they seem, Samuel. There is still much I need to explain, but once I have, I promise you it will all become clear." Or at least, she hoped it would; there was no way of telling just how they would react to what she needed to say. How could someone just accept that everything they knew about their own history was wrong?

"We're back at Empire," declared Adam, as the camper began to pass the first few antiquated houses. It was fast approaching eleven o'clock, but a few of the buildings still had lights shining in their windows and TV sets flickering. "Where am I heading to anyway? Back the way we came?" Signs for the I70 and Denver began to appear on the side of the road. Passing the small sheriff's station, he saw it was in darkness. He wondered if they would be standing point out on the mountain all night.

"We need to head south," said Oriyanna, leaning forward in her seat.

"South, why south?" Adam could see her anxious expression in the rearview mirror. It was all he could do to keep his eyes on the road and every time he looked away, he longed to look back at her.

"Because... I need to get to Austin."

"Texas? Austin, Texas?" quizzed Sam. "That's miles away, and we're meant to be heading to San Francisco. What the hell is there in Austin?"

"Not what," she replied, "but who! I promise you, it will all be clear once I have explained it. Once we are clear of the area and out of danger, I'll tell you all I know." She paused, the thought of it filling her with dread. "You are going to need an open mind, though. Remember everything you have seen and experienced tonight and it might be easier for you to accept. No modern Earth-Human has ever known the things I need to say, nor should any Earth-Human know them, but things have changed."

"It's nine hundred and eighty-six miles to Austin," Adam cut in, fiddling with the SatNav and suddenly realising he'd just been referred to as an Earth-Human. Route 40 came to an end and he guided the camper onto I70. It felt good to be on the faster moving freeway, there was still plenty of traffic about, helping them to blend in a little. Despite that, he still felt vulnerable in the RV. It was big, bulky and even with the steady flow of cars he felt as if they stuck out like a sore thumb.

"The ones who shot you down, who are they?" asked Sam.

"Long ago we were one and the same people. Thousands of years ago, a war tore us apart. Like me, they will appear no different to you, which is what makes them so dangerous. You could pass them in the street and you wouldn't know." Oriyanna's voice was low and foreboding.

"What was the war about?" Sam desperately needed to piece it all together. He'd spent many years of his life protecting and guarding people. It was seeming like Oriyanna was about to become his next customer, only the stakes this time seemed much higher. He was used to babysitting rich businessmen, politicians and the occasional developer; this was on a whole other level.

She fidgeted uncomfortably in her seat. "The Earth!" she replied. Oriyanna looked him right in the eye. "What they desire has never changed. I don't know how or when it will happen, but I have no doubt they plan to kill everyone and they won't stop until they have wiped you off the face of this planet!"

Sam tasted blood in his mouth and realised he was chewing the loose skin on his lip again. "We— we will take you— take you to Austin," he said, his voice shaky as her words sank in, "I don't think we should keep hold of the RV, though. The Sheriff took our details back there, so we'll be very easy to find. All the major interstates have traffic cameras on them, which can automatically read your number plate – hell, we've probably driven through a few already."

Adam felt a chill run down his spine. "Oh God, I never even thought of that," he whispered, as if talking too loudly might give them away. Sam was right, once they found no trace of Oriyanna, he had no doubt they and the RV would be in the spotlight once again, after all, they hadn't seen another vehicle back up on Trail Ridge.

Sam began programming the SatNav. "I'm going to route us to Austin, steering clear of as many of the main interstates as possible," he said. "Tomorrow, we'll look to ditch the RV. Hopefully, one of the towns we'll pass through has an office where we can drop it back. Once we've done that, we'll hire a car, but not from the same firm." His mind was racing through ways to help them drop off the radar. He didn't know at this point in time if they were even on the radar, but he didn't plan on being complacent. In a flash, the SatNav pinged happily, letting them know it had figured out a new route. It was actually about twenty miles shorter, but what they gained in distance they lost in time. It would take another four hours going via the smaller roads and even then, they had to touch on a few interstates. "Once we've got new wheels tomorrow, we should be okay to get back on the main roads," he said, thinking swiftly. "Let's just get through tonight first and see how it goes." Oriyanna placed a hand on Sam's shoulder. He flinched once again, waiting for her to zap him, or whatever the hell it was she could do.

"Thank you both," she said sincerely. "I have no idea how hard it must be to have this dropped on you. I'd have understood if you just kicked me out and left me on the side of the road."

Sam forced a smile. "For the record, I still think you're a nut job, but I always like to err on the side of caution, and you might be telling the truth." He backed the smile up with a wink. "What I need from you is the whole story. I need to know everything, so I have an idea of what we're facing, including what the hell that thing is we found with you."

Oriyanna nodded her head. "Of course. It's the least I owe you." She turned the object over in her hand and Sam was transfixed, watching it glow at her touch. "I really don't know where to start, though," she said. "There's so much to tell, and some of it, I fear you will find impossible to understand."

Adam glanced in the rearview mirror, catching her eyes and making his own heart flutter. "Well, it's one hell of a drive down to Austin," he said, reluctantly looking away and back at the road. "We have plenty of time, so maybe you should just start – at the beginning."

Chapter 8

Finch was drained and badly needed to sleep. The two hours he'd managed to get on the flight to Paris had done nothing but amplify the fatigue he was experiencing. He'd tried to close his eyes and grab an extra hour on the flight to Denver; however, as the minutes and hours ticked by, his anxiety grew, making any kind of rest an impossibility, no matter how much his body and mind craved it.

The 'Fasten Seatbelt' sign clicked off as the jet came to a stop next to the terminal building. The Denver night sky looked dark and brooding. A variety of randomly-sized puddles littered the tarmac. The city had obviously been party to a heavy rainstorm at some point during the evening. Stepping into the disembarkation tunnel, Finch immediately switched his phone on. By the time the Blackberry found a signal and he had enough network coverage to make and receive a call, he had reached immigration. His new documents didn't arouse the slightest bit of suspicion in the border guards. As the stern-faced official handed him his passport, the phone beeped twice. Finch stuffed the passport back into his jacket and accessed the handset. It was a message from Buer. 'Roddick will meet you at Denver,' it read. In true Buer style, it was brief and to the point. Finch hadn't expected for one minute that it would reveal any more details about his urgent and immediate return to the States. Clearing the baggage reclaim, he headed straight for customs, not even bothering to wait for his small overnight bag. The time was swiftly approaching eleven pm. The airport still had a steady flow of people hurrying around, but in comparison to JKF, it was quiet. Within five minutes, Finch was through customs and on his way to the arrivals hall. It seemed as if he'd been living a day of constant darkness, the two quick trips both east and west bound between America and Europe meant he'd continuously been following the night. Even now, it would still be a good six hours before dawn. Whatever was happening was big, and he doubted there would be much chance to catch up on sleep for some time.

Roddick Laney was standing with the usual diverse collection of people who were always waiting on the other side of the barrier in arrivals, no matter what country or airport you found yourself in. People eager to catch that first glimpse of a loved one, or limo drivers who were keen to make the pickup and get on to the next job. Neither Finch or Roddick would be pleased to see each other. Finch felt himself growing angry just at the sight of the lummox, as he remembered how Roddick had commented about being a few minutes late at the pickup in Kuala Lumpur.

Finch spotted him first from a good twenty meters back, leaning lazily on one of the barrier poles, dressed in an ill-fitting suit which appeared to have been ironed with a cold Mars Bar. Roddick was busy leering at a small group of college girls, who were being showered in hugs and kisses by their doting parents. It crossed Finch's mind that he could just slip right past the useless idiot and out into the night, get a cab and vanish, not even have to worry about Buer or any of the others. He could hole up somewhere safe and just wait for the virus to do its thing. There were plenty of places a guy like him could hide and not be caught. He'd felt the same back in Paris. The desire had been there, to just carry on in into Europe and not look back. Whatever the issue was that had arisen in the seven or so hours he'd been away could sort itself out. He had done enough.

As Finch pondered the idea, Roddick looked away from the small family reunion and spotted him. He raised a lazy hand in greeting, before turning and heading for the terminal doors, leaving Finch to make ground in order to catch him up. Purposely, Finch stayed a few feet behind so there was no need to engage in conversation before absolutely necessary. True, Roddick might know some of the details about what had happened, but he doubted it.

Like Finch, Roddick was second generation Earth-Breed; they had been bred especially for the operation. The first of the Elders who had arrived some eighty years ago had set about the program, developing them so they could operate unnoticed by the Watchers. The likes of Buer had remained solely in the background. The first generation had helped set up the investment firm which cemented their place in modern society, allowing them to accrue wealth and assets. Finch's generation had been bred to infiltrate governments and businesses, to discover the identity of the four Watchers and see through the final steps of the plan. The likes of Roddick envied the ones like Finch, the Earth-Breeds who held the important roles. The ones who had been developed with abnormally high IQs. From birth, Roddick had been destined to be no more than a general dogsbody, never possessing the brain power to go to the best colleges and hold the powerful jobs. Positions in businesses and governments were beyond his reach. Finch was in no doubt that now he possessed The Gift, Roddick would envy and dislike him even more. He was sure that even the other Earth-Breeds who were on Finch's level would feel the same way. He didn't care, it wasn't his fault that he'd proved to be the best at what he did, nor was it his fault that he'd been handpicked to help head up the hunt for the Watchers and ultimately deal the striking blow in their demise. In truth, he'd always seen himself as superior to them, and now, even they couldn't deny it. Sure, by the time all this was over there would be other Earth-Breeds given The Gift, Buer had told him so, but he was the first, and as far as Finch was concerned, that spoke for itself.

Slowly, over the last nine years, they had selected their targets. Remy had been the first one who had drawn their attention, even before he took the role as President. Back when he was just a Senator, he had shot to power, storming the elections at the end of the second Obama Administration. Thanks to an adoring public, his election was a landslide victory. His beliefs and ideas on unity and peacekeeping had been a giveaway. As soon as Finch was in close enough for day-to-day contact, it had been easy to gain a small sample of hair from the Presidential pillow. Any normal DNA scan would have shown nothing different at all from any other man or woman on the planet, but they knew exactly what to look for. Traces of his true roots were there if one knew how to find them, and find them, they did. Next came Francis Tillard, a man of the cloth who had spent many years carrying out aid and missionary work, feeding the starving in the less fortunate countries of the world. He became Archbishop in the year after President Remy had gained power. Tillard was also hotly tipped to be a future Pope. On the surface, President Remy had been a devout Catholic, often in close contact with Tillard during his many leisure visits to France. It was their unusually close friendship which had given them away. It sickened Finch to see Tillard promoting a belief system he knew to be false. It reminded Finch of the old days he'd been taught about as a boy, when his masters were all one people and worshipped as gods. The whole thing had been a mockery from the beginning. During one of the presidential trips to France, Finch had secured a DNA sample from the Archbishop, and as they suspected, it confirmed Tillard's true identity and target number two was acquired. The next to be uncovered was Jaques Guillard, an EU Politician from Brussels. As with the previous two, it was his actions and policies that eventually gave him up. Guillard was a keen financier and had been vital in holding the Euro Zone together following the collapse of the Greek and Portuguese banks. By eventually securing the financial wealth of the United Kingdom into the Euro, he'd managed to put together rescue packages that had saved the single currency. His idealistic views that one day the world could be united under one monetary system were as celebrated as they were ridiculed. To Buer and the others, it was blatant Arkkadian politics.

The last piece of the puzzle was Euri Peterson. Zeon Developments, his green energy company, had first drawn their attention when they announced the development of cheap and stable hydrogen-fuelled engines. These developments had progressed fast, too fast, and in the last eighteen months the first of the Boeing X54 Oxy-Hydrogen Jets had been rolled out on test, and more quickly followed. The engine was a good few years beyond current technology. Peterson had been the easiest to get to, not protected and shut away like the other three. His true identity was soon uncovered, just as the rest had been. Finch had learned that throughout the ages, the four Watchers varied their involvement with Earth affairs – there were times when they had acted as mere observers, no different than any other person you would pass in the street. Then, like now, there were periods when they became more involved, helping to give humanity a gentle nudge in the right direction. No one knew how many generations of them had come and gone over the long years since the Great War. During times where they acted as mere observers and guardians, it was possible for them to live here for many years. The ones who held the public roles, like the four he'd dealt with, couldn't serve as long. Questions would surely be asked when a famous face never grew old or died. For the past fifteen months or so, his people had known who the targets were, and it had just been a matter of time before each pawn was in place. The G8 Summit had come and gone, with only two of the four in the same city at the same time. It was essential that his people took them in one go. With each of them holding high-profile positions, any one of their deaths would have made the news and alerted the others that something was amiss. Also, the kind of security afforded to Guillard and the Archbishop had not been so easy to get around on home soil. Whilst patience was key, Buer had been becoming increasingly anxious to take care of them all. President Remy would have been an easy target at any point with Finch working so closely to him, but the other three would have been a little trickier. Plans were put in action for a global strike on them all, but it would take much more time to get the players into position. In the end, it was their ideals and visions that had been their downfall. In the few months following the discovery of Peterson, President Remy, along with other Heads of State had arranged a World Summit; this was an event not limited to just governments. From heads of religion to heads of business and politics, they were all invited. Finally, each of them would be within a few miles of each other, like fish in a net. Any plans to take them out singly had been immediately scrapped.

Finch followed behind Roddick as he pushed open the swinging glass door, not bothering to hold it in place. Finch caught it just before it swung shut. Roddick made his way to a bright red Chevrolet Impala which was double parked in the taxi rank, a penalty ticket now securely fixed to the screen. Roddick tore it off, leaving a sticky residue in its wake and tossed it onto the passenger seat. Finch was in no mood to sit up front and ride shotgun. There were a few questions he needed to ask Roddick during the drive to wherever Buer was holed up, but sitting up front would just put pressure on him to hold more conversation than was needed. Opting for the rear seat, he jumped in and fastened his belt. Roddick's lack of personal hygiene had apparently not been limited to Malaysia. Despite the cool damp night, the slight, musty smell of his body odour greeted Finch's nose. Silently, Roddick gunned the engine and launched the Chevy out into the light traffic.

"Where are we headed to?" Finch asked, leaning forward slightly in his seat.

"Downtown," Roddick grunted, eyeing him in the rearview mirror, "Buer and a few of the others are at the Hotel Monaco. It's about a twenty-five-minute drive."

Finch rolled his eyes, *Great* he thought. *Twenty-five minutes of enduring Roddick and his blatant perspiration problems.* The only blessing was at this late hour traffic would be fairly light. Roddick was never one to dawdle and tonight was no exception. He seemed to be driving even faster than normal. "You're not hanging around are you?" Finch observed as Roddick carried out a rather risky overtake on a large truck.

"Instructions from Buer were to get you to the hotel as fast as possible," he replied flatly.

"I'm guessing you probably don't, but if you have any idea what the hell this is all about, I'd like a heads-up." Even if Roddick knew, Finch didn't expect him to spill the beans. Roddick eyed the rearview mirror again, taking his eyes off the road for longer than Finch felt comfortable with at these speeds.

"Sure I know," he replied cockily. "But Buer wants to run through it with you himself. All I can tell you is that there's a world of shit going down right now and you're in the centre of it." He smiled sarcastically in the mirror.

Had his safety not been in Roddick's hands, Finch could have quite easily reached around and ripped his stupid, chubby face off. "Yeah, well thanks for the info."

"You're more than welcome," Roddick sneered, obviously pleased he had one up on him.

In a little over fifteen minutes, Roddick was guiding the Chevy through downtown Denver. A few high rise buildings lit up the stormy night sky, but it was nothing compared to New York, this city seemed to have a slightly more relaxed feel to it. Life here obviously wasn't quite so fast-paced and in-your-face. Finch couldn't deny Roddick's sense of direction; it was his one blessing. The guy could look at a map or drive a route just once and know exactly where to go. He was also pretty handy behind the wheel. It was those attributes which had guaranteed him the job as a driver. Whilst it was lowly and menial work in the eyes of many of the Earth-Breeds, Roddick was the best at what he did. He hadn't been dealt the best hand in life, but he'd certainly played it the best he could.

Almost bang on the twenty-five-minute mark as he'd predicted, Roddick delivered the Chevy to the front of the Hotel Monaco. It was an older, restored building. From the outside, it gave the impression of being a little retro with an art deco feel to it. It appeared expensive, but then again, Buer had never been one to skimp on personal luxuries.

"They're in the Mediterranean Suite, sixth floor," Roddick said, pointing to the top of the hotel. "I need to go park, but you can get out here."

Finch didn't bother with any thanks. Why should he? Not only did he dislike the guy immensely, but he'd also just been party in delivering him to Buer. He never liked his meetings with Buer, and this was one particular meeting he was dreading. He unclipped his belt and stepped out onto Champa Street, pausing for a few seconds to gaze up at the top floor.

"Don't even think of doing a runner," mocked Roddick from the driver's window, as if he'd read his mind.

"Fuck you!" spat Finch, much to Roddick's delight. Laughing, he gunned the Chevy and with more wheel spin than was needed, launched it up the road. Finch watched him get to the lights and turn right. Allowing himself a deep breath, he walked into the lobby.

The hotel was plush and grand, but not overly done. There were certain aspects to the decor that reminded Finch of parts of the White House. He didn't bother to speak to the receptionist who was regarding him eagerly, waiting to help; instead he went directly to the elevator. There was certainly no expense spared in this place. Even the elevator-car had an attendant in it. Finch couldn't even begin to imagine what a mind-numbing job that must be, spending your whole working day in a box going up and down. 'Not to worry' he thought, 'you don't know it yet, but soon we'll be putting you out of your misery.'

The elevator attendant delivered Finch to the top floor. He didn't get a tip. Following the brass plated signs, Finch navigated his way to the back of the hotel where the suite was located. The door was auto locked from the outside, and having no key card, he had to knock. It felt like an eternity passed before he heard the sound of footsteps from the other side – though in truth, it was only a few seconds. He just wanted to get inside and find out what all the fuss was about, take whatever shit was coming his way and get on with whatever job they needed him to do.

Mitchell Banks answered the door. Mitchell was a fellow second generation Earth-Breed. He was a few years older than Finch and of similar height and build, but his brown hair looked uncombed. It seemed Finch wasn't the only one having a bad night. Although Mitchell didn't hold a job like Finch, he was still one of the more intelligent ones. Mitchell was a whizz with computers and Earth-Tech. His very presence at the hotel meant they were using the Mediterranean Suite as a temporary ops centre. Mitchell and his small team would be busy hacking into networks with the help of their government and law enforcement placements, gaining them up-to-the-minute access to any information they needed, no matter how classified.

Mitchell looked a little shocked, but also seemed relieved to see him standing there. "Robert!" he exclaimed, and Finch noted he looked both tired and stressed. "You had best come in; Buer is waiting to see you." Finch slipped past him and into the suite, which consisted of a grand-looking bedroom area with a good-sized separate living room. At one end of the lounge was a large, oversized dark hardwood desk. Trestle tables lined one side of the living area, where banks of laptops had set up. Members of Mitchell's tech team were busy sorting a mess of wires out. It didn't look as if they had been there that long and things weren't quite up and running yet. Out of the other faces in the room, Benjamin Hawker was the only other he could place. Hawker, like Banks, was a computer genius. Last Finch had heard he was working on defence programs somewhere in the US government. From his spot in the lounge,

Finch saw Buer seated behind the large wooden desk, already looking as if he owned the place. A glossy black telephone was glued to his ear, a grave and angry expression on his face.

Buer looked up from his call and glared, making Finch feel like a naughty child outside the principal's office. Buer ended the call immediately. "Robert, there you are," he said, rather more calmly than Finch had expected. "Take a seat." He gestured to the chair opposite his. "I did wonder after speaking to you in France if you would actually get on that plane." Buer watched him through stone-cold eyes.

"The thought never even crossed my mind," Finch lied. The sheer calmness Buer displayed was making him feel even more uneasy about the situation.

"Robert, I have a question for you." Buer leaned back in his chair and clasped his hands together. "That night, back in Malaysia, was there any possible way that one of them made a call, or spoke to someone before you took them? Was there any way at all they might have gotten a sniff as to what was happening?"

"Not a chance!" replied Finch, a little too hastily, "All three were asleep when we drugged them, they never suspected a single thing. As for Remy, the poison in that water would have killed him in seconds."

Buer watched him, his eyes narrowing, Finch could see the anger that had obviously been seething away just below the surface was about to erupt like a volcano. Suddenly, he shot up out of his chair and swiped a glass off the desk, causing it to shatter against the wall, soaking the very luxurious green and cream striped wallpaper in sticky orange juice. In seconds he was around the desk, his hand clamped around Finch's throat. In one fluid movement, he lifted him off the chair by his neck and rammed him into the wall, knocking an ornate oil painting to the floor.

"*Then why!*" he boomed in a voice like thunder, "*why* did our orbital craft shoot down three Arkkadian scout vessels a few hours ago?"

Finch could only just register what was being said to him. Buer's hand was clasped so tightly around his neck, he couldn't even draw breath. As the life was being strangled out of him, he knew that his millions of tiny robotic life sustainers were busy delivering oxygen to parts of the body that needed them most, prolonging the amount of time he could survive without a breath. Finch had no idea how long that might be, and he didn't want to find out. Desperately, he tried to kick his feet and gain some purchase on the carpet, but the more he struggled, the higher Buer lifted him. He clamped both hands onto Buer's arms and tried to push him away, but the other man's grip was vice-like and strong as steel. The only time it would relent was when he was ready.

"How can you explain that to me?" As Buer spoke he lifted Finch away from the wall and slammed him hard back against it, over and over.

Finch felt the booming voice resonate throughout his entire body as Buer abused him. He felt himself gain another few inches of height. His eyes seemed as if they were going to pop out of their sockets. Then in a flash, and right at the point when unconsciousness began to pull at him, Buer released his grip, leaving Finch to fall to the floor like a rag doll. For a few moments, it was all he could do to get a breath into his lungs. His windpipe felt crushed. A few seconds later it began to feel better, his breath came easier and the pain ebbed away. The Gift was working its magic; the tiny passengers who had stopped him from being strangled were now busy repairing the damage done by Buer's strong, iron-like hands. Finch hadn't planned on having to find out just how quickly they could repair an injury so soon, although now, he was in no doubt that if he hadn't had them he would either be dead or in serious need of medical help. Stealing a glance around the room he saw that the five or so guys setting up the tech unit hadn't even flinched at the outburst. He flush with embarrassment; he hated seeming weak. Gathering up his strength, Finch got to his feet. Buer was already sitting back down at the desk, as if nothing had happened.

Buer watched him gingerly sit down and straighten out his shirt. "As I said," he began calmly, "a few hours ago our orbital craft intercepted and destroyed two Arkkadian scout vessels."

"I thought you said there were three," Finch cut in, his neck and throat back to normal.

"I did. Two were destroyed, the third was hit but managed to evade the last strike. It went down hard and fast. The reason you're in Denver, Robert, is because the craft crashed about eighty-five miles west of here in the Rockies."

Dread swept through Finch's body. No wonder they'd been in such a panic to get him back. "Were there any survivors?" he asked reluctantly.

Buer nodded his head slowly. "Yes, I'm afraid so. The US Military picked up the craft as it came down; they scrambled helicopters and local troops to the area. Thankfully, we have General Stone on the inside. It's a stroke of luck for us that he's, one, in the US at the moment, and two, in charge of troops in this area. He's currently commanding out of Buckley, Aurora. He took charge of the operation and issued orders for ground troops to shoot first, not to take anyone alive. He hoped the situation could be dealt with fast and before anyone higher up overrode his decision."

"Well, it sounds as if the matter's been taken care of then," said Finch, feeling relieved. "We have time to plan before they can send any more craft."

Buer shook his head, "No, Robert, it's not taken care of at all. You see, one escaped the crash site. Thankfully the other two on board were already dead. There's no way anyone should have survived it. I've seen some of the satellite images of the area, and it's one hell of a mess. I don't need to tell you how someone might have survived, do I?" Finch didn't need telling, he had just experienced the magical healing powers he now possessed first hand. "It's not hard to do the math here, Robert," Buer continued. "It's just over two weeks since Malaysia. We know any communication takes a little over seven days to reach them from Earth, then another seven days to get here. Something in the plan you executed went *wrong*!" Buer emphasised the last word in a growl.

"Impossible," denied Finch. "I killed all four. As I said, the three that I executed were taken in their sleep. Remy was poisoned and that's not to mention the fact that none of them would have been travelling with the technology to do such a thing." Finch was running the night over and over in his head. The only weak link he could think of was President Remy. While he hadn't seen him die, the lab which developed the deadly poison he'd put in the water had assured him it would only take seconds to work. Even if they were wrong, how the hell had he managed to get a message out?

"Let's just say for argument sake – so to speak," said Buer, pondering the problem aloud, "that the poison you gave Remy wasn't quite as fast as we thought it would be. Say the lab was wrong, and his system managed to fight it for even a minute."

"But it was still impossible to get a message out," Finch cut in, immediately regretting his outburst.

"I know!" Buer shouted, slamming his fist down onto the desk so hard, it made the telephone receiver jump into the air. "You're smarter than this, Robert; surely you can see what I'm getting at here?" he growled.

"You think he contacted someone here, someone on Earth?" gasped Finch, the penny finally dropping.

"I certainly think that someone on Earth sent the message," said Buer. "Maybe they were contacted and maybe they weren't. The death of the President and the sudden disappearances of the others was all over the news by the next morning. Whatever happened, there is someone else here who knew who they were, someone capable of sending that alert out."

"You really think they have a fifth Watcher here?" The very notion seemed impossible to comprehend; it went against everything they knew.

"Maybe not a Watcher, but I have no doubt at all that they had someone here behind the scenes, maybe more by luck than judgement. What I want to know, is how this oversight happened, how was it missed?"

Finch saw how the balance was shifting. Ultimately, the proverbial buck was going to have to stop somewhere. Sure, Buer was in overall charge, but Finch had been the lead Earth-Breed in the search for the Watchers. Buer was looking for a scapegoat and Finch had no doubt he was the one lined up to take the fall.

"How could we have known?" Finch asked. "We had them under observation for just over a year. We had lines tapped, emails hacked and there was no indication at all that they were in contact with anyone." There was no way Finch was going to be held accountable for this. "Surely what's important now is damage limitation. We have to hope that no more are on their way, that this is just a scout crew sent to see what's happening. If that is the case, we have a good two weeks before more arrive. The virus will be well at work by then, so no matter what happens, it will be too late." Finch was eager to steer the conversation away from Buer's control, trying to factor the blame his way.

Buer sat for a few seconds considering Finch's words, running a hand absently over his chin. "Two weeks if we're lucky, Robert," he began. "By then, the virus should be half way through its process, but we both know they have the ability to easily cure it. No doubt a few billion will be dead, but it's not enough. It needs a clear four weeks to take full effect. My main concern right now is the Tabut. I'm in no doubt that one of those craft carried the Key Tablet. I just hope it was either lost, or aboard one of the ships that we destroyed, but I doubt it. If they reach it in the next few days, then it's all over. You should have tried harder to extract the location of the artefact!"

Finch shrank back in his seat. He'd wondered when the conversation would swing to the Tabut. With this latest development, Buer would be even keener to locate and destroy the device. Finch knew deep down that he'd personally been a little complacent about it before, thinking it was a waste of time trying to find something that had been buried for thousands of years. But now the game plan had changed. If there was even a slight chance the survivor carried the Key Tablet, they had to be found and taken care of. "So..." began Finch tentatively, "where are we on locating this survivor?"

"Nowhere!" snapped Buer. "After the crash General Stone had the site locked down. FBI and local law enforcement sealed off the area." Buer tapped the space bar on his laptop, bringing the screen to life. A daylight Google Map view of the area lit up the screen. "This road here is the only one that runs near the crash site. The actual site of the wreck is about a mile or so to the east." He hovered a finger over an area of dense forest. "The military got to the scene within about thirty minutes. A lone survivor was seen running from the crash site, ground troops and tracking dogs gave chase for about three quarters of a mile, to here." Buer traced his finger over the forest to a river. "General Stone's direct order to shoot the target still stood, and one of the soldiers got a shot off and hit her in the leg. The soldier involved stated he saw her fall into the river and get carried off downstream."

"She?" questioned Finch. "It was a woman?"

Buer nodded. "Yes, description is a female aged in her twenties with blonde hair."

"Do you know who it is?"

"I have an idea," Buer replied, staring at the satellite map as if it would suddenly yield some piece of important information. "I believe her name is Oriyanna."

"Oriyanna." Finch let the name roll off his tongue. He knew it, but couldn't quite place why. "I recognise her name," he admitted thoughtfully.

"You should. She is a very high ranking Arkkadian Elder. She was one of the first to return here, years before the war, before any of us had The Gift; back then, she was nothing more than a science officer."

"So you knew her?" Finch was intrigued; Buer and the other Elders had lived for longer than Finch could even conceive. He longed to have seen some of the things they'd seen and shared some of their experiences. He only knew Earth as it was now; he found it hard to imagine the planet without its bustling cities full of skyscrapers and cars.

"Yes, long ago, right back before the war." For a brief second, Buer seemed different, as if he was remembering better times. He almost seemed vulnerable. "But then things changed, the war came and we were on different sides. It's thanks to the likes of her that we were cast out and left for dead." His expression changed and in an instant, the old Buer was back.

"Do you think she could have drowned?"

"Information from the troops under General Stone's command reported that the river was very swollen and fast flowing from all the recent rain, not to mention the downpour the area suffered earlier. The troops said it was highly unlikely anyone could survive the waters, especially with a gunshot wound." Buer halted briefly. "But do I personally think she drowned? No! Not for a second."

Finch heard a knock come from the door to the suite. Benjamin Hawker, who was busily working in front of a laptop shook his head in disgust at the interruption and went to answer it. Roddick's voice drifted through the room. He was obviously back from parking the car. From his seat, Finch watched as he dashed through to the bedroom, keen to be out of the way. "Is it possible that the Key Tablet was on her craft?" Finch asked, drawing his attention away from Roddick and back to the conversation.

"I'm certain her craft would have been the one carrying it," Buer said gravely. "As you know, the Tabuts were created after the Great War, one held here on Earth and one held on Arkkadia. The plans to build it began before the war; however, back then it was never more than theory. Oriyanna was heavily involved in the project, so I'm almost certain she will be in possession of it." Buer paused briefly and glanced at the bank of technicians beavering away at the side of the room. "There is a slim chance we could use tonight's events to our advantage." He grinned slyly, as if it were nothing more than an afterthought.

"How so?" Finch could see no possible way a positive could be drawn from what was happening.

"We know that although they eventually managed to build both the Tabuts, the project was never one hundred percent stable. If we can obtain the location of the one here on Earth, as well as the Key Tablet, there might just be a way we could deal a fatal blow to Arkkadia, one that will most certainly seal our success and literally remove any risk of them being able to strike back at us."

"I'm listening," said Finch, relaxing back into his seat. If there was the slightest chance he could help to turn things around, while at the same time further his own social standing, he wanted in.

"I don't have time to run through the details now, but our top brains are working on it as we speak. I'll fill you in on it when I know more. All you need to know, Robert, is how vital it is that you locate Oriyanna and if she has it, the Key Tablet. General Stone is still at the crash site. There's a chance it might still be found there. If it is, I'll let you know."

"When I do find her, which I will," said Finch confidently, "what do you want me to do?"

"We need her alive. She will certainly know the location of the Tabut. As an absolute last resort you have my authority to kill her, but it must be in the event of you having no other options – do I make myself clear?"

Finch nodded slowly, absorbing all the information. He had a feeling he was soon going to be out on the road. He would relish the chance to track down another Elder. If this Oriyanna girl was out there, he was confident he could find her. "Crystal clear," he replied, smiling confidently. "What's the media coverage on this? I take it there is some press attention from the crash?"

"Well, you can always rely on any Earth government to cover these things up," grinned Buer. "The official press release is that a jet containing three domestic terrorists was shot down over the Rockies and they are currently searching for one survivor. They have roads in and out of the area on lockdown; any vehicles leaving the zone are being searched. If she surfaces we *will* find her." The sound of Mitchell clearing his throat captured Buer's attention.

"Sir," he began, "we're up and running now. We have full access to local law enforcement and all military radio communication, as well as CIA and FBI. The access codes General Stone provided are working. We're also tapped into their real-time satellite surveillance system."

"Good work," praised Buer. "Robert and I will be with you in a minute. I'm just bringing him up to speed."

Mitchell shot Finch an encouraging look. He had obviously witnessed Buer's outburst having been engrossed in his work.

Buer continued. "We have to work on the assumption that Oriyanna is in possession of the Key Tablet, I believe she will ultimately try to reach the Tabut, but now she's on her own. It's highly likely she will look to make contact with whoever sent the alert. Our problem is, we don't know where the contact is, nor do we know the location of the Tabut, so we don't even know where to start looking." There was a slight hint of desperation to Buer's voice. There weren't many Elders above him. Finch certainly didn't fancy having to answer to any of them, and Buer was undoubtedly sweating it out at the moment. He had the look of a man on the edge.

"I'll find her!" Finch said confidently. "I'll start right away."

Buer studied him, seemingly weighing up his worth. "I can't emphasize enough how crucial it is, Robert, that you don't fail us on this. If she reaches the Tabut, then our chances of success are practically zero. This task was entrusted to such a small number of us. It's taken us many years to get where we are today, not just the eighty years I've spent here on Earth. Failure now is not an option."

Finch knew what he was getting at. If they failed now, none of them would be spared. Punishment would be swift and fatal, of that he had no doubt. His brain started running through just where the hell he should start looking for this girl. "Do you have access to the police records for all the vehicles stop checked and searched leaving the area?" he asked.

"I imagine Mitchell will be able to get those for you," replied Buer. "Let's see what we have so far." he stood up and gestured for Finch to join him at a bank of laptops which were now whirring away on the other side of the room. Roddick was standing with two of the tech team, one of them being Ben Hawker, the other guy he didn't recognise. The three men were busily scanning online maps of the area. "Mitchell, can you access the local police computer records for any licence plate numbers that were checked leaving the area?" asked Buer, standing behind him. Mitchell was busy working on a screen that held the FBI seal. He was obviously deep into their system, gleaning any information he could find.

"Sure, no problem!" he replied confidently, switching screens. In a few seconds, he was into the Clear Creek County Sheriff's Department system, navigating it expertly he found the call stack list. "This is an on-going list of all active and closed jobs for the whole department over the last twenty-four hours," he said, tapping the screen with his finger. "The nearest Sheriff's office to the crash site was in the town of Empire, but they called in aid from Idaho Springs as well. These messages here, highlighted in red, are either still awaiting an officer, or are major incidents still running." Mitchell scanned down the list; the majority of jobs which had come in over the last few hours were all red, obviously with activities up in the mountains, there was no one free to deal with the day-to-day stuff. Within a few seconds, Mitchell had found the incident log for the crash. The initial description just said

'Aircraft down, one mile east of Trail Ridge Road'. Mitchell selected the incident and it narrowed down the location by providing a grid reference. He ignored this, as well as the more in-depth write up. It was no more than a detailed cover story, cobbled together by the military. He scanned down to the officers running log of events. "Hmm, not many vehicles on here," he summarised, scanning the screen with well-trained eyes. "Not really surprising. It was a pretty wild night up there, by all accounts." Finch watched him slowly scroll down the message, taking in bits here and there but primarily it was all useless police talk and jargon. "Ah, we have one vehicle here," said Mitchell pointing to the screen, "A Dodge pickup stopped at ten pm, driver a Mr. Brian Slater, passenger Mrs. Amanda Slater, heading to Denver. Obviously a negative search of the vehicle." He turned to Finch. "What exactly are you hoping to find here?" he asked. "All the vehicles listed will have been searched and left the area."

Finch shrugged. "I don't know yet, just a bit of a hunch and I need to start somewhere. How much time has passed now since the crash?"

Buer checked his watch. "I was notified just after eight pm, and it's now a few minutes after midnight, so around four hours."

"You said the military was on site inside an hour?"

"That's right," replied Buer. "The local police were on scene first, but told to stay clear and just set up the roadblocks. The first sighting of her was around half an hour after the crash, when the first ground troops arrived with General Stone."

"So she's been unsighted now for three hours. How much manpower is up there searching the area?" Finch was still trying to piece it all together. He suspected she would be well clear of the cordoned area by now.

"Four helicopters with heat sensitive cameras," replied Mitchell, switching screens again. "Around forty ground troops and five dog units." He ran his hand down the list, reading it off. Finch did the numbers in his head, visualising the cordon.

"So in three hours, even if she was averaging six miles an hour on foot, which would be hard on that kind of terrain, the furthest she could have made it is eighteen miles." He paused. "I would say without doubt she's well clear of the area by now. Those choppers cover a lot of ground. They can easily tell a person's heat signature from that of an animal. Even if the ground and dog units didn't find her, they should have." Finch glanced at Buer, whose expression said it all. "I need to see more of that call log."

Mitchell scanned down another few pages on the incident report. "We have another vehicle here," he said, in a slightly disinterested tone. It was obvious he thought this was a waste of his time. "Ford MTR Freedom RV, registered to Freeway RV Rentals in Denver, Colorado." Mitchell paused as he clicked to the next page. "Two passengers, both male, one a Mr. Adam Fisher, the other a Mr. Samuel Becker, both British citizens. Notes say they're heading to San Francisco. Looks like the Sheriff searched the vehicle, negative result." Mitchell began to scroll again.

"Stop!" cried Finch.

Mitchell lifted his finger off the scroll bar. "Why? It says here search, negative result – look." He pointed to the screen.

"Just check for me. Is that the largest vehicle to pass through since the crash?"

"There were only two, the pickup and the RV," said Mitchell, running his eyes down the rest of the log.

"I need to know everything you can find on the two occupants." Finch looked up at Buer, who for the first time since his arrival, had a slight smile on his face.

"You think that's the missing link?" Buer asked hopefully.

"It stands to reason. It's a large vehicle with plenty of places to hide someone." He glanced at the screen. Mitchell was busily finding out what he could about the two Brits. "I'm guessing two guys on a road trip are going to be in their twenties or thirties, not married. Let's say they find this girl, or she flags them down?"

Buer knew exactly what was being implied. "You might be right, Robert. As I said, I knew her long ago, she can have certain... effect on men. She's most definitely the kind of girl they would choose to help."

"Okay, here we go," Mitchell cut in. "Both passed through US Immigration today," he checked his watch. "Sorry, I mean yesterday, and they're both in their early thirties. Visa details list Adam Fisher as a freelance writer, not married." Mitchell clicked and changed screens. "Samuel Becker, listed as unemployed but formerly British Military, also unmarried." Mitchell clicked two thumbnail-sized photos and their immigration pictures filled the screen.

"That's our boys!" exclaimed Finch. During his time working on Presidential protection he'd learned to trust his gut. His foresight was rarely wrong. "We need to find that RV."

"Are you sure, Robert?" asked Buer, a slight hint of doubt still in his voice.

"Yes, sir. I'm certain." He turned to Mitchell. "I need you to get into the Freeway RV system and bring up the hire agreement." Mitchell nodded and went to work. "I'm guessing it won't be too much trouble seeing as you've already hacked the FBI and local Sheriff's Department tonight."

"No problem at all," he replied.

"They should have at least one cell phone number listed. And then I'm going to need to you to run a cell locate program for me. We should be able to get a GPS location. At the very worst, we can see what cell mast that phone is pinging off." Finch allowed himself a little smile of satisfaction. Of course, if he was wrong, he would look like an idiot, not to mention the time that would have been wasted. But he wasn't wrong. He could feel it in his bones. "We should know what direction they're headed in within half an hour," he said to Buer.

"I hope for both our sakes that you're right on this. Despite what's happened over the past few hours, you've always served above and beyond what we expect of you. I'm going to trust you on this." Buer patted his shoulder with a heavy hand. "You're going to be taking Roddick with you," he added, and Finch cringed internally. "As you know, navigation is one of his strong points."

"He has more than one?" Finch cut in, feeling cheated. Buer treated him to a look which made it clear he was overstepping the mark.

"You'll also need to be in contact with us here. You can't concentrate on driving and speaking to us simultaneously. We don't want you running yourself off the road." Finch knew the matter was non-negotiable. As long as he got it dealt with fast, he wouldn't need to suffer Roddick's company for too long. "We have suitable weapons here for you to take with you, as well as an FBI identity badge and card. It might be of use. If it turns out she's with the two British guys, then kill them both – is that clear?" Finch nodded. "It's also imperative that you recover the Key Tablet if she's in possession of it, and that you take her alive. In the kit we've prepped for you, there's a vial containing the same serum you used in Malaysia. Do not kill her, unless you have no other option."

"Understood," said Finch, as he turned to leave.

"Oh, one more thing, Robert!"

"What's that, sir?" He stopped a few paces from the laptops and turned around.

"When you do find her, just be careful and remember what the objective is." Finch stared at him, a puzzled expression in his eyes. Buer continued. "As I said before, Oriyanna can have a certain effect on some men."

Finch shook his head dismissively. "Oh, don't worry about that. I know what I need to do."

"No, you don't understand. In the old times, before the war and even after it, Oriyanna spent many years here on Earth. She was seen by the ancient people as a goddess. There were many Earth men who left their wives and offered themselves to her, even as sacrifice."

"With all due respect, sir, times have changed a little. Trust me, I know what I have to do no matter who she is… or was." Finch turned and left the room, knowing there was much to prepare before he hit the road. Roddick offered him a sly smile as he passed by. Obviously, he already knew they were going to be working together. Roddick wouldn't be happy about it either, but on the flip side, he would enjoy the fact that his mere presence was pissing Finch off. With about ten minutes to fill before they would be ready to leave, Finch made his way to the bathroom and grabbed a quick shower. *Maybe leaving my bag at the airport wasn't such a good idea*, he thought as he stepped into the steaming water. He'd left himself with no choice but to stay in the same clothes. The conversation with Buer kept running through his head as he washed. What was it with this girl that had Buer so shaken up? Surely she was no different to any of the others he'd killed.

Closing the faucet, he stepped out of the shower. The water had revived his tired body a little, but it had done nothing to freshen his clothes up. Within minutes he was dressed and back at the row of laptops. Roddick wandered over lazily and joined him, whilst Mitchell was busy working on the cell phone number he'd acquired from the information on the Freeway RV's rental agreement.

"Looks like we're going to be partners," Roddick said, with a slightly cocky grin on his face.

Finch pasted on a false smile. "Well, you'd best not fuck up on this or we'll both be dead."

"Oh, don't worry. I'll just be doing the driving… and a little shooting if needed. I've got your back."

The thought of Roddick having his back offered no comfort whatsoever. Finch checked his watch and saw it was getting on towards one am. They needed to get moving and soon. Every second that RV was on the road, was putting them further onto the back foot.

"Okay, here we go," said Mitchell, a slightly relieved tone in his voice. "I managed to get Adam Fisher's cell phone number from the rental form. It's registered with a UK-based provider – unfortunately, at the moment I can't get it to GPS locate; the British phones can't always be tracked as accurately as the US ones. I just tried pinging it to see what cell tower it's on, but the data is thirty minutes old." He pointed to the screen and Finch couldn't believe his luck. The cell tower was about twenty miles west of Denver; they had actually been driving toward him the whole time.

"Where do you think they are?" asked Finch, his excitement growing by the second.

"It's hard to tell," said Mitchell, looking at the map with interest. "There are lots of roads they could be on, but my guess would be either the 470 or 285. Both are west of the city."

"Is there any way you can get the cell to register on the network and give us a more up-to-date location?" Finch questioned.

"Sure, I can call the number, let it ring once and hang up."

"Do it. I just hope it won't spook them. With any luck, the phone will be on silent anyway." Finch knew it was a gamble, but with the cell data being half an hour old they could already be miles from the last location. He watched Mitchell dial the number, placing the cell on speakerphone. After a few seconds the phone rang once. Mitchell hung up immediately and turned his attention back to the screen. He pinged the number again using the cell phone location program.

"Good, good it worked," he said, sounding relieved. "Okay, it still won't let me get into the GPS function, but the cell tower info has updated. The phone is now registering on a mast that's five miles east of Castle Rock." Mitchell zoomed in on the map. "I'd say they're still moving." He scanned the screen. "Most likely, they're on I25 or one of the smaller side routes heading south, toward Colorado Springs. They could be anywhere from thirty to forty miles southwest of here."

The information was all Finch needed to know. The police report had stated the RV was heading for San Francisco, but if that were the case, why the hell were they heading south? "Where are you going?" he whispered to himself, staring at the small cell tower dot on the monitor. "Get your stuff together Roddick," he grinned. "We leave in five minutes!"

It was time to go hunting.

Chapter 9

Adam's soft cotton tracksuit bottoms were ill-fitting in almost every way: baggy around the waist and far too long in the leg, but still Oriyanna was pleased to be out of her damp and dirty flight suit. As well as the bottoms, he'd lent her a dark blue hooded top, which felt as if it were made of the same material as the trousers. Both were soft and comfortable, as well as feeling warm against her skin. Unfortunately, the top was also a little on the big side. Adam was a good five to six inches taller and the sleeves came down over her hands and required rolling up, just like the tracksuit legs. Taking a few moments to study her reflection in the mirror, she ran her fingers through her wet and tangled shoulder-length blonde hair. Despite washing and towel drying it, her hair still looked a mess. The small comb they'd provided her with wasn't really up to the job of sorting through it. Sam had given her something called an 'elastic band' to tie it all back with. Collecting up the damp mess of hair, she secured it in a makeshift ponytail. It wasn't ideal, but at least it didn't look quite so untidy. The tiny shower cubical in the RV was not the most comfortable way to bathe, but there was no denying she felt better for the semi-warm shower and change of clothes. As she tried to make the best of her appearance in the mirror, the RV bumped over a pothole in the road, making her grab the sink for support. The whole bathroom shook violently with the jolt, knocking the shampoo from its hook and sending it crashing into the shower tray.

The last few hours had been tough. She still regretted the way she'd needed to transfer to Sam. It had taken a good fifteen minutes for him to fully recover. She'd held him in her mind for longer than she liked; a few seconds was the most people could generally handle. Much longer periods, like the one he'd been subjected to, always took more time to recover from. Oriyanna glanced into the sink. The Key Tablet bounced around a little in the bowl. She brushed her hand over its cool surface, making it hum and light up. She knew she'd been lucky; firstly, just surviving the crash had been a miracle. She didn't know how long she'd lain in the forest after they came down. The sound of a helicopter had woken her. Thankfully, any injuries she'd suffered had already healed, enabling her to get away. For a few seconds the memory of the chase through the forest rushed through her mind, just as she'd shown it to Sam. Oriyanna rubbed her thigh where the wound had been and smiled as she recalled waking up in the seat cavity, not knowing where she was. As soon as Sam had spoken to her, even though she couldn't see him, she'd known she was safe. There was something in his voice that she trusted. It had seemed like an eternity passed, lying there in the dark whilst the Sheriff spoke to them. Had he been a little more meticulous, things could have turned out very differently. There was still so much she didn't understand. The four Watchers were dead, that much she was sure of, but how the enemy had gotten to them was still a mystery. So far, from what Sam and Adam had told her, nothing else had changed in the last two weeks. There were obviously events in motion that had not yet come to pass. She felt sure though, that any day now something would happen, it was just a matter of what, and when. Sam was confident they could reach Austin within the next day or so. Getting rid of the RV would cost them time, but he'd insisted they needed to change vehicles. Oriyanna had seen it in him during the transfer; he'd experienced battle. He had courage and training that would no doubt prove vital to this situation. Adam was more of an intellectual. His reasoning and understanding would also prove valuable. What she had sensed in them both had earned her trust one hundred percent. Even with Sam's experience, she still felt on edge. With every passing minute she expected to be stopped and searched again. The soldiers in the forest had meant to kill her, and she knew that wasn't normal practice. Someone who knew exactly who she was had issued the order. The thought chilled her to the bone. How many of them were here? And how had they not been discovered? For the moment, there were far too many questions and not enough answers. Oriyanna adjusted her hair one last time, purposely prolonging having to go back up front. Prior to showering and changing into Adam's clothes, she'd promised to tell them everything she knew. The problem was, there was no easy way to explain the information. How could she tell it all to them in a short, concise manner? There was just too much to explain, not to mention the questions that would no doubt follow, but they deserved to know and if they were going to help her, they needed to know. Taking a deep breath and a last glance in the mirror, she left the cubicle and made her way to the front of the vehicle to join them.

* * *

"We're just south west of Denver," said Adam, glancing in the rearview mirror at her. "How are the clothes?" It seemed strange seeing her in his things. The baggy and unflattering attire did nothing to take away the way she made him feel. His stomach skipped every time he looked at her; he liked and hated the feeling, all at the same time.

"Not too bad," she replied. "A bit on the big side, but better than being in my dirty uniform." She sat down and readjusted the bottom of the pants which had slipped down and caught under her bare feet.

"When we stop and ditch the RV, we can try and find something a little more your size," he added.

Oriyanna smiled in appreciation. "Thanks. I need you to tell me everything you can about the death of John Remy and the disappearances of the other three. Did Sam say you were there when it happened?"

"Kind of," replied Adam. "It was around two weeks ago now, in Kuala Lumpur, Malaysia, at the World Summit. It was the first of its kind. It was seen as a chance for heads of state, business and religion to come together. The US President spearheaded the idea just over a year ago. I was only there to cover a story for the Financial Times, and I left the morning after it all happened so I don't know too much." Adam glanced at the SatNav. The miles were slowly ticking down, but they hadn't even made a dent in the journey yet. "Anyway, it was four people who disappeared in all, not three. The head of the President's security detail also vanished. They're still not sure if he was involved, for the past two weeks the media have been reporting that it was a massive heart attack that killed the president."

"Who was this security guy?"

"Robert Finch," Adam replied, splitting his attention between the road and the rearview mirror as he spoke. "He's currently wanted for questioning, but as far as I know, they don't have anything on him other than circumstantial evidence. His face has been on the news all over the world. He's also on the FBI's Most Wanted page."

"Do you think this Finch guy is involved then?" Sam cut in.

"He has to be," Oriyanna replied hastily. "John Remy, as well as the other three who went missing, possessed The Gift. There's no way Remy could have suffered a heart attack. I don't know who this Finch guy is, but I need to find out."

"Wait a second," said Sam, shifting slightly in his seat so he could face her, "are you telling me that those guys were all the same as you, and all from wherever it is you're from?" He shook his head in disbelief.

Oriyanna nodded. "Yes they were. I did say sometimes things are not as they seem."

"Just how many of you are there here?"

"Usually only four," she replied, her stomach lurching a little. She was dreading explaining it all to them. "John Remy was nearing the end of his second term in office as president. Once he stepped down, his period as a Watcher was to end. The one who was set to replace him is already here on Earth. It's vital that any new Watcher spends a few years here before taking up their post. The ones who killed John Remy and took the others obviously didn't know about him, or we wouldn't have discovered anything was wrong until it was too late." Deep down, Oriyanna feared that it might already be too late, but she didn't bother raising the point.

Sam narrowed his eyes. "Okay, none of this really makes much sense. Why would you have people here? And how come no one else knows about all this? And what is a Watcher?" Sam wasn't sure just how much more he could take. He had the feeling though, that what he already knew hadn't even scratched the surface. He massaged his temples and chewed at the loose skin on his lip once again.

Oriyanna glanced down at the sleeves which had already slipped down over her hands. "We come from a planet called Arkkadia," she began awkwardly. "It's around six hundred light years from Earth."

Adam drew a sharp breath in through his teeth. "How long did it take you to get here again? Those disappearances were only two weeks ago."

"The journey time between Arkkadia and Earth is just over seven of your days," she replied.

"So it's possible to travel faster than light then?" Adam asked excitedly.

Oriyanna had known this would happen. She hadn't even gotten started and already the questions were flooding in. She shook her head. "No, you can't travel faster than light in an object with mass, it's a scientific impossibility," she said matter-of-factly.

"Then how—" began Adam.

"Look, it's going to take me a while to explain it all. I'll try and cover any questions you have a little later," she snapped. It sounded as if she was being hard on him, but unless she was strict, explaining would take even longer.

"Okay, sorry," he replied, sounding a little dejected. "I'll try my best just to sit and listen, but I warn you, I'm a writer and reporter so it goes against my nature." Adam took his eyes away from the rearview mirror and stared intently at the road ahead. The night was gradually growing clearer. Light clouds made silvery, mackerel-like patterns across the moonlit sky.

"Thank you." She patted his shoulder, feeling a little guilty for the way she'd spoken. "As I said, Arkkadia is around six hundred light years from Earth. Our sun is close to the constellations of Lyra and Cygnus, so it's visible from Earth." She paused as a patrol car shot past them, its blue lights flashing brightly in the night. They all let out a long, relieved breath when it took a left hand turn off the main road and went about its business. "Arkkadia," she continued, "is a little under twice the size of this planet. We don't have a great deal more landmass though, as much of our planet is covered with water. I am led to believe that around ten years ago, one of your deep space telescopes actually found our planet and highlighted it as a place likely to contain life." A wry smile formed on her face.

"Did you know about that, mate?" asked Sam. He liked the way that no matter what the subject, Adam usually had some knowledge of it.

"I vaguely remember something about it, but it was a long time ago now. It's the kind of thing that makes the tail end of the news for a day or two then just gets forgotten about."

"It's funny though," Oriyanna continued. "A deep space telescope was how our ancestors first found the Earth — close to fifty thousand years ago now." Much to her surprise, neither of them cut in or interrupted. "Back then, the Arkkadian people were much like you are now, just taking their first tentative steps off the planet, looking to the heavens and wondering if life could possibly exist somewhere out there. We don't have droves of information about our ancestors who first came here, but I will tell you what I can." She arched her back slightly, stretching out a niggling travel pain from the seat. "As I said, when our ancestors first found Earth they could do nothing but look at deep space images and wonder if any life could exist here. From what we understand, it was that way for almost three hundred years. After nearly three centuries of research and development, our whole planet marvelled at the invention of an engine that would make deep space exploration possible." She looked fleetingly at Adam. "Don't worry, if you really want to know how it all works, I'll tell you later. I also understand that your best minds are working on a similar project, although you are many years away from being able to put it to practice." He glanced in the rearview mirror and smiled in appreciation. "Once they knew the technology was stable and after many more years of testing, three craft were sent here. They found Earth to be in the grip of your last ice age. Much of the northern hemisphere was one big ice sheet. The southern hemisphere and around the equator were slightly warmer, but it wasn't the paradise they'd thought it would be. Exploration of the warmer regions of the planet found it to be teeming with life of all kinds. For the first time in our history, we knew that life existed elsewhere, that we were not alone. Geological scans of your planet also found it to be rich with precious metals and minerals. But that was not the most amazing discovery, not by far. They found a semi-intelligent race that your history calls Genus Homo. Like us, they were bipeds and seemed similar in height and build, although they were covered in much more hair and had a much darker skin tone. What our ancestors found most remarkable was the fact these creatures used tools and weapons for hunting. The first mission took two of these creatures as specimens, one male and one female. After two weeks' initial exploration, they returned to Arkkadia with the creatures as well as geological survey maps of Earth." Oriyanna stood up and stretched her back again; the seat was really not that comfortable. "Can I get some more water, please?" she asked, turning to the fridge.

"Sure," replied Sam," just help yourself." They had cleared the southern tip of Denver's city limits now. Adam took them onto State Highway 85, heading toward a town called Sedalia, avoiding the need to use I25 with its ever-watchful traffic cameras. Despite the fact the road was small and narrow in places, the lack of traffic still enabled them to progress at a fairly decent pace. The roads here were clear and dry; the storm which had hammered them earlier had petered out just south of Denver.

Oriyanna returned to her seat and took a mouthful of water before screwing the cap back onto the bottle. "From the records we have of those first missions," she continued, "we know they carried out genetic testing on the Genus Homo creatures that they took. It showed them to be what we call an evolutionary dead end."

Adam rubbed his eyes a little, they were starting to feel sore and sleep-deprived. "I'm sorry, what does that mean exactly?" he asked.

"It means they had evolved as far as they could. From what we can tell, they had been at that state of evolution for tens of thousands of years, if not longer. They just didn't possess the genetic ability to progress any further." She paused for a second, wondering how to cover the next part. "We were a very different people back then," she said awkwardly. "The governments that ruled Arkkadia were keen to carry out mining operations on Earth, and they knew that precious metals and stones from this planet would be near on priceless." She stopped and looked away to the side, avoiding eye contact with either of the men. "They sanctioned a genetics program to develop the Genus Homo breed for mining purposes. They took a small amount of the Genus DNA and mixed it with our own to create a cross breed; in effect, they bridged the evolutionary dead end and created a new race in their image. It was a race bred for the sole purpose of working. Intellectually, they were back engineered and didn't possess a high enough intelligence to have any grasp of who their creators were or the technologies they possessed. Ethically, I don't know how they could ever have done it. I guess they saw it as a far cheaper alternative to transporting large numbers of Arkkadians to Earth and paying them a wage."

"So you're telling me," snapped Sam angrily, "that you created us as slaves! Is that where this is going?"

Oriyanna turned back to face him. He looked flushed with anger. "Please understand, Samuel, that our ancestors were a very different people. It was thousands of years ago now," she pleaded, placing her hand on his shoulder. Sam immediately relaxed a little at her touch. "Over the next two hundred years, our ancestors carried out mining operations all over this planet. During that time, they continued to develop and advance the new worker species that they'd created. They called them Adamites. In our language it means those who are of the ground. The project also had a name with which you will be familiar – Eden. Even your name is derived from those early worker species they created, Adam." He flashed her a quick look in the rearview mirror but didn't cut in. "Over time they introduced females into the population so they could reproduce themselves. I am ashamed to say that our ancestors were as hungry for wealth as they were for power. They ruled the Adamite people with fear, killing any who became too weak to be of use."

"Don't beat yourself up too much," Sam sympathised. "There are plenty of people on Earth just like that. I guess the apple doesn't fall too far from the tree, as they say."

She nodded. "Yes. Unfortunately, we have noticed very similar traits in you over the years." Oriyanna took a swig from the water bottle and placed it into the drinks holder at the side of her seat. "As I was saying, for around two hundred years our ancestors came and went from Earth, studying it and mining what they could. But the whole operation halted when a massive disaster fell upon Arkkadia. Our home planet was hit by a meteorite. Despite their ever-growing technology and understanding of the stars, there was nothing they could do to stop it, it wasn't even spotted until it was too late. The impact almost wiped us out completely. I know Earth suffered a similar event millions of years ago, which led to many early species being wiped out; this was a similar extinction-level event. At the time, we had no craft on Earth or on other exploration missions. The only people not on Arkkadia were in a space station that orbited the planet; they witnessed and recorded the whole event. Massive tsunamis washed clean whole continents, enough dust was thrown up into our atmosphere to block out our sun, the impact winter it created lasted for thirty-eight thousand years." Oriyanna stopped and wiped at her eyes. She'd seen the ancient footage of the event which had nearly killed her entire race many times as a student. Despite the dislike she felt for her ancestors, the images still horrified her. She took another sip from the water and carried on. "The event cast us back thousands of years, we lost everything, our race turned into scavengers who were almost no better than the Adamite people we had left on the Earth. Our rich technological history almost passed into myth, and very little evidence of the great race we once were survived."

"You weren't kidding were you when you said it would be hard for us to grasp," said Sam. His stomach was experiencing the first few pangs of hunger, but the selection of corn chips he'd picked up back in Empire didn't appeal in the least.

"I know, I'm sorry. I will try to keep it as simple as possible. I must sound crazy, but I promise you it's the truth. If you'd rather, I could show you." She raised her hand, prepared to pass the information to Sam through touch.

"No! no, you're good. Just telling me is fine," Sam replied hastily, leaning away from her a little.

Oriyanna smiled. "I thought you might say that." She lowered her hand and began fiddling with the Key Tablet, turning it over and over as if it were some sort of stress reliever. "Anyway, as the impact winter began to end we started to get back on our feet, a mere shadow of who we used to be. Steadily, over hundreds of years, we began to rebuild. Stories of our ancestors had almost turned into legend, but as we rebuilt, traces of our old civilisation were found. Slowly we came together, united out of the tragedy of near-extinction. Our new civilisation longed to regain some of the knowledge that our ancestors were rumoured to have possessed. Stories of the Earth and the race that had been left behind were now nothing more than what you would call folk tales. Then, as the first of our astronomers began to use technology to look to the skies, they made a startling discovery. There was an ancient structure still in orbit around our planet, a relic left from the old days. I was born around a hundred and fifty years after its discovery. I remember studying what had been found when I was a student. The information they had gleaned from it was unbelievable. The very first of our astronauts to go there found that amazingly, the reactors were still running. It still had power. The crew were still onboard; obviously long dead, but with no moisture in the air everything was preserved, almost appearing new. Over time, we learned how to access their computer systems. The information held on them changed the way we thought overnight. They discovered detailed plans on how the craft had worked and enabled us to once travel to the stars. Instantly our technological understanding advanced hundreds of years. The most ground breaking discoveries though, related to Earth. Not only did they find satellite images of this planet, but also star charts and equations on how to navigate here. The thing that shook us the most though, was learning about you. It was true, not only had we once visited this planet, but a race created by us had indeed been left here. Over the decades, speculation of what might now be on Earth was rife. You had been left unhindered for tens of thousands of years. Many believed that an advanced civilisation would now reside here, whilst others believed you would be extinct, having gradually died out over the years."

"I hate to butt in," began Adam, "but we're going to need a gas station pretty soon." He glanced at the fuel gauge nervously, as it crept even further into the red. Using the RV's computer, he found the fuel range guide. "It says we have just over twenty miles before empty."

Sam leaned forward and investigated the SatNav. "We should be fine. We're just less than twenty miles outside of Castle Rock. There'll be a station there. Just drive as fast and as economically as you can." He returned his attention to Oriyanna as she rolled up her sleeves for about the tenth time. "So how and when did you become involved in all this?"

"The subject fascinated me as a child. I was born into a time when they were just beginning to grasp the technology and understanding of how to rebuild the craft that had once made it possible for us to travel here. As a student, I was naturally talented in math and physics, as well as many other areas of scientific study. Our education systems were not too dissimilar from yours back then."

"Hold on a minute," said Sam, shifting in his seat to try and relieve the dull ache gradually forming in his neck. "You were born – before your people had even returned to Earth? Just how long ago was that?" He was trying to run the math in his head, but couldn't quite believe the answer.

Oriyanna looked a little uneasy. "Just shy of six thousand years ago now," she replied awkwardly.

For a few seconds, and not for the first time that night, Sam sat there looking a little like a fish which had just been caught and laid out on the river bank with its mouth gaping open. "Oh, right. Okay," was all he could manage; he had given up trying to question anything now. It was much easier to just accept it and carry on.

"When I was roughly twenty-nine Earth years of age I became involved in the final stages of the program that was rebuilding the craft our ancestors had once used. The engines we developed were exactly the same. It had taken us decades to understand the physics behind it. Like I said before, these engines do not enable us to travel faster than light, due to the fact our craft have mass. Not to mention the fact that as you approach speeds of that nature, time virtually bends around you. The faster you go, the more time bends. If it were possible to travel many times faster than light, you would virtually be travelling in time. While a few days might have passed for you, many years would have gone by for everyone else. Even if it was possible, it would be highly impractical." Oriyanna paused, briefly allowing them to get their heads around the concept.

"Okay, I have a feeling I'm really going to struggle on this bit," sighed Sam, already confused. "Just try and keep it as simple as you can."

"Do you have a piece of paper I could use?" she asked.

"Yeah – sure," he said, opening up the glovebox and fishing out the hire agreement.

Oriyanna held it up. "Right, let's say this corner is Arkkadia and this corner is Earth." She ran her hand diagonally across the sheet. "This represents the distance between the two planets."

"Okay, I'm with you so far," said Sam. He looked as though he wanted badly to understand what she was saying.

"Now the fastest way to get from this point to this point is how?" she eyed him, enjoying the look of confusion on his face.

"By making them co-exist at one singularity!" cut in Adam, looking rather smug. Sam turned his attention to his friend, who for the first time in a good few hours had a triumphant smile on his face.

"How the hell do you know this shit?" he asked in amazement.

"What can I say? I like to read," he responded, grinning.

Oriyanna enjoyed the banter between the two men. The atmosphere was about as relaxed as it had been since she'd met them. "I'm impressed," she said. "I know the theory behind this has been looked at on Earth. Unfortunately, as I said, you're still a good few hundred years, if not more, from being able to put it into practice. I know that NASA is hoping to harness it in the next hundred years, but I fear they may be in for disappointment, unless they experience a real breakthrough. I would add though that the amount of power required to create a bend in space that spans six hundred light years is massive, and far more than the engines on our spacecraft can manage."

"So, you're telling me," said Adam, "that even after all these years, the technology your ancestors used and you redeveloped is still the same?"

"It is. There comes a point where you can only develop something so far and then it's impossible to improve. This is how it is. I didn't say that a bend in space that big was an impossibility, far from it. I just said that as far as our spacecraft are concerned, it's impossible. So what we do is create a series of smaller bends, one after the other, and pass through them. Thus the time it takes to travel from Arkkadia to Earth is just over seven days – seven days and six Earth hours, to be precise." Sam caught himself nodding his head, as normally as if he'd just been told what day of the week it was. He reached for a fresh bag of corn chips, his hunger pains now in full swing. Cracking them open, he immediately regretted it. The first mouthful made him feel a little sick. He needed some proper food, not to mention some sleep.

"You said earlier," he began, ridding his mouth of the corn chips with a very dry swallow, "that there was a war between your people."

"Yes, I will come to that in a second. I'm sorry, it's quite a task getting all this down into a brief account."

"It's okay," Sam replied, his mouth feeling like an old, dry plimsoll. "I'm just keen to know what we might be up against, that's all."

Oriyanna smiled weakly. "I'm not sure you really want to know," she said, staring at the bottoms of the pants which were once again swamping her feet. "As I was saying, we had finally rebuilt and under-stood the technology our ancestors once possessed. Due to the work I'd done; I was selected to go with the first team to return to Earth. We sent two craft in the first instance."

"What year was this?" asked Adam, trying to ignore the pungent cheesy smell of Sam's snack food.

"Around three thousand eight hundred BC on your calendar," she replied. "We found a world very different from the one our ancestors knew. The ice age had long since ended, and the topography of the planet looked vastly different. What had once been frozen wasteland, was now lush and fertile. The temperature around the equator was much higher than we ever experience on Arkkadia. It was like paradise. The most amazing discovery of all though, was you, the human race, left behind by our ancestors. Whilst you were in no way technologically advanced, you had progressed from the primitive work slaves who had been left here. Testing showed your DNA had evolved and become almost identical to ours. All over the planet, small civilisations had cropped up. Many different cultures and skin tones had developed; it was a rich tapestry of life, far more fascinating and diverse than we could ever have conceived. The first race of people we encountered were the Sumerians, who lived in the region you know as Iraq. Back then it was rich and fertile, nothing like the desert which occupies the area now. On our arrival, they literally fell before our feet. We learned through them that they worshipped the gods who had created their ancestors. Not only were those gods worshipped, but they were also feared, for they had bound them to slavery. The people had become free when those gods left and never returned. Over thousands of years, and through many forms of civilization, the story lived on, albeit a little embellished from what had actually happened. Each generation feared that one day their gods would return. They saw us as their ancient gods and believed we had returned to enslave them once again. To them we were known as the Annunaki, in their language it meant—"

"Those who from the heavens came," Adam cut in in a low voice, though he didn't take his eyes off the dark road.

"You know this story?" she asked, a little surprised.

"Not fully. The guy I got friendly with in South America, the one I told you about earlier, he spoke about a dig he'd done in Iraq on an ancient Sumerian city. He mentioned the Annunaki. He said though that the gods they worshipped came from a planet called Niribu. Back in twenty twelve, a whole host of conspiracy theory nuts actually thought that Niribu was going to collide with Earth when it passed through our solar system. Of course, it never happened."

"It never fails to amaze me just how much useless crap there must be in that head of yours," laughed Sam as he contemplated another mouthful of the corn chips.

"No, Adam is right," Oriyanna defended. "That is just what they believed. Niribu was what they called our planet, the fact that they thought one day it was going to return to Earth was a just a metaphor for how they believed their gods would one day return to enslave them. They couldn't understand the concept of spacecraft and space travel, although in their records, it does detail how the human race on Earth was created using jars and vials. Whilst they could never understand the true science behind it, what they wrote was not far from the truth. As with most beliefs on Earth, over the centuries accounts become embellished and distorted. As I was the only female on the mission, they actually thought me to be the embodiment of Nammu, the female goddess whom they believed gave birth to the Annunaki gods." Oriyanna paused as the glow of a petrol station appeared on the horizon.

"At last," said Adam in a relieved tone. They were still a good ten miles from Castle Rock, but he wasn't taking any chances. The fuel gauge needle was now pinned hard on empty. He swung the RV onto the forecourt, jumped out and began to fill the tank. Sam turned back around in his seat. He'd been twisted facing Oriyanna for a good few miles and his neck felt as if it were going to seize.

"How far do you intend to drive tonight?" she asked, absently watching Adam pump gas into the tank. He used his credit card to pay for the fuel, before heading across the brightly lit forecourt to grab some supplies from the small store.

"Colorado Springs," Sam replied, rolling his aching neck in his hands. "It's only another fifty miles or so, should take just over an hour. It's a big enough place to ditch the RV and pick up a new set of wheels. Tomorrow, if Adam and I drive in shifts, we should be able to cover almost the whole distance down to Austin." They sat silently whilst watching Adam waiting at the counter behind a guy who was taking an age to pay for his goods. After what seemed like an eternity, he finally emerged from the small shop and hurried across the forecourt before jumping back into the cab handing them both a cold can of Pepsi.

"Thought we could all use a little sugar boost," he said enthusiastically. His expression showed his mind was already working out how he could transfer all this to a story. Despite the grave situation they were facing, some small part of him was naturally intrigued and excited about what they'd learned.

"What is it?" asked Oriyanna, studying the can with interest and turning it over in her hand.

"It's just a fizzy drink, look!" Adam cracked the ring pull and took a swig, exaggerating his movements. Oriyanna copied, screwing her face up as the drink hit her tongue.

"You actually drink this stuff?" she asked in amazement. "What's in it?" She handed the can back to him to place in the spare cup holder.

"I find it best to try and not think about that," he laughed, pulling off the forecourt and back onto Route 85. Sam had drained his drink in a few swallows and began working on Oriyanna's unwanted can.

"Right. Where was I?" she said thoughtfully.

"You were just telling us about the first trip here and your contact with the Sumerian people," prompted Sam. He though he sounded crazy even saying it.

"Yes, that's right –well, that first mission was only for two of your months. We briefly studied the cultures that had sprung up all over the planet, finding that the most advanced ones were in the Mesopotamia region. No matter where we went, the people cowered and feared us. Various religions had sprung up, all with different ideals. The only

141

common factor was that every single one worshipped a creator, a being or god that had made them."

"You don't have religion on your planet?" asked Sam. Despite being a hardened atheist, the idea seemed strange.

"No, not at all. We have always studied science. The prospect that we had a creator or someone to worship has never featured at all. We find the whole concept quite puzzling, really."

"Well, when you look at the facts and how you've explained things to us," began Adam, "it's not surprising you were worshipped. They could never have understood the technology you possessed. I mean, it's only in the last few centuries that our modern culture would have been able to grasp it."

"No, indeed, I do understand. The Earth-Humans seem to have a deep need to believe in something; you are obsessed with it. Over the last few decades, we've seen a steep increase in people turning away from faith, as your developing minds began to question the idea more. Like the friend you met in South America, many people now believe it possible that you were created by another race. It's like you all know something doesn't quite fit, but for many, it's easier not to believe or question it. Over the years, we've seen how your religions and beliefs have killed far more people than they've saved. It's a very dangerous thing when in the wrong hands, although on the flipside, it can have an overwhelming power for good. It seems you have no way of finding a balance."

Sam nodded his head, taking another drink from her can. "You don't need to tell me," he said, suppressing a burp, "I've seen far too many good men die, because the people we were fighting had blind faith in their god. I've never truly believed in any of it, but hearing what you're saying, and knowing without doubt that it's all untrue kind of rubs salt into the wounds, if I'm honest."

"I understand," sighed Oriyanna. "I am truly sorry, we never meant for any of the wars to happen that were fought in the name of religion. We believed that as you progressed technologically, you would hold science in higher regard than belief. We were very wrong." She paused and stared absently out of the side window for a few seconds. The passing headlights of a car snapped her back from the daydream. "Anyway, as I said, we returned home after two months. The trip had gained us more information than we could ever have imagined. On our return we were all offered The Gift. It was a brand new technology back then, developed on theories and plans we had found aboard the space station over a century ago. It was and is still held as an honour, given to those who serve or do a great deed in the name of our race. The same governmental system has ruled our planet now for thousands of years, thanks to it. The only time it was ever thrown into doubt was during the Great War."

"So you don't have elections or people with differing views?" quizzed Adam. "How does that work? It sounds almost like a dictatorship to me."

"No, not at all, it's nothing like that. We view your methods and systems as very primitive. It's not just religion that causes your wars, it's the barriers you build between the countries and continents and the differing views of your governments. Only when you learn to break those down and become one will you know true peace and unity. The formation of alliances such as your European Union and NATO, as well as the single currency, are the first signs of you taking such steps, although you are still many, many years away from achieving what we have. It is our hope that you will get there in the end. Then you will be ready."

"Ready for what?" asked Sam, draining the last of the Pepsi and crushing the can.

"To learn en masse who you really are. It has been our hope and vision all along that one day, our two worlds would stand together united. You are drawing ever closer, but you're not there yet. You see, we view you almost as a parent views a child. We were responsible for your creation and as such, we see it as our duty to help and guide you when necessary. Unfortunately, there were those on Arkkadia who developed a different view, and it was those people who caused the war that eventually divided our people and ultimately led to what's happening now."

"How did it happen?" asked Adam, glancing back at her in the mirror. It felt good to take his eyes off the road briefly; the constant strain of driving was starting to take its toll.

"We had been studying and living here among you for almost a thousand years. Eventually, over generations, the Earth people stopped fearing us and began to trust us, although they never could see us as anything other than god-like beings to be worshipped. We lived mainly among the Sumerian people and also with the early Egyptians, and then, many years after the war, we also came to study the Mayan people. Our teachings helped them understand the planets within your solar system and how to chart the stars. We helped them understand the science of math and how to keep time, and use calendars. From our influence, their culture thrived and their early cities grew in size and wealth. However, our studies were not limited to Earth. During that millennia, we searched deeper into space than our ancestors ever had, looking for other planets such as Earth and Arkkadia. We found many that sat in the right orbital distance from their star, but all were either gaseous or just barren wastelands, devoid of any life or the vital conditions needed to sustain it. We became increasingly aware of just how unique our two worlds were. It was then when things began to change. There were those within our government who started to believe that we should look to claim the Earth, to colonize it as a second home to help safeguard our future. They had seen how easily we had nearly been wiped out before and feared the same thing could happen again. Unfortunately, within their plans they had no room for the descendants of the people our ancestors had made. To them, the Earth-Humans became a mistake that should never have happened. In their view, you had been created by us and were a race that should never have existed, and therefore, they saw no issue with destroying you." Oriyanna hung her head and gazed at the floor. "Their thinking caused a divide among our people; tensions grew as we tried to resolve it peacefully. Unfortunately, there were cities here on Earth that were under control of those who felt the same. Overnight, the peaceful mediations broke down and the massacre began. Our opponents didn't hold back, and slaughtered entire city populations, taking control from the Earth-Humans. The war between us had started. Fierce battles took place both here and on Arkkadia, and we fought to protect you for nearly a century until in the end, those who had sought to destroy you were driven from Arkkadia and banished to Sheol, a small mining planet around one hundred and fifty light years away. Sheol had been terraformed some three centuries earlier. Whilst we had made the atmosphere stable and breathable, it had never been a planet we thought to colonize due to it being so close to its sun; it's uncomfortably hot. Our operations on Sheol had long since ended. Before they fled there, it was merely used as an outpost. In the last few months of the war, our armies struck the surface of Sheol hard, destroying their craft and ability to reach Earth and strike back. The only structures to have survived were the mining colonies, deep below the surface. The last of their resistance to fall was here on Earth. They still held control of the two cities that they had claimed right at the start of the war. The occupants knew they had nothing to lose and made retaking them virtually impossible. In the end, the destruction of those cities was ordered and they were laid waste." Oriyanna glanced up at them, tears welling in her eyes, and as she blinked they streamed down her face. "It was a painful time for us, and I can still remember it all," she said, embarrassed by her distress.

Adam dug into the side pocket of his door and retrieved two tissues. "The Bible tells a story of how God destroyed the cities of Sodom and Gomorrah because they were found to be full of sin. I'm guessing that story is a rough account of what you just described," he said, reaching back and handing them to her.

Oriyanna wiped her eyes and cheeks, nodding her head. "Yes, although over the years it's become altered somewhat to fit your religion. The Earth people who witnessed it had no grasp of the weapons we used."

"So, how have events led us to where we are today?" asked Sam. "I don't mean to sound stupid, but all that was thousands of years ago."

"After the war, we remained in regular contact with Earth. Some of us, myself included, spent many years actually living here, looking to guide the people toward science. We began to study the Egyptian people in greater detail, as well as many of the other fascinating cultures that had begun to develop across the globe. Around two thousand two hundred and seventy BC, the Sumerian culture began to collapse and a new Arkkadian empire rose up in our honour; even aspects of our native language began to appear in their spoken words. The empire lasted for almost one hundred and ninety years. In the end, wars between men, which we had no interest or involvement in, led to the end of this period. Then, for many years, we slowed down our visitations to Earth. We backed off our direct involvement in human affairs. The last race of Earth-Humans we had in-depth involvement with were the Mayan people, around two thousand eight hundred years ago. They were a fascinating culture. Much like the Sumerians, they built cities that were well ahead of their time. Toward the last days of the Mayans, a sanction was passed on Arkkadia to leave Earth to develop. No matter how we looked to teach those early civilisations, they just couldn't grasp who we actually were. It was far too soon. It was then that the Watchers were introduced. Four Arkkadians would live among the people of Earth, and they would be seen no differently to any other Earth-Human. Amazingly, after we left Earth and the Watchers took over, we saw a large backward step in your technological development. Without us there to directly guide you, much of what we had taught died out with the cultures we had taught it to. It confirmed what we thought. You were not yet capable of understanding and mastering technology the way we'd hoped. At times throughout Earth's history, the Watchers have taken a more active role. When needed, they would help to give you a gentle nudge in the right direction. The four who have just been killed held such roles. Their primary purpose though, above all else, was to safeguard your future against the ones who tried to destroy you."

"It's all just too much to take in," said Sam distantly. "What about stories in the Bible? You refer to our Earth years as BC. You're aware of the belief some people hold in the birth and life of Jesus?"

Oriyanna nodded earnestly. "I thought you might ask about that," she said thoughtfully. "Just remember what I said. Many important historical figures have been Watchers; Arkkadian people here in your best interests. You also need to remember how historical events that happened thousands of years ago, particularly those that hold precedence in Earth religion, get altered over the years. Many religions that see Jesus as the son of God seem to forget that it wasn't until three hundred and twenty-five years after his recorded death that he was viewed as such. Until then, he was just seen as a prophet and leader, and in today's culture he would just be viewed as a visionary and a great humanitarian. Many of the people who follow the Bible choose not to question the massive gap that exists between the time of his birth and death."

"So it's all wrong then?" questioned Adam.

"You must remember that back then, there was no real way of recording things accurately, not like you have now. In the three hundred years that passed before he was viewed as the Messiah, the true accounts of who he was and what he done became altered dramatically. The whole story of his birth is not at all accurate, in truth, he first appeared here on Earth as a man. It was hoped by us that he would be a great leader, one to unite you. Unfortunately, differing views and the

147

ever-raging struggle for power between Earth-Humans eventually led to his execution."

"So the accounts of his crucifixion are correct then?" The writer and reporter in Adam had well and truly taken over, and whilst his mind was still struggling to comprehend what Oriyanna was saying, he was hungry to learn as much as possible. He also found the exotic tone of her voice relaxing; he liked listening to her.

"No, they are actually very close to the truth," she replied. "Like every Watcher who has been here, he possessed The Gift. How else do you explain how he rose from the grave? Like the way you saw me heal earlier. It was no miracle, although back then it was seen as such."

"Well I'm still finding it hard to believe what I saw and it's just over two thousand years later," cut in Sam.

"More like two thousand two hundred years," Oriyanna corrected. "Your calendar is a little off, but we won't go into that." She gave Sam a small grin as if to say, 'It's okay, I can forgive your ignorance. It's not your fault'.

"Wow," gasped Adam. That's quite a mind fuck – I mean I've never been religious in the slightest but hearing it first hand is, well…" he drifted off for a few moments. "You could really open a can of worms with what you know."

"There are clues recorded in the texts, it's just how you choose to understand them. I have studied many of your religious scriptures with interest over the years. Jesus is actually recorded as saying, *My kingdom is not of this world*. It all comes down to your personal interpretation."

"What about that strange metallic thing you seem to be so reluctant to let out of your sight? Where does that feature in all of this?" asked Sam, keen to steer her off the subject of religion. While he didn't hold any belief in it himself, it was hard to hear that many of the conflicts he'd seen and been involved with were all for nothing.

"Are you sure you want me to go through this now? You have already been burdened with so much information."

"Let's just get it all over and done with," he said, noticing the first sign for Castle Rock on the side of the road. There would be no need to stop now, the full tank of fuel would be more than enough to see them through to Colorado Springs. Reaching forward he cranked the heat up a little on the dash; since the soaking they had received a few hours ago Sam was struggling to keep warm. He felt chilled right down to his bones.

"Very well," she agreed. "Just before the war, we had begun to look at ways to create much larger bends in space, and whilst the journey and communication times between our worlds was never excessive, we longed to find a way to properly unite our two planets. We began to experiment with the amount of power needed to make a bend in space that big. Unfortunately, when the war broke out, our work halted. After the war we had the resources to start the project again, but no matter how we tried, we just couldn't build an engine that could generate enough power. In the end we realized that the answer to our problem was both here and on Arkkadia."

"How so?" asked Sam, trying to rub a little heat into his cold hands by holding them over the hot air vents.

"We discovered a way to tap into the planet and use the massive amount of energy it creates. In actuality, there was no need for an engine to be built; we learned how to use the planet itself as the engine."

"And you managed it?"

"We did, although the technology has never been one hundred percent stable. Its use is never without risk." Oriyanna stared uneasily at the glowing metal object in her hands.

"So how does that feature?" asked Sam, gesturing at the small card she held.

"We constructed two devices, one here on Earth and one on Arkkadia. It was tested and used a handful of times, but we found huge risks came with its use. In the end, it was decreed that the Tabut should only be used as a last resort under extreme circumstances. The one here on Earth was left dormant and this," she held the artefact up, "the Key Tablet, was taken to Arkkadia. This is the first step used to turn it on. The second is the biometric signature of an Arkkadian Elder."

"And you believe that whatever is happening here will warrant you using this device?" asked Sam sceptically.

"I don't know. Once I find out exactly what is happening here, I can decide. It may well be our only option. At best, it will take another two weeks to get more craft here from Arkkadia. If I activate the Tabut, it will bridge the distance between our worlds instantly."

Sam shifted further around in his seat to face her, starting his neck to aching again. "The Tabut," he began, "is that what it's called?"

Oriyanna nodded her head, "Yes, although you will know it by a different name."

"There are records of its existence?" Sam asked, sounding a little confused. "If that's true, then how come no one has tried to find it and use it?"

"Oh, but they have," she said, smiling knowingly. "Many people have searched for The Ark, but none have ever found it, nor do they know what its true purpose is."

"The Ark of the Covenant?" gasped Adam. "You are talking about the Ark of the Covenant here, is that right?"

"Yes, I believe that is the name it's most commonly known by on Earth."

"And you know where it is?" he asked, his voice full of amazement.

"Of course I do," she grinned confidently. "It's in Egypt, deep under the Great Pyramid of Giza."

Adam's concentration on the road wavered and the wheels of the camper scuffed the verge, making it shake violently. He snapped the wheel left and corrected his mistake, and then took a moment to gather his thoughts. "So, is that the purpose of the Great Pyramid then?" he finally asked. "I know that for years they believed it to be a burial chamber, but no bodies were ever found inside."

"It is," she answered. "The position and alignment of the pyramids help to harness the Earth's energy through the ley lines they sit upon, and these form part of a much larger and invisible grid network that covers your whole planet – you just haven't learned how to harness it yet. Once the Tabut is activated, the Great Pyramid helps to capture and amplify the power of the Earth's magnetic poles. In effect, the structure acts as massive harmonic resonator which produces the huge amounts of energy needed for the Tabut to work."

"So the Arkkadian people built that structure here – thousands of years ago?" quizzed Adam.

"Indeed, but with the help of the Earth-Humans," she replied, enjoying the conversation. Not only did she seem to have some kind of mental connection with Adam; he was well educated and smart. She'd also noticed the way he looked at her, and it made her feel warm inside. "It still amazes me," she continued, "that you have scholars here on Earth who believe the Egyptians built that structure unaided." She smiled at the thought. "You can't even replicate it now – how would you ever have built an eight-sided, perfectly symmetrical pyramid that's lined up exactly with magnetic north all those years ago?"

"Eight-sided?" asked Sam, confusion blossoming in his eyes.

"Yes, although the pyramid appears to have four sides, it actually has eight."

"Oh," Sam replied, not really wanting to get into an in-depth discussion about the geometry of the building – his head was spinning enough as it was. "My knowledge of this sort of stuff is pretty lacking," he added truthfully, "but I'm sure they never found anything inside the pyramid. It was empty when they opened it up."

"The Tabut was held in what you call the King's Chamber," began Oriyanna, "but it was far less stable above ground. After much theorisation it was moved below the pyramid, under the lower chamber.

Beneath the structure itself we found the power of the ley lines was far greater and amplified, with the help of the aquifers that run deep under the plateau. We also used a highly sensitive and conductive metal, that's not found here on Earth, to line the chamber with." Oriyanna handed the Key Tablet over to Sam. "No one has ever found the chamber that houses the Tabut, even if the lower chamber is pounded with ground radar, it would never show up. We knew as the knowledge of your ancestors was lost you would look to things such as the Great Pyramid in wonder. You could say we planned ahead and made sure you'd never find it, until we were ready for you to do so."

"I'm guessing this is made of the same stuff then?" he asked, still marvelling at the way it hummed and glowed at his touch before handing it back to her.

"Yes, the Tabut and the chamber, as well as the Key Tablet, are all made of the same material; we call it Taribium; it's a mixture of three different ores found on my planet. It's both a conductor and an amplifier, it vibrates and glows at your touch because it's picking up and amplifying the energy from your body. This is only a very small amount, the chamber and the Tabut contain thousands of times the mass of this small piece. The energy it can harness from the planet is tremendous."

"So, what exactly are the risks then, if you turn this thing on?" Sam asked warily.

"If singularity with Arkkadia is held for too long, it will cause major seismic activity on both our worlds. Just powering it up and tapping into the Earth's magnetic poles will cause an electromagnetic pulse powerful enough to fry every circuit board on the planet. Televisions, phones, computers, aircraft – everything will be useless." Her tone was flat and serious.

Adam just nodded; he didn't really know what to say. It was all just too much for him to grasp at the moment. After a lingering pause he said, "And if it turns out you need to get to Egypt, have you thought about how you're going to get there? You're not even on the right continent." It seemed like a stupid question in the light of what they'd just been told, but it was all he could think about.

"I don't know," she replied, sounding a little subdued. "My first concern is getting to Austin; I didn't plan for all of this to happen."

"I'm not too sure how much more of this I can take in," groaned Sam, rubbing his temples again.

Oriyanna placed her hand back onto his shoulder. "I'm sorry, I can't even begin to imagine how hard all this must be for you both to understand. This man, Robert Finch," said Oriyanna, changing the subject, "you mentioned he was the head of President Remy's Secret Service rteam?"

"He was," replied Adam, glad to be on to something he had a chance of knowing a little more about. "There's been no trace of him since the night the President died."

"Is there any way I can see a picture of him?" Oriyanna asked, desperately needing to piece the whole situation together.

"Sure, my phone is in the glove box. As long as we have a good enough signal, Sam can get onto the FBI website."

Sam opened the glove box; it was big enough to fit a small child in and full of their travel documents. After about a minute of rummaging around he finally located it, and the moment his hand clasped around the cool metal, it rang. The shrill tone of the incoming call made them all jump. Sam tore it from the compartment and flipped it over. 'BLOCKED' flashed up on the screen briefly, before it rang off. Sam stared at it for a few moments, as if expecting it to ring again. His mind raced. *Why would a blocked number call once and ring off?* he thought. All their close friends knew where they were; even if Lucie phoned, Adam's home number would have been identified on an international call. Something didn't sit right; a bad feeling grew quickly in the pit of his stomach. "My god, I think they're trying to track your mobile," he said quietly. the idea occurring to him in the same instant he said the words.

"Who's tracking what?" asked Adam, leaning over to try and hear better. The road surface had changed and roughened, increasing the constant hum of the tyres over the tarmac.

"I said, they're tracking your phone, or at least, I think they are."

"How the hell do you know that?" shrieked Adam, his voice an octave higher than he would have liked.

"I don't know, it's just a hunch. The number was from a blocked call and they only let it ring once. Calling your phone would have made it register on the network." Sam paused for a minute, thinking it out again. He was desperately trying to remember back to the many close protection courses he'd done after leaving the army. He had covered this – how it was possible to locate a kidnap victim if their phone was switched on. "There are programs out there that will give you the location of any phone, if you have the number. It's like when you share your location with a friend so they can find you, only with this program, you don't get asked permission, they just pump in your number and it displays the info on a map. It's only really used by government and law enforcement, but I have no doubt that they would be capable of doing it, seeing as how they had an operative that close in to the US President." It felt strange using the word operative to describe this Finch guy; however, Sam found it helped him put a real-world face on the situation.

"How accurate is it?" asked Oriyanna nervously.

"It depends. If they can get in and ping it from the GPS, then we're talking a few feet. If not, then maybe ten miles at the most."

"Turn it off then," cried Adam, reaching across the cab and trying to snatch the phone from Sam's hand. The movement of his body caused the RV to veer dangerously to the left, crossing the road into the oncoming traffic. The blaring sound of a car horn snapped Adam's attention away from the phone; wrestling with the steering wheel, he pulled the lumbering vehicle to the right, narrowly avoiding the oncoming car that was frantically flashing its lights in warning. The oversteer sent the camper fishtailing across both lanes, and its wheels found the loose gravel and grass of the verge, causing the back to snake uncontrollably as it built momentum. As time seemed to slow down, Adam fought with the steering wheel, pulling hard to the left and right as he tried to control the slide, but it was too late. The back slid around further until he was looking at the disappearing tail lights of the car he'd just missed. Somewhere below them, the transmission screamed in protest at the change of direction as the rear of the RV smashed through a wire fence, collecting up a line of old wooden fence posts with a series of sharp, splintering crashes which reverberated up through the steering wheel. Finally, the camper came to a stop, in a billowing cloud of dirt and dust that seemed to engulf them. For a few long moments, Adam sat there, still gripping the wheel, his knuckles turning white as he watched the dust motes settling in the headlights. He forced back the dry prickly feeling in his mouth, brought on by the momentary panic, and released his grip; his fingers were aching from how hard he'd had hold of the wheel. "Is... every— everyone okay?" he finally managed to gasp. He glanced back at Oriyanna and saw her picking herself up off the floor; she'd slipped off the seat and slid against one of the large cupboards. Apart from being a little pale she seemed unscathed. Sam was braced hard into his seat, his feet rammed into the foot well and his arm wedged against the door, holding him in place.

"That is precisely why I like to do the driving," he chuckled, letting out a long breath. He pointed to the other side of the road, which was heavily lined with trees. "Might have been a messier outcome if you'd veered off that way." He looked back at Oriyanna, who was busy rolling up her baggy clothing. "That's crash number two for you tonight," he joked.

"That one was a little easier," she replied, trying to smile. "Is there much damage?"

"Not sure, hopefully only a few dents and scratches, but I need to check."

"Sam, the phone," pleaded Adam. "Turn it off!"

Sam held his free hand up defiantly. "Wait. Just wait a second," he barked. "I need to think this through, but first let me just see what damage you've done." Taking the phone with him, he flung open the door and jumped out into the night.

"Can they really find us from that phone?" said Oriyanna nervously.

"Yeah, I think so. I need to speak with Sam. This is one subject that he does know more about than me." Adam was trying to speak as calmly as possible, but wasn't making a very good job of it. No matter how much the subject matter fascinated him, he was well out of his depth, and sinking further down the rabbit hole with every passing minute.

"I will go along with whatever he suggests," she said, glancing out of the side window to try and see him. "It's been many years since I was last on Earth, and things have changed a great deal."

"It's not too bad," said Sam clambering back into the passenger seat. "Just cosmetic damage to the rear, no punctures or bits hanging off that might snag. Give the engine a try; I just hope it's not flooded." Adam turned the ignition, almost holding his breath. The engine fired up first time and they all breathed a sigh of relief. Gingerly, he selected first gear and eased them back onto the road.

"Now, will you please switch off the phone?" he begged.

"Not yet, no, I've had an idea. It's risky, but it might give us the upper hand here, plus I need to show Oriyanna the photograph of that Finch chap." Sam unlocked the screen and loaded a browser window.

"What the hell are you thinking?" pleaded Adam. "It will lead them right to us!"

"I know it will," replied Sam as the FBI page loaded. "That's the idea." He found the 'Most Wanted' picture and passed it back to Oriyanna. "Here you are, does he look familiar?"

She stared at the image for a few seconds and began shaking her head, "No, sorry, I have never seen him before, but he must be involved. I'm guessing that whoever they used to get that close to John

Remy wasn't a face any of us would recognise." She paused to think and handed the phone back. "That's my main concern, I don't know how many of them are here or who they are. They got someone into the US Secret Service, he was even in charge of security for one of our Watchers."

"Sam, for Christ sake, will you either switch off that phone or explain to me why you think it's such a great idea to let them find us?" Adam was starting to panic and he hated to seem weak in front of Oriyanna, but the truth was he wasn't good at this kind of stuff. Sam, however, was cut from a completely different cloth. Adam had no doubt that some small part of his friend was relishing the challenge they faced.

Sam looked at him, a sly smile spreading on his face. "Aren't you just a bit curious to get a look at who is after her?"

"No, not really!" Adam snapped. "I'd rather stay as far ahead of them as possible, if I'm honest, and how the hell did they even get my number?"

Sam dug out the rental agreement that Oriyanna had used for her demonstration earlier. "It's on the rental form," he said, waving the paper in the air. "The license plate of the RV is bound to have been recorded when we were stopped. It wouldn't take a genius to get our information from the rental firm." Adam's face was growing whiter by the second. "Look, if I'm right, they called your phone to make it register on the network; that means they can't get a GPS fix on it – if they could, it would never have rung. All they will have is a rough idea of where we are. Are you with me so far?" Adam nodded his head reluctantly. "So let them follow us, then when we get to Colorado Springs we can ditch the RV and leave your phone in the cab. I'll switch on your Google Mapping app and fire up the GPS, and if they're still watching us, which I bet they will be, it will provide them with an exact fix."

"I really don't know about this," said Adam shakily.

"Look, this kind of stuff is my thing. Trust me." He patted Adam on the shoulder. "I need to know who we're fighting here, and the only way I can do that is by getting a look at the enemy."

"Sam is right," agreed Oriyanna. "It is a risky move, but it's pointless just running, they will find us eventually and as much as I am dreading it, the only way I'm going to figure out exactly what they are up to is by getting in close."

"No, no, no," groaned Adam, "there is no way I want to get that close, getting a look at them from a distance is bad enough, but one-on-one – no way!" He shook his head in protest. "And do you really expect them to tell you what's going on?"

"Not for a second," she replied shaking her sleeve down for what felt like the hundredth time. "I don't need them to speak to me. I just need to get my hands on them."

Sam's eyes were wide with a mixture of excitement and nervous energy brought on by the developing plan. "You want to try and get in that close?" he gasped.

"No, not for a second, but I think it's the only way."

"This is just crazy talk," Adam protested. "For one, we don't know when they will catch up to us, or how many there will be. You might not even have time to get ready for whatever the hell it is you're planning to do. Just turn the phone off and let's concentrate on getting to Austin."

"Just relax," insisted Sam sternly, "chances are they're a fair few miles away right now, they won't be breathing down our necks anytime soon. If I switch it off now, they'll know we're spooked. Just get us to Colorado Springs, mate, one step at a time." Sam offered Adam an encouraging smile.

"It seems I'm somewhat outnumbered, doesn't it?" he conceded reluctantly.

"Yep, you are, sorry," laughed Sam. It felt good to finally have something to do, a plan to focus on. In his many years of military service and protection work, he'd never been the one to be hunted, he had never been the one running. It just wasn't the way he liked to work.

"Okay, I'll go with it, but for the record I still think it's a pretty shitty idea. It's just – I don't know; this seems too big. If what Oriyanna said is true, how can we make the difference?"

She sat forward in her seat and placed a reassuring hand on his shoulder, just as she'd done with Sam earlier. "Sometimes, Adam," she began softly, "just one or two people can make more of a difference than an entire army." He watched her smile in the rearview mirror and his heart skipped a beat.

"Oh, and just one more thing," Sam cut in, "when we get to the city we need to find somewhere to buy some hardware."

"Hardware?" repeated Adam, snapping himself out of the near trance-like state Oriyanna had inflicted on him once again.

The smile on Sam's face stretched almost from ear-to-ear. "Yes, hardware. We're going to need some guns."

Chapter 10

Due to the late hour, traffic on Interstate 25 was light. Since clearing Denver and getting onto I25, Roddick had kept the Impala gunned, and a few miles out of the city the interstate was dry. The rainstorm which had pounded Denver hadn't made it that far. Thankfully, due to the dry, empty road, they had hardly dropped below ninety for the last fifty miles. Finch glanced down at the FBI badge in his hand and ran his thumb over the cool, imprinted metal surface. Whilst the new government ID was a fake, it still looked as real as any genuine one. It felt good to have a powerful form of identification in his possession again. While his previous one had been the real deal, this would no doubt serve just as well on members of the public, and allow him the ability to question anyone he may need to, without having to get nasty. Finch had no real issues with inflicting pain when the situation arose, but actions like that often drew unwanted attention, not to mention how time consuming and messy it could be. Stealth and speed were the name of the game now.

"We're about thirty miles outside of Colorado Springs," said Roddick nonchalantly, keeping his attention firmly fixed on the road while watching out for the slightest sign of a police patrol. "I'll start backing off in a few miles until we get an update."

"Okay, get us to within ten miles of the city; hopefully by then we'll have news from Mitchell," Finch replied, tucking the badge back into his jacket pocket. Roddick nodded in agreement as he manoeuvred the Chevy into the fast lane and swept past a worn out, rusty red pickup truck with a busted tail light. The driver flashed his headlights in annoyance as they passed him as if he were standing still.

Conversation had been pretty light between them since leaving the hotel, which suited Finch just fine. With the window cracked down just a little and some cooling air blowing from the fans, he'd even started to get used to the slight odorous stench that Roddick seemed to emit twenty-four hours a day. While there was no question that he would rather be working alone on this, the benefit of having Roddick as a driver couldn't be ignored. Finch knew he would have wasted a good ten minutes messing with maps and SatNavs, searching for the fastest route out of the city. Roddick had taken a quick look at the map and somehow managed to imprint it into his brain; while he had the Impala's navigation system as a backup he never once looked at it. Mitchell had estimated the RV to be around forty miles ahead of them as they'd left the Hotel Monaco. Forty miles was not a great head start when you were in a much slower vehicle, and there was no way it could cover ground as fast as the Impala. They would be managing a steady fifty miles an hour at best. From the cell tower information, Mitchell also strongly suspected they weren't using the interstate. As Finch and Roddick had left the hotel, Mitchell had gained a link to the traffic camera system on I25. There was no trace at all of the RV having been logged by any cameras, which also pointed to the fact it was on one of the smaller, less surveilled roads. Being on the back roads was more than fine as far as Finch was concerned; it would just serve to slow down their pace even more. From the centre console, his Blackberry suddenly lit up and vibrated loudly, causing it to dance around the small plastic cubby hole. He reached down and snapped it up, answering the call promptly.

"It's Mitchell," said the voice on the other end. "Looks like I was right about the back roads, I just gained access to Adam Fisher's Visa account. His card was used at Texaco Gas Station on State Highway 105, about ten miles south of a small town called Sedalia and just west of Castle Rock."

"How long ago was that?" asked Finch, his heart rate quickening.

"Not recently, I'm afraid," he began. "It was around ten minutes before I called his phone, when you were back at the hotel. I've only just managed to get into his financial records. I'm working on Samuel Becker's now but it will take me a while, it looks like all the financial transactions over the last day have been from Fisher."

"No problem. Do you have anything else for me?" he asked, annoyed that the information was that old.

"The phone is still switched on and shifting gradually south on cell tower locates. I'm looking at State Highway 105 now, that's the one they're using and runs almost parallel with the interstate. There are a few turn offs but if they stick on it heading south, eventually they will have to come out onto I25. I've run a few hypothetical calculations and if they do take the interstate, I'm expecting them to ping the traffic camera about five miles south of where the roads meet." He paused for a second; Finch could hear the hum of conversation in the background. "That should be in about ten minutes," he concluded. Finch sat silently, nodding as he absorbed the information; the fact that the phone was still switched on pleased him. It meant the call had either not been heard, or it hadn't spooked them at all. Glancing to his right he caught Roddick shooting inquisitive looks at him, obviously keen to be part of any update.

"Can you try and access the gas station's computer system," asked Finch, "they may have CCTV at the site. If the cameras are networked back to a main server, we may be able to get some images from the forecourt." While he was eager to end this as quickly as possible he was also enjoying the chase – he liked having the opportunity to show off his skills. It was frightening how quickly you could find someone with a few basic snippets of their personal information, and the right training on how to exploit it.

"Sure, I'll get right on to it," replied Mitchell, "I'll call you back in a few minutes."

"Well?" Roddick asked expectantly, as Finch ended the call.

"Back your speed off a bit now," said Finch, scanning the dark highway for a mile marker. "Mitchell thinks they're going to join this interstate in about ten minutes, it looks like they're on a state highway that runs parallel to us over there," Finch gestured to his left, where a line of dark, brooding mountains filled the horizon.

"That highway merges with this road at a town called Monument," replied Roddick in a flash. "I saw it on the map earlier; I think we're a little over ten miles from where they meet."

"Good, let's slow it down just a little," cautioned Finch. "We don't want to get ahead of them. At this pace, you'll cover that distance in about seven minutes. You've done a good job of gaining ground." Praising Roddick didn't come naturally but he did deserve some credit – thanks to his directional sense and Finch's intuition, they were well and truly back in the game. Finch relaxed against the headrest and began thinking through how it would all play out when they located the RV. He would ultimately need to deal with the two males first, and he suspected his toughest challenge lay in Sam Becker. With his army service, he was no doubt used to a little hostile action; the writer wouldn't be so difficult to deal with. Finch immediately decided that ideally, Becker should be the first to die. Once they were both dealt with he would shoot the girl, not fatally, but enough of an injury to slow her down and give him a chance to inject the serum. Once that was done she would be putty in his hands. The sharp vibrations of his phone snapped him away from his scheming daydream.

"Not good news on the gas station front," began Mitchell, not bothering to introduce himself this time. "They have cameras, but the system is down for maintenance work."

"Shit," Finch swore under his breath. "Not to worry, it was only an outside chance anyway," he sighed.

"However," Mitchell continued, his voice picking up a little, "the license plate just pinged off a southbound traffic camera on I25, about five miles past Monument. It's a little sooner than I estimated, but they're heading toward Colorado Springs."

"Front or rear facing camera?" asked Finch quickly, sensing the net was closing in. He was also keen to prove he hadn't put all his eggs in the proverbial single basket by chasing off after the two Brits.

"Front facing!" said Mitchell eagerly.

Finch's heart rate picked up again. "Can you send the image to my phone?" he asked calmly, suppressing a rising sense of anticipation.

"Can do," Mitchell replied. Finch could hear the clicking of keys as Mitchell went to work back in the hotel room. "Okay, done. Should be with you now." As he finished speaking, Finch felt the handset vibrate against his ear, notifying him of new email.

"Excellent work," he praised. "Keep tracking them as best you can and let me know when you have anything further." Finch ended the call and hastily switched to his emails, selecting Mitchell's message he waited for the image to load. "Pick up the pace a bit, but not too much," he instructed, as the picture slowly materialised on the small screen. It was taking forever. "They are on the interstate, about fifteen miles ahead."

"No problem," replied Roddick confidently as he put his foot down, taking them up to a steady seventy-five miles an hour. Even at that speed, they would be gaining ground on the lumbering RV, with every turn of the wheels.

At last the image loaded, and Finch got his first look at their quarry. Using the navigation button he zoomed in over the windscreen; the image was a little grainy and pixilation began to set in as he enlarged it. Staring intently at the CCTV picture, he could still clearly see two people sitting up front, one driver and one passenger. He scrolled the picture down a little so just the top half of the windscreen was in view, affording him a slightly better look at the area behind the driver. Just visible through the grainy, enlarged image was an outstretched arm, holding onto the back of the driver's seat. There was a third person in the vehicle. A wide grin spread across his face. "*Gotcha!*" he muttered smugly under his breath.

Chapter 11

"God bless America and its constitutional right for people to bear arms," exclaimed Sam as the RV came to a stop outside the Colorado Springs Gun Emporium. "Where else in the western world would you find a twenty-four hour armory, open to the public?"

"All this is great," said Adam, securing the parking brake and stretching out a cramping pain in his leg, "but you're forgetting one thing."

"And what would that be exactly?" Sam was already fishing his wallet out of the glove box.

"That constitutional right doesn't include holiday makers. It's for US citizens. They won't sell you any weapons, you don't have the right forms of identification." Sam slowly tucked his wallet into his jeans, as the truth of what Adam had just told him sunk in.

"Shit," he spat in frustration, "I never even thought about that, how could I have been so stupid?" He sunk into the seat, looking deflated. He'd become so caught up forming the plan, he hadn't even considered this problem. Sam glanced out of the window at the brightly lit shop. "Why the fuck didn't you say something before?" Adam shifted around in the driver's seat – despite the major hole in Sam's plan, it did feel good to stop driving. His eyes stung from the constant glare of oncoming headlights.

"I'm sorry," he began, "it didn't really dawn on me until we got here. Plus, I kind of took it for granted that you might have thought of a way around it, after all, this is your thing. You know, guns and stuff." Adam had been against the hare-brained plan from the start, but the thought of going head first into the hornet's nest that no doubt awaited – without Sam having any kind of weapon to defend them with – just made it worse.

"I'm sorry," Oriyanna cut in, looking worried, "what is the problem exactly? Don't they sell what you need here?"

"Oh they sell it, alright," groaned Sam, "there are enough guns in that shop to kit out a small regiment. It's just – I might have a little trouble actually buying them. You see, American citizens can purchase firearms if they have the right police checks and identification. I have my British Passport and driver's license as identification, but that won't be enough. I can't believe I didn't think about it."

"So now, why don't we all see sense," said Adam, as calmly as possible, "and crack on to Austin, but we start with you turning my phone off." He released the parking brake and engaged reverse.

"Wait!" cried Oriyanna. Her outburst had Adam jamming the brakes on hard, jolting the RV harshly. "Just go in with what you have, I will take care of the rest."

"What are you talking about?" asked Sam.

"I'll put it as simply as I can," she said slowly. "Show them the identification you have; I can make them see whatever it is they need to see. Trust me."

"Is that more of that hocus pocus shit you pulled on me earlier?" Sam demanded.

"Very similar." She smiled.

"How the hell do you do that, anyway?"

"Let's just say that the thousands of years of evolution I have over you has enabled me to use slightly more than the ten percent of my brain that most Earth-Humans can use."

167

"And you can really do this?" asked Adam warily. He could fast see the excuse to get out of Sam's crazy plan slipping away.

"Of course I can, no one knows more about what is at stake here than me, and if I was in any doubt I wouldn't be wasting my time." After all that she'd shown and explained to them, she sounded a little annoyed at Adam's skepticism.

"It's settled then," concluded Sam. "Let's get this done." He opened the door and jumped down into the parking lot. Adam climbed down out of the driver's seat, a little more reluctantly. Oriyanna and Sam were a few paces in front of him, already heading for the door. The whole idea sounded crazy, and he suspected they would be thrown straight out of the shop. Regardless of anything else, Oriyanna looked odd in his clothes that were much too big, and her hair appeared as if it had been dragged through a hedge backwards; not to mention the fact she wasn't wearing any shoes. Adam picked up his pace and joined them, and as they reached the entrance the large automatic doors hissed open.

After spending a good few hours in the dimly lit camper, the bright artificial light of the Gun Emporium was an assault on Sam's eyes. It also served to snap him back into the real world. Being in the camper and hearing what Oriyanna had told them had made him feel cut off and distant from everything else. The shop was a good reminder that despite all he'd learned, things were still ticking along normally for the rest of humanity; for now, at least. Sam took a deep breath, enjoying the smell of gun oil; it made him feel at home and brought back fond memories of his army days. The walls behind the sales desk were lined with all kinds of firearms and boxes of ammunition stacked high, while the shop floor sported a mixture of tactical and outdoor pursuit style clothing as well as a good range of shooting accessories and survival gear. Sam clocked the two staff who had the unlucky pleasure of working the night shift. The guy behind the counter looked to be in his early fifties, he was obviously ex-services and still sported the same buzz cut he'd no doubt worn in his younger days. In an attempt to hold on to the youthful look, he'd dyed it jet black, and it resembled a bizarre wig. Sam could tell from his attire that he was obviously making the most of his staff discount; the clerk looked as if he'd fallen through one of the tactical clothing racks and come out fully dressed. If World War Three were to break out then and there, he was already fully kitted out for combat. His younger, fresher-faced male colleague was busy sorting through a range of hiking boots; he didn't look as if he'd ever fired a weapon in his life. Sam guessed he was no more than a college kid, trying to fund his education.

The hard-faced clerk behind the counter watched them suspiciously as they walked into the store, all blinking in the bright light; he made his way around the large U shaped counter to get a closer look at his customers. The younger assistant glanced up briefly at the sound of the shop doors, but soon returned his attention to the mass of boots he was sorting through.

"Is there anything I can help you guys with?" the clerk asked with a hint of suspicion in his voice. Sam walked over to him confidently and placed his hands on the glass counter. The display cabinet below was full of seemingly lethal hunting knives.

"Sure, I'm after quite a bit actually," he said brashly. "Firstly, my friend over there," he gestured to Oriyanna, "had a little boyfriend trouble earlier this evening, hence her slightly shabby appearance." The clerk nodded his head in understanding, as she made her way over to the counter. "I'm guessing you don't have the best range of ladies wear in here, but if you could point her to something that fits a bit better than the potato sack she's in now it would be appreciated. Some shoes would be good also."

The clerk took in her dishevelled appearance warily. "I'm not sure what kind of trouble this guy caused you, Miss, but I can call the police if you'd like?" He offered Oriyanna a sympathetic smile as he leaned on the counter. "I don't mean to speak out of turn here, but whoever this guy is, he must be a fool to be messing around a pretty lady like you."

"Thank you for the offer but I'm fine, really, "Oriyanna said softly, returning his smile, and the moment he looked into her eyes she knew she had him; it was now or never. Slowly she reached across the glass service counter and took hold of his hand, not breaking eye contact with him for a second. "It's a very kind offer though," she continued, wrapping her hand over his.

"You're more than welcome, Miss," he said, sounding a little distant. Sam glanced nervously over at the shoe stand; thankfully, the assistant was engrossed in his work; he collected up a pile of boxes that came up to under his chin before balancing his way through to the back storeroom, bumping the swinging door open with his back. Adam, on the other hand, was transfixed watching Oriyanna work; he still stood close to the entrance, near a small display of camouflaged thermos flasks, pretending to browse through the stock.

"There is something you can help us with, though," purred Oriyanna in her hypnotic tone. "My friend Samuel needs to purchase some firearms from you."

"No problem," the clerk nodded in his trance-like state, his eyes locked onto hers as if they were sharing a romantic meal in a fine restaurant.

"Serve him with whatever he wants; it's quite alright for you to do that." He continued to nod his head like those dogs Sam sometimes saw stuck on a car's parcel shelf. "When you ask for his identification, you will be satisfied with whatever documents he produces, it's perfectly fine for you to accept them as legal documentation. They will be all you need to see." Oriyanna broke her contact with him and stood back from the counter. As if a light switch had flicked on in his mind, the clerk snapped back to his normal self. "You were telling me where I might be able to find some clothes?" Oriyanna smiled, switching her attention away from the clerk and gazing around the shop.

"Yes, of course. Just toward the back of the store you should find something in your size." He pointed over toward a rack near the shoe stand. "If you need any help just ask Josh, my assistant."

"Thanks for your help," she concluded, gesturing for Adam to join her at the back of the store. The clerk's eyes followed her across the shop floor; once he'd seen her locate the correct stand he turned his attention back to Sam.

"Okay, what else is it I can do for you?" he asked politely, any hint of suspicion in his voice now gone. Sam's heart rate picked up a few levels, there was no way of knowing if this was going to work, other than jumping in with both feet.

"I need some firearms," he said as confidently as possible, taking his driver's license and passport out of his pocket and pushing them across the glass counter. The clerk collected them up and spent what seemed like an age studying the documents.

"These all seem to be in order," he said, nodding his head in satisfaction. "I may need you to fill out a few forms, it depends on what you're after." He turned to a small photocopier on a table against the wall and took two copies of the passport.

"I'll take two of those Ruger LC9s," Sam began, feeling a little of the stress drain from his body, "two spare clips and two boxes of Black Hills nine millimetre hollow points." The clerk nodded his approval and retrieved the requested items, placing them on the counter. "Do you have anything a little more tactical?"

"Sure," the clerk replied helpfully. He unlocked a display case near the cash register and fished out a small black carry case; unclipping it and turning it around for Sam to see.

"Very nice," exclaimed Sam, running his eyes over the contents. "FNP45 with spare clips, suppressor and added Trijicon sight, very nice; very nice indeed." Sam picked the weapon up and weighed it in his hand, the gun was well balanced and completely at home in his grip.

"You know your guns, son," said the clerk approvingly, watching as Sam raised the weapon up and checked the sight.

"Yeah well, that's what ten years of army service does for you, followed by four years of close protection duties." Sam placed the weapon back onto the counter with a clunk.

"Ah, thought I sensed a soldier in you," beamed the clerk. "William Thomas," he said happily, extending his hand across the counter. "Twenty-five years with the United States Army myself." Sam took his hand and pumped it up and down a couple of times. Exchanging banter was all very well and on any other day, he'd have been more than happy to chew the fat and share a few war stories with William, but he was keen to get this finished as fast as possible. He didn't know just how long whatever Oriyanna had done would last.

"Pleased to meet you," Sam replied politely.

"Always happy to help a fellow ex-serviceman," William continued. "Is there anything else I can get you?" Sam scanned the knife display under the counter as casually as if he were picking out a ring in a jewellery shop.

"I'll go for one of those Linder Yukon hunting knives," he said, pointing out his choice through the display cabinet. "Also, I'll take a good strong tack bag, some duct tape and a good pair of binoculars. Oh, and do you have any army surplus?"

"We sure do," beamed William. Sam could see he was more than happy to be selling this much stock in one go. "Since things died down in the Middle East, we've been getting truckloads in from the government. What is it you're after?"

"Half a dozen flash bangs and the same in smoke grenades." Sam thought he was pushing his luck, but he went with it.

William laid the knife out with the other goodies. "You're supposed to be currently military or law enforcement to purchase the flash bangs," he said, scrunching his face up and pausing for a brief second. "But as I said, I'm always willing to help an ex-serviceman out, so on this occasion, no problem. I keep that stuff out back; I won't be a second. Grab yourself a tack bag." He pointed to a small selection of bags opposite the counter. "The Patrol Ready ones are pretty good value, our local Police Department uses them," he added as he turned and disappeared into the rear storeroom. Sam grabbed the bag and gave it a once over – it wasn't quite as robust as his old army one, but it would do the job.

As Sam unzipped the bag and placed it on the counter, Oriyanna and Adam made their way up to join him. "Not bad, not bad at all," he commented, taking in her new attire. Adam had managed to find her a good quality pair of black cargo trousers and a North Face fleece. She also had a pair of sturdy walking trainers on. "You do seem to have the ability to make almost anything look good," he said, giving her a sly wink. Despite her slender and delicate frame, she looked quite purposeful in the new clothes, resembling some kind of female assassin you might see in a spy movie.

"Thanks," she said, brushing some imperceptible dust off her new fleece before setting the price tags down on the counter. "At least this stuff fits me, I wouldn't go as far as saying I look good in it though. It's a little more cumbersome than my normal day-to-day clothing; all your stuff feels so heavy."

"You've been busy," observed Adam, gesturing toward the small arsenal of weapons on the counter. "Do you really need all those guns?"

"I have no idea, but I don't plan on being caught short," smiled Sam, pleased with his new toys. He watched as William returned from the back storeroom carrying a small wooden crate containing the rest of the kit. Sam watched him place it on the counter and began to pack the guns into his new tack bag. "I think that's the lot," he said, pausing to opening the lid of the crate and admire the latest additions to his collection.

"Right, I need you to fill out these forms." William pulled them from under the cash register and handed them to Sam. "Also, I need to take your thumb prints; new law I'm afraid. They changed all the paper-work last year, gotta do it for any tactical weapons sold." He added a small ink pad to the variety of papers. "There's space at the bottom of the form here for your prints." He pointed to two small squares next to where Sam needed to put his signature. "I'll just ring all this up while you finish those off." Adam took over packing the tack bag so Sam could complete the paperwork; he held each gun as if he was handling a dangerous animal.

Sam signed the last form before covering both his thumbs in black ink and transferring his prints to the paperwork. "All done," he said, pushing the documents across the counter. "What's the damage?"

William ran an eye over the papers, nodding silently in approval before returning his attention to the cash register. "I've given you a fifteen percent Forces discount," he said, looking up from the screen and smiling, "in total you're in for four thousand five hundred dollars."

"Not a cheap night in all," said Sam, letting an exasperated breath out through his teeth and digging his travel Visa card out of his wallet. "This should be good for the lot." He handed the card to William, who slid it into the chip and pin machine. It took a few seconds to authorise before spitting out a receipt.

"Looks like you guys are all set," he smiled, handing over the receipt. "Have a good night."

Sam thanked him for his help, collected the bag up and left the store behind Adam and Oriyanna. The cool, fresh night air felt wonderful as he stepped outside and relaxed properly for the first time since enter-ing the Emporium. The bag felt heavy, yet reassuring on his shoulder, and the purchase had literally wiped clean his prepaid travel Visa card, but it had saved him using any cards that were directly linked to his own bank account. He had no doubt that by now, they would be scan-ning financial transaction for both of them, and whilst letting them come to him was part of the plan, he didn't for a second want them to know they were armed. With the right amount of digging, someone could no doubt find a record of the card he'd used to pay, but it would take much longer to find. In situations like this it was key to stay one step ahead of your enemy, while still letting them think they had the upper hand. Reaching the RV, Sam slung the bag into the passenger foot well and climbed in, resting his feet on top of it. He took a moment to use the navigation system and find the nearest hotel. "Well now, that's very apt," he mused, as the results came up on the small, dimly-lit screen. "There's a Quality Inn two blocks from here, and just off the interstate." He pointed to its location on the map.

"Garden of the Gods Road?" questioned Adam, squinting at the screen. "Are you kidding me?"

"My thoughts exactly," smiled Sam. "It's our best bet, though; they even have a small diner and take-out next door, once we get a room you can go grab us some food. I'm not sure how long we're going to be waiting."

Adam drove them out of the car park and onto the road. The small digital clock on the dash was blinking two AM at him, and he felt as if he hadn't slept or eaten properly in days. The meal at the diner in Denver had only been around six hours ago, but it felt like a lifetime, and a very different lifetime at that.

In just under five minutes they reached the hotel. Sam made Adam drive around the car park once, while he clocked which rooms would afford the best view of the RV and car park. The hotel looked to be freshly renovated; it had a slight motel look about it with the room doors facing out onto covered walkways that went up four floors.

"Just park us up here mate," said Sam, pointing to an empty space right in the middle of the car park. "It doesn't look that busy, so we should be able to get the pick of any of these rooms." He pointed to the four floors on the east facing wall. "Preferably second floor or higher for a good vantage point."

Adam guided the RV into the spot picked out by Sam, the lengthy vehicle actually ending up occupying two spaces, but now wasn't the time to worry about breaking a few parking laws. "I'll go in and get us a room then," he said nervously, cracking the door open and letting the fresh breeze drift into the cab.

"Okay, remember, second floor or higher on the east facing side of the hotel," Sam stated as he unlocked Adam's phone and turned on the location sharing option in Google.

"I best come with you," Oriyanna cut in. "We can't have you using your real identification, you might need my skills." She shot them a half-cocked smile.

"Good plan," agreed Sam, nodding his head.

Reluctantly, Adam crossed the car park toward reception, closely followed by Oriyanna. He already felt as if invisible eyes were all over them, watching his every step. The thought sent shivers down his spine, amplified by the stiff breeze which carried the scent of food from the nearby diner; it flared hunger pains up from deep down in his stomach. Even if he were presented with a plate of the finest roast beef, he doubted if he could take a mouthful, the sick feeling brought on by panic and worry was running riot all through his body. He didn't like Sam's plan and the later the hour grew, the worse he felt. He had a bad feeling about the whole thing, a very bad feeling indeed.

Chapter 12

None of the staff on cleaning duties in the small Subway restaurant were paying any attention to the red Chevy Impala and its two male occupants, who sat on their forecourt right outside the eatery's large glass frontage. Finch glanced at the reflection in his wing mirror and watched a spotty-faced young male wiping down a long, bar-style table before tucking the cloth into the back pocket of his food stained trousers.

"It's a shame they're closed," grumbled Roddick, shifting uncomfortably in his seat. "I could go for a sandwich right now."

"Even if they weren't, this is no time to be thinking of your stomach!" spat Finch as he turned his attention back to the Days Inn car park across the street. The Ford MTR Freedom stood proudly in the nearly empty parking lot, like a prize hovering just out of reach.

Mitchell had phoned them just over fifteen minutes ago with the urgent news that he'd managed to obtain a GPS location on Adam Fisher's phone; it had pinged at The Days Inn on Garden of the Gods Road. At the time, they'd only been one junction off the correct exit – less than ten minutes later they had found the RV.

Finch removed the clip from his Glock and checked it was full, for the second time in as many minutes. Something about the situation and the speed in which they'd ended up finding the camper wasn't sitting right with him; removing the silencer from his kit case he attached it to the muzzle before checking the clip for a third time.

"How many times are you going to do that?" groaned Roddick, staring at the gun in Finch's hand with clear annoyance.

"Shut up, it helps me think," Finch replied curtly, tucking the pistol back into his body harness. "You haven't even checked your weapon yet!"

"That's because I don't need to," said Roddick confidently. "It was all in order when we left Denver and being as it hasn't been used or even taken out of the harness, I'm guessing that it's still fine." His voice held a sarcastic tone that Finch really didn't care for. "What's the problem here anyway?" he asked, focusing on the RV. "It's right there, what are we waiting for?" He sniffed loudly, and Finch gritted his teeth in disgust.

"Hearing you make stupid fucking comments like that makes me realize why you're nothing more than a driver." Finch glanced across at him in frustration. "Doesn't this seem odd to you at all?" Roddick merely shrugged his shoulders, not taking his eyes from the vehicle across the street. "Why would you book into a hotel if you have an RV? Also, that phone is still pinging away on GPS from inside it, why would you turn your phone's mapping on when you reach your destination, and then forget to take it to your room?"

"You think they wanted us to find them?" Roddick asked doubtfully.

"I don't know, but something is up. The other guy, Samuel Becker – Mitchell said he'd worked as a close protection operative after leaving the army. He's had similar training to mine, I think we need to be careful not to underestimate him, that's all."

Roddick nodded his head slowly. "To be fair, you don't even know if the girl is with them. All this might be for nothing."

"Oh, she's there," Finch retorted, furious that Roddick would question his judgement. "The police log said they were going to San Francisco. It also said that when they were stopped, there were only two occupants in the vehicle. You saw that photo, they have someone else with them, someone who that inept sheriff didn't find. Why the hell are they now miles south of where they should be, and carrying an extra passenger?"

"Okay, maybe," said Roddick distantly. While he was as keen as any of them to put an end to the night's events, there was a small part of him that wanted badly to see Finch fall on his face. "So what's your plan? After all, as you said, I'm just a driver." He made no attempt to hide the sarcasm in his voice.

"Well I don't plan on sitting here with you all night, if that's what you mean." Finch unclipped his seat belt and cracked open the door. "I'm going to make enquiries at reception, see what I can find out. You can stay here, keep your eyes on the hotel and if for some unknown reason all this starts going south, just try and be of some help." He didn't wait for the comment that would no doubt follow; he pushed the door open and climbed out into the car park.

* * *

Sam laid the array of weapons out on the small single bed and began meticulously checking them. Although they were all new, well-oiled and had never fired a bullet in anger, it was just a natural process for him, plus it made him feel normal. Opening a fresh pack of hollow points, he loaded both Ruger pistols before flicking the safety on and off a couple of times, testing the fluidity of the guns' mechanics. Satisfied they were both in order, he placed them to the side and began to prep the FNP45. Once loaded, he attached the silencer and double checked the gun's balance by pointing it at the hotel room door. "Anything to report?" he asked, looking up at Adam who sat to the side of a large window, his eyes fixed intently on the car park below.

"Not a thing," he replied nervously. "You know, all this might be for nothing and a waste of valuable time, how can you be so sure that they're even looking for us?" As he spoke he didn't take his eyes away from the window. Sam hadn't allowed any lights to be turned on, other than the small shaver light above the bathroom mirror; even then the bathroom door was closed to almost latching point, allowing the thinnest bead of light through. It was just enough to keep them from stumbling around blindly in the dark.

"I can't be sure, but I know one thing – we're going to find out." Sam stood up and followed the line of the wall along to the window. "Here take this." He offered one of the Rugers to Adam.

"No way," said Adam, shaking his head. "The last time I fired a gun was on the range on that day you organised – that was over two years ago – not to mention the fact the recoil almost busted my hand." He glanced at the pistol uneasily.

"That was a much bigger weapon, this won't have anywhere near that amount of kickback." Sam thrust the gun forward, prompting Adam to take it. "Trust me." Reluctantly, Adam took the weapon and turned it over awkwardly in his hand.

"So do I just pull the trigger?"

"Almost," said Sam encouragingly. "You need to take the safety off first, it's this clip here." He demonstrated, clipping and unclipping the catch a few times. "Always keep it on until you think you might need it." Adam looked at him doubtfully. "Trust me mate, even a child could use this gun, it's that simple. I'll take over obs in a sec, you need to go and grab us some food. It could be a long night. If we see no sign of anyone by morning, I promise we'll push on."

Oriyanna appeared from the bathroom, opening the door just enough to slip her slender frame through before pushing it back into place. Her hair looked tidier, thanks to being dampened again and combed. She crossed the room and perched on one of the single beds. "Is that weapon for me?" she asked, eyeing the spare pistol through the gloom.

"It is, are you familiar with our weapons?" Sam crossed the room, staying clear of the large window and collected the gun up before handing it to her.

"Not overly, but I understand how it works." She took hold of the Ruger and unclipped the magazine without guidance.

"I'm sure you would rather have something from home," joked Sam, "these must be a little antiquated to you."

"A little, but they will do the job," she said seriously.

"Adam is going to grab us some food, I'm not sure what you normally eat, but—"

"Anything with meats or vegetables is fine," she cut in smiling. "Remember, I'm really the same as you, I don't eat anything you would find strange." The tiny grin on her face made Sam feel a little foolish. "Just don't get any of that fizzy stuff I tried earlier!"

"Are you sure it's safe for me to go out?" asked Adam, glancing back at them briefly.

"Like you said, they might not even be following us." Sam joined him at the window. Two large fuel tankers had just pulled up, as well as a rusty old family estate car with three slightly overweight children crammed into the back. The equally large parents got out and began pointing the kids in the direction of the diner. "Just head down and blend in, you'll be back in ten minutes." Truthfully, Sam didn't want any of them heading out but it had been hours since they'd eaten, and staying fed and well hydrated was as crucial as being armed. Reluctantly, Adam switched places with Sam; he fished a red McLaren baseball cap out of his bag and affixed it to his head, before he removed a lightweight black jacket and slipped his arms into it, pulling the collar up around his neck.

"Ten minutes maximum, you say?"

"Ten minutes," Sam reassured. "Oh, and don't forget to take this." He handed Adam the Ruger, "Just tuck it into the back of your trousers and for fuck sake, don't let it fall out! If you see anything you don't like the look of, come straight back – follow the line of the hotel to the end of the car park, and don't expose yourself by shortcutting across it."

Adam reached out and reluctantly took the gun, tucking it into his waistband. He adjusted his top and coat to conceal the weapon, which felt cold and alien against his skin. Turning his back on Sam he got to the door and gripped the round brass handle. "I don't know," he began, releasing his grip, "wouldn't you be best doing this?"

"I need to be here. What if someone turned up while I was away? You're just going to get a take-out, think of it like that. Oh, and so we know it's you when you get back, knock twice before you unlock the door. You have the key, right?" Adam patted the pocket of his faded blue jeans, causing the key and fob to jingle; he glanced at Oriyanna who sat on the bed, watching them both with interest.

"Be quick!" she said encouragingly, her voice as soft and musical as ever.

"Okay, fuck it," sighed Adam, and before he could think about it any further he slipped out onto the walkway and hurried to the stairs. The sheltered outer corridor acted like a wind tunnel, whipping up and amplifying the stiff breeze. Shivering, he readjusted the collar on his jacket and picked up the pace. Adam glanced down at the parking lot; the family were slowly making their way across to the diner while the two truck drivers were busy enjoying a coffee and cigarette break by their cabs, both deep in conversation. He'd half expected something to grab him the very moment he stepped outside. He felt exposed, almost naked. Reaching the stairs, he descended the three floors as fast as he could, and by the time he was pacing along the building line he felt a little better. No boogie man had found him, yet. Despite it being almost three AM there were a few people about, attracted by the all night food service offered at the diner. It was obviously a well-known venue for people not wanting to venture too far off the interstate; the steady hum of its ever-flowing traffic drifted through the night air occasionally, amplified on the wind.

Just going to get take-out, just going to get take-out, he repeated in his head. He didn't dare look around, and like a child hiding under a duvet, he kept his head down and hoped for the best, only looking up occasionally to check on his progress. The brightly lit restaurant began to strip away the darkness, glancing up Adam saw he was close; he'd made it, almost. He could see the family from the car park now, standing inside and waiting to be seated. He was close enough to hear the hum of people talking and the clinking of cutlery. The hunger he'd felt not twenty minutes ago came back fast, and for a brief second he began to think of what he was going to order for them all and how they would have a nice meal before trying to get some sleep. No one was coming for them, tomorrow they would reach Austin and everything would be alright. The door was close now; maybe twenty feet at the most, he could even read the 'OPEN' sign behind the glass. Engulfed by the temporary euphoria of having survived the short walk, he didn't hear the rushing footfalls behind him, nor did he hear the crack of the gun handle as it came down hard on the back of his skull.

* * *

Finch rounded the Impala and stepped up the slight grassy incline which separated the forecourt from the pavement. He walked down a few yards, staying clear of the hotel's line of sight. Satisfied that he was now free to cross unseen, he paused for a second as a lumbering lorry trundled by, heading toward the interstate. As it passed it swept up a mixture of fine grit and litter that whipped up around him, causing Finch to squint. Once it was safe, he crossed the road swiftly and waited for a brief second by an untidy looking bush that marked the end of the hotel's grounds. The car park had suddenly turned quite busy; two tanker drivers were having a good chat and setting the world to rights, whilst a rather rotund family were eagerly heading for the diner. Staying alongside the bushes, Finch crossed the car park and headed for the reception, fishing the FBI badge from his back pocket as he walked. Suddenly something caught his eye: a dark silhouette of a figure dressed in a jacket and baseball cap was briskly walking along the far wall of the hotel, sticking to the shadows and not straying out into the car park where the lighting was better. Finch didn't wait to think it over; he went with his gut. Cramming the badge back into his pocket he unclipped his gun and held it low to the side, obscuring it from prying eyes. The hunched-over figure glanced up briefly before looking back down and hurrying on. Finch knew that unless they turned around, he would never be seen rushing in from behind. Sinking into the same shadows, Finch used the building line as well. Snippets of the conversation between the two drivers cut in and out between his footfalls. He was gaining ground, fast. Whoever this was, the diner was obviously the place they were heading to, nothing else was open apart from the Esso gas station across the street. The figure was almost at the door; it was now or never. He glanced around quickly, no one was watching from the car park and the people in the restaurant were too caught up in their own miserable lives to notice what was happening outside. In one final rush, Finch covered the last ten yards in a few quick, meaningful strides, and as he went he turned the gun in his hand and brought it down hard. The butt of his pistol contacted with the baseball cap in a satisfying crunch. Instantly, his quarry's legs buckled and the figure went down. Finch was ready for the fall and in one swift movement he caught the body, dragging it off to the side of the diner behind a small line of young sapling trees.

Finch turned the limp, unconscious body over and permitted himself a broad, satisfied smile. While Sam Becker would have been his preferred target, Adam Fisher was a close second place. Glancing around for a second time, satisfied he hadn't been seen, Finch fished his phone out of his pocket and dialled Roddick's number. It rang for a frustratingly long time before his usual nonchalant voice finally answered.

"Sorry, left my phone on silent. "What's up?"

"See the diner opposite, just to the left of the hotel?" growled Finch.

There was a pause. "Yeah, I see it," Roddick finally replied, still sounding disinterested.

"Get over here now. Don't come in via the hotel parking lot though, drive toward the interstate and use the entrance at the far end of the diner's parking lot, keep the building between you and the hotel and drive around to the trash cans.

"Okay, I'm on my way. What's happening?"

Finch heard Roddick turning the engine over. "I've got Adam Fisher. I need to secure him in the car, and then we both have a room service call to make!"

* * *

"He likes you, you know," Sam said, taking his attention away from the window to glance at Oriyanna across the dusky bedroom; she was sitting on one of the single beds with the Ruger by her side.

"What, and you don't?" she asked, sounding a little dejected. Sam shook his head and returned his attention to the parking lot. The large white body of the RV stood out against the night like a beacon.

"Of course I do," he replied, sounding a little exasperated. "If I didn't, I wouldn't be so keen to be putting our lives on the line. What I mean is Adam *likes* you!" Sam emphasized the 'like' with his fingers, drawing imaginary punctuation.

"I'm sorry, Samuel, I really don't know what you mean" Oriyanna said, sounding a little confused.

"You know, for a superior being you really aren't that bright," Sam chuckled, checking his watch; the fluorescent hands glowed dimly in the darkened room. Adam had only been gone for five minutes, but it seemed like an hour. Sam craned his neck to the right and looked at the roof of the diner; Adam should be in there right now, waiting for their food. "You really don't know what I'm getting at here, do you?" he asked, looking back at her briefly, and through the darkness he could just make out a flash of understanding wash across her face.

"Oh!" she gasped. "I'm sorry, I'm still not completely up to speed with some of your phrasing and terminology. And for the record, I'm not a superior being, just a little more evolved, that's all." Her face flushed with embarrassment at the misunderstanding.

"I wouldn't worry, you're probably a bit too old for him anyway," laughed Sam. "Although you do look bloody good for your age." He paused and strained to look down the outer walkway, certain he'd just seen a shadow or two moving in the nasty orange lighting outside. "Do you have someone back home?" he asked, his nerves about as highly strung as they had ever been. The flap of loose skin on the inside of his bottom lip begged to be worked on, but he resisted.

"No, I don't really have…"

"Shhh!" he hissed, holding one of his hands up and cutting her off.

"Is it Adam?" asked Oriyanna, her voice barely a whisper; instinctively, she slid her hand from her lap and wrapped it around the cool rubber grip of the gun.

Sam waved her back urgently with his hand. "I don't think so," he whispered as calmly as possible. "I just saw what looked like two shadows at the end of the corridor." He heard Oriyanna slide from the bed and take cover. Silently, Sam slipped from his seat and ducked down below the ledge. Pistol in hand, he shuffled right on his knees, hoping to get a better view. He didn't need to move far, and before he'd travelled half the length of the large window, two dark shadows passed by, blocking out what little artificial light was flowing in through the window. Sam held his breath and moved backward on his bum, as fast as he could. Reaching the bed, he rounded the foot of the divan and joined Oriyanna who was crouched down staring at him, her eyes wide but defiant. Sam forced a breath into his lungs, trying to steady his nerves; he hoped whoever the shadows belonged to came from a room further down. In the deathly silence he heard their footsteps on the glazed tiles outside, he longed to hear them carry on past their room and fade out, but they didn't. Right outside the door, the footsteps stopped! Sam clicked the safety off his pistol and drew in two more long deep breaths, slowly breathing out through his nose.

Quickly he moved his body around and got to his knees, resting his elbows on the soft mattress for support – it wasn't an ideal shooting platform but it would do. Sam levelled the gun at the door and took aim, just as a key was pushed into the lock. He wasn't going to let them open it. Expertly, he squeezed the trigger off twice, one shot at head height and another slightly lower, the soft yet reassuring, *pfft, pfft* of the silenced weapon filled his ears as the slugs left the barrel and slammed through the freshly painted plywood door, splintering the surface with two short sharp *cracks*. Sam heard a muffled cry and the sound of a body hitting the tiles; at least one bullet had found its target. In one swift movement he was on his feet and rounding the foot of the bed, the gun aimed squarely at the door, arms braced in a shooting position. As he closed the distance the door burst open, and he squeezed off another two shots at head height as the figure of a smartly-dressed man charged into the room, blindly returning fire. Instinctively, Sam ducked and the stranger's shots slammed into the back wall, shattering a mirror with a deafening crash and showering the dark grey carpet with shards of broken glass. Sam stayed low and kept his forward momentum. The distance between them now was too short to get off another round. Opening his arms Sam grabbed the stranger's legs and lifted up with his body as hard as he could. He felt the assailant's body rise up off the ground, gravity took over and the male cartwheeled over Sam's back and hit the floor with a thud.

* * *

Finch checked the zip tie restraints that bound Adam's hands and feet one final time before throwing his red baseball cap in beside him and closing the boot. The blood from the wound on his head was smeared down the side of his face, but the gash had already started to clot, stemming a little of the bleeding. It was a nasty wound, but in no way life threatening. He didn't intend to kill him just yet, until he had safely secured the girl and gotten away he couldn't risk it. Should things go wrong he might need him – Finch had no idea what Oriyanna had told the man. He strongly suspected it would be far easier to break Fisher than it would be to break her. Rounding the car, he joined Roddick by the driver's door. "They're in room thirty-three," he said quietly. "We'll leave the car here and walk over; sleeping beauty back there should be out for a good few hours, so we have plenty of time."

Roddick nodded his agreement, "I'll follow your lead," he said. "And what if she isn't with them?"

"I'm not even thinking about that right now," growled Finch as he walked away from the Impala and approached the ground floor wall of the hotel. "She's in there, trust me!"

"Are you going to knock?" asked Roddick, staying a few paces behind him as they slipped into the same shadows that Finch had exploited not five minutes ago.

"No, of course not!" he hissed. "They'll be expecting him back any time soon and we have a key, why the fuck would I knock? When we get there, just let me take charge. Oh, and keep your voice down." Quickly and silently Finch crossed the span of the hotel's outer wall, before arriving at the concrete stairway. The small enclosed space still smelt of fresh masonry paint from a recent rebuild. Taking two steps at a time, Finch climbed to the third floor in under a minute, and pausing at the top he waited for Roddick who had dropped back a good few feet tackling the stairs. Finch stepped away from the wall and counted the doors. "It should be the fourth one down," he whispered, "when we get there, pass the window as fast as you can, unfortunately there's no way we can get to the room without walking by it." Small wall lamps hung sat above each door, illuminating the brass room numbers; the lights filled the outer corridor with an artificial orange glow. Reaching into his jacket, Finch removed the Glock from its holster and expertly unclipped the safety, all in one swift movement. Glancing back at Roddick who was a little red-faced from the three story climb, he saw he already had his gun in hand. Finch raised the weapon and beckoned him forward. As quickly as possible he paced along the line of doors. Passing the darkened window of room thirty-three he readied the key; Roddick was with him every step of the way.

Reaching the door, he slipped the key into the lock with ease, and the moment he did, two rounds slammed through the door. Finch felt a sticky wetness spray the left hand side of his face as the taste of blood filled his mouth. Turning the handle, he glanced left and watched Roddick's legs buckle and collapse, the right hand side of his face a bloodied mess from the one round that had found its target. As his companion hit the glazed tile floor, Finch barged the door open and stormed into the darkened room. Instinctively, he weaved left as the soft silenced sound of two more shots filled the air; one of the rounds hammered past his ear, far too close for comfort. Blindly, Finch fired off two rounds hoping one would find the gunman; brief flashes of light from the silenced muzzle engulfed the room like crazed lightning, closely followed by the shrill sound of breaking glass. Finch saw the gunman, who he guessed would be Sam Becker, running at him and hunched low. It was too late to avoid contact; strong arms grabbed his legs and began to lift. As his body rose off the ground his centre of gravity altered, the room turned upside down and he wheeled over the gunman's back before hitting the deck hard.

* * *

Sam was still on his feet as the assailant hit the floor. Spinning around, he planted his sturdy Caterpillar boot into the side of his head, and even through the thick rubber sole he felt a satisfying crunch as the guy's cheekbone shattered from the impact. Sam stepped back and aimed his gun at the stranger's head.

"Stop!" cried Oriyanna, as she shot to her feet from behind the bed. "I need him alive!" It was all Sam could do to ease the pressure from the gun's trigger; it was almost at its critical load point, just one slight flex of his finger and the next hollow point would be sent charging from the barrel and straight into the unconscious guy's head, ruining the new carpet. "Don't do it, Samuel," she continued calmly. "It's over. Please, I need him alive!" Oriyanna approached him, closed her hand around the barrel and gently forced Sam to lower his weapon. "Once I find out what I want to know, it will be my duty to kill this man, not yours." There was a new, purposeful tone to her voice that Sam hadn't heard before, and it snapped him from his adrenaline-fuelled state and brought him back to the real world with a bump. "You need to get that body out of the walkway," she added, "we can't have anyone seeing it."

Sam glanced down at the stranger. His face was badly bruised and cut, and blood flowed from a gash in his cheek. Sam was sure he could even see some mashed up bone somewhere in there – his boot had really done a job on the guy's face. He made his way quickly to the door, which had swung closed in the melee. Raising his gun, he swung it open, and saw that the assailant's companion was slumped in a crumpled mess on the floor. Stepping over his tangled legs, Sam saw where one of his bullets had hit its target. The right hand side of the man's slightly chubby face was missing; the other side was peppered with splinters of wood from where the slug had exited the door. His head, from the upper cheekbone to the eye socket was gone, a mixture of red and white gunk was slowly leaking out onto the glazed red tiles. Sam didn't need to check for a pulse or fire another shot; he was deader than a doornail. Tucking the pistol into the back of his trousers, he grabbed the stranger by the legs and dragged his heavy carcass into the room, laying it out under the window.

"Can you get any information from him?" he asked, gesturing to the unconscious one, his voice croaky and dry. "You know— if he is one of you?"

"If he's only unconscious, then yes," she said, kneeling down and looking intently at the face Sam had just crushed with his boot. "I don't think he is an Elder though, not many of them were left after the Great War. I certainly don't recognise him." She looked up at Sam for a second. He picked up no hint of fear from her, throughout the last few minutes she'd remained deadly calm. Oriyanna slid a hand into her back pocket and removed the Key Tablet. "I need you to take this while I work on him, if he is like me, I can't risk him picking up on its energy." Sam nodded and took it from her, quickly tucking it into his jeans. Oriyanna watched as he concealed it before she turned her attention back to the unconscious male. Lifting his thick set, heavy arm, she took hold of his hand and closed her eyes. Without the benefit of a lucid subject, she would need to concentrate much harder.

* * *

Through the depths of unconsciousness Finch felt her presence, and desperately tried to bring himself around. It felt as if he was stuck at the bottom of a deep pool of liquid, as thick as molasses, and unable to reach the surface. Her mind enveloped his, and like a thin spidery hand she wrapped herself around his deepest thoughts, probing and exploring his memories. Finch knew what she was after, but the harder he tried not to think of it, the more prevalent the memory became. The instant the thought of his conversation with Buer and his time at JFK popped into his head she had it, extracting everything he knew like a hacker, downloading information in droves. Even through his unconsciousness, he felt his body weakening. Summoning all his mental strength, he tried to swim to the top of the dark pool holding him, desperate to wake. It was too late to stop her learning his secrets, but he wasn't out of the game just yet. The deep, throbbing pain in his cheek told him he was close to breaking the surface, close to waking. She continued to hold his hand, her grip as tight as a vice; then in a flash the sensation was gone – she'd released him. Full consciousness flooded back and his eyes snapped open.

* * *

Sam sat on the end of the bed and the adrenaline started to fade from his body. He watched Oriyanna kneeling beside the smartly-dressed assassin who had just tried to kill them. Despite all that he'd learned over the past few hours, part of his brain still refused to believe it all. The arrival of the two armed men had made it all seem far more real though. He watched Oriyanna grip the guy's hand and close her eyes. Sam removed his gun and checked the safety was still off. From Oriyanna's position, he couldn't get a clean line of sight to the man's head, but he wanted to be ready if things took a turn for the worse. She was leaning so close into him it almost looked as if she was offering first aid or comfort. The seconds ticked by like hours, until finally, she let the man's hand fall and turned to face Sam, her face was as pale as the finest of porcelain. Sam knew instantly that she'd learned all she needed to know. Before he had time to speak, he watched in horror as Oriyanna's head snapped violently sideways, and even in the darkness he saw blood spray from her mouth and nose. Sam shot to his feet and raised the gun, trying to get a clean shot, but the guy moved too fast. He looked on helplessly, as in one swift movement the stranger got to his feet, his arm secured tightly around Oriyanna's neck. Despite the poor light, Sam could see the Ruger in his hand, the barrel pushed tightly into her temple. Sam raised his own gun and aimed it squarely at the stranger's head. Now standing, the man was a good six inches taller than Oriyanna, the side of his face fully healed, and there was no sign of the impact from Sam's boot. Gaining clear line of sight, Sam took up the trigger pressure and prepared to fire.

"I wouldn't do that if I were you, Mr. Becker," the stranger growled. "Not if you want to see your friend Adam again." His eyes were wide and fierce. In all the commotion of the past few minutes, Sam had completely forgotten about Adam. Hearing the stranger say his name was like a slap to his face. Instantly, Sam relaxed his trigger finger, but kept the gun trained squarely at the man's head.

"Okay – I'm listening," he said calmly. Sam glanced at Oriyanna, who was starting to come around; the cut on her face already healing over.

"Finch," she croaked, "he's Robert Finch!" The sound of her voice prompted the stranger to increase the pressure on her neck, and her legs started to jolt violently. It took a few moments for Sam to register what she'd said; the man standing in front of him bore no resemblance to the picture he'd looked at earlier on Adam's phone.

"I'll do the talking, if it's alright with you!" snapped Finch, turning his attention to Sam. "It seems we have a situation here, Mr. Becker." Finch took two steps back toward the door, and Oriyanna's legs scooted backwards as her feet struggled for purchase on the carpet. Sam's mind was reeling, looking for any possible way to tip the scales back in his favour.

"It would appear so," he replied. "What is it you want?" Sam watched as a sly, deadly grin spread across Finch's face.

"I'm here for two things," he began. "The girl and an artefact I suspect she has with her." Finch cocked his head to one side, trying to read Sam's facial expression. "I have no interest in you or your friend, you didn't ask to be part of this. Just let me take what I need and you're both free to go."

"How do I know you haven't killed him?"

"You don't; you have to trust me. Let me have the girl and the Key Tablet and I'll let you have Adam back; his head might need a Band Aid, but apart from that he's unharmed. You have my word."

Sam glanced down at Oriyanna; both her hands were gripped around Finch's arm, trying to relieve some of the pressure on her neck.

"Samuel, don't!" she croaked.

"I thought I said I'd do the talking," Finch growled, raising his arm up just enough to lift her feet off the floor. Sam was sure he was going to snap her neck at any moment. "So, Mr. Becker, I have the girl, all I'm missing is the Key Tablet. I hope for all your sakes that you know something about it."

Sam swallowed hard, trying to ease the dry feeling at the back of his throat. "And if I do know something?" he asked.

"Then, just like I said, you both go free."

Oriyanna's eyes were pleading with him to do something. "And if I just shoot you now?" hissed Sam, weighing the options.

"Then your friend dies, one of my men has him downstairs," said Finch. "If I don't come back, he'll be executed; I expect they'll be kind enough to leave his body in the parking lot for you." Finch took another step backwards; his gun was pressed so tightly against Oriyanna's temple that her whole head was being pushed to one side. "This isn't your fight, Mr. Becker, just let it go."

"If just half of the shit I've learned tonight is true, then this is very much my fight," retaliated Sam, taking a step forward and matching Finch's movement.

"Enough *chitchat!*" shouted Finch, raising his voice. "Either give me the Key Tablet or your friend dies, it's that simple."

Sam looked to Oriyanna; she was still trying to prise Finch's arm away from her neck but her strength was no match for his, and she looked desperately into Sam's eyes and silently mouthed, "*No.*"

"I can't give you the Key Tablet," said Sam, as calmly as possible.

"Why not?"

"It's not here," he lied, praying Finch wouldn't make some attempt to search him. "I can get it for you, but it's going to take me some time."

"I don't believe you," spat Finch, his voice full of venom.

"Fine, just kill us all then." Sam lowered his pistol and threw it onto the bed. Oriyanna was watching him in disbelief, her anguished face full of confusion. "Take her if you want, you can even keep hold of Adam." Sam took a step back and raised his hands in surrender; his plan was a longshot, but if it worked it would keep them all alive for now, and buy him some time to think. "You see, Finch, I knew someone was after us, that call you made earlier tonight to Adam's phone gave you away. I wanted you to find us. Sure – I didn't plan on it ending quite like this, but sometimes shit happens." Sam was growing more confident by the minute, he just hoped that Oriyanna could grasp what he was trying to do. "Way before we got to Colorado Springs, I hid the Key Tablet. Oriyanna knew you would be desperate to get your hands on it. I know your background, Mr. Finch, we've both worked in similar circles. I'm sure you would have done the same; tactically, it's the only option. Do you really think it would be here, if we knew you were coming for us?"

"So what are you proposing?" growled Finch, his voice brimming with frustration. He wanted badly to phone Buer and tell him he'd fulfilled both of his objectives.

"You keep both Oriyanna and Adam – you can contact me on Adam's number in five hours. When you do, I want proof of life and you'll let me speak to him. Once I'm satisfied he's alive, we'll arrange an exchange. It's no use trying to extract the information from her, only I know where it is. Think of it as an insurance policy." Sam even managed to treat Finch to a confident grin.

Finch nodded his head reluctantly; he couldn't risk killing them both now, if what Sam had told him was true he might never find the Key Tablet. Even if Oriyanna did know, she was unlikely to break. "Alright, Mr. Becker, I can live with that", he conceded. "Just know that if you try and fuck me on this, not only will I kill your friend, but I'll make it my personal responsibility to ensure he dies as slowly and as painfully as possible. Is that clear?"

"Crystal," replied Sam confidently. Inside, he was raging like an angry bull, and the temptation to grab the gun and shoot Finch through the head was overwhelming. He could almost envisage watching the hollow point slam through the man's skull.

"I'm going to leave now, Mr. Becker. Don't follow me or your friend dies. You'll hear from us in five hours sharp, and if by then you don't have the Key Tablet, he dies."

Oriyanna put up another desperate struggle, and Finch slammed the butt of the Ruger into her head, knocking her unconscious. Sam winced at the sound and saw fresh blood trickle down Oriyanna's cheek. Finch tucked the pistol into his holster and threw her limp body over his shoulder, then turned away and left the room. Sam watched helplessly as his shadow swept past the window and vanished.

Chapter 13

The soft sand felt as fine as Demerara sugar beneath Adam's bare feet. Oriyanna took hold of his hand, her soft skin brushing against his as they entwined fingers. Just her touch caused his heart to skip a few beats. White sand stretched as far as the eye could see, small lazy waves gently broke around their ankles as the crystal clear blue waters of the ocean found the shore. Further out to sea, hundreds of tiny islands sparkled in the evening sun, like jewels. To the east, a large blood red moon filled the sky, it's smaller twin looming on the horizon, rising proudly behind the most breathtaking mountain range Adam had seen in his life. Its deep red glow juxtaposed against the snow covered peaks, setting them like an oil painting against the dusky sky.

"It's the most beautiful thing I've ever seen," Adam gasped. He stopped and turned to Oriyanna. In an instant he realised he had lied, no vista on Earth or anywhere in the universe could have the same effect on him as the sight of her face.

She smiled warmly and took hold of his other hand. "You need to wake up now Adam," she said, in her usual soft musical tone. "You need to help me. You need to help us!"

"Can't we just stay here?" he pleaded, gripping her hands tightly.

She shook her head, her blonde hair fluttering in the breeze; it almost glowed in the evening sunlight like golden fire. "This isn't real, Adam. You do know that, don't you?"

He nodded his head, "I know," he replied painfully.

"The place where we really are is not safe; we're both in danger." The soft expression on her face changed to one of fear. "Please, Adam, wake up! Help me, help us both!"

"What happened to us?" Adam suffered a spinning, falling sensation in his stomach which spread like a spiral throughout his whole body; he gripped her hands tighter, hungry to hold on to the illusion. It felt as if some unseen force was pulling him away.

"They took us both," she replied, her voice sounding distant. "They know things, they got into my head. Please, Adam; this is no longer about just saving your people." She grew even more distant, sounding like a disjointed voice on a long distance telephone call. "They know too much now, and once they have the Key Tablet, they will destroy us all – both our worlds. You need to help me!" Adam felt himself rising up above her; his arms seemed to stretch out even as his hands still clung to hers, trying to hold on. He imagined himself as a balloon at the end of a long tether, a tether that was about to *snap*. Instantly, Oriyanna was gone, as was the beach, the mountains and the jewel-like islands. He started to reel back into reality and there was nothing he could do to stop it.

* * *

Buer released Oriyanna's hand and re-secured it with a zip tie to the back of the shabby wooden chair. As he zipped it closed, small strips of blue paint flaked off the damp wood and fluttered to the dusty concrete floor. He stood up and backed off a few paces, her head had slumped forward and now rested on her chin, restricting her breathing. As a result, deep raspy sounds resembling snores came from her partly open mouth. Adam Fisher sat next to her, secured to an identical chair. Congealed blood matted his brown hair to his head, and deep red stains ran down his jaw line, from the wound Finch had inflicted a few hours ago. He was still out for the count, but it wouldn't be long before he was awake and lucid once again. Buer was sure that when he did wake up, he was going to wish he hadn't.

"Well?" asked Finch expectantly, as Buer took his piercing grey eyes away from Oriyanna and turned around.

Following the shootout which had ended Roddick's miserable existence, he'd called Buer with the news. Buer had listened intently to the update, just cutting in with the occasional "I see," and "Okay!" On the whole, Buer had been happy with the work Finch had done; as suspected, he saw the loss of Roddick as being no more than a necessary casualty of war; collateral damage and nothing more. Finch had feared there would be some backlash against his failure to immediately secure the Key Tablet, but surprisingly, Buer had been quite understanding and for once had seen things from Finch's point of view. On the flip-side, the news that he'd captured the girl had been met with nothing more than a curt, "Well done Robert." Buer had instructed him to head south out of the city until he reached the outskirts of the Cheyenne Mountain State Park, once there, he'd been told to find a suitable place to secure the two prisoners and await Buer's arrival. The old rangers' cabin just off Rock Creek Canyon Road had been perfect. It looked as if it had been abandoned for a good few years, while the flat, but slightly overgrown field to the front of the building served as an ideal landing platform for the Explorer helicopter which Buer had arrived in, not half an hour ago, accompanied by two smartly dressed bulky males, Michael and Rick Malone. Like Roddick, the two brothers were lower intelligence Earth breeds, and they had been Buer's security detail for the past couple of years. Until now it had been an easy job, as he hardly ventured out into public and opted to stay mainly in New York at the investment firm. Finch had no issue with either of them; they both possessed a quick wit and sense of humour that seemed to keep Buer entertained.

"I see she got into your head," said Buer with a sly smile. "It's a good job you managed to take her, she knows as much as you do about the virus."

"Yeah well, that wasn't part of the original plan," replied Finch, a little embarrassed. "Sam Becker was a little handier than I first suspected, plus he'd managed to get a gun. If it wasn't for The Gift, we wouldn't be having this conversation."

"You were lucky, Robert. Things could have ended very differently." He paused and glanced back at their two unconscious guests. "Can we trust this Sam Becker to deliver the Key Tablet to us?"

"I'm sure of it," replied Finch, "he won't risk us killing his friend. I'll be making contact with him soon to arrange the transfer."

Buer nodded in approval, "Excellent. Once we have the Key Tablet, we can move to strike a deadly blow to Arkkadia, one that will take them years to recover from." Buer smiled. "I hope you're feeling up to another foreign excursion Robert, this time I'll even be joining you."

"So, I take it you managed to glean what you needed from her?" Finch wasn't too keen on having Buer constantly breathing down his neck; he would almost rather have had Roddick to deal with.

"Oh yes, once we have conducted the exchange, we'll be heading to Egypt. The Tabut is located deep under the Great Pyramid of Giza."

"But we researched that location years ago," said Finch, looking confused. "It was one of the first places highlighted by our science teams as being most likely to house the artefact."

Buer turned his attention back to Adam, who was starting to move. He was still out of it, but coming around fast. "I know, all the information we had pointed to the Great Pyramid. However, we thought they had moved the Tabut long ago – who would have thought there was a secondary level to the lower chamber."

"Really?" exclaimed Finch. "How do you intend on reaching it? I was always told that the whole building was examined. There was never any trace of another level found."

"You need the Key Tablet to open the shaft that leads to it. Once you reach the Tabut chamber, you need it again to access the chamber itself. Then it's needed for a third time to activate the Tabut. My biometrics will read no differently to theirs, so we won't even need the girl to turn it on for us. The Tabut on Arkkadia was prepared before they left, the moment we activate the one on Earth the process will begin, and once singularity is achieved, we'll send through an explosive device big enough to destabilise the Tabut on Arkkadia. The result for them will be disastrous."

Small moans and groans began to come from Adam, causing Buer to glance over at him in annoyance. His eyelids were starting to twitch as his head lolled from side-to-side, like a drunk waking up on a park bench.

"How so?" asked Finch eagerly, ignoring the painful sounds coming from across the small, dank room.

"It will cause a chain reaction across their entire planetary energy grid, a chain reaction so great, it will cause an immediate pole shift. The area directly around the Tabut will suffer an explosion of massive proportions." Buer grinned.

"And you're sure this can happen?" asked Finch. It seemed almost impossible that a situation which had been disastrous for them a few hours ago, could be turned around so swiftly.

"Of course!" growled Buer, the grin washing from his face in an instant. "Do you doubt what I say?"

Finch held both his palms up. "No, not at all," he fired back quickly.

"We have one other matter to deal with first," continued Buer. "The one who sent the alert which brought her here in the first place." He looked over at Oriyanna; her raspy, rhythmic breathing was slow and steady. "It's just one person, a man; he's in Austin, Texas. That's where they were heading. Turns out that your old boss was due to retire after he stepped down as president, and his replacement was already here. Like I said back in Denver, Robert, it was an oversight that never should have happened, but as it turns out, things may well now work in our favour. You must get that Key Tablet."

"I will," said Finch, nodding his head. "And what do you want done with her?" He pointed to Oriyanna's unconscious body. "The drug is good for another few hours at most."

"Once we have the Key Tablet, kill her, we don't need her anymore. I'll be sending a small team to Austin to take care of our friend there, and I'll leave it to your discretion in regard to our two British friends. Kill them if you wish or let them go – they're as good as dead anyway."

Finch watched as Buer left the room and headed through to the small living area of the cabin. The first beads of light were starting to seep through the cracks in the boarded up windows, capturing thousands of tiny dust particles in the air and illuminating them for a few seconds before they passed back into the shadows. The cabin was a shithole, but it had served its purpose. Finch checked his Seamaster; it was time to call Sam Becker. Once he had the Key Tablet, they could kill the girl and put an end to the whole situation. He understood now what Buer had meant when he'd warned him back in Denver. Oriyanna was beautiful in a strange and haunting way, but it didn't detract from who she was; when the time came he wouldn't think twice about putting a bullet into her brain, and even if it felt like destroying a fine and rare work of art, he didn't care. He turned his back on the two guests and grabbed his Blackberry. It was time to make that call.

Chapter 14

The shrill, old-style ringtone of Adam's iPhone raised Sam from an uneasy sleep. Fumbling around in the early morning light, he managed to find the handset. Squinting through tired eyes he saw 'BLOCKED' flash up on the screen, just as it had the previous night. With a shaky hand he pushed his thumb on the answer tab. "Yeah!" he croaked.

"Is that Sam Becker?" asked the stern male on the other end of the line, the voice was unmistakably that of Robert Finch. Sam had only spoken to him briefly the previous night, but he would recognize his overconfident tone anywhere.

"It is," he replied sharply. The sound of Finch's voice had swept away any sleepiness in an instant; Sam's heart rate picked up, as adrenaline rushed through his veins.

"Good, we have a transaction to make this morning. I trust you haven't forgotten our terms?"

"Of course not," Sam snapped. "I hope you've remembered my terms Finch, I want proof of life and I need to speak to Adam." Sam rubbed his right eye as he spoke, ridding it of some sleep.

"Of course, although I'm not going to let you speak with him. I don't want him influencing your decision to hand over the Key Tablet. I'll send you a time and date stamped video, to prove we haven't killed him – that will have to do."

Sam mulled over the proposal for a few seconds and listened intently for any background noise which might give him a clue as to where they were. "Okay," he said reluctantly. "It goes against my better judgment, but I'm going to have to trust you."

"That you will, Sam," Finch replied cockily. "How do you want the exchange to go down? I trust you're not hoping for us to give you your friend before we have the Key Tablet?"

Sam smiled to himself in the early morning gloom of the RV, he'd known they were going to try and play it this way. Following the departure of Finch, he'd closed the room up and left the hotel. Taking the RV, he'd driven a few miles and parked next to a reservoir on the edge of a flashy golf course. He'd been just in time, too; as he trundled up the road three police cars, blue lights flashing, had shot past and swung into the parking lot of the Days Inn. Sam had left Finch's partner with almost half his face missing, and he was in no doubt the room would now be a major crime scene. The local police would have been there all night and likely the majority of the next day, desperately trying to piece together what had happened.

On reaching the reservoir Sam had checked, cleaned and reloaded the weapons. Finch had helped himself to the Ruger that Oriyanna had on her; however, in some kind of weird tradeoff, he'd left the Glock that had fallen from his hand when Sam floored him. As for the Ruger he'd given to Adam, it was likely in Finch's possession, too. Once satisfied that everything was in order, Sam had tried to get some sleep, which hadn't come easily. He'd managed to grab a few unsettled hours, tossing and turning on the double bed. The day ahead was going to be long and stressful, and as impossible as it seemed, Sam knew he needed to rest. During his army days, he'd spent many a far less comfortable night in the field, sleeping on the ground in all manner of conditions with only his hard, uncomfortable rucksack as a pillow. Even though many of those occasions had been in hostile situations, Sam had still managed to sleep better then than he had in the past few hours.

"I had a feeling you were going to say that," Sam replied, stretching a little and he heard the joint in his knee crack. "So you want me to leave the Key Tablet and just wait for you to call and tell me where to pick him up?"

"That about sums it up, Sam." Finch sounded overconfident. Sam wished he could reach down the phone and rip his throat out.

"And what about the girl, Oriyanna. Is she still alive?" Sam had taken a big gamble in letting Finch take her, the fact he hadn't just shot her on sight meant they had some use for her. He only hoped that hadn't changed; he knew without doubt that once they were done with her, she would be killed. He just hoped he was in time to rescue her.

"She is – for now," Finch's voice sounded suspicious. "What do you care anyway, Sam? She's caused you nothing but trouble; I did you a favour taking her off your hands."

"You're right, I don't really care," he lied. "Okay, if you won't release Adam until you get the Key Tablet, the pickup will be on my terms. Is that clear?" Any negotiation like this was nothing more than a tug of war for the balance of power. Finch held all the cards, but Sam had the ace, and he needed to set the balance back in his favour.

"I'm listening."

"There's a reservoir a few miles up from the hotel we were at last night, look on a map and you'll see it. It's toward the end of Garden of the Gods Road and next to a golf course. Around that reservoir there's a public footpath. Are you with me so far?"

"Yes, of course I am. Just tell me where I need to collect it from," Finch barked.

"On the east side of the reservoir there's a wooden bench seat. The Key Tablet will be secured below the seat – be clear that I'll have no contact with you during the pickup. Once you have it, I'll expect a call detailing the location to collect Adam." There was a long pause from the other end; Finch was obviously thinking through the proposal, and from the slight echo on the line Sam suspected he was on speaker phone and others were listening, maybe even someone who called the shots. While Finch was undoubtedly more than just hired muscle, there was obviously someone higher up the food chain giving the orders. Sam had dealt with plenty of people like Finch before, they always had delusions of grandeur and the idea that they were far higher in the scheme of things than they actually were. Often the greatest weakness in those like Finch was overconfidence; it bred complacency, and it was that complacency which Sam was hoping to exploit and force him into making a fatal error.

"Okay, that will work," he finally replied. "The pickup will be made in an hour. Once I have possession of the Key Tablet, I'll need thirty minutes to confirm its authenticity. Then you will be told where to collect your friend. If those terms are not acceptable to you, I'll just kill him now."

"The terms are fine; once I have the video I'll get the Key Tablet into place. The pickup will be in an hour, as you said." Sam checked his watch. "So that would be half seven?"

"Seven thirty it is," Finch replied flatly. "We'll speak again soon, Sam." The line went dead.

Sam eased himself off the bed and drew back the tacky floral design curtains; they matched the tasteless double duvet which was now covered in a mixture of dry blood and dirt from the previous evening. Sam rolled it into a sloppy bundle and placed it at the foot of the bed. Standing in the kitchen area, he took a wistful look around the camper. *We should be out hiking in the Rockies now,* he thought. *Not fighting for our lives.* The sharp beep of Adam's phone snapped him out of the daydream, the message had a media file attached. Sam opened it and waited for what seemed like an eternity for the file to load. When the screen finally came to life, he saw Adam tied to a chair and barely conscious, his head lolling from side to side as small groans of pain and discomfort slipped from his mouth. Sam could see a dark red blood stain on the side of his face. Watching his friend in that state made him want to kill Finch even more, and at that point, he made a promise to himself that one way or another, he would end Finch's life, no matter how long it took. Next, the camera swung right, bringing Oriyanna into view. She was more out of it than Adam. Sam suspected they'd used some sort of drug on her. She was bound to an identical chair, head slumped forward, and her hair had come out of its ponytail and fallen forward, hiding her face. Even if they'd treated her to a beating, there would be no sign of it now. The cameraman moved back, including both of them in the frame. The room they were in looked a mess. Sam could see boarded up windows behind where they were sat; long angled streams of sunlight were leaking in between the wooden boards. Just to the side of Adam stood an old table and two more chairs, the same as the ones they were tied to. The camera focused on them both for a few seconds before whipping away, and the room blurred as the lens moved far too quickly for the camera to process. It settled on Finch's face; he'd turned it around to record himself.

"There you go, Sam" he began smugly. "Thought I'd give you a two for one deal, as you can see they are both alive. Later when we kill the girl, I'll be sure to send you a video, too. I want to make sure she's awake first; after living for so many years, do you think she'll beg for her life or just accept her fate?" The look on his face was stone cold. "Make sure that the Key Tablet is where you said, or the next video you get will be your friend dying!" The camera turned again and a blurred shot of the ceiling whipped by; after that the camera turned to the floor, and then the video ended. Sam reloaded the file and watched it through twice, looking for some clue as to where they were being held. It had to be somewhere fairly close; Sam felt sure they wouldn't be more than twenty miles away. However, nothing in the video gave him any clue, it didn't help that the area was totally alien to him. Locking the screen, Sam tucked the handset into his cargo trousers. Digging in the tack bag, he removed a roll of duct tape and slid it over his wrist, like a large, oversized bracelet. The Key Tablet was still securely in his rear pocket, where he'd put it after Oriyanna had handed it to him. Opening the side door, Sam climbed down into the car park; the early morning April air was brisk and the wind had died down, leaving a crystal clear blue sky. As he walked, his breath clouded momentarily in front of his face. Birds were just beginning to sing from their hidden perches within the thin line of trees that surrounded the reservoir. Picking up the pace, Sam saw a morning dog walker with a large Alsatian approaching him. The old woman walking it looked far too small to control an animal of that size. She treated Sam to a polite nod in greeting as she passed by, leaving an invisible wake of cheap scented perfume that smelt more like air-freshener. The dog took a moment longer to have a sniff around Sam's legs, before a sharp whistle from its owner sent it running off down the gravel path. The well-kept fairways and greens of the golf course stretched out to the side, covered in dew that glistened in the morning sun. Sam suspected it wouldn't be long before the first players started their rounds.

It took about three minutes to reach the bench, and stopping by its side Sam gave himself a second to look around, scanning for any more dog walkers or joggers. The old lady and her Alsatian were just visible on the far side of the water, too far away to see him. Crouching down on the cold sharp gravel, Sam removed the Key Tablet from his pocket. It picked up his body's energy immediately, and the hum seemed to be even stronger in his cold hand, almost making it sting. He looked at it for a brief moment, unable to quite grasp the importance of the strange alien artefact. He placed it on the bench and slid the duct tape off his wrist before peeling off a long strip, biting it clear of the roll with his teeth. Grasping the Key Tablet, he held it in position under the bench and applied the tape. Sam pushed up hard on the underside of the wooden seat, securing it in place; he peeled off a second strip and applied it to the bench, forming a cross. Standing up, he took another good look around, making sure no prying eyes were watching his strange behaviour. It seemed odd to think that an item as important as this was being left taped to an old wooden bench next to a golf course. If things went according to plan, it would be back in his possession in a few hours, along with Adam and Oriyanna. Satisfied the job was done, he jogged back to the RV. He still had work to do before it was collected.

The Sunday morning traffic was sparse as he drove back toward the interstate. As he passed the Days Inn he glanced into the car park; three police cruisers were still parked, not far from where the camper had been. A throng of onlookers stood outside, gawping up at the third floor. The sight of two rather large women in gaudy pink dressing gowns amongst the crowd even made him smile a little. No matter where you went in the world, people were always the same, all eager to watch someone else's misfortune or get in on the latest gossip. Sam kept the RV on Garden of the Gods Road; passing under the interstate he followed the SatNav toward the university campus. The trip only took a few minutes on the quiet roads. Situated next to the university, Sam saw what he was looking for. Opposite the campus was a large shopping village, and many of the students obviously used the parking lot to leave their cars over the weekend. Driving past, Sam took in the array of older, slightly tatty cars.

Pulling off the road and into the car park, he brought the RV to a stop, climbed out and removed a flat head screwdriver from the tool kit in the side utility compartment. It didn't take him long to find what he was after. The small, metallic grey Mark Two VW Golf GTI was just the job, Sam had owned one in his early twenties, he knew exactly how to get in and start it without the key. Taking the screwdriver, he forced it hard into the lock and turned; the knob inside popped up first time. Sam glanced around quickly before jumping in, the car smelt of damp and stale fast food, and a variety of wrappers and bags from various junk food establishments littered the passenger foot well. Jamming the screwdriver into the ignition he repeated the process. Reluctantly, the engine turned over but didn't fire – the battery had obviously seen better days. Depressing the clutch to take some of the pressure off the

engine, Sam tried again and held his breath. This time the engine fired
and spluttered a few times, but didn't die. Revving the engine, he selected first gear and crept the VW over to the camper. He loaded their
luggage quickly, putting the tack bag into the boot. As a last thought he
went back to the RV and removed his phone and their passports from
the glove box, before tossing the keys onto the passenger seat. In a few
days someone would report the RV as abandoned, and the rental firm
would get it recovered. Any fines or charges for just leaving it would
have to be worried about later, if they were even alive to do any worrying. Leaving the car park Sam checked the time; he had thirty-five
minutes. As the VW warmed up, the pokey engine came to life. It felt
small and nimble compared to the camper and despite its age and odd,
musty smell, it was much nicer to drive. Covering ground as quickly as
possible, Sam headed back to the reservoir. On the way, he stopped at a
garage and filled the Golf with as much petrol as he could squeeze into
the tank. Before paying, he blindly grabbed a selection of sandwiches
from the kiosk's chiller cabinet, as well as a pack of energy drinks and
a four pack of bottled water. Leaving the garage, he opened a packet
of ham and cheese sandwiches. The instant he smelt the cold meat he
was ravenous, and finished them both in a few bites. Steering with one
hand, Sam freed a bottle of water from the pack and cracked the top off.
He could feel the start of a dehydration headache brewing. Draining
the cool liquid in a few long swallows, he opened a second bottle for
good measure, finishing the contents just before arriving back at the
car park. He didn't need long to sort out his observation point, he'd
selected it the previous night when scoping out the area.

Pulling into the car park he saw a few more vehicles had arrived in
the time he'd been gone. The odd jogger and dog walker were busy
with their morning routine, and far off across the course he could
see a couple of people teeing off. Sam scanned the reservoir; the thin,
matchstick-like structure of the bench was just visible across the water.
He alighted from the car and fished a pair of binoculars from his tack

bag in the boot, constantly looking around as he went. He felt exposed and naked. There was a good chance Finch already had eyes on the area; Sam knew if the roles were reversed he would have the whole vicinity plotted up.

Securing the binoculars around his neck, he placed the FNP45 in his waistband and hid it with his fleece. Sam felt like kicking himself for not purchasing a couple of Kevlar vests from the armoury. He'd been lucky last night, just one on-target shot would have put him out of the game.

Returning to the driver's door, he removed the small screwdriver from the ignition and hid it in the door pocket. Satisfied that at first glance the car didn't look stolen, he walked briskly to a small wooded area and got into position. The bush provided just enough cover to hide him from the view of anyone using the car park. Whoever was collecting the Key Tablet would be walking away from him. Once they reached the bench, they would be too far off to spot him in his hiding place. Sam made himself as comfortable as possible – as with any surveillance jobs he'd been involved in, the order of the day was hurry up and wait.

* * *

Finch gunned the Impala and headed away from the rangers' hut in a cloud of dust. Buer had ordered him to collect the Key Tablet on his own; the previous night's events had left them short on both manpower and vehicles. Mitchell and another of his small team were already on their way, but it would be an hour or so before they'd made the trip from Denver and another hour before they had an operational base set up. Buer had chosen to stay at the lodge with the two drone-like meat heads he'd arrived with, worried that there might be some kind of attempt by Sam Becker to free his friend and the girl. Finch had thought it unlikely, as he had no clue where they were hiding. There was no doubt that Becker was a skilled soldier and pretty handy, but he wasn't that good. More importantly, Finch didn't really want nor need anyone to go with him. Even after Roddick had been shot and he'd had his face crushed with a size nine, he'd still managed to get the job done. After all that, just picking up the Key Tablet from under a bench would be a piece of cake. Hitting the state highway Finch increased his speed, and despite the lack of food and sleep over the last twenty-four hours he was feeling rather good about himself.

Once he'd acquired the Key Tablet, Buer had requested that he come straight back. He wanted confirmation from the girl that it was the device and not some tin pot ploy to dupe him into taking a fake. Once that was done, the girl was going to die. Finch wanted to be the one to pull the trigger, but he suspected Buer would want to do it. The fate of Adam Fisher had been left up to him, and he was still undecided on whether to hold up his end of the deal or not. Once he had the Key Tablet he might just shoot him, it would be more fun than letting him go. Plus, he owed some kind of payback to Becker for stamping on his face, even if there was no trace now that the assault had ever happened.

The drive to the reservoir took just over twenty minutes. Finch checked his watch; he had five minutes before the pickup. It was close enough. Becker was bound to have the Key Tablet at the pickup point by now. Pulling into the small gravel parking lot, he scanned the other vehicles. There was no sign of the RV, which meant one of two things: either Becker was long clear of the area, sat up waiting for a call that he would never get, or he was somewhere nearby, watching his every move. Finch hoped it was the latter; he would relish the chance to lead him back to the lodge. Once there, he would kill him as well.

Climbing out of the Chevy he set off along the gravel footpath. Following the water's edge, he could see the bench at the far side of the reservoir. The fact he was so close to completing his task just made him feel even smugger. The sound of an early morning golfer hitting the ball on the sweet spot drifted through the air. The ball caused a nearby flock of birds to take flight in a frantic jumble of squawks and flapping wings. Smiling to himself, Finch watched them pass overhead as he reached his target. This was it, the moment of truth. He glanced around for a second, almost expecting Sam Becker to appear out of nowhere and take him on, but he didn't. Finch knelt down and gripped the bench. Using the grey wooden slats for support he looked underneath; it was there, a cross of black duct tape secured to the underside of the seat. Frantically, he whipped it off and the tape came away in one whole piece. Stuck to the adhesive was a strange rectangle of metal. Finch gawped at it for a few seconds, not quite able to believe he actually had it. There was no way this could be fake. The artefact looked like no metal he'd ever seen on Earth, strange inscriptions that he recognised as written Arkkadian ran down its surface. Carefully, as if it were now the most delicate thing in the world, he peeled the tape away. The minute his skin touched its surface the metal hummed and glowed. Even in the bright morning sunlight he could see it. *Becker actually handed it over* he thought to himself in amazement. Sam Becker's desperate attempt to save just one person had just sealed the fate of an entire planet. Grinning contently, Finch tucked the Key Tablet into his suit jacket and walked hastily back to the car.

* * *

Sam watched as a Red Chevrolet Impala rolled into the car park. From his position he didn't get a clear view of the driver, but he heard someone get out of the car and slam the door. Checking his watch Sam saw it was seven twenty-five; if this was the person collecting the Key Tablet they were early. Moving slightly to adjust his field of view, he stared intently at the first small section of path visible from his hiding place. He could hear the rhythmic crunch of the driver's feet on the gravel for a good minute before he saw him. Patience offered its reward, as the profile of Finch strode into view. He was dressed in the same suit as he'd worn on their first run in, although it was looking a little worse for wear now. Finch looked like a party goer who'd fallen asleep in a park wearing his best clothes, and then woke up the next morning and discovered he had to walk home.

Where the view afforded vision, Sam kept a watchful eye as Finch made quick progress around the path. As he approached the bench, Sam switched to the binoculars which were already focused perfectly for the distance. He watched as Finch removed the tape and looked at the artefact for what seemed like an eternity. As soon as he tucked the Key Tablet into his suit jacket, Sam left his hiding place and hurried back to the car. Finch was too far off to recognize him as he fired up the VW and pulled out of the car park. The small road that led to the reservoir was a dead end, there was only one way Finch could come out and it was the perfect choke point to pick him up on. Reaching the end of the road, Sam purposely turned away from the junction that led to the state highway and headed in the opposite direction. After about two hundred yards he slid the Golf in behind a large pickup truck and waited. The view of the junction wasn't the best, but he would see the red Chevy when it appeared. There was no way that Finch, who would be concentrating on the road, would see the little old VW parked and hidden. Sam also had the added bonus of being in a new vehicle.

As the minutes ticked by, Sam's heart rate increased. He hated how time always seemed to pass much slower in situations like this. Finally, the Impala arrived at the junction. Sam could just see the vehicle positioned to turn left, just as he'd suspected. Watching it move off, he waited until he was out of sight and crept the VW forward, pulling out and away from the parked truck. Gunning the engine, he closed the distance to the junction as fast as he could. Thankfully the road was clear, allowing him to pull straight out. The Impala was a good two hundred yards ahead and carrying out an overtake on a bright blue SUV. Sam waited for it to pass and drop out of sight before dropping down a gear and closing the distance. He felt far more comfortable with a vehicle between them for cover. Staying behind the SUV he followed Finch to the interstate, where he took the on-ramp and headed south. The Sunday morning traffic was still quite sparse, offering few vehicles to hide behind. He remained calm and focused, resisting the growing temptation to get in closer. They stayed on the interstate for what seemed like ages; Sam kept an eye on the trip counter, which revealed a good seven miles had clocked by before he watched the turn signal finally come on ahead of him. Mirroring the Impala, Sam guided the VW onto the off-ramp and slotted in two cars back as they took State Highway 115. Tree-covered hills began to rise up to his right, and he felt sure that they would soon be heading that way. Wherever Finch had them was going to be somewhere out of the way, making any attempt to escape hard.

After a few miles the two vehicles turned off, leaving him directly behind the Chevy. Sam eased off the accelerator and let the gap build. He was confident Finch wouldn't have noticed him following. He'd been more than cautious, but trying to carry out surveillance on your own was an almost impossible task, and sooner or later, you were bound to get burned. After another three miles he watched Finch swing the Impala right onto a small unkempt road, the tyres kicking up dust as he went. Sam backed off further and waited for him to disappear over a small hill before making the turn. The dust trail was as easy to follow as the car, and staying a good two hundred yards back he kept pace. As the VW cleared the hill Sam knew he'd arrived, to his right was a small, dilapidated lodge-type building. At the front, sitting proudly on an overgrown field, stood a jet black Explorer helicopter. Sam hit the brakes and pulled left, as the Impala bumped its way up a rough access road before coming to a stop. He rammed the VW into reverse and backed up over the small hill, hiding the Golf from view. He slid out of the car silently and crept forward on his hands and knees. Finch was out of the car and scanning his surroundings, no doubt looking for any signs of a tail. Sam raised the binoculars and focused on the lodge.

It definitely fitted the type of building he'd seen on the video. Taking a quick look around, he watched Finch head inside, slamming an old wooden screen door behind him. Either he was satisfied that he hadn't been followed, or he knew Sam was close by. One thing was certain, in the next few minutes Finch would know he was there and with any luck, Sam would get the chance to kill him.

Chapter 15

Oriyanna's plea for help still resounded in Adam's head like a ringing bell, and as his eyes blinked open he felt as if he'd been hit by a train. The pain raging through his head was so acute it unfocused his eyes; even squinting didn't do much to bring the room into view. Somewhere, in a different part of the building, he could hear the dull drone of men talking, although he couldn't make out any words. Adam tried to lift his hand to rub the pain throbbing like a pulse behind both his temples, but neither of his arms wanted to work. It took a few moments to realize why; he was bound to a chair and his ankles had suffered the same fate, paralyzing him to the spot.

Claustrophobic panic began to set in. He could hear someone breathing heavily next to him, and turning his head he saw Oriyanna, bound and unconscious. In an instant his panic turned to anger. Her head and body had slumped forward so much that the restraints were all that held her delicate frame in place. If they were cut she would have instantly fallen forward onto her face. He shifted in his seat. Something cold and uncomfortable was digging into his back, and what little movement he had did nothing to relieve the discomfort, until he remembered what it was. The gun! Sam had given it to him just before he left the room. Adam tried to piece things together. After taking the gun he'd walked to the diner, but he never made it. Somewhere in the dark car park, someone had been waiting for him. His anger changed to dread. If Oriyanna was with him, what the hell had happened to Sam? Surely he would have put up a fight to help her, which could mean only one thing. He was dead. Adam let his head drop in solace and winced at the constant, throbbing pain behind his eyes. It felt as if someone was trying to push them out of their sockets from the inside. He felt warm tears pooling in their corners, and keeping his eyelids shut he tried to hold them back, but it just created more to follow. One tear after another slowly dripped off his face and down onto his dirty blue jeans. *Oriyanna trusted us to help her,* he thought, *and we let her down. Now Sam's dead and we're going to be next.* He needed desperately to wipe the tears away. If she came around now and saw him bawling, it would do nothing to help their situation. Ignoring the pain, Adam craned his neck down and wiped both eyes in turn on the shoulders of his jacket, smearing the blood on his face. He still had the gun, but with both hands bound to the chair it might as well be on the other side of the room. Adam tugged at the zip ties binding his hands, and the old wooden chair creaked in protest. Despite the aged appearance of the timber, it was obviously still strong. In one of the other rooms a roar of laughter erupted, followed by some more inaudible chatter. He tried to count the voices, from what he could make out there were three, all male. He glanced around frantically, looking for something he might be able to use to get free. On the far side of the dank and run-down room, he spotted a rusty old kitchen knife sitting on a worktop, but like the gun, it was of no use. For a brief second he thought about trying to stand and shuffle back quickly towards the wall, in the hope the chair would shatter, but the commotion would only bring whoever the voices belonged to charging into the room, way before he had time to react. Feeling beaten and downtrodden Adam slumped in the chair, allowing the restraints to take his weight for a second. As the plastic bit into his wrists the pain brought back the memory of Sam, dropping the keys outside the diner. Much to his friend's amazement he'd managed to fish them out of the grating they'd fallen through. It had hurt like hell, but somehow, he'd manipulated his hand through the small gap. If only he could do the same thing now. Having only discovered this strange ability the previous day, he wasn't sure if it would work a second time, but it was worth a try. Adam closed his eyes to concentrate; as he did he heard heavy footsteps enter the room. *I'm too late,* he thought, not wanting to look up and accept his fate.

"Mr. Fisher," boomed one of the voices he'd heard from the other room, "I would wish you a good morning, but unfortunately for you, there's nothing good about it!" Adam looked up reluctantly. The guy standing before him was a man-mountain; he resembled an aged wrestler, the kind you see years after retirement, still looking impossibly huge. "You're probably wondering what happened," the man continued. "Would you like to know?"

Adam nodded slowly; he could feel the goliath's eyes boring down on him, as if they had a physical weight of their own. "Is Sam dead?" he asked croakily, not sure if he really wanted to know the answer.

A booming laugh filled the room; it almost seemed to resonate through Adam's body. "No, he isn't dead." The man took a few deep breaths to stifle his amusement. "In fact, as we speak, he is doing a deal with my colleague. You met him, in a manner, last night." The guy paused. "Right at this moment, good old Sam is trying to save your life." He raised his eyebrows, as if Adam should be showing him gratitude.

"What's the deal?" Adam thought he already knew, but he needed to hear it himself.

"It's quite simple; the Key Tablet that Oriyanna had in her possession, in exchange for you."

Adam's stomach lurched. Somehow, through their combined unconsciousness, Oriyanna had reached out to him. He could hear her in his head once again. *Help me Adam, help us both!* Her words seemed to repeat in his mind.

"Any minute now, my colleague should be back with the artefact. Once we've confirmed its authenticity, you will be released."

"What about Oriyanna?" Anger brewed in him once again, like a smouldering fire being fed the oxygen it needed to ignite. In small movements hidden by his seated position, he adjusted his right hand and applied gentle upward pressure on the restraint.

The male started laughing again, as if he'd just heard the funniest joke in the world. "Oh, poor Adam," he coaxed, cocking his head to one side like a bird watching its prey. "Did she get into your head?" He crossed the room, forcing Adam to halt his escape attempt as the guy moved around behind Oriyanna and yanked her head back by her tangled blonde hair. Towering over her, he gazed into her pallid face. "You see, Adam, this one can be a bit of a mind fuck. You wouldn't be the first man to fall for her, but you will certainly be the last." He let go of her hair, and Oriyanna's head slumped forward. "Who could blame you? Many years ago, before all this, I had similar feelings for her. But in time we all change, and I've had a lot of time to change, Adam. Lifetimes, in fact." He strode the distance between their two chairs in one go, and came back around to the front. "As nice as it is to see her again, and I must say the years have been kind, this is where she gets off the ride."

"So you plan to kill her?" asked Adam, trying to sound calm and in control. He began to apply pressure to his hand once again. The upward motion forced his bones together, and he felt the sharp plastic tie biting into his skin.

"Yes. I'm sorry, but that's precisely what I plan to do," he said, his voice almost apologetic. Outside, Adam heard the sound of car tyres on gravel, followed by a door slamming shut and rapid footsteps. The massive hulk of a guy looked up at one of the boarded windows, as if he could see through it. "I do believe my colleague is back. Hopefully for you, this whole ordeal will be over within the next few minutes. Please excuse me." Adam watched him turn and leave the room. It was perfect timing. Now free to apply more pressure, he squeezed his hand together into a point and pulled up hard. Adam's bones slid slightly out of position, giving way to the upward movement against the plastic. Gritting his teeth, he felt his skin begin to tear; if he wasn't careful the sharp plastic would peel his skin off, like the rind of an orange. But he wasn't going to give up now. Suppressing a cry of pain which badly wanted to escape, he upped the pressure one final time, and the pain he experienced made him see stars behind his closed eyelids. Right at the point where he thought he could take no more, his arm jerked violently upward and his hand snapped free of the plastic tie. For a second he just held it before his face, like a baby discovering the appendage for the first time. His wrist had been cut by the action, but not badly. He glanced at Oriyanna; her head was beginning to move from side-to-side, the deep rhythmic breathing had slowed; he thought it wouldn't be too long before she was awake. Adam could hear voices again from the next room; someone was talking excitedly. Returning his attention to the restraints he reached around and took hold of the tie securing his left hand.

Wrapping his fingers around it he pulled hard, stretching the plastic as much as he could. It was hard, but in his adrenaline-fuelled fury it gave a little. Ignoring the biting pain in his fingers, he kept up the pressure and began to wriggle his left hand free. Using the right as leverage sped the process up, and in a flash, it whipped loose. His feet would be another matter altogether, the realization that he couldn't squeeze a foot through the plastic restraint immediately sunk his spirits. Sure, he could operate the gun, but he was still attached to the chair; still unable to stand and help Oriyanna.

The conversation continued next door. He still had a few seconds, and he thought it was pointless giving up now. He leaned forward and studied the ties holding his feet. They were secured around the legs of the chair and a supporting strut braced the legs apart, meaning he couldn't just lift the wooden legs up and over the restraints.

Leaning further forward and almost toppling over, Adam tested the strut with his hand, keeping one planted on the floor for balance. The wood was much thinner than the thick slats on the back which had held the ties around his hands. It also seemed softer, probably from being so close to the cold damp concrete floor. Using the heel of his hand, Adam hit the strut. More pain exploded up his wrist, as the vibration of the impact reverberated through his bones. The strut moved a little, but not enough. Hiding the second impact with a cough he hit it again; this time the wood cracked and a quick look confirmed it; the strut had broken where it joined the leg. Adam grasped the round wooden spindle in his hand and wriggled, pushing down and completing the break. Frantically, he pulled the strut free; lifting the chair he slipped the legs away from the zip ties and stood up. Every bone and joint in his body sang with relief. The voices from the other room suddenly grew louder. In a panic, he sat down and positioned his hands and feet back against the chair, making his aching muscles scream in protest. He watched in silent horror as the man-mountain came back into the room, sporting a wide, triumphant grin. He knew instantly they had the Key Tablet. Sam had made the trade and in the next few minutes, he would either be dead or free; the thought made his bowels churn and bile rose into his throat.

"Your friend did very well," beamed the man, opening his fist to reveal the glowing Key Tablet "Once I get confirmation from your girlfriend here that it's the real deal, you'll be free to go. After you watch me shoot her, that is."

Adam slid his hand up under his coat and felt the cool rubber grip of the Ruger against his fingertips. His own body hid the movement well. He couldn't quite believe they'd missed the weapon. As unobtrusively as possible, he slid it from his waistband and fumbled blindly for the safety, remembering what Sam had shown him back in the motel, the whole time keeping his eyes on the grinning man.

"It's time for sleeping beauty to wake up," he proclaimed, removing a syringe from his pocket with the other hand. He pulled a plastic cap off the needle and squirted a little fluid into the air. Adam needed Oriyanna awake, he knew this was leaving things to the last minute, but there was no way he could carry her and defend himself at the same time. He watched the guy slide the needle into her neck and depress the plunger before removing it and standing back. The reaction was almost instantaneous. Oriyanna's eyes snapped open and her head rose rapidly; it was like seeing someone receive a shot of adrenaline. Adam watched her wide, crystal blue eyes fix on the giant who was standing before her.

"*Buer!*" she growled in a tone Adam had never heard her use before.

"Nice to see you again, too," Buer replied with a grin. "I hate to wake you up just to kill you, but I have to show you something. I'm sure you'll understand." He unfolded his massive fist once again revealing the Key Tablet.

As Adam continued to watch them, he found the safety and slid it off. The small click never caught Buer's attention; he was focused completely on Oriyanna. Adam adjusted his grip and prepared himself for the right moment.

The instant Oriyanna saw the Key Tablet, Adam knew what this Buer guy had meant about confirmation. Her face said it all, and no words were needed. Adam tried to move his hand, whip it around and fire the gun, but fear of failure had frozen him to the spot. He watched Buer smile maniacally at the sight of her face. Feeling totally useless Adam looked on, as tears welled up in her large blue eyes.

"That's all I need to know," grinned Buer. He turned and left the room. Before Adam had time to say anything he was back, a gun clenched firmly in his hand. "It all ends here, Adam," he said calmly. "Once she dies, you'll be free to go." There was a false note in his tone which told Adam differently. He knew he was next, but first Buer seemed determined to make him watch Oriyanna die. Adam frantically looked across at her, her face was defiant as tears rolled down her cheeks. Suddenly, in his head, he heard her words again.

They know things, Adam. This is not just about saving your people anymore, once they have the Key Tablet they will destroy both our worlds. Help me, help us both!

Buer raised the gun; Adam watched his finger take up the trigger pressure. In the same instant, the paralysis which had held him in place let go. Back in Afghanistan, he'd been helpless and unable to save the young girl, this time would be different. He couldn't watch a second person be executed, especially not Oriyanna. The fury which had been smouldering inside his chest ignited like wildfire. Adam whipped his hand around from behind the chair, levelled out the gun, and squeezed the trigger three times. *Bang, bang, bang* echoed through the room. He watched Buer crumple as the shots slammed into his stomach and lower abdomen. As he fell, Adam squeezed off another round, *bang*. It slammed into the top of his shoulder, shattering the bone and lodging itself deep into his body. Before Buer's gun hit the deck Adam was on his feet, and in one swift movement he kicked Oriyanna's chair over, sending her crashing painfully to the floor. Ignoring her surprised cry, he stamped frantically on the legs and backrest, snapping the aging timber like twigs. A large, thick-set male appeared at the door with his gun raised, and on seeing Adam free, he squeezed off two shots. Adam suffered an odd, numbing pain as one round grazed across his arm, ripping his jacket and jumper. Beneath his clothing, warm blood leaked from the injury, he knew he had been hit but it wasn't serious, no more than a flesh wound. In his frenzied state, he barely noticed.

"Adam, give me the gun!" cried Oriyanna. She was free of her restraints and on her feet behind him; without thinking he handed her the pistol as another three shots hammered into a boarded up window behind, sending the slats crashing to the floor. Oriyanna returned fire; expertly, she dropped the male with a round which slammed through his neck, spraying blood across the dirty, damp walls. A second male came into view and instantly took cover behind the door lining; it was his first and last mistake. Remembering how Sam had killed Finch's partner through the door at the hotel, Oriyanna levelled the gun and fired two shots into the plaster; a second later, his body slumped to the ground and fell across his already dead friend. Adam raced for the broken window, picking up one of the spare chairs as he went. He swung it around his body and sent it crashing through the jagged broken glass. Oriyanna was right behind him, instinctively he grabbed her wrist and pulled her toward their escape route. "The Key Tablet!" she cried. "They still have it."

"If we stay here and look we might both end up dead," pleaded Adam. "*Come on!*" Oriyanna wrenched herself free and rushed to Buer's body; he was writhing around on the floor in a pool of blood, like a snake which had been cut in half.

"*Where is it?*" cried Oriyanna, frantically running her hands over his blood-soaked clothing. The sound of heavy footfalls from somewhere in the building snapped her out of it. Glancing through the door she saw Finch heading up a corridor at the far side of the adjoining room. He was breaking into a run, drawing his gun as he went. "Adam, go. *Go!*" she cried, waving him away with her free hand. She stood up and backed off, firing the last shot in the gun for cover. Finch replied with a hail of gunfire. One round slammed into Oriyanna's right shoulder, the force of the impact throwing the now-empty Ruger from her hand and sending it crashing to the floor. Stumbling backwards, she followed suit.

Adam saw her go down and dived away from the window. As he scooped her up with his good arm, another bullet slammed through the plaster, covering them both in a fine white powder. Finch was close, in a second he would be on them. He lifted Oriyanna and thrust her forward, sending her through the broken window. As soon as she was clear he jumped through. A round whizzed past his ear. Oriyanna was already on her feet. Adam grabbed her hand and started running, the bright, clear morning sun stinging his eyes. "*Go, go!*" he encouraged. The sound of Finch's gun broke the morning silence; Adam saw the turf kick up to his left as a bullet lodged into the ground. Without warning, a figure appeared in front of them at the far edge of the field; Adam saw the barrel of a gun pointing at them, glinting in the bright sunlight. It was all over; with Finch behind them and someone in front they had no chance. Adam watched the figure training his gun in their direction; it took him a second to process what was happening. This latest player was frantically waving his arm left, gesturing for them to get out of the way. Another round from Finch kicked up the grass at Adam's heels; instinctively, Adam guided them left as instructed by the stranger. As the distance between them closed, Adam realized who it was.

* * *

Sam kept the binoculars trained on the old lodge; Finch had been inside for just over two minutes. If he was going to hold up his end of the deal, he would be calling any second now. Sam dropped the lens away from his eyes and blinked for the first time in what felt like ages. Across from the helicopter, a small family of deer were enjoying the cover of the long grass. Sam got to his knees and shuffled back to the Golf, but the astute creatures sensed his movement and immediately took flight into the trees. Lifting the boot, Sam removed the tack bag and grabbed two flash bangs and a smoke grenade, before throwing the bag onto the back seat. He wanted it easily to hand. Tucking the devices into the various pockets of his grubby cargo trousers, he stayed low and began to descend the small hill toward the lodge. He had a fair bit of ground to cover, with not many places to hide from view. It was a massive gamble. If they had just one sharpshooter on lookout, Sam knew he would be dead before even hearing the shot. Dropping into a drainage ditch, he removed Adam's phone and checked. No one had called, Sam made sure it was set to silent and vibrate before putting it back in his pocket.

The unmistakable sound of gunfire shattered the still, cold air, sending a flurry of nesting birds squawking frantically from the trees. Three shots in all, followed by two more, then two more. Whatever was happening inside was not an execution. Sam could tell by the blast sounds that there were a few different weapons being fired; the brief gaps between shots told his well-trained ears that a fierce gun battle was underway. He launched himself out of the ditch and started running toward the lodge. As he ran, he saw a chair come crashing through one of the windows that faced out onto the overgrown field. Sam cut right and hit the field running, the long grass whipping at his ankles. He removed the pistol from his waistband and kept it low, keeping his eyes fixed on the freshly broken window as he went. He watched in amazement as Oriyanna came reeling out backwards, hitting the ground hard. The gaping frame was instantly filled with Adam's body as he climbed frantically through; the moment he dropped clear another shot cracked loudly from inside the building. Sam stopped dead and raised his weapon; he knew that whoever had fired the shot would be next through. He watched Adam pull Oriyanna to her feet, wrenching her forward like a rag doll. Frantically, Sam tried to wave him left, away from the window; he couldn't get a clean shot and risked hitting them. As the distance between them reduced, Adam saw what he was trying to do and ducked out of the way. Behind them and closing ground fast was Finch, his suit jacket flapping behind him as he ran. He raised the gun and fired – the shot missed. Breathing slowly, Sam took aim, it would be almost impossible to hit Finch from this distance with a pistol. He cracked off two shots, being mindful to conserve his ammo; they missed, but forced Finch to dive to the ground in a slightly over-theatrical manner. The covering fire was enough; Adam was only yards away now. "Keep going," Sam cried, "there's a car just over the rise, get in!" Adam nodded in acknowledgment as he passed by, dragging Oriyanna behind him. Sam caught sight of blood running down over her right hand; but her face held a grim and steely expression, he recognized it as the fierce desire for survival.

Sam held his ground and got low in the long grass, watching Finch struggle to his feet and look hurriedly around. Seizing the right moment, Sam stood up and fired another singe shot, which missed and kicked up a bevy of dust about two feet from where Finch was standing. For a few seconds they stood weighing each other up, like gunmen in an old Wild West movie. The sound of skidding tyres on gravel broke the tension. Adam had reversed the VW up over the hill and drawn level with Sam. Leaning across the car he flung the passenger door open like a getaway driver, "Sam, go! *Get in!*" he cried. Sam watched Finch turn and sprint toward the Chevy on sight of the small VW; he had a good sixty yards to cover. Sam took two steps back, keeping a cautious eye on him before turning and making toward the passenger seat; he slammed the door as Adam hit the throttle and sent the car lunging forward in a hail of dust and gravel that sprayed up under the front wheel arches in an array of bangs and clatters.

* * *

Becker didn't have much chance of hitting him from that distance; the last two rounds had proven that. On the flipside, he was too far off to take down, unless he got very lucky. Finch picked himself up off the floor and readied his gun. *Where the hell did he come from?* Finch thought to himself. The whole journey back to the lodge he'd kept half an eye on the rearview mirror. Not a single car had followed him from the parking lot. En route back to the cabin he'd purposely driven a little faster than normal and overtaken a couple of cars, hoping to draw out any vehicle on his tail. Sam Becker had obviously been one step ahead of him, waiting somewhere away from the car park and able to pick him up on his route back. It was the second time he'd underestimated him; there wouldn't be a third. As he stood up, the sound of a shot echoed through the air, Finch jumped right in blind reaction, not knowing if he was avoiding the round or offering himself right into its path. Across the field, he and Becker seemed to lock eyes for a few seconds, neither of them sure quite how to play the next move. From the rise of the hill Finch heard an engine revving loudly, and watched a small grey hatchback rush down the rough, unmade road. He knew in an instant that Adam had reached whatever vehicle Sam had come in. Finch stepped back a few paces; he needed to reach the Chevy if he was going to have any chance of catching them. When Becker turned and ran toward the car, Finch sprinted back across the field, his eyes fixed on the red Impala which was still a good sixty yards away.

After Buer had shown Oriyanna the Key Tablet, he'd come back through to the living area of the cabin and handed it to him, with instructions to put it somewhere safe and out of the way. Taking possession of the Key Tablet, Finch had watched Buer take one of the brothers' guns off the small uneven coffee table where they were playing cards and stride back through to the dilapidated dining room. Finch knew in that instant he wasn't going to be given the honour of killing the girl. Following Buer's orders, he'd gone through to what had once been the sleeping quarters, and stowed the Key Tablet in Buer's briefcase. As he closed the latches, the gunfire had started. At first, he thought Buer had gone a little over the top and chosen to empty his gun into both of them as payback for the trouble they'd caused, but the sound of the Malone brothers rushing to Buer's aid warned him something was amiss. Thanks to Buer's order he was a good thirty seconds off the pace. Rushing back to the room he'd seen his boss in a crumpled mess on the floor, writhing and kicking about from more than one gunshot wound. The girl was leaning over him, obviously searching for the Key Tablet. Finch had gotten a few rounds off from down the hallway, one had even hit her, but only in the shoulder. By the time he'd made it through to the room, they'd already made good their escape.

Running flat out, he reached the Impala. He could still hear the VW's tyres screaming on the loose gravel, and it wouldn't take long for them to reach the road. Finch fired the engine and floored the accelerator, the Chevy hung in a wheel spin for a few seconds before it finally found enough purchase to move forward. The suspension screamed in protest when he slammed over the bumps and potholes in the unmaintained road, and driving as fast as he dared, he flew down the gravel track. Through the dust cloud he watched the VW make the state highway and turn right. Finch kept his foot to the floor, the back of the car snaking like crazy on the loose road. In a few seconds he'd descended the hill, getting a clear view of the highway that allowed him to pull straight out, only lifting his foot off the gas to prevent the car from spinning. When the tyres touched the tarmac, the whole car stabilized and picked up speed. Hitting the redline with every gear shift, he raced the Impala down the road as fast as he could. The VW looked old but it certainly wasn't slow, in fact, it almost seemed to be gaining ground on him. As Finch reached top gear he began closing the gap; slowly at first, then much faster. It almost seemed to Finch as if they were slowing down. Then, in silent horror, he watched transfixed as two long, black cylinders were thrown from the passenger window, hanging in the air for a second before hitting the tarmac and bouncing down the road toward him. It was too late and the road was too narrow to swerve. He closed his eyes, pinned the throttle to the floor and hoped for the best.

* * *

The Golf appeared to take off as Adam launched it over the brow of the hill. For a split second, the suspension was at full stretch before gravity took over and slammed the car back down with a thump. Wrestling with the steering wheel, he managed to hold the car straight.

The state highway ahead was clear, and in one slightly out of control slide, he hit the tarmac. As soon as the tyres found solid ground the Golf snapped violently into shape. Kneeling on the passenger seat, Sam watched the Impala careering dangerously down the gravel track, almost lost in their dust cloud. Finch was coming, and he was coming fast. Unzipping the side pocket of the tack bag Sam selected two more of the flash bangs. Oriyanna watched him with testing eyes, a smile forming on her lips when she realized what he was going to do. Fresh, wet blood still matted the fleece to her arm; it ran down the inside of her sleeve and covered her right hand. He was sure that given a few minutes, she would be just fine. If anyone had to get shot, she was probably the best one to take a bullet.

"Are you hurt at all?" Sam shouted to Adam over the screaming engine.

"Not badly, a bullet grazed by my arm but is isn't serious." Sam nodded and returned his attention to Finch, who had reached the road. He watched Adam glance in the rear view mirror, his eyes wide with fright when he saw the Chevy coming after them.

"When I say so, you need to back off the throttle a little. I need him to make some ground on us," Sam instructed. "These should slow him down a little." He waved the two small explosive devices in the air.

"Just tell me when," replied Adam, nodding his understanding.

Sam glanced at the speedo. They were up over a hundred miles an hour and the Impala seemed to be keeping pace with them. At that speed, Finch would be covering too much ground to take evasive action. "Okay, now bring us down to about eighty!" Adam eased off the throttle. Through the dusty rear windscreen, he watched Finch gaining ground. Without looking, Sam reached to his side and wound down the window. Using signs and trees as markers he counted out the distance between the two cars. He needed to be spot on. Sam pulled the safety pins on both devices, counting out the gap once again in his head; the Impala was just three seconds behind them now. He released the spoon-like safety handles on both flash bangs and immediately dumped them out of the window. Sam watched as the cylinders skidded down the road. Finch had no chance to avoid them, and as the two black tubes bounced up under the front of the Chevy, they detonated in unison.

* * *

The joint explosions roared through the Impala like a clap of thunder. Confined to the space under the car, they had a similar effect to a firecracker going off in someone's hand. Thousands of tiny, razor sharp shards of metal from the pair of one pound devices slammed up into the engine compartment, severing coolant hoses and fuel lines as they went. Their siblings, who were eager to cause just as much damage, instantly shredded both front tyres with a loud *pop* which seemed feeble in comparison to the larger explosion.

The car lifted slightly as the sound of the detonation forced Finch to open his eyes; it slammed up under the foot well like a rabid jack hammer. The bonnet instantly dipped when both tyres blew, causing the alloy rims to smash down onto the tarmac; bright white sparks kicked up from the wounded wheels, showering both sides of the car. Finch lost the ability to steer as the crippled Chevy slewed down the road, and in a futile attempt to regain control, he wrestled with the steering wheel, simultaneously jamming his foot hard on the brake. Unseen to Finch, fluid gushed out of both front brake lines while he mashed the pedal into the floor. As the front of the car began to pitch left, the bare wheel rim dug hard into the tarmac, pivoting the Impala like an Olympic pole-vaulter. Finch could do nothing but sit back and endure the ride as the back of the car lifted clear of the road, turning his whole world upside down. As the world began to right itself, the road was gone. Finch's face smacked into the steering wheel as the front bumper slammed down hard into the soft verge, bringing the beaten car to an immediate stop. For a few seconds it seemed to hang there, like a playing card impossibly balanced on a table, while gravity decided which way it wanted to send him. The world went the wrong way again, and the Impala pitched over onto its roof, destroying a small crop of young trees with a series of cracks and scrapes.

* * *

"Fuck me!" shrieked Sam in delight as he watched the Chevy cartwheel off the road and shrink into the distance. "Now that's what I call taking care of business." He spun around and plopped back into the passenger seat, smacking his fist triumphantly onto the grubby dashboard. "Did you see that?" Sam cracked open the glove box and took out their phones. "Time to get rid of these as well," he continued. "We don't want them tracking us any longer." In one swift movement he tossed away both handsets, craning his neck out of the open window as he watched them hit the tarmac and smash into pieces.

Adam nodded silently and allowed himself a sigh of relief. Even though the Impala was nothing more than a smoky speck in his rearview mirror, he didn't let off the accelerator for a second. The events of the last few minutes were rushing through his head like a steam train. Reaching up, he adjusted the mirror to get a better look at Oriyanna, saw she was still sitting silently on the back seat. She'd turned almost comatose and he wondered if the blood loss was getting to her this time. Her legs were drawn up to her chest and her arms were wrapped around them. "How's your shoulder?" he asked, not knowing if he should expect a response.

"The Key Tablet," she said distantly, "you gave them the Key Tablet." She turned her attention to Sam, who was still beaming from ear-to-ear. "*You gave it to them!*" she shrieked, dropping her legs and launching herself forward. Sam instinctively backed off as much as he could in the small car as she rained a torrent of punches down on him from the back seat; some finding the back of his head and shoulders. "*Why did you do that?*" Her voice sounded manic, nothing like her usual soft gentle tone.

"Whoa, hold on a second," cried Sam, lifting his arms up to defend the blows. He managed to spin around on his seat and push Oriyanna back with a forceful hand. "I just saved your fucking life, again! By my count that's twice now in twenty-four hours!" His shove sent her reeling back into the rear seat. "It wasn't part of my plan to leave there without it, we were lucky to just get away with our lives!"

Oriyanna stared back at him, and a little of the fire in her seemed to dissipate. She dropped her head. "I know. I'm sorry," she said solemnly. "Things have changed." She lifted her head to look at him; Sam could see fresh tears welling up in her wide eyes. "This is no longer just about saving you," she said flatly. "Now that they have the Key Tablet, they can destroy my world. While they had us, they got into my mind. The one who did it, Buer – I saw what he's planned. I saw what they're doing here."

"And?" asked Sam expectantly, his anger at her outburst immediately gone.

Oriyanna held his gaze, the way she had back in the RV when they'd first met. "Yesterday, they released a virus to your population. In about eighteen hours, it will start to appear all over the world, and if untreated, in a month almost every living person will be dead!"

Sam felt as if he'd been punched in the stomach, a cold chill ran through his whole body. Instantly, perspiration chilled on his back and under his arms. "Can it be stopped?" he finally managed to ask.

"If I had the Key Tablet and I could reach the Tabut, then maybe," she replied, running the numbers in her head. "But I'd need to be there within the next few hours, which is impossible. I don't even have the Key Tablet now, so I can't see a way of preventing it altogether," she continued helplessly. "This virus is going to hit and many people are going to die. I just hope it can be stopped before the number of dead runs into the billions."

"What about your home, Arkkadia?" asked Adam, his voice shaky and a little broken. Not for the first time in the last few hours, he couldn't quite comprehend what she'd said.

They both listened in horror as Oriyanna explained Buer's plans and how he intended to use the Tabut against her home world, she went on to explain in greater detail what she'd learned about his plans for Earth and the virus. As she spoke, they entered an area where trees began to line the road, casting shadows in the morning sun which flickered through the dirty windows, it gave the effect of someone turning a light on and off, over and over again. After Oriyanna had told them all she knew, she sat back and gazed out at the trees as they sped by.

Sam sunk into his seat. "I'm sorry," he said quietly. "I had no way of knowing, I just wanted to get you both out alive. I would never have handed it over if I'd known."

Oriyanna leaned forward and rested her hand on his shoulder. "I know. I'm sorry for the way I acted. We may need to change our plans now, though. Firstly, I need to make contact with Xavier; the Watcher in Austin. There is no longer time to reach him, Buer has already sent a team to kill him."

Sam stared blankly out of the window, also transfixed by the blur of passing trees. "Can you contact him in time?" he asked.

"Yes. I didn't want to risk it before, but now I don't have any choice. I can make contact by telephone."

"We'll stop at the next town or service station, and you can make the call," said Sam sympathetically.

"And then what?" asked Adam. He wasn't sure just how much more his nerves could take; the euphoria at having escaped with his life had just been whipped away.

"Then I need to get the Key Tablet back," she replied. "I don't know where they took it after I saw it back at the lodge. It wasn't on Buer after you shot him, and we can't risk going back now to try and recover it. We would be killed and everything would be lost."

"I was worried for a second you were going to ask me to turn around," said Adam.

"No, there's no need, I know exactly where they will be taking the Key Tablet. All we need to do is make sure we get there in time."

Chapter 16

Xavier stood holding the phone to his ear for a good few seconds after Oriyanna had disconnected the call. Absently, he watched two squirrels squabbling over a nut in his yard, the small grey animals providing a tempting distraction as they jumped and pounced on each other, both eager to be the victor and claim the prized piece of food. Watching the mammals was far more appealing than processing what he'd just been told. He knew things were going bad the moment he'd gotten the panic alert from John Remy two weeks ago, and over the past twenty-four hours, 'bad' had turned into the proverbial 'worst'.

Thanks to the wonder of internet forums, he'd been able to keep a fairly close eye on developments in the Rockies; the news never reported what was really happening when it came to secretive events such as that. The thread relating to the downed craft had first appeared on a board he often looked at called 'Above Top Secret', one of the most popular online conspiracy forums. Although much of the information on there was no more than people's personal theories, occasionally a story would break with some worth. The conspiracy nuts had been having a field day since the death of President Remy and the disappearance of the three delegates, as well as Robert Finch, who was still a wanted man. Xavier knew the moment he'd seen the story appear on the news that Finch was most definitely involved, he also knew that no matter how hard the authorities looked, they would never find him. If you knew all the facts, it didn't take a genius to piece the events of that unfortunate night together. Countless threads had sprung up on the forum since that day, and almost everyone had a different opinion to offer, and some even went so far as claiming the CIA had killed them all, including the President. From stories of a New World Order to secret cults and sects, almost every angle had been covered, apart from the actual truth. The funny thing was, the real truth behind what was happening was far more mind blowing than even the most imaginative of theories. The only continuity between the many posts was that somehow, all three of the missing delegates, as well as the dead President, must have been linked. Despite the unprecedented tragedy of the night, some of the crazy posts had been quite entertaining to read. Xavier had felt odd studying them and actually knowing the truth.

Then, on the very same evening he'd been expecting contact from home, he'd seen the thread appear. 'Suspected Alien Craft Crash' had been the poorly-worded title. The variety of posts and accounts had all missed the real truth, but there had been enough information to confirm his worst fears. The general consensus was that something had crashed in The Rockies that wasn't built on Earth. Xavier had immediately sent a second broadcast home using the Micro-Wormhole Radio Transmitter; he'd feared the seven-day transmission period would take too long and he'd been right. At first the sound of Oriyanna's voice on the phone had brought a massive wave of relief; however, all that soon changed once she'd explained in length the events of the last twenty-four hours. As she spoke, he'd been able to do nothing but listen in horror. The news of the virus would have been bad enough on its own; the fact that Buer was here on Earth and had the Key Tablet was nothing short of disastrous. This was certainly not the way he'd envisaged his one-hundred-year duty on Earth would start.

Xavier slowly placed the handset back on the charging cradle, the phone beeping as it made contact with the base. The slightly smaller of the squabbling squirrels had gotten the upper hand and went sprinting up a nearby tree, triumphantly storing the prized nut in his fat cheeks.

He didn't know how long he had. According to Oriyanna, Buer had already sent a team to kill him and it could be a matter of minutes before they arrived. It all depended on just how many of them were here and how widespread their infiltration into society had been. Xavier ran a shaky hand through his thick dark hair and considered his options. The urge to take immediate flight and escape his home was immense. Immense, but impractical, since there was work to do and he couldn't leave until everything was in place. Besides, it wouldn't take him long to get things in order. Pacing through the ground floor of the large two story house, Xavier made his way to the study.

Plonking himself into the leather office chair, he turned on his Mac-Book Pro. As the small computer powered up he slid open the bottom drawer of the desk and removed his Smith & Wesson 500 from the small gun safe. Flicking out the barrel, he spun it and checked each chamber was full. Satisfied that everything was in order, he flicked his wrist and snapped the barrel back, placing the heavy weapon onto the desk with a metallic clunk. Even though he knew it was only his imagination, the MacBook seemed painfully slow to reach the home screen. When it finally loaded, he immediately opened Safari and selected the first of the many online travel agents to pop up via the Google search engine. Oriyanna needed three flights to Egypt, and he took a little comfort from the fact that she had secured two Earth-Humans to help her. They had obviously proven their worth with all they'd gone through to protect her over the last few hours, and the fact they were all still alive and relatively unhurt was nothing short of miraculous. That aside, he would have given anything to be with them now. He'd felt practically useless during the last few weeks, living each day in fear that something big was about to happen and that when it did, he would be powerless to stop it on his own.

Eyes fixed on the small screen, Xavier ran a generic search, seeking the fastest way to get them out of the country from their current location in Canon City, Colorado. Much to his despair, there weren't a great deal of options. The only direct flights to Cairo left from Washington or JFK. The fastest and only option was a flight out of Albuquerque to JFK with a one hour stop at the New York airport, before they could pick up the direct flight to Cairo. None of the X54 fast jet services ran routes into Egypt. Xavier loaded Google Maps and checked the distance from Canon City to the airport, shaking his head at the five-hour drive-time the page displayed. It was still the fastest option, and even if they risked driving back to Denver they would have to wait six hours for a flight once they arrived. Providing they could reach Albuquerque within five hours, they would get to the airport just in time to check in for the flight to New York. Satisfied it was the only option, Xavier immediately booked three tickets. As the payment cleared he loaded a fresh screen and began searching for his own flight. Ideally, he would have liked Oriyanna to reach him so they could travel together, but that was now out of the question. He had no choice but to make his own arrangements and meet her in Cairo.

Scanning the options, he found that the flights from Dallas were a little kinder, but still not direct. Xavier's ticket would first send him to Washington with just a half hour to wait before he picked up his connecting flight. Running the numbers, Xavier estimated that all being well, he would arrive in Egypt about an hour and a half ahead of Oriyanna and her two companions; he should even be able to meet them at the airport. Switching screens again he wrote down the booking reference. Oriyanna had no travel documents whatsoever; he just hoped she could use her talents to get aboard the aircraft, or they were all in trouble. With their booking complete he switched his attention back to his own journey. Printing off his e-ticket, Xavier shut the Mac-Book down and removed his U.S Passport from the desk drawer. It was the first time he'd had to use it; the document was genuine but

the paperwork he'd needed to obtain it was not. Gaining Earth identification was not an issue, prior to taking up his position Xavier had
been provided with all the basic documents needed to slot neatly into
Earth culture. While none of them had been genuine, not even the best
forgery expert would have been able to tell. Along with the new identity came access to the vast legacy of wealth, built up over long years by
the many generations of Watchers who had come before. Given more
time, he would have had no issues getting a passport for Oriyanna,
but time was not something they had and she would have to make do.
The thought of things going wrong at the airport, that she might not
be able to get on the flight, made Xavier feel sick. He pushed it to the
back of his mind and concentrated on the matter in hand, getting out
of the house and disappearing as fast as possible.

Sliding the chair back under the desk he tucked his freshly printed
ticket and the passport into a small black rucksack before slipping
on a lightweight, waterproof jacket. Picking up the gun he zipped it
safely into one of the large front pockets. He would need to remember
to ditch the weapon before arriving at the airport; the Earth-Humans
were more than a little obsessed with members of the public who tried
to take guns into such places. Striding up the stairs two at a time,
Xavier reached his bedroom. Opening the wardrobe he froze at the
sound of a car pulling up on his drive. Ducking down he crept across
the plush carpet and peered over the bottom of the window, just in
time to see three well-built and suited strangers alight from a metallic grey Ford Galaxy. Almost in unison, they removed silenced pistols
from their hidden body harnesses. Instantly forgetting the need to pack
some clothes, Xavier grabbed the rucksack and rushed across the bedroom. He needed to get out of the house, and fast. Hurrying down
the hallway he paused by the spare room as three loud knocks echoed
through the house. The previous owners, who had been involved in
the precious metal and jewelry trade had installed a panic room, and
while he had no intention of using it and becoming trapped like a rat in

241

a cage, it might just help throw the three assassins off his scent. Ducking into the spare bedroom he placed his bag on the floor and slid back a large mirrored door, exposing a second solid metal door behind. He hoped it would be enough to make them think he was inside. Xavier left the room, scooping up the small rucksack as he passed. He made it to the bottom of the stairs as the front door came crashing in. Xavier was fitter than most Earth-Humans in their early forties, and at just over six feet tall he could even come across as quite intimidating if the situation called for it. He certainly had nothing against standing his ground, but three against one were not the kind of odds he favoured.

Hurrying away from the stairs he stopped by the study and grabbed his wallet and mobile, as a flurry of urgent footsteps rushed through the reception hall, smacking against the terracotta tiles. He knew the house well and avoided bumping into them by going back to the living room via the walk through kitchen. He could hear the armed intruders splitting up; heavy feet ran up the stairs while the other two accomplices reached the kitchen, missing him by a matter of seconds. Hurriedly he crossed the living room and slid out of the large French patio doors, ducking around the back wall of the house for cover. He allowed himself a brief second to steady his nerves before crouching down below the kitchen window and sneaking along the building line. The neighbor's fence was only thirty feet away, but to Xavier it seemed like miles. Staying low he reached the wooden barrier between their properties. Preparing to launch himself over he froze. He didn't have the number to call Oriyanna back; sure, he had his mobile, but the number was on his home phone. The handset was still on the coffee table in the living room, and he'd rushed right past it as he left. He felt nauseous at the stupidity of the error; this was no time to be going back. Weighing the options up for a second he knew he had no choice. He needed that phone. Without it, he'd never be able to contact her. Cursing under his breath he retraced his steps along the back wall. A few gardens down a dog was barking as a young child screamed excitedly, no doubt fully engaged in a game of fetch. Xavier needed them to be quiet so he could hear what was going on inside. Reaching the patio doors, he peered hesitantly into the living room, confirming the phone was sitting right there on the table where he'd left it. Factoring out the glass it was no more than fifteen feet away – so near and yet so far given his current circumstances! Cautiously he grasped the sliding door handle but retreated almost instantly, when one of the assassins strode boldly into the lounge, a mobile phone pressed to his ear. Xavier could just make out his side of the call as he sauntered closer to the window and stopped.

"We're searching the house now," said the man in a frustrated tone. "No, no sign of him yet."

A muffled call from one of his colleagues upstairs drew him away. Using the very slight reflection on the glass Xavier watched him turn and walk away, heading for the hall. The guy upstairs had obviously found the panic room. It was now or never. Reaching up, he slid back the patio door just enough to squeeze his stocky frame though. He could hear all three of them upstairs, involved in a heated conversation. Xavier grabbed the handset as footsteps pounded on the ceiling. Darting back across the living room, he slipped through the narrow gap and silently closed the door. This time he didn't pause, he kept low and ran as fast as he could, staying crouched down all the way to the fence. He didn't know if his neighbors were home and he didn't care; the thought of facing them was much more appealing than fronting up against the three intruders. Throwing the rucksack over first, he gripped the wobbly cedar wood capping of the fence panel. Pushing up on his legs and using his arms as a pivot he half jumped and half rolled over the five-foot panel, making it creak and shake dangerously. His feet slipped away the moment they found the soft, damp earth of the flowerbed on the other side, planting him firmly down on his ass. For the first time in long minutes, Xavier breathed deeply. Leaning back against the slats he took a second to gather his composure. The neighbors' Collie, Angus, was watching him curiously from across the garden, his tail wagging at a hundred miles an hour, making his whole rear end move from side-to-side. Xavier didn't know his elderly neighbours Mike and Claudette Haskins well enough to easily explain why he was trespassing on their property, he just hoped they were busy inside with breakfast. From his lazy spot in the sun, Angus came bounding over to him eagerly, tail still wagging madly. Immediately, Xavier was treated to a torrent of licks and nudges from his cold wet nose. "Fine guard dog you are," he whispered to the excited mutt, giving him a rub behind the ears. Xavier could hear one of the men had returned to the Galaxy; the vehicle's side door slammed shut before heavy footsteps crunched across the gravel drive and went back into the house. Keeping Angus occupied with a plenty of rubs and pats he listened as all three of the intruders left his property, the Galaxy's engine firing up before he heard it pulling out of the drive, the wheels spitting up a hail of gravel as they went. *They're leaving!* Xavier thought to himself, relieved. *I might actually be able to go back and grab some clothes.* That was as far as his idea formulated before an earth-shattering explosion ripped through the bright, idyllic Sunday morning air.

Chapter 17

Finch heard the sound of the Explorer's rotor blades thumping the air before he even reached the brow of the small hill. He wasn't sure how long he'd been unconscious for, but judging by the fact it was almost nine AM, he guessed around thirty minutes. After flipping over, the car had slid down a small embankment, hiding the wrecked vehicle from view; any passing motorists would have been completely unaware of the stricken Chevy. Waking up upside down, only held in place by the seatbelt, he'd managed to get free, only to be deposited squarely onto his head after unclipping the seatbelt. The walk back seemed vastly further than he'd driven; amazingly he'd covered about a mile and a half before the crash. Clearing the crest of the hill he saw the chopper, it was getting ready to depart, the long overgrown grass around the aircraft pinned hard to the ground in an almost perfect circle which stretched out around it like a purpose made take-off and landing pad. Buer had obviously fully recovered from the mêlée of bullets that Adam Fisher hit him with. Thankfully, not one of them had been a head shot, although Finch couldn't help thinking things might have been a bit easier for him if Buer had been killed. There would be some pretty tough questions to answer yet again; and as yet, he couldn't quite piece it all together. How the hell did Fisher get a gun? If it had been Becker, it would have made a little more sense. Fisher was just some freelance writer – combat and firearms were something that certainly wouldn't come naturally to him. All that aside, he'd obviously grown a pair of balls and somehow managed to escape. If it wasn't for the shit that was bound to be heading his way, Finch could almost respect the bravery Becker had shown.

Parked not five feet from where the Chevy had been less than an hour ago, Finch could see one of their black rental SUVs. It looked like Mitchell had just arrived from Denver; it was going to be a wasted trip. Reaching the edge of the field he jumped over the small drainage ditch and made his way toward the building, as he got closer the turbulent air from the spinning blades plastered the dirty, crumpled suit to his skin as a bevy of loose dirt and grass whipped up around him. Buer was standing out front, shouting instructions at Mitchell and another from his team who Finch recognized but couldn't place; they were both leaning in, trying hard to hear what was being said over the roar of the Explorer's engine. Buer spotted him from a good fifty yards away. His glare hit Finch like an iron fist and he slowed down, like a child reluctant to approach an angry parent. As Buer ended his conversation, Finch watched Mitchell and his scruffy colleague climb into the SUV and head back up the bumpy road leading to the lodge. They both looked fed up and sleep deprived as they drove by. Buer stood and watched them leave before turning and going back inside, wrestling for a brief moment to open the screen door which was firmly pinned shut by the helicopter's downdraft. Finally managing to prise it open, Buer held the rickety timber frame in place with his strong back, gesturing for Finch to go in first.

"Do you know what makes me angrier than anything, Robert?" Buer said, more calmly than Finch had expected. As he spoke, he made his way through to the old kitchen and dining area. The lifeless bodies of the Malone brothers were still slumped in a heap, on top of each other in the doorway, blood pooling in a thick sticky puddle around them. Buer halted by the smashed up chair Oriyanna had been bound to and absently kicked a few pieces of the broken timber out of his way. "There are undoubtedly times when you really do excel in your duties," he continued, not giving Finch a chance to speak. "But then there are times when I really have to question your abilities." The only sign that Buer had been involved in the gun battle was his dirty, scuffed black leather shoes. He must have had the luxury of a change of clothes, the pinstriped black trousers and open collar blue shirt looked freshly laundered.

"What happened?" Finch asked cautiously.

Buer ran his eyes around the room, pausing momentarily on the two dead bodies, "What happened, Robert, was that Adam Fisher had a gun on him." He paused for a second, and Finch could sense Buer's eyes boring into him, seeking some kind of reaction. "Somehow," he continued, "and for the life of me I can't figure out how, he managed to get out of his restraints, and the fucker shot me – *four times!* Can you please explain to me how that happened?"

"I can't," replied Finch truthfully. There was no excuse for what had happened. He had obviously forgotten to search Fisher properly, or just taken for granted in the heat of the moment that the man was no real threat.

"I'm guessing the fact that you arrived back here on foot means your attempts to go after them were also less than successful?"

Finch could see the fury smouldering away in Buer as it had back in Denver; the memory of how he'd almost been strangled made his throat close up. Instinctively, he began to rub his neck. "I almost had them," Finch replied weakly, "but Becker had some small explosive charges. I think they were flash bangs. Whatever they were, they did a job on the Chevy, it's about a mile down the road on its roof." Sam Becker was turning out to be a real thorn in his side. Finch just hoped he would get the chance to meet him again, if he did, he would end his life.

Buer nodded slowly, taking in every detail, "So, Oriyanna is still alive, as well as the two British men," he summarized. "It's not ideal, but at least we have the Key Tablet."

Finch relaxed a little; despite all that had gone on, he'd managed to secure the one thing Buer had desired most; capturing the girl had also led to him learning the location of the Tabut.

"All that aside, Robert, your mistakes cannot go unpunished."

Finch tensed up again. Surely Buer couldn't be that angry, even though the girl was still alive they undoubtedly had the upper hand and that was solely down to him. Before he had time to put his side of the argument across, Buer shot his arm out and grabbed Finch's shirt, pulling him forward in one powerful movement, popping several buttons off his shirt as he went. With Finch's feet scrabbling for purchase, Buer dragged his struggling body through to the living room and slammed him down hard onto the coffee table which still held the unfinished game of cards. The wooden legs immediately gave way with a splintering crack, sending Finch and the cards crashing to the floor. Finch suppressed the urge to beg Buer to stop; he couldn't seem weak; it was best to just take what was coming.

"I think your mistakes come from your overconfidence," Buer growled, pinning him to the broken table top, his eyes wild with fury. "What you need is a little something to focus your mind, something to stop you from taking your eye off the ball." With his spare hand Buer reached into his shirt pocket and took out a small silver metallic disk, no bigger than a guitar plectrum.

"No, please!" cried Finch, deciding that if he was going to beg, now was the time to start – he knew exactly what the disc was for. The Gift had saved his life more than once in the last twenty-four hours, and he didn't want to give it up without a fight. Attempts to fend off Buer's assault were nothing more than futile and just delayed the inevitable. With a fist of steel, Buer drove down hard into Finch's gut, knocking all the air from his lungs. The blow instantly halted Finch's struggle, as he gasped for breath. Buer flipped the disc over in his fingers like a magician with a coin, and all Finch could do was watch through wide, tear-filled eyes. With amazing dexterity, he flipped the disc around and held it between his thumb and forefinger before pushing it down hard onto Finch's forehead. As the disc made contact with his skin, a series of small, pin-sharp prongs sprung out around its circumference. Within a second they had secured themselves into his flesh, like a microchip on a circuit board. Even if he had the strength to struggle, it was already too late. Gasping to regain his breath a jolt of electricity passed through his entire body, and he convulsed momentarily like a heart attack victim being treated with a defibrillator. The charge instantly deactivated and killed the billions of microscopic Nanobots in his body. In less than a second, he'd been returned to mortality. As the pain of the shock gradually subsided, the small pins retracted. Laying still and powerless on the broken table, his heart pounded and sweat dripped off his brow as he watched Buer remove the disc and slip it back into his pocket.

"This is only temporary," said Buer, his voice calmer and almost apologetic. It was frightening how quickly his demeanour and mood could change. "You need to focus, Robert. Once we have completed our task, I will make sure you're given back what I've just taken." Buer stood up and his full height appeared mountainous from Finch's sprawled out position on the floor. Much to his surprise, Buer even offered a supporting hand to help him up; begrudgingly and a little warily he took it. "We still have much to do," he continued, as Finch tried to dust down the wrecked and dishevelled suit. It seemed as if he'd been wearing it for a week. "I'm taking the Explorer to Colorado Springs Airport to meet Mitchell. You can come with me, seeing as you don't have any transport now. He's arranging for one of our jets to come over from Allentown. As soon as it arrives and refuels, we leave for Egypt. In less than twenty-four hours the virus will start to appear, and we need to make sure we get there before they close the airports."

"Do you think they'll try to recover the Key Tablet?" croaked Finch, watching Buer cautiously as if he were a rabid dog.

"Oh, I'm almost counting on it," replied Buer. "Which is why I'm keen to get out of the country as soon as possible. I doubt that's the last we have seen from our three friends. When I took the information from Oriyanna it also gave her access to my mind. She knows exactly what we are planning—" An incoming phone call cut him off. Instantly, Buer fished the handset from his pocket. Finch listened to as much of the conversation as he could – it sounded like Mitchell's voice on the line. He rubbed the circular scratches on his forehead caused by the pins; the small injury was scabbing over and itching like crazy. Without The Gift to repair the damage, he'd be left with a ridiculous looking mark for a good few days. "That was Mitchell," said Buer, ending the call, "he's just heard from the team taking care of Oriyanna's contact in Austin."

"And?" asked Finch, trying to ignore the prickly sensation on his forehead.

"The house was empty but they found a panic room on the first floor, they believe he was inside but they couldn't confirm it. The house has been destroyed, if he was in there he's dead, but I'm not taking anything for granted. She could have easily been in contact with him before they arrived." Buer paced through to the bedroom and retrieved his briefcase. "We need to get moving, that jet will be arriving in the next few hours. If you're lucky, you might even get to shower and change on the way to Cairo, you're starting to stink worse than poor old Roddick."

* * *

Vacantly, Adam watched the elderly waitress in a pink pinny balance two oversized plates of burger and fries away from the serving hatch and across the busy diner. Despite it only being just after nine AM, someone was about to tuck into a meal bigger than he could manage for dinner.

"So, how long do we have before this virus appears?" he asked Oriyanna, before forking a heaped pile of scrambled eggs into his mouth. He didn't feel much like eating, but the lack of food over the last day was making him feel rough, the dull aching pain from his head injury still at work. The two pain killers he'd necked a half hour ago had done nothing but take the edge off a little. The wound had healed, leaving a nasty scab he was constantly fighting the urge to pick at.

"I'm not sure," Oriyanna replied, staring at her half empty glass of orange juice, "twelve hours or so, a day at best."

"I need to phone Lucie," Adam sighed. "I need to warn her!" He pushed his half eaten breakfast away and reached for the basic prepay mobile that Sam had bought half an hour ago from the local hyper-market. Having purchased a phone, toiletries and some more clothes for Oriyanna, they'd all headed to the large disabled toilet at the back of the store. Taking turns at the sink they'd managed to get a pretty decent wash, although a shower was what each of them really needed. A bit of soap, deodorant and a quick brush of the teeth with a change of clothes had been better than nothing. Sam had also expertly dressed the small wound on Adam's arm caused by the one shot which had hit him; thankfully it hurt worse than it actually was. Allowing Oriyanna some privacy, they'd both turned to face the wall while she washed and changed into a new pair of faded blue jeans and a white, lightweight sweater. Her latest gunshot wound had healed before they'd even arrived in Canon City, much to the continued amazement of Sam.

"I need you to keep the line clear," she said, reaching over and taking his hand. "Once Xavier has phoned back you can call your sister." Her touch instantly relaxed him, but as soon as she removed her hand the panic and dread began to return. He wanted badly to take hold of her hand again, not only to make him feel better; he wanted to feel the way he had back on the imaginary beach when she'd been inside his head. Oriyanna sensed the longing in him and offered up a weak smile as a consolation.

"So who is this Buer guy?" asked Sam, breaking the somewhat awkward silence. Adam pulled his plate back and tried to force down some more breakfast.

Oriyanna switched her attention to Sam. "Back before the war," she began, thankful for the interruption, "when we first returned to Earth, he worked with me. I think he was in charge of the second or third team to come here," she said, swilling the remainder of her orange juice around the glass. "When things changed he became one of the main figureheads for the resistance against the Earth-Humans. Toward the end of the war, many of their Elders were killed in the bombing of Sheol. He was one of the survivors. He's not the head of their people, but he will be high up in the order of things and definitely the one in charge here at the moment."

"But the guy who took us, Robert Finch, he had the same healing abilities you do, yet you say you don't know him?" Adam cut in. He'd been amazed to learn in the car that the guy who'd abducted them both and chased them from the rundown lodge was the same guy who'd been the head of President Remy's Secret Service Team.

"No, I have never seen him before. Over the years they have obviously replicated the technologies we possess on Arkkadia. I didn't get much from Buer except for the details of what they're planning, but from the little information about Robert Finch I did manage to retrieve, I believe he was born here on Earth. I suspect he would be one of many, bred especially for the task. It's the most logical explanation as to how they managed to operate unnoticed; the events that are unfolding now were put into motion decades ago."

Adam nodded, thoughtfully chewing his breakfast, "And Xavier, is he as old as you?" he asked after forcing down a mouthful of slightly overcooked bacon.

"No, nowhere near," she smiled. "Anyone who becomes a Watcher was never around before the Great War, they would be too easy for the likes of Buer to uncover. Almost all of those who become Watchers are given The Gift as part of the role. As I said before, The Gift is only given to those who do a great service or offer great personal sacrifice for the betterment or good of our people." Oriyanna knocked back the rest of her drink, wincing slightly at the acidity. "It's been a long time since I had an orange," she added, "they remind me very much of a fruit we have back home." She placed the empty glass back onto the table and eyed Adam's full glass; he pushed it over to her, not feeling much like the drinking it anyway.

"So, how many are there like you?" asked Sam. Despite all they'd been through, he realized he still knew very little about her.

"Around ten thousand now," Oriyanna began, tucking into the fresh drink. "Very few in comparison to our total population, which is just under four billion. The majority of our people tend to live for around one hundred of your Earth years. Your genetics have evolved to be the same as ours, over the last few centuries we have seen that Earth-Humans are living longer and longer." Adam pushed the plate away for a second time as the sound of smashing crockery came from the kitchen. The loud noise made them all jump.

"Are you finished with that?" asked Sam, eyeing up the remaining food.

"Yeah. I don't know how you can feel like eating at a time like this," Adam pointed out.

"I don't really feel like it; just don't want to waste the food." Sam grabbed the plate and began squeezing ketchup onto the remainder of Adam's cold scrambled eggs. "You should have eaten more as well," he said to Oriyanna through a mouthful of food.

"I'm fine," she replied, "those sandwich things you had in the car weren't too bad. The phone suddenly lit up and played a very annoying tinny ringtone that for some reason, none of them had been able to change. The ringing phone earned them a few disgruntled looks from a family on the next table, as Oriyanna snapped it up and struggled to work out how to answer it. In the end Sam snatched it out of her hand and pressed the antiquated answer button before handing it back to her. He and Adam both sat watching pensively, trying to get the gist of the conversation taking place. There wasn't much talking from Oriyanna, she listened intently to Xavier, her eyes wide and staring past Adam, fixed somewhere in the middle distance. After a few very long minutes, she placed the handset back on the table.

"Well?" asked Sam, raising his eyebrows.

"We need to get to Albuquerque; Xavier has booked three tickets for us to Cairo, via New York."

"Albuquerque!" exclaimed Sam. "How far is that?"

"About five hours from here," she replied, "you do know how to get there, don't you?"

"No, not a clue; in case you forgot, I'm not a local. We were meant to be on holiday."

"It's okay," Adam cut in, getting to his feet with the phone clasped tightly in his hand. "We'll find it. When do we need to leave?"

"Now," she said urgently.

"Give me two minutes, I need to phone Lucie. I want to do it outside on my own, if that's alright?"

"Sure," said Oriyanna, smiling sympathetically, "but please, be as fast as you can, we can't miss the flight." She watched Adam head for the door, side-stepping around an unruly child dressed in a bright yellow Mickey Mouse jumper. The young boy was running riot, and weaving around other peoples' tables. "So, do you have anyone back home you need to call, Samuel?" she asked.

He shrugged. "Not really, I never knew my parents. I got passed from pillar to post as a child and lived with more foster families than I care to remember. Adam is about the closest thing to family I've ever had." Sam gazed around the busy diner, it was packed with people from all walks of life, innocently grabbing a Sunday morning breakfast before heading out for the day, all totally oblivious to the tragedy that was about to strike. He found himself wondering how many of them would die, how many loved ones would be lost. He fought the urge to jump up on the table and scream at them all to go home and lock their doors; sometimes there was a lot to be said for ignorance. He started to think about the simulated forecasts he'd seen during his army days, they looked at how quickly a highly-contagious disease could spread through the population. The results for some of the nastier man-made viral agents were horrifying; he didn't even want to consider how much worse this alien strain might be. Even if they managed to reach the Tabut, and Oriyanna could stop the virus, the death toll would be massive. In military terms they were now on damage limitation, and it was never a good position to be in.

"What about you?" he asked, taking the spotlight off his disjointed life and forcing the grim thoughts to the back of his head. "You must have friends and family back home."

"Not really," she replied a little distantly. "My parents died thousands of years ago; I can't expect you to understand what life is like for my kind. Although we are genetically almost identical, our culture is very different from yours."

"Must get a bit lonely. You know, being practically frozen in time like you are."

"It can be, yes. I think it's impossible for you to grasp what it's like to have lived for as long as I have. Normal human life is so brief, it's no more than the blink of an eye. I have seen so many things, so many changes. Both our worlds have turned many times to bring us to this point. If these are destined to be my final days, then so be it, but I won't be going down without a fight." She offered Sam a slightly uncomfortable smile that said she wasn't as brave as she was trying to sound. Underneath her ancient and tough exterior, she was still little more than a frightened girl.

"So, is Xavier safe then?" he asked, changing the subject. He could sense her unwillingness to delve too far into her personal affairs.

"No, not really. Three men turned up and tried to kill him about twenty minutes after I called, I just reached him in time."

"He got away though, right?" asked Sam. "Didn't you just speak to him?"

"Only just; they thought he was hiding in the house so they blew it up. He is meeting us in Cairo," she said bluntly.

"You said he booked three tickets?"

"Yes, why?"

"I was wondering if we would be coming with you."

"You don't want to?" asked Oriyanna, her voice full of concern. "Both of you have saved my life more than once now. I can't think of two people I'd rather have with me through all this."

"It's okay, I'm more than fine with seeing this thing through. I know Adam would go with you, even if I didn't. What else are we meant to do? Just sit around and wait to die?"

"Thank you," she said gratefully, smiling in relief.

"Do you really think we can do this?" he asked, keeping an eye on Adam on the phone outside; he was pacing up and down the pavement beside the diner, the phone glued to his ear. Sam wondered how he could even begin to approach the subject with Lucie. What the hell would you say? *Oh, hi sis, yeah we're having a great time here in the States – oh and by the way, there's a deadly plague about to strike so you might want to lock up the doors and windows, see you when and if we get back!* It certainly wasn't a call he would want to make.

"There is a chance, albeit a slim one," she replied flatly. Through the window she watched as Adam ended the call. He didn't head back inside; instead he just stood there, looking out across the car park. "We need to get going," she said, standing up and heading for the door. Sam followed behind, stopping at the counter to pay for their food before following her outside. Adam was still standing in the same spot, deep in thought.

"Did you speak to her?" asked Sam, placing a hand on his shoulder. Adam flinched slightly as the touch snapped him from his thoughts. His eyes looked red, as if he'd been trying not to cry. Sam knew that if Adam lost his sister, he'd be almost as devoid of family as Sam was, and it wasn't a nice way to be.

"Yeah, I woke her up, I didn't even think of the time difference. She was trying to sleep before she goes to work tonight."

"And? Did she think you were crazy?" asked Sam, trying to keep his voice as positive as he could.

"At first she thought I was joking, then she thought I was purposely trying to scare her. I think in the end she believed me, but I'm not sure." Adam had a puzzled expression on his face, as if he were still trying to figure it all out himself. "I told her to stay inside and keep an eye on the news. I asked her to seal up all the doors and windows as well."

"Well done, that's just what she needs to do," said Sam encouragingly, "I just hope it's not too late, I mean, this thing could be all around us now, we could even—"

Oriyanna fired a look his way that made him think twice about saying the rest. Sam was sure that Adam must be thinking the same thing, they could already be carrying the virus, without even knowing. One thing was certain, in the next few hours they'd know for sure.

"So do you have any idea where we are going?" asked Oriyanna, deliberately changing the subject.

"Nope, not a clue," Sam replied, trying to sound lighthearted. He scanned the packed parking lot until he saw what he was after. "One sec, I'll be right back," he added. Boldly, he strode over to a parked BMW and rammed his elbow through the window, the sound of smashing glass echoing across the car park. Not caring who was watching, he reaching into the BMW and grabbed a Garmin SatNav from the windscreen before walking hurriedly back. "Now I do," he smiled, tossing the device to Adam.

"Is getting arrested part of the plan then?" growled Adam, holding the SatNav as if it were poisonous.

"We're already driving a stolen car, I figured one more theft wouldn't matter. Besides, it's for the greater good."

"Yeah well, I'm not sure the local police department would accept or believe your mitigating circumstances," Adam replied as they reached the VW. Sam jumped into the driver's seat and rammed his screwdriver key into the ignition, bringing the engine to life.

"According to this it's just under three hundred and eighty miles," said Adam, fixing the device to the windscreen. "How long do we have to get there?"

"Five and a half hours at most," Oriyanna replied from the back seat. "The flight from New York leaves at six; Xavier said we need to be there no later than five o'clock."

Sam swung the Golf out onto the road and sped away from the scene of his latest crime. "I'd best put my foot down then," he replied, following the monotone female voice on the SatNav as it directed them toward the interstate. "And pray we don't get pulled over." Sam manoeuvred the little VW around a fuel tanker and just managed to clear a set of traffic lights as they turned red. "I don't even want to think about how you're going to get on that plane without a passport," he called back to Oriyanna, not taking his eyes off the road.

"Let me worry about that," said Oriyanna, leaning forward and raising her voice in order to be heard over the screaming engine. "I got you those guns, didn't I?"

Chapter 18

Annie Martin made three mistakes. Two of them occurred the moment she arrived at Albuquerque Airport; the third wasn't really her fault. Ultimately, all three combined into some strange act of fate which ultimately saved her life. Annie's first mistake was leaving her handbag attached to the hanger on the luggage trolley while she sat waiting for her friend, Sue, to come out of the ladies' toilets. The second mistake was leaving her handbag unzipped with her passport clearly on display. The third mistake, and the one that was no one's fault – except maybe her parents – was the fact that she was a blonde, twenty-nine-year-old female who bore a very small resemblance to Oriyanna, who in turn was in desperate need of a passport, something authentic that she could use. The fact that side by side the two girls looked different didn't matter, Oriyanna could make the officials see whatever she wanted; however, the more the document appeared to be hers, the easier the job would be.

With the dexterity usually more akin to the most talented of pickpockets, Oriyanna walked past the bag and palmed the passport straight into her pocket. Annie, who sat with her back to the trolley, wasn't even aware she was there. Even the elderly couple waiting to check in for their flight home to Miami didn't notice, despite the fact they were both looking directly at Oriyanna as she committed the crime. Nervously, Adam watched on from across the check-in hall, worrying that the theft of the girl's passport was just another crime to add to the growing list of offences they had racked up in the past few hours. Watching Oriyanna slip the document into her pocket and make good her escape, he allowed himself a small sigh of relief; whether or not she could actually use it was another matter. Her ability to mess with peoples' minds had worked a treat back in Colorado Springs; trying get out of the country on a stolen identity was a completely different kettle of fish.

Thanks to Sam's heavy right foot and the good fortune of not seeing a single police cruiser on their side of the interstate for over three hundred miles, they'd covered the distance in just over five hours, which included one speedy pit stop at a service station for fuel. Pulling into the short stay parking lot next to the terminal building, Sam had transferred a few essential items of clothing from both their cases into his hiking pack before tossing the rest of their stuff into a large recycling bin; the guns also suffered a similar fate. There was no way they could get the weapons on board the plane, even with Oriyanna's talents. This left them with a major problem, not only did they have no idea what they were walking into once they arrived in Egypt, but they'd also be unarmed. Sam had a contact in Gaza from his close protection work, but with his phone smashed and abandoned on the road back in Colorado, there was no chance of him being able to arrange anything.

Adam checked the departure board above the ticket desk, where Sam stood waiting for their documents to be printed. The American Airlines flight to JFK was on time, and as Oriyanna approached she gave him a sly wink, patting her hand on the pocket containing the passport triumphantly.

"Nice work," he said as Sam approached them, clutching the tickets. "Are you sure you can do this?"

"No problem," Oriyanna replied, a little more confidently than she actually felt. "Let's have a quick look at my new name." She removed the passport as boldly as if it was her very own, "Annie Martin," she read aloud, raising her eyebrows. "Not too bad!"

"Well, at least the hair colour and age are about right," said Adam, looking at the girl's picture." You do know you've just ruined her day?"

"Ready to get this done then?" Sam chipped in before she had a chance to do more than shrug her shoulders in a *never mind* fashion. He handed them both a small cardboard travel document folder. "The good news is we check in now for the flight to Cairo as well. Once they check your tickets and passport here that's it, until immigration in Egypt."

"So how does this all work?" asked Oriyanna, looking at the desk. The final check-in call for their flight to JFK had just been announced over the tinny PA system.

"It's quite simple," began Adam, "when you get to the desk the lady will ask for your tickets and passport, she'll check you in and confirm your seat for the next flight as well." He took the ticket folder from her and removed the documents – the name 'Oriyanna Summers' was printed boldly on the front of both tickets. Her lack of second name had forced Xavier to invent one; the booking wouldn't process without it. "Be aware, though, that the name on the ticket and the name in your passport are different, so just do what you need to do – okay?"

"Don't worry," she replied, taking the tickets off him, "I can do this. Adam, you come with me, I might need you." She reached down and took hold of his hand, her touch had its usual effect and instantly he felt as relaxed as someone sunbathing on a tropical beach.

Hand in hand they approached the desk as Sam followed a few paces behind; without the luxury of Oriyanna's calming touch it felt as if his heart was going to hammer its way out of his chest – everything came down to the next few minutes. Reaching the desk, he watched as she draped her arm over Adam like a love-struck teenager. Whatever she was planning, was in full swing.

The aging female check-in clerk who looked as if she'd fallen face first into a makeup counter greeted them with a wide, beaming smile. "Good afternoon, how many are checking in today?" she asked politely.

"Three," replied Oriyanna confidently. "My fiancé, myself and the best man," she turned to Sam, taking his passport and tickets which were poised ready in his hand. "We are going to Egypt to get married," she chirped, treating Adam to an affectionate squeeze. "I can't wait to see the Pyramids and ride on a camel." Oriyanna handed her the documents, putting her own to the bottom on purpose. The check-in clerk began sifting through them individually, carefully matching up Sam and Adam's passports to their tickets.

"Sounds wonderful," the clerk replied, glancing up from the desk, "I've always wanted to go there." She turned her attention to Oriyanna's ticket, glancing over the details and as she opened the passport, Sam held his breath.

"Oh, please excuse my photo," he heard her say. Daring to look, he saw her hand was on the clerk's, covering her perfectly manicured nails. "I was having a really bad day, and now I'm stuck with it, but I guess it's fine, isn't it? I mean, to be honest there's nothing wrong with it, is there? It's just fine! Besides, I can get it redone when I become Mrs. Annie Fisher, I never really liked Martin anyway. It's a boy's name."

"It's not that bad," the clerk replied, as if she were having a perfectly normal conversation, but there was a hint of distance to her voice which told Sam she wasn't quite as lucid as she'd been a few minutes ago. He watched Oriyanna remove her hand, and instantly there was clarity again in the woman's eyes. Oriyanna was obviously satisfied the job had been done. "Are you checking any bags?" she concluded.

"No, thanks," Oriyanna replied.

"Travelling a little light, aren't you, if you're getting married? There was a hint of suspicion in the woman's voice, "None of you have any bags?" She took their boarding passes out of the printer but kept them securely in her hand.

"We did – I mean, we do," cut in Adam. "Last year we flew to London to visit my sister and BA lost all of our luggage. Since then, Annie refuses to let an airline take our bags." He rolled his eyes. "We sent it all via UPS a few days ago, it's already waiting at our hotel in Cairo. What with the transfer and all, well, if the wedding dress went missing I'd never hear the end of it! We just have this one bag to carry on." He reluctantly let go of Oriyanna and took the bag off Sam, holding it up for the clerk to see.

The woman nodded her head in understanding as he placed his arm around Oriyanna's waist. "No problem," she said, her suspicion giving way to a wide, helpful smile as she started tucking the boarding passes into their passports. "Your boarding cards for both flights are here, so make sure you don't lose them. You can go straight down to your gate; they'll be boarding soon."

"Thanks," beamed Oriyanna enthusiastically as she took them from her. "Have a good day." She handed Sam and Adam their documents as they left the counter. "See, I told you it wouldn't be a problem," she whispered to Adam. "Although it will be much easier when you eventually do away with your strict border controls – it's all very primitive."

* * *

Gritting his teeth against the uncomfortable, ripping pain caused by the blunt razor, Finch gingerly dragged the metal blade down his cheek, trying his best to see what he was doing in the small, steamed up mirror. The shower and washroom facilities aboard the Gulfstream jet were no bigger than you'd find in a modest sized motorhome. Finch didn't really care, having been devoid of any kind of personal hygiene for over a day, even a wash in a toilet bowl would have been acceptable. Tapping the clogged razor into the small china sink, he turned his attention to the goatee beard they'd given him back in Allentown; he didn't care much for it. Taking a small pair of nail scissors from the grooming pack he'd found on board, he set about cutting it back to a length the razor might be able to handle. After another five minutes and a few shaving cuts that would now have to heal in their own good time, his clean shaven face stared back at him once again. Even without the beard, he still looked significantly different to the man he'd been back in Malaysia, but now they were so close to the end it didn't really matter. In the next few hours the virus was going to hit the Earth with a sucker punch. He couldn't wait to see how humanity would react; the thought of the chaos that would undoubtedly follow excited him. Having taken off from Colorado Springs, Buer had explained that as soon as they activated the Tabut, an EMP would instantly fry every electrical circuit on the planet. It would add nicely to the chaos caused by the outbreak, and make it even harder to control.

A slight popping in his ears told Finch they were starting to descend into Caracas, Venezuela. The small, sixteen-seater jet only had a range of just over five thousand miles, consequently the trip to Cairo would be a three stage journey. Once refueled, they would cross the Atlantic to Lisbon, Portugal, and from there they would fly on to Egypt. Finch quickly changed into a pair of lightweight, beige combat style trousers and a plain white tee-shirt that he'd picked up at the airport in Colorado Springs. Suitably dressed, he made his way through to the luxurious main cabin which looked more like a strange, elongated living room than an aircraft fuselage.

"There have been no transactions on either Becker's or Fisher's accounts since the fuel purchase," said Mitchell, as Finch sat down and clipped his lap belt on. Buer was sitting opposite the technician as he worked on a laptop. "It looks as if they're well and truly off the radar, sir, the last mobile phone location we had was five miles south west of the lodge."

"Okay, keep an eye on it for me," Buer replied. "If we have learned one thing over the last few hours, it's that we can't underestimate any of them. It seems Oriyanna got very lucky when she stumbled across those two. I don't think for a second that she will just leave it alone now; she knows what we are going to do. Now there is a threat to Arkkadia as well, she will be even more determined. One thing I am sure of is that we are a good few steps ahead of them, they won't have had the benefit of a jet at their beck and call. They'll be using the airlines."

"I'll run a check of outward passengers, but with no clue as to where they'll be flying from, it might take some time," said Mitchell, as a small pocket of turbulence shook the cabin.

"Do it, with any luck they'll close the airports down before they even get there." Buer shifted in his seat and switched his attention to Finch. "Feeling better now, Robert?" he asked.

"A little." Finch was in no real mood to maintain niceties with Buer, from the moment he'd helped him up off the floor he'd been acting as if nothing had happened.

"I hope you're not still brooding over what happened back at the lodge," Buer smirked at him from across the aircraft.

"No, not at all," he lied. "I think I just need to rest, it's been a long couple of days." Finch watched as the jet swept through some light cloud, revealing the sparkling blue waters of the South Atlantic. The jet continued its fast descent as they sped along the Venezuelan coast.

"Once we're back in the air I'd get some rest, it's going to be a busy day. I have General Stone and a few men from Allentown en route as well, they'll be meeting us in Cairo. I'm not taking any chances in regard to our three friends. I thought it best to pull Stone from his cover now, once things start to develop with the virus, the military are going to be all hands to the pump."

"Sir," Mitchell interrupted, "I ran a search for their names on all outgoing flights from U.S airports in a five-hundred-mile radius of where you last saw them."

"And?"

"Samuel Becker and Adam Fisher checked in for a flight from Albuquerque to JFK two hours ago, they also have an advanced check-in for a connecting flight to Cairo. Sir, they'll be in the air now!"

"Just the two of them?" asked Buer, looking out of the window as if he expected the two men to swoop in and destroy him like some bird of prey.

"I have a female passenger who checked in with them under the name of Annie Martin."

"Clever girl," Buer muttered to himself. "She's using a fake or stolen passport; I'd guess stolen, as it's not in her name and she wouldn't have had time to get one made."

Mitchell went back to work on his laptop, quickly tapping away at the keys. "I've just checked the flights they're on, and without delays we'll be on the ground four hours ahead of them," he concluded.

Buer smiled to himself as the jet dropped the last few feet and hit the runway with a jolt, shaking them all in their seats. "Well, Robert," he began, "it looks like you just might get the chance to dish out a little payback. Hopefully, this time you won't fuck things up!"

Chapter 19

The aircraft on the map crept along at a painfully slow pace. Adam had been transfixed by it for the last half an hour or so, watching intently as they drew ever closer to the Egyptian border. Sam and Oriyanna had both been asleep for the majority of the twelve-and-a-half-hour flight, Oriyanna's head pillowed against his shoulder for the last few hours. Although it had caused a little pain to develop in his neck, he didn't want to wake her. Sleep had been a luxury Adam hadn't been lucky enough to benefit from. He'd managed the odd half an hour here and there, but had never dropped off properly, always aware of the usual background noises experienced during air travel. The constant drone of the jet engines, the low murmuring chatter of passengers and cabin crew as they went about their business. Rolling up the sleeve of his jumper for what seemed like the hundredth time, careful not to wake her, he rubbed and scratched at the blotchy rash which had sprung up on his arm. The constant urge to give it attention had done nothing but make it redder and angrier as time passed. To make matters worse, a similar patch had started to blossom on his upper thigh. Adam couldn't see it, but the nagging, itchy pain beneath his cargo trousers felt exactly the same as his arm had, when it first drew his attention a few hours after leaving New York. It felt as if something was crawling all over the affected area of skin.

Leaning forward he freed the tepid bottle of mineral water from the netted pocket of the seat in front, unscrewed the cap and took a swig. As the dull pain from his head injury finally began to subside, another headache started, almost in conjunction with the rash. It felt like the ones he always got when he was working in a warm country, if he failed to take on enough fluids. The empty bottle in Adam's hand was the third one he'd drunk on the flight, but so far, it hadn't shifted the pain at all. Trying to take his mind off the ailments, Adam slid the window blind up halfway, immediately bathing their line of seats in the strong afternoon sun. Far below the blue, jewel-like waters of the Mediterranean stretched out away from the desert. The small aircraft on the map was obviously far from on scale, if it were to be believed, half of the 747 was now over the coast of Libya whilst the first class seats and the pilot were in Egypt. It made Adam think of a riddle-like problem someone had once told him.

If a plane crashes and half of it lands in one country and the other half in another, where do you bury the survivors?

It wasn't the most taxing of problems to work out for anyone with half a brain. You wouldn't need to bury the survivors.

The sudden influx of light caused Oriyanna to stir in the seat next to him. Adam slid the blind back down and returned his attention to the cabin, searching for a steward. He needed another bottle of water, his mouth feeling drier than the desert below. As she slowly blinked her eyes open, the rash on his arm began demanding his attention again. Adam slid his hand up his sleeve and went to work on it, simultaneously moving his shoulder to get some of the feeling back. Oriyanna yawned and stretched her legs out, and accidently kicked the seat in front, much to the annoyance of its occupier who purposely tutted loud enough for them to hear.

"Where are we now?" she asked quietly, her voice still sleepy.

"Just crossing into Egypt," Adam replied, scratching at the inflamed section of skin. The patch on his leg began to kick off, as if it were jealous of the attention its sibling was receiving. Sliding his hand out of the sleeve, Adam froze in horror at the sight of fresh wet blood on his fingers.

"Where did that come from?" asked Oriyanna urgently, instantly awake.

"My arm, it started itching not long after we left JFK." He rolled his sleeve up to reveal the rash, the top layer of skin had almost worn away from the constant scratching, leaving a bloodied mess, as if someone had rubbed sandpaper over the skin. It looked much worse than it had half an hour ago. "I've got a rash on my leg, too." Oriyanna didn't need to say a single word, he could tell by the look on her face what she was thinking. "It's just a rash though, right?" he asked in a panic. "I mean, I had pretty bad eczema as a kid, maybe all this stress has caused it to flare up."

"Have you noticed anything else?"

"Only my head hurts like crazy," he replied, his voice growing shakier by the second. "But different to how it felt after Finch took me, it's more like I haven't drunk enough water. I've had three bottles whilet you were asleep but nothing seems to shift it."

Oriyanna grasped his arm and examined the irritated skin, her eyes wide and alert, before placing her hand on his forehead. "You're running a temperature, too, can't you feel it?"

"I don't know," he whined, suddenly nauseous. "I just thought it was starting to get a little warm in here." Adam could feel a state of panic coming on. "Do you think..." he couldn't even bring himself to say it.

"*Ladies and gentlemen,*" the captain's voice announced over the intercom, "*I will soon be activating the fasten seatbelt sign for our approach to Cairo International Airport, we expect to have you on the ground in around thirty minutes. It's a warm pleasant evening down there, air temperatures are in the region of twenty-one degrees centigrade, that's seventy fahrenheit.*"

"Well, at least it's a damn sight warmer than it was back in Denver," said Sam, rubbing his eyes. "Shit, did I need that sleep. I don't remember a thing after..." he trailed off. "What's the matter with you two?"

"How do you feel?" asked Oriyanna.

"A little knackered still, but I just woke up. Why?"

"No, how do you *feel*?" she repeated impatiently.

Sam noticed the bloodied rash on Adam's shaky forearm, "Oh— what the fuck is that?" he cried in disgust.

"It came on just after we left JFK, he has one on his leg, too, plus he is running a temperature. Are you showing any symptoms?" Oriyanna was desperately trying to sound in control.

"I— I don't know," Sam stammered, rolling up his sleeves and patting down his legs, as if he were trying to brush off an invisible army of ants. "No, I'm fine! And what do you mean by symptoms?"

"I didn't say anything before," began Oriyanna. "I didn't want to make you both hyper aware of what to look for." She took hold of Adam's hand, but on this occasion even her touch didn't help the way he was feeling. "This virus starts by attacking the skin," she said seriously, "it's likely those who contract it will get a series of rashes and sores to begin with. After that, it turns every cell in your body against the other—"

"Okay, stop!" pleaded Adam, snatching his hand back. "I don't need to hear it. How long do I have?"

"I'm not sure," she replied truthfully. "I think maybe twelve hours at most before you can't function properly, then another hour before..." She couldn't bring herself to say it, and she didn't need to. "Adam, I'm so sorry," she concluded, dropping her eyes and feeling helpless.

Adam slumped dejectedly back into his seat, "I— I don't know what to do. What can I do?" he pleaded, gazing at Oriyanna through frightened eyes. A disturbance further back in the aircraft caught her attention, unclipping her lap belt she knelt on the seat and looked back down the fuselage. Three rows down, two male flight attendants were attending to a young boy of no more than ten, his frightened face was covered in red rash-like blotches which had started to bleed. She could just make out similar blemishes on both of his pale arms. The commotion was drawing the attention of a number of other passengers, causing the hum of background chatter to raise in volume, as if some unseen person had a remote control and was gradually cranking the volume up. Scanning the rest of the cabin, Oriyanna made out at least nine other passengers with similar symptoms, though the young boy looked to be the most advanced case and was the one drawing the most attention.

"It's started," she said, sitting down and refastening the lap belt. "You're not the only one, Adam," she continued, as if it would offer some comfort. "There are at least nine other sick passengers that I can see. How many people are there in this cabin?"

"I'm not sure," replied Sam, glancing around and mentally calculating. "Maybe a hundred and fifty, why?"

"That means just over six percent of people in this cabin are sick." She ran the numbers with the speed of a computer. "If we look at this as a cross section for the global population, it would mean that already over four hundred and fifty-five million people are sick, and that's inside the first twenty-four hours."

"What can I do?" Adam cried. He'd started to scratch at his other arm and the skin was showing the first signs of blotching.

"Drink plenty of water," replied Oriyanna comfortingly, as she pulled his hand away to stop him. "I know that sounds crazy, but you're going to lose lots through sweat as the fever sets in, if you don't replace it you will feel worse." She found her half-finished bottle under her seat, unscrewed the cap and handed it over. "Drink it," she encouraged.

"Is there nothing you can do?" exclaimed Sam. A mounting panic was starting to set in throughout the cabin. A stewardess rushed by, her hands covered in blood. Sam couldn't make out if it was hers or not. The worried chatter of the other passengers continued to rise, as more and more people realised what was happening.

"We need to get on the ground and to the Tabut," replied Oriyanna, keeping her voice deliberately calm.

"Why, what's the fucking point?" spat Sam, raising his voice over the growing bedlam. "We don't have the Key Tablet now, thanks to me. We don't have any weapons, what the fuck can you do? Nothing! That's it, game fucking over!"

The monotone bong of the intercom cut Oriyanna off before she could tell him to calm down.

"*Ladies and gentlemen,*" came the captain's voice, only this time it wasn't as calm and routine as it had been a few minutes earlier. "*We have a developing situation on the ground, air traffic control has asked us to remain in a holding pattern over Cairo for the time being.*" There was a long pause as the cabin noise suddenly dropped into a deathly silence. "*In the last few minutes they have halted all air travel, I'm being advised that with immediate effect all airports have been closed. They are working on a way to get us down as I speak, I'll update you—*"

The intercom went dead and a small, subtle shockwave rippled through the cabin. As the intercom died, so did the cabin lights and every inbuilt headrest TV screen. The silence brought on by the captain's announcement held on to the passengers of Egypt Air Flight 205 pensively, as if every person was straining to hear the same sound; but the sound they all longed to hear was gone.

The engines had stopped.

* * *

From the small café style bar at Cairo International, Xavier watched in horror as the Arabic subtitled BBC News program began to report the epidemic. Having landed an hour ago he'd cleared customs and immigration before heading to the arrivals hall to await Oriyanna.

Judging by the news report, the first cases had been reported while he was in the air. Over the last few hours, the story had gained pace. As more and more hospitals around the world began to report cases of the mysterious virus, the story had taken over the news completely. It had hit so suddenly that the initial reports were sketchy at best. From the forty minutes of coverage he'd seen, Xavier had learned that the first cases had appeared in China, England, Australia and the USA, and then like a bushfire, it had spread within hours, touching countries all over the globe. Some reporters in China were claiming people were already dying; the Chinese Government had almost immediately denounced it as a lie.

Xavier checked the arrivals board, the Egypt Air flight from JFK was still showing as on time but the growing military presence at the airport was making him uneasy. Something was happening, something big. As he stared at the LCD arrival screen it erupted into a flurry of activity, as every single flight's status changed to '*Cancelled*', prompting a wave of dissatisfied and shocked cries from those waiting to greet friends and family. The background noise became so great that no one noticed the tannoy announcement which first came in a hurried torrent of Arabic. Xavier didn't need to wait for the translation, like all of his kind he could speak, read and understand every widely-used language on Earth. They were closing the airport! After the announcer had finished in his native tongue he switched to English.

"*Cairo International regrets to announce that due to a developing situation, we are closing the airport with immediate effect. Please vacate your current building via the nearest emergency or non-emergency exit.*"

The queue at the information desk was becoming massive, as those waiting either chose to ignore the request or just didn't hear it. People began jostling for position and pushing each other out of the way. Xavier watched two Arabic men hurling a torrent of hurried insults back and forth before they became engaged in an all-out fist fight. Frozen to his chair, he watched as a number of soldiers marched into the arrivals hall and immediately began evicting people. Those who chose not to go quietly were grabbed and dragged from the building before being deposited roughly onto the pick-up and set-down area out front, like a gang of unruly drunks being ejected from a bar. Xavier couldn't quite understand why things were happening so fast, the virus was only on its first day and only hours old. Somewhere on the planet a research lab must have obtained an early sample and realized its deadly potential, it was the only explanation for the sudden turn of events. The crack of gunfire echoed across the arrivals hall, as one of the soldiers fired two rounds into the air in a desperate attempt to restore order. Xavier had seen enough, and collecting his bag he pushed his way through the ruckus and left the airport.

The hum of the nearby main road greeted him as he paused by the taxi rank. He didn't know what to do. Somewhere up there was Oriyanna's flight; closing the airports was one thing but what were they going to do with the thousands of flights currently in the air? They would have to land them somewhere and quarantine the passengers – the aircraft wouldn't fly forever. Not for the first time in the last few weeks, he felt useless. There was no conceivable way he could see her getting to him now. He knew Buer would ultimately be trying to reach the Tabut, and he knew that on his own and unarmed he had practically no hope of being able to stop it. Part of him wanted to hail a cab and head out to the plateau, while the other part was screaming to stay near the airport in case things changed. Standing frozen outside the arrivals hall, Xavier felt as if his body wanted to tear in two, until a beaten up beige Mercedes screeched to a halt right in front of him. Xavier watched as an unshaven, dishevelled man jumped out of the car, left the engine running and dashed toward the building, only to be stopped by a soldier who had taken up a post at the door. The part of him which was keen to try and reach the plateau won, and without thinking he rushed over to the old Mercedes and climbed in. Slamming the vehicle into reverse, he gunned the engine before leaving the ever-building chaos of the airport behind. Despite the developing events, the highway outside was still packed with Monday evening traffic, and for the moment things seemed relatively normal. It was a stark and strange comparison to the scene he'd just left behind. Xavier's mind was reeling, and he had no idea what he would do when he eventually got there. One thing had become clear though, he had to try and do something, even if he died in the attempt.

Staying clear of Cairo city centre, he sped through the smaller out-laying town of Al Abajiyyah, following signs for Giza. It seemed as if he was working blind, there was no way of knowing just how much time he did or didn't have. Buer could still be thousands of miles away, caught up in the chaos he'd caused, or he could already be in Egypt, maybe even out at the plateau. The thought didn't bear thinking about. Not for the first time, Xavier pushed his worries to the back of his mind and concentrated on the task in hand: getting there and not getting killed. As he approached the El Rawda bridge the labouring traffic eventually came to a compete standstill. Cursing under his breath Xavier joined a queue of cars, all trying to cross the muddy waters of the Nile. The afternoon sun streamed in through the dusty windows, making it uncomfortably hot. The vehicle's air conditioning had seen better days and even with it cranked up high, it did nothing besides offer a feeble trickle of foul, eggy scented air which only added to the unpleasant stale tobacco smell in the cab. Xavier wound the window down and leaned out, trying to see what the hold-up was. Up ahead, an old bus appeared to be broken down right on the bridge, steam pouring out of the engine compartment. The passengers who were gradually disembarking stood in a line by the railings, looking out over the river. A few cars back, someone began sounding their horn impatiently, as if their annoyance could suddenly fix the situation. Leaving the window down to try and let a little fresh air into the car, Xavier forced himself to relax into the seat and wait it out. His mind drifted back to Oriyanna and what it must be like to be stuck up in the air, thousands of feet above the city. Suddenly, he felt a small pulse race through the car. Immediately, the waiting traffic fell silent as every engine died in unison, leaving the bridge bathed in an eerie silence. One of Xavier's questions had been answered; he now knew exactly where Buer was. Unlike the majority of other road users, Xavier knew there was no point trying to restart the Mercedes. Abandoning the stolen car, he set out on foot; he still had a good few miles to cover. Among all the uncertainty, one thing was definite: in the next two hours, fate would decide the outcome.

* * *

"So then, Karim," said Finch, leaning forward to read the portly tour guide's name badge, "how would I go about getting some tickets to tour the inside of The Pyramid of Khufu?"

"Tickets go on sale at seven thirty AM," the guide replied in perfect English. "They only let around two hundred and fifty people in a day, so you need to arrive early to avoid disappointment." The small wooden hut was uncomfortably warm. Karim had the benefit of a desk fan blowing in his face, and selfishly, none of the flowing air was making it as far as Finch's side of the counter.

"And what about evening tours? My friends and I were hoping to go in tonight. We are especially interested in visiting the lower chamber."

"I'm sorry, sir," Karim replied suspiciously, "tours finish at five thirty, we have just locked up for the night. Besides, the lower chamber has been shut off to the public for some time now, the passageway down is too dangerous. I'm not even sure if we will be open tomorrow, the news is saying something about all tourist attractions staying shut. I'm waiting for an update from my boss in Cairo." Finch watched Karim start scratching at a red blotchy rash on his neck, and his hands also looked a little on the sore side. Karim obviously wasn't privy to the exact symptoms of the virus which was now busy at work on his body. If he had any idea, he wouldn't be so relaxed.

"So, there is no way you can personally take us in then?" Finch removed his wallet and fanned out a large wad of American hundred dollar bills. For a brief second, he saw the temptation flash across the guide's eyes.

"No, I'm sorry," he said firmly.

"What? Don't you have the keys?" Finch probed. "This is a lot of money, more than you must earn in a year."

"I have the keys, but I could end up in prison if I were caught. I have a wife and child who depend on me. I'm sorry, sir, but it has to be a no," the guide concluded, shaking his head.

"Prison," muttered Finch, raising his eyebrows in surprise. "Surely that must be better than dying?"

Karim's brow creased slightly as he tried to register what the strange, pushy American had said. "Dying?" he repeated, "Why would I—"

Finch whipped the silenced pistol up and over the counter and shot the guide squarely in the head. For a few seconds, Karim's thick legs held his body weight as a thin line of dark red blood ran down into his left eye, the confused expression still stuck on his face as if he were a living photograph. Finch watched as the inevitable happened; Karim's legs eventually gave way and he fell to the floor in a heap.

"I did you a favour," whispered Finch, as he ducked in behind the counter and began going through the dead tour guide's pockets, eventually finding what he was after clipped to a keychain on Karim's belt. The small bunch of padlock keys seemed rather unimpressive compared to the building they opened, there were no other keys anywhere in the small ticket office. He just hoped the keys would unlock whatever barrier or door sealed off the lower chamber. Tucking the gun into his waistband and hiding it under his shirt, Finch left the small office, flipping the sign on the door to 'CLOSED' as he went.

"Chatter on many of the government lines is suggesting they might close the airports in as soon as thirty minutes," said Mitchell, when Finch climbed back into the Volvo.

"That soon!" exclaimed Buer from the front seat. "Originally, we estimated it would take just over twenty-four hours for them to reach that point."

"It seems the CDC in Vermont got hold of some of the very early cases. The U.S government has a good idea of what they're facing, although they're not making it public knowledge." Mitchell shut down the iPad and placed it on the seat next to him; he always seemed to be glued to some kind of computer screen.

"Are we in?" asked Buer, turning his attention to Finch.

"The guide couldn't be persuaded with hard cash," he replied, tossing the keys to Buer who caught them with lightning fast reflexes.

"That's funny, I thought most things in this part of the world had a price. I take it you had to use other means?"

"You could say that," Finch grinned, placing the large Volvo into drive and creeping forward. Despite the developing situation everywhere in the world, there were still a good few tourists hanging around the area. Those who'd spent the whole day out exploring the plateau's many treasures might not even be aware of the unfolding events. Finch glanced in the rearview mirror; former General Harrison Stone was behind the wheel of an identical vehicle, following them. Finch could just make out his grey hair behind the steering wheel; he looked too short to have ever been anyone in a position of authority. Accompanying him were three of Buer's security team, Tom Ellis, Mike Hardy and Troy Jennings; hired muscle no different than the Malone brothers who would have no doubt been here, had they not been killed back in Colorado. Despite the gravity of the event, it was a relatively small team. The theory was simple, get inside the structure, then get to the lower level. From there it was up to Buer and what he'd managed to learn from the girl to make it all happen.

Finch abandoned the Volvo in an area designated for coaches. The last tours had left almost an hour ago, the only people now wandering around were roaming souvenir sellers and those families with hire cars enjoying the quieter evening period. Unless it was cancelled, more coaches would be pouring in once it got dark, bringing droves of eager tourists to watch the night time light and sound show. With events developing as fast as they were, Finch doubted there would be a party here tonight.

"You take up position outside," instructed Buer, leaning into Stone's vehicle. "Keep your eyes peeled, there's no point in us taking walkies. Once we get below ground, they'll be useless."

"No problem," replied Stone. His military experience meant he was more than used to taking orders. "Are you expecting company?"

"I doubt it, but stay alert," barked Buer. "Mitchell just checked, the flight Oriyanna is on is still inbound, and they won't land for almost an hour yet. There's a very good chance we will reach the Tabut before they land. If we do and it works – well, let's just say I don't think they'll be giving us any problems."

"And Xavier?" asked Stone.

"No sign of him. I think we can assume he was still at the house back in Austin when we destroyed it."

"If it's all the same with you, sir, I don't like to assume anything" said Stone bluntly.

"Fine," Buer replied. "Sit tight, it's going to be a long, but historic night." He patted the top of the Volvo and went around to the back, opening the trunk.

"Are you sure that's going to cause a big enough bang?" asked Finch, eyeing an explosive device in Buer's padded flight case. "It doesn't look like it would do much damage."

"The explosion doesn't need to be that big!" snapped Buer furiously. "When it detonates, the Tabut on Arkkadia will be active. The explosion will be amplified millions of times and it will cause more damage

279

than you could ever imagine. Now stop questioning and start helping." Buer clipped the case shut and handed it to Finch, who carried it by the shoulder strap. Taking the weight of the device he felt his back sag a little; it was heavier than it looked. Buer slammed the trunk lid down with a sharp crack before taking the Key Tablet from his pocket and examining it for a second. "Let's get moving," he instructed. "Mitchell; you're with us, I doubt I'll need it, but we might want your tech brain for something." Mitchell dropped in behind Finch as they walked out onto the flat-packed sand; a light evening breeze was starting to kick up a little dust which swirled around their ankles as they walked toward the Great Pyramid. The structure loomed oppressively before them, dwarfing even Buer's massive frame.

* * *

From across the plateau, Stone watched the three figures grow-ing smaller by the minute as they approached the ominous ancient structure. "Okay, let's kit up" he began. "I want line of sight on all four corners. Stay in contact, I've set the radios to channel four." He fished the small handsets out of the glove box and distributed them, keeping one for himself. "Anything remotely suspicious, call it in. We can't have this going south on us, Finch knows only too well how un-forgiving Buer can be about avoidable mistakes." He clicked his ra-dio on and keyed the mic, sending an immediate squawk of feedback through the Volvo. "Keep your guns in their covert harnesses. There are still tourists about, and we don't want to raise any suspicions." Stone cracked the door open and jumped down onto the sand. After the chilly air-conditioning inside the Volvo, the warm afternoon desert air hit him with the same intensity as opening an oven door. "Ellis, you and Hardy take the far side. Jennings, you take the back corner nearest to us. I'll take the front; I want eyes on the main entrance." The three men, all decked out in matching desert combat attire, nodded in understanding. "Once you're in position, check your radios, then remove the batteries and put them in this, until after the EMP." He handed them all a metallic zip bag. "Keep your phones switched on, that way you'll know when it's hit. After that maintain radio silence unless you have something to report." Stone went to the back of the rental and took three large Camelback bottles out of his holdall. "You're going to be out there for a few hours, so take these," he continued, handing out the bottles one at a time. "It will cool off considerably when it gets dark in the next hour, but stay hydrated. Is that clear?"

His instructions were met with a united "Sir" as they all tucked their drink ration into large hip pockets on their matching trousers.

"Okay, let's move out!" Stone concluded. Following the same line as Buer had a few minutes before, he headed out across the plateau toward the Pyramid. To his right, the Sphinx sat pensively, as it had for thousands of years, a stone guardian keeping a watchful eye on all that passed her by.

* * *

Finch climbed the rough cut stone steps first, the stolen bunch of keys in his hand. As he ascended he kept an eye on the few tourists below, making the most of the last light of the day to grab a few photos of the famous structures. They were going to have a nasty wakeup call when they got back to their hotels. He wondered how many of them had developed the rash and headache during the day but chose to ignore it, putting it down to the hot weather. Reaching the bar-like metal door he paused and examined the chunky padlock which secured it in place. The door seemed almost new, its predecessor had obviously failed to stand up to the harsh conditions of the desert like the Pyramids had. Shuffling through the keys he found one that showed the same manufacturer's symbol as the padlock. The key slipped in on the first attempt and clicked the lock open with ease.

"We're in," he said, turning back to glance at Buer and Mitchell who were waiting behind him. Finch took one last cautionary look around before cracking the door open and slipping inside.

The air in the entrance corridor was cool and damp; it smelt as if it had been sealed up in the pyramid for a thousand years. Thankfully, the lighting system was still on, negating the need for using torches. Following the entrance passage Finch led the way, and the deeper he went, the damper and cooler the air became, the lighting system casting the walls in an eerie orange glow. Following the downward sloping tunnel, Finch came to a switch in the passageways. The iron grated prison-style door which led further into the bowels of the structure was what he was looking for. The brightly lit tourist route switched to an upward passage which carried on to the Main Gallery.

"This is it." Buer's thunderous voice came from behind. It echoed off the cool stone walls, amplifying it so it sounded deeper and louder than normal. In the dim artificial light Finch checked the padlock. It bore the same symbol as the one on the main entrance. None of the other keys looked as if they matched, but holding his breath, he tried the same key. It fit. Whoever was in charge of the security had one set of locks for the whole site. It made sense, really, there was nothing inside the pyramid to actually steal. Finch swung the metal door open, and it squeaked loudly on its unused hinges, the shrill shriek echoing off the walls and bouncing off into the depths of the darkened corridor before him. The darkened stairs looked to descend forever, and if there were any lights in the bowels of the structure, they weren't on. Buer took his torch and clicked it to life; the beam sliced through the perpetual darkness like a dagger.

"I'll take it from here," he boomed confidently. "Mitchell, you come up front with your flashlight as well. The next chamber is a good twenty meters or more below ground, so we have quite a climb."

After a few minutes the stairs levelled out into the lower chamber. The chilled air had cooled enough for Finch to see his breath in the torchlight, as it bounced off the smooth flat walls. To his right, the room raised up onto a roughly cut platform which had a deep channel carved through the middle. "So, what are we looking for?" he asked, adjusting the flight case on his shoulder.

"Over here," came Buer's voice though the darkness. "We need to get down there." He pointed his torch to a pit directly opposite where they had come out of the access tunnel. Finch made his way over and peered into its mouth. Buer's torch cast back the darkness, finding the bottom around ten feet below. The base of the well-like feature was made of smooth rock. "That's where we need to be," claimed Buer, scaling the protective railing. "Take this," he said to Finch, handing him the Key Tablet. "I want us all to be ready before it comes down."

Finch and Mitchell watched as Buer jumped down into the pit, hitting the bottom with a thwack that bounced back up the shaft to meet them.

"I'll go next," said Mitchell, sitting down and sliding himself over the edge. Reaching up, Buer was able to catch hold of his feet and lower him down.

"Pass the case down," called Buer. Using the long shoulder strap, Finch leaned over the edge and lowered the case, until it was just a few feet from Buer's outstretched arms. Praying he wouldn't drop it Finch let go and hoped for the best. Through the gloom he saw Buer catch it and slide the case down his body before placing it on the floor. Finch tucked the Key Tablet into his pocket. The strange object seemed to be glowing brighter than ever, and there was no distinguishable difference between when he had or didn't have hold if it. Sliding his rear over the dusty rock, Finch eased over the edge. Buer wasn't there to support his feet, and with a flurry of scrapes and scratches he fell over and bumped down the side, hitting the hard rock base with a thump. The moment he hit the deck the seemingly solid rock floor shifted with a mechanical whine, stone grinding on stone causing a series of sharp cracks to echo through the chamber. Slowly at first, but with gathering pace, the base descended deeper beneath the pyramid than anyone had been for more than three millennia.

The drop lasted for about ten seconds before the stone elevator came to a grinding stop at the bottom. Buer ran his torch around the seamless circular wall; it seemed as if they were lodged in a stone tube. "Pass me the Key Tablet," he said, holding his hand out. Removing it from his pocket, Finch handed it over, the strange metal had stepped up its unusual glow another notch, and the vibrations coming off the metal were almost audible. "We must be close now," Buer exclaimed, holding the artefact up. "This thing is going nuts." He placed the Key Tablet against the curved stone as Finch and Mitchell looked on, both praying that something would happen. It was a good hundred feet back to the top, and with no means to climb they would be truly stuck. As the Key Tablet completed one circuit of the stone wall, a sound echoed up the shaft sounding like the release of gas under pressure. Part of the wall dropped away below the platform, revealing a perfectly smooth glass-like corridor that luminesced subtly of its own accord in the gloom. The metal appeared to be the same as that of the Key Tablet. The odd tunnel stretched down about another hundred feet before coming to an end. Buer stepped out of the lift shaft, and the moment his feet touched the flat glowing surface it started to shine brightly around him. Finch and Mitchell both quickly followed suit, and the gentle hum of the unearthly material resonated through their shoes and up their bodies like a tuning fork.

"I've never seen anything like it!" exclaimed Mitchell, staring around in wonder.

"No one has seen this for thousands of years," replied Buer, his eyes wide and triumphant. "Come on, we are almost there." Leading the way, Buer headed down the strange glowing passageway.

"What is this stuff?" asked Finch.

"Taribium," answered Buer, glancing back. "It's not a natural metal, it's a combination of three different ores found on Arkkadia – it's both a conductor and an amplifier." Buer reached the end of the corridor first. Unlike the featureless flat walls, it was beautifully inscribed, one side displaying an intricate tableau of the Earth as seen from space, the other an equally impressive etching of Arkkadia. It even appeared to be in scale; Arkkadia stood proudly, the larger of the two planets. Spanning the gap between them was a double helix style engraving which connected and joined the two worlds. Beneath the awe-inspiring picture ran a written engraving. The strange language matched the inscriptions on the Key Tablet.

"Is that Arkkadian?" Finch asked in a low voice.

"It is," Buer replied flatly, examining the diagram. "It says, 'Joined In Unity, Two Worlds As One'. The Tabut chamber will be just behind this door."

"Door?" questioned Mitchell. "It looks like a dead end."

"Things are not always as they seem," replied Buer, holding the Key Tablet up to a small smooth panel in the middle of the engraved surface. As the two metals made contact, they glowed with the colour of white hot steel for a brief second, before another loud hiss filled the air. The inscribed wall parted in the middle, breaking its perfectly seamless appearance. Earth and Arkkadia separated as the two halves drew back to reveal a breathtaking room, decked in the same mysterious metal as the corridor and the Key Tablet. The Tabut sat directly in front of them on a matching altar. Two long, smooth and rounded poles ran down either side, extending past the body of the artefact by three feet at each end. The main body was decorated lavishly on all four sides in a pattern resembled something you'd see carved onto a fine piece of wooden furniture. Sitting proudly on its flawlessly smooth top were two winged beings, one facing toward the east side of the room and one to the west, their backs arched as they looked jointly to the heavens.

"It looks just like the Earth's history books depict it," said Mitchell as he gingerly walked into the room, almost expecting to fall through the shimmering floor. Looking down, he could see his own upside down reflection staring back at him. The only thing that stopped the chamber from being a seamless metallic box was a small groove which cut the room perfectly in half. It ran along the floor, under the Tabut, up both walls and across the ceiling.

"This device was seen by the eyes of man long ago," said Buer. His voice fell flatly in the room, the walls failing to bounce back any echo. "They would have used Earth-Humans to help construct this room. It stands to reason that it fell into legend, the only thing becoming distorted over the years being its true purpose. Back in the early days, they would never have been able to comprehend its true meaning." He approached the altar and reverently ran a hand along the surface of the Tabut. Despite the coolness of the room, the metal was warm to the touch and glowed at the point of contact, leaving a strange trail of light as his fingers passed. "I have longed to see this for more years than either of you can comprehend."

"Why is the room cut in half?" asked Finch, bending down to examine the groove.

"When singularity is achieved, the west side of the room will sit in Arkkadia, the east will sit on Earth. In two hours from now, you'll get to see for yourself," replied Buer, unclipping the flight case and examining the bomb. Clipping it shut again, he carried the case across the room, placing it at the Arkkadian end of the Tabut. "When the two worlds join it will automatically appear in Arkkadia. When that happens, I'll power down our side, breaking the contact. They won't have time to react; it will detonate twenty seconds after singularity." Returning to the centre of the Tabut, Buer stood before the Ark like some manic preacher at an altar; bending down he inserted the Key Tablet into a small slot at the base, precisely in the centre. The vibrations in the room immediately grew louder, reminding Finch of the static heard if you were standing too close to an electrical substation. "After the EMP, I'll take the bomb out of the case and prepare it," Buer concluded, walking toward the east side of the device. He raised both hands and clasped the two poles, as if he were going to lift it up from one end. The moment his skin made contact, a pulse of electrically-charged air pounded through the room, throwing both Finch and Mitchell to the floor.

Chapter 20

Sam shot up from his seat and clambered over Oriyanna. Reaching across Adam he flung up the window blind and stared out. "We're still about eight thousand feet off the ground!" he exclaimed, glancing at the dead engines in a cursory manner. "This bird will glide without its engines, but if we can make it safely to the ground from this altitude, I don't know." He gazed down at the desert below; they might have descended a good twenty thousand feet from cruising altitude on their halted approach into Cairo, but they were still frighteningly high.

"We have two hours," Oriyanna cut in, seeming oblivious to the crippled state of the aircraft. "In two hours, the Tabut will hold enough power to achieve singularity. Once that happens, we lose all hope of stopping the virus and saving my home from that bomb."

"Yeah, thanks for adding to the pressure of the situation," snapped Sam. "You might not even get to worry about the if's, but's and maybe's. The chances of anyone walking away from this when we do hit the ground are slim. You have a better chance than most, hell, you fell from fucking space and you're still here. The rest of us won't be quite so lucky." The panic in the cabin was spreading; barely twenty seconds had passed since the EMP hit the aircraft. Flight attendants were trying to keep the situation calm, but failing miserably. Despite the lack of attention from their passengers, they continued to bark out crash landing procedures, as if they were nothing more than auto-mated machines.

"Oh well," Adam said in a resigned tone, "at least I won't have to worry about dying from the virus." It seemed strange, but it was almost a relief to know that the last two days of hell were coming to an end. Sure, the world would turn to shit over the next few weeks, but at least he wouldn't be there to witness it.

"You're not dead yet," Oriyanna reassured him, her eyes wide and defiant. "None of us are!"

Sam could already sense a slight dropping sensation in the pit of his stomach as the 747 lost altitude. He unclipped his belt and climbed up onto the seat, studying the cabin. "There are seats right at the back, by the toilets. Follow me." Climbing down off the seat, Sam grabbed Oriyanna and pulled her into the aisle. "This plane is going to go down nose first. The longer we glide, the further down the nose will dip. People at the front won't stand a chance," he said hurriedly as they rushed toward the back, closely followed by Adam.

It was strange to witness first-hand, how different people were re-acting to their impending doom; the sick people in the cabin had been forgotten. Some families were frozen, clutching hold of one another, while other people prayed and still more cried. Dying was one thing, having time to actually think about what was going to happen was another. As they reached the back Sam was aware of plane angling forward, and the further he walked the more of an uphill struggle it became. The more the pitch changed, the more the panic around them grew. "Strap yourself in!" he shouted over the commotion. "When I say so, tuck your head between your legs and brace." He wanted to say, *kiss your ass goodbye*, but somehow, the expression didn't seem funny anymore.

Craning his neck to see, Sam glanced down the line of seats. From their position in the centre column, it was hard to estimate how high they were. He could just see the desert below; it was coming up to meet them fast. "We've got about thirty seconds," he shouted. "Get ready!" The passengers who sat by the windows were transfixed, staring wide-eyed at the swiftly approaching ground. Daring one last look, Sam could see the tops of trees and houses. *Oh shit*, he thought, *we're coming down in a built-up area.* A shudder ran through the whole plane as the pilot desperately tried to make the most of the hydraulic pressure and apply the air brakes, but it was a fruitless endeavour. "*Now! Brace!*" Sam shouted, his voice almost lost in the mêlée of panicked cries which had reached fever pitch.

The nose of the 747 hit the ground first, just as Sam had predicted. The impact tore through the cockpit, crumpling it like an old tin can and immediately killing the pilot and flight crew who'd been working bravely to try and save the stricken jet. As the aircraft screamed nose first along the ground, it collected up and smashed through a line of cars which had also been rendered useless by the EMP. One by one, their fuel tanks exploded around the fuselage. When the rear of the jet dropped, its massive wings sliced through the roofs of shops and houses on either side of the road, tearing off the silenced engines. The assaulting volley of masonry continued to pummel the plane until it tore through the airframe of both wings, ripping them off in a hail of sparks which instantly ignited the remaining jet fuel held in the massive tanks. Fire rained down like white hot hail, as the centre of the fuselage was engulfed in flame. As gravity took hold, the tail section slammed down into the ruined street, the impact immediately making it break away and come to an abrupt and neck-jolting stop when the tail fins wedged firmly between two shops at a crossroad. The remainder of the aircraft still had momentum and smashed over another road, sliding through a line of trees and splashing into the yellow-brown waters of the Nile where it came to rest, jet fuel spilling out onto the water, creating a river of fire around the fuselage as it burned.

"Still alive, still alive, still alive," Adam muttered repeatedly, his eyes tightly closed, his head buried deep in his lap. Oriyanna sat in an identical position beside him, clasping his hand tightly. Sam next to her was doing the exact same thing. The cries and screams of the other passengers were lost to the ear shattering sound of metal tearing and glass breaking. Adam felt the rear of the aircraft hit the ground; the force vibrating up through his body, shaking every bone. The abrupt halt in forward motion made him lurch painfully forward and the lap belt dug into his stomach, winding him and forcing his eyes open. The rest of the aircraft was gone, and two rows ahead of him nothing remained. The rest of the 747 lay in a crumpled heap at the end of a road, half of its massive bulk in the river. The street before him resembled a war zone which had just been carpet bombed. The cries of the dying and injured who spanned the gap between the two chunks of aircraft suddenly filled his ears as realisation struck him. They'd survived.

"Are you hurt?" cried Sam over the hellish noise, his eyes open, frantically searching about and absorbing what had happened.

"No, I don't think so," Adam replied in amazement; though the sores and rashes were still there, he seemed otherwise uninjured. *Buer's virus might just get to kill me yet,* he thought. Those who weren't near enough to the crash to be killed or injured were starting to appear, rushing to help anyone shouting loud enough to be heard over the cacophony of noise. Somewhere below them a fire was burning in their part of the aircraft. "We need to get out of here!" Adam shouted. The tail section had wedged itself at a forward angle, almost hanging them out over the road below.

"We need to try and climb down," said Oriyanna, weighing up their options. The thirty or so other passengers who'd been lucky enough to be seated at the back of the 747 were all still sitting in their seats in shock, seeming unable to believe they'd survived the landing. "Let me try," she added. With the dexterity of a cat, she unclipped her belt and slid down onto the back of the seat in front. Expertly she climbed over it and dropped down another row, bringing her to where the plane had split. Using the back of the seat and the floor of the cabin which formed a rough 'V', she scooted her way along until she reached the aisle. Positioning her legs in the walkway, she pushed herself out and slid down the carpet. Reaching the end of the makeshift slide, she dropped over the edge and fell the last six feet to the ripped up tarmac below. "No problem," she called back confidently. "Just follow the same route I took."

A few onlookers who'd been watching her daring escape began unclipping themselves, all eager to get out of the plane. Sam helped a couple of stunned students out of their seats and down into the aisle; Oriyanna waited at the bottom and caught them as they dropped. It was going to take some time to get everybody down; a few people were still frozen in fear, too scared to even remove their belts. Feeling selfish, Sam pushed Adam forward and followed him down the carpeted aisle and onto the street below. As much as it pained him, there wasn't time to help everyone. Further down the road, smoke was billowing out of the main body of the plane. People were frantically trying to help, but the heat of the burning jet fuel kept them back.

"We'd have been in there if you hadn't moved us," Oriyanna commented, watching the nightmarish scene through wide blue eyes. One by one the other survivors were freeing themselves from the tail section, and as they reached the street they all stopped and stared in horror at the burning wreckage.

"It's odd," said Adam, watching with the rest, "there are no sounds of sirens coming to help. Unless the survivors here can get those people out, they'll die. We have to do something."

"There are no sirens," replied Sam, "because that EMP fried everything. That's it, no more laptops, no more iPhones, no more cars. No more anything! Someone just pulled the plug on the planet."

"We don't have time to help those people," Oriyanna cut in, already working out the direction they needed to head in. "We have to get moving." She rushed over to one of the panicked locals, who seemed frozen to the spot, unable to work out who he should try to help first, "How far is it to the plateau?" she asked the stunned man. The confusion on his face wasn't from the scene before him, or from the fact that despite all that was happening, one of the survivors was asking for directions to one of the area's main tourist attractions. He simply didn't seem to understand English. Oriyanna realized her mistake and immediately switched to his native tongue, asking the question again in perfect, unbroken Arabic. The sudden change in language seemed to surprise him even more. Sam watched on as the confused man eventually managed to give Oriyanna the information she needed. "It's about six or seven miles," she said, hurrying past them. "We need to head this way." She waved her arm down an adjoining street, away from the wreckage. "The nearest road bridge over the river is about a mile upstream."

"What about Xavier?" said Sam, remembering they were due to meet him at the airport.

"I don't know," she replied sadly. "We have to assume he's out of the game. We don't have time to go to the airport and try to find out."

Sam nodded and turned his attention to Adam, who was looking worse by the minute. "Can you make it?" he asked, noticing the dazed look in Adam's eyes. A feverish sweat had broken out on his forehead.

"Only one way to find out," Adam replied, following Oriyanna. "I know one thing, we didn't come this far and go through all this for me to just sit down and give up when we're so close." Sam tucked in behind them as they picked their way through the debris and rounded the back of the broken-off tail section. The scene behind the aircraft was just as disastrous. The straight road leading down toward the river was more like a demolition site than a suburban street. For a good three hundred meters, the houses and shops on both sides had been sliced away at the roofline. Around a hundred meters behind the rear of the jet, the tangled and crumpled wings lay almost directly opposite each other, wedged on top of two demolished buildings. Sam couldn't even begin to make out what the buildings had once been. Among the vast array of mangled, man-made materials were other more organic parts. People who'd been unlucky enough to be caught in the street when the 747 hit the ground hadn't stood a chance. It was far worse than anything he'd ever witnessed, in any of the war torn countries he'd served in. The worst of suicide bombing scenes couldn't hold a candle to the chaos and devastation caused by the downed Boeing. Sam found himself wondering about the thousands of other flights which would have been in the air when the EMP struck. The scene before him wouldn't be a unique one; all over the world, aircraft must have literally fallen from the skies.

The smashed wreckage of a dark blue Nissan pickup caught his eye. The vehicle was securely planted in the front of what had once been a hardware store. "Hold up a second," he called, "we may have something here." Crunching over the broken glass, Sam climbed into the wreckage. The two police officers in the vehicle were well and truly dead, both slumped over the top of each other.

"What is it?" called Oriyanna. "We don't have much time, Samuel. Please, we need to get going!"

"Feel free to crack on," he called back, "that is, if you fancy going into this thing unarmed. I know I certainly don't." Using his right leg as a pivot, Sam gained as much purchase on the passenger door as he could muster and tried to pry it open. After a few good, hard tugs, the door finally gave and opened with the reluctant sound of metal grinding over metal. "Adam, give me a hand here," he shouted, leaning in over the dead passenger. Sam felt like kissing the corpse at the sight of his Smith & Wesson M&P 537 pistol, still secured in its holster. Unfastening the weapon from its harness, Sam slid out the clip. All fifteen rounds were there, as well as one in the chamber, ready to go. "Here, take this," he said, handing the weapon back to Adam who was standing behind him, watching with interest. "These guys were in the right place at the right time," he commented, climbing further into the cab and reaching over the driver.

"I guess it depends on whose point of view you look at that one from," said Adam, examining the gun. "Are there any more?"

"Yeah, the driver has an identical weapon," Sam replied, using both hands to lever the body toward him. "I just need to free him a little to— there we go." The limp body finally moved, and Sam almost fell back out of the cab. Reaching over, Sam unclipped the pistol and slid back out into the shop. "I need to check the rear cab," he added, handing the second gun over. "Is there anything else we need?" Pinning his body flat against a display cabinet full of door locks and other household security items, Sam shimmied down the side of the police pickup.

"Some flashlights," called Oriyanna from the gaping hole in the front window. "We might also need some rope." Passing the guns out to her, Adam jumped over the counter and landed on the dead body of the shop owner, who was sprawled out on the floor, a large knife-like shard of broken glass wedged tightly in his neck. Ignoring the gruesome scene and with his shoes slipping in the sticky blood still seeping from the wound, he reached up and ripped three torches from the display and placed them on the counter. "Why do we need rope?" he asked.

"No time to explain now. Trust me," she shouted, as an explosion shook the air, causing some of the remaining intact window to shatter onto the ground. "Just be quick, we only have a few hours."

Following the line of the counter, Adam was making his way to the back of the shop, when a sudden wave of nausea washed over him. He doubled over and vomited onto the floor. Clutching hold of the work-top for support, he continued to retch repeatedly. Cold sweat started running from his already clammy brow.

"Are you okay?" Oriyanna's concerned voice came to him as she joined him in the store, resting a supportive hand on his back.

"I'll be fine," he said breathlessly, wiping his mouth on his sleeve. "If I get too sick, promise me you'll go on with Sam," he added.

Oriyanna nodded her head in understanding, "It won't come to that," she reassured him. "You *will* make it."

"Let's get that rope and get out of here," Adam said, changing the subject. "Every second counts, right?"

"Right," she agreed.

Shakily, Adam reached the stand that held a variety of different thicknesses of rope. Each one was hung on a rail so customers could reel off their required amount. "How much do we need?"

"A couple of hundred feet," she replied, trying to convert the measurements in her head. "That should easily do it, get some thick enough to take your weight." Selecting one which looked as if it could lift a small family car, Adam hastily began reeling the thick, white rope off the roll, wrapping it around his arm the same way he would usually roll up the lawnmower cable. Not bothering to measure it out, he kept going until the roll spun empty.

"Got it," he said, clambering back behind the counter and stepping over the contents of his stomach, which had joined the dead clerk's bodily fluids. "Sam, are you done?"

"Almost." Sam's voice came from the back of the pickup. After squeezing his way behind the vehicle, Sam had managed to jam open the crumpled tailgate, giving him access to the back cab. Reaching in, he slid out a large black canvass holdall and zipped it open. "Hello, beautiful," he whispered, staring wide-eyed at the contents. Had he not known better, the turn of good fortune might even have made him reconsider his lack of belief in the big man upstairs.

* * *

Xavier wiped the sweat off his brow and sat panting in the sand. With his back pressed hard against the limestone base of the Sphinx, he looked out across the plateau toward the Great Pyramid which loomed ominously against the night sky. The plateau, usually bathed in an awe-inspiring array of floodlights now lay silently beneath a blanket of darkness. Following the EMP, he'd had to cover the last few miles on foot, navigating the panic-ridden streets. While the loss of the world's constantly running media machine had halted incoming reports of the virus, word of mouth was still at work, prompting a widespread vein of fear to run through the population. Those who had chosen to stay out on the streets were there for no good reason. Over the last few miles, Xavier had seen widespread looting and an array of vicious attacks which thankfully, he'd managed to stay clear of. It was truly frightening to witness how in just a few short hours, law and order had broken down, giving way to outright anarchy. Thinking through his options, he turned his thoughts briefly to Oriyanna and the two who had been travelling with her. Not long after the invisible pulse which crippled the planet, he'd heard one plane come down a few miles to the east. In the distance, far off over the desert, he'd seen a second aircraft on its fatal and final descent toward the ground. He'd been too far off to hear the impact, but the rising plume of thick black smoke that soon followed confirmed his fears. There was no telling just how many people had been killed by the activation of the Tabut; it made him wonder if Oriyanna would have actually been able to bring herself to use it. In the old days when it had first been placed on Earth, there had been no complicated electrical systems to worry about, but at the present point in the Earth-Humans' technological evolution, they relied heavily on such things. Unfortunately, unlike the electrical systems on Arkkadia, the ones on Earth were not immune to the powerful EMP that was produced.

Staying low, Xavier left the Sphinx behind and hurried across the sand toward the smaller ruins of the Queen's Pyramids, which lay directly in front of his target. The plateau was dead silent apart from a stiff warm breeze that occasionally swept through the ancient buildings, creating an eerie whistling sound. Even the Tourist and Antiquities Police, who usually kept a watchful eye on the priceless monuments were gone. Reaching the first of the small pyramids he ducked down and kept his back to the front wall. Xavier took a second to catch his breath before racing along the line of small structures. Finally reaching the smallest pyramid he laid flat, chest pushed into the ground. Peering around the corner and allowing his eyes to adjust to the darkness, he could just make out a faint green pinpoint of light which bobbed and moved around at the corner of the Great Pyramid. Through squinted eyes, he watched it, mesmerized, for a few seconds before his brain registered what it was. Someone was standing guard and they had a radio. Whoever it was had somehow managed to save their small piece of electrical kit from the EMP, someone who knew it was coming. Xavier lay there for long seconds, looking hungrily at the dark opening into the structure. Somehow, he needed to get inside. He'd lost track of time and had no idea how long there was left, but he felt sure it had to be less than an hour now. He might even be too late. From his position he ran his plan of attack through his head a few times; the element of surprise was certainly on his side, but he was in no doubt that whoever the radio belonged to would be armed. Silently counting to three and taking a deep breath, he sprang from his hiding place and hit the ground running. The crack of gunfire tore through the deathly silence and a round slammed into his shoulder, followed by another which hit him square in the stomach. It made him double over and face plant into the ground hard. Raising his head from the sand he watched as the green light came swiftly toward him. Xavier closed his eyes and waited for the head shot that would end his life. He heard a shot ring out and bounce off the old limestone buildings. A sudden cry of pain made him look up; to his surprise, he was still alive. Amazed, Xavier watched as the green light staggered around in front of him, its owner now close enough to be revealed. The grey-haired man, dressed in full desert warfare attire, staggered wide eyed, clutching a gaping wound in his neck. His mouth opened and closed a few times before he fell to the floor with a thump. Through the darkness came a volley of shouts and footfalls, before three more sharp cracks of gunfire silenced them.

* * *

Hunkered down low in the old cemetery, Sam pressed his eye to the high powered night vision sight on the sniper rifle he'd found in the back of the police pickup. Thankfully, the battery pack had been out of the piece of kit, saving it from the EMP. Turning the weapon on its two-legged support stand he swept it along the base of the pyramid, taking in as much detail as he could through the strange green light. "There are two men stationed at both corners," he whispered to Oriyanna who laid next to him, her body pressed tightly against the ground. "I suspect there are two more posted at the back, but the scope can't reach that far." In the moonlight, he saw her nod her head in understanding. Glancing to his left he checked on Adam who was laid in almost a fetal position, his face blotchy and sore. Sweat had soaked his dark grey tee-shirt to his skin. Despite his ever-worsening state, he'd managed to keep pace over the seven-mile hike to the plateau, and the sight of him laid out on the ground made Sam wonder just how much more he had to give. The journey from the crash site had been fraught with danger, and on more than one occasion, Sam had needed to draw one of the pistols he'd recovered from the dead Egyptian police officers to ward off would-be attackers. The EMP had done nothing but escalate the civil unrest, and things had started to fall apart swiftly. "I need to try and draw the other two out," he said in a hushed voice, returning his eye to the sight and adjusting it slightly. Through the darkness he heard the sound of heavy footfalls, somewhere off to his left. Not taking his eye from the scope, he watched as the older of the two men who he'd had in his sights drew his gun and ran toward the sound, firing off two shots as he went. Sam cursed under his breath, the shot ruined; whoever was out there had really cocked it up. Following the armed figure in the sight, Sam squeezed off a round and watched as he immediately dropped his weapon and flung both arms up to his neck before falling to the ground. He knew it was a lucky shot. Swinging the rifle around he dispatched the other guard with a clean headshot; he had no time to register what was happening. Moving with expert precision, Sam swung the barrel of the gun toward the corner of the structure and waited. Through the darkness he caught the sound of shouting, as the two unseen guards realized they were under attack and came rushing to help their colleagues. The first one came into view, rounding the corner of the pyramid with his weapon drawn and ready. He had no chance. Sam breathed slowly out of his mouth and squeezed the trigger; before his finger had even reached the stop the man was dead. The baseline of stones swept past quickly as he swung the weapon back, searching for the man's friend. The few seconds' advantage had given the last gunman a chance to cover a little more ground, but he still had no idea what direction his attackers were shooting from. Sam clicked the next round into the gun without having to take his eye off the target. *Crack* – the high calibre round hit the gunman square in the upper cheek, snapping his head back and making him fall backwards in an almost comical manner.

"What's happening?" Oriyanna asked urgently.

"Someone else is out there," he replied, sweeping the area for any more guards. "Most likely some poor tourist or tour guide. I think they shot him."

"Did you see them?"

"No, and we don't have time to go looking now. We need to move." Sam reached into the holdall and removed two flashlights. "Can you carry the rope?" he asked Adam, who was just beginning to pull himself upright.

"Yeah," he replied in a croaky voice. "I'm not done yet." Over the past few hours, Sam had seen a completely different side to his lifelong friend. Instead of defeating him, the virus seemed to have made Adam more determined. His steadfast resolve to see the situation through was admirable. "Let's go – while I still can," he added, getting to his feet as a wave of shivers ran through his body. Leaving the rifle behind, Sam took up one of the pistols, holding it in the ready position. Staying low, the three of them covered the uneven ground as quickly as possible.

"You lead the way," Sam prompted, beckoning Oriyanna forward with his gun. Silently and with her usual feline stealth, she swept past him and rushed up the stairs to the main tourist entrance.

"It's open," she whispered, swinging the door inward. The darkness seemed perpetual; not even the bright new moon provided any hint of light. Oriyanna removed a flashlight from her trouser pocket and clicked it on, the gun poised and ready in line with the beam of light which sliced deeply into the descending passage.

"How long do we have?" asked Adam, using the cool stone wall for support.

"I'm not sure," she replied, heading down the passage. "Ten minutes, I'd guess; maybe less. Singularity hasn't been achieved yet."

"How do you know?"

"Trust me, you will know when it happens," she replied, reaching the crossroads style switch point. "It's this way." She swung the metal, cell-like door open and aimed the beam of light into the tunnel before heading down the steep slope.

Adam tried to keep pace on his shaky legs; the length of rope around his neck was starting to feel like a millstone. Gripping the loose rope banister for support, he fought to stay upright as they descended into the darkness.

"Can you feel that?" exclaimed Sam in a low voice as they broke out into the lower chamber; the walls were resonating like a double bass string.

"Every second, it's drawing enough energy from the Earth to power a country the size of China for a month," Oriyanna replied, clicking her flashlight off. The light coming up the well-like shaft in front of them was enough to see by.

"I guess that's why you needed the rope," croaked Adam, reaching the railing and leaning on it for support. Looking over, he could see the source of the light far below. "Is there no other way to get down?"

"No," Oriyanna replied bluntly, examining the drop for herself. "It's like a lift, the base is at the bottom and you need the Key Tablet in order to bring it back up. At the bottom is a corridor which leads to the Tabut chamber, it's still open at the moment. Once the Tabut has enough power, the corridor and the entrance to the chamber will seal automatically."

"So we have to climb down there, not knowing who or what is at the bottom, and hope that we don't get shot?" said Sam doubtfully, taking the rope from Adam and starting to uncoil it.

"It's the only way down," she replied, testing the strength of the railing. "This should hold it." Taking the end of the rope from Sam, she tied it around the thicker middle post before leaning back on it to test the knot. "Can you make the climb?" she asked, turning to Adam.

"I really don't know," he admitted, his whole body shaking in the cold air. "I feel like I'm burning up, but inside I'm chilled to the core."

"You need to try," Oriyanna encouraged. "I'm not going to let you die like this."

"I think it's a little late to worry about that," said Adam, smiling weakly. "It's okay; you do what you need to do. Don't worry about me," he concluded, stifling a coughing fit.

"Things are not always as they seem," she said, swinging herself up and over the railing. "There is always hope." Leaning back and allowing the rope to take her full weight, Oriyanna began the descent.

* * *

"Six minutes," said Buer, pacing across the chamber and kneeling by the bomb. "Six minutes and this will all be over." He flicked the power switch, bringing the weapon to life. The preset clock began counting back from six minutes and twenty seconds. "Make sure you're both on the east side of the room when it happens, I don't want either of you getting caught on the wrong side of the fence."

"You don't have to worry about that," replied Mitchell, looking back at him from the mouth of the long corridor. "I have no intention of going anywhere."

"You're both about to witness an event that none of our people have ever seen, an event that hasn't happened in over three millennia." Buer checked his watch again. "Five minutes!"

* * *

Oriyanna swung herself clear of the corridor and landed neatly on the stone base of the lift shaft. Looking up, she watched as Adam began his descent. It had been more than three thousand years since she'd seen the Tabut used, but she could tell by the deep tone echoing through the walls that there were only minutes left, and there wasn't time to wait. Removing the gun, she planted her back against the smooth stone wall and peered into the long, glowing passageway. She could just make out the figure of a man standing in the entrance to the chamber. Glancing upward, she saw Adam still had around thirty feet to go. Sam had obviously seen her move into position and guessed what she was about to do. He wasn't waiting for Adam to clear the line; he was already on his way down and catching up fast. She knew it was exactly ninety-six feet from the shaft to the chamber. The constant drone of the machine would mask her footsteps, but how far would she get before she was seen? The man glanced down the passage briefly before turning his back – it was now or never.

She launched herself into the glowing corridor, flicking the gun's safety off as she went. *Sixty feet* she counted silently, *forty feet.* Raising the gun she discharged a round; the bang was ear-splittingly loud in the narrow space. The shot missed and her target span around, shock and surprise visible on his face. Oriyanna was closing ground fast. She didn't wait, and firing another shot she hit him. It wasn't a fatal wound but he went down, clutching his side. Things happened fast; almost immediately the familiar figure of Finch filled the opening, his body silhouetted against the brighter glow of the chamber room behind. Raising his weapon he fired, and there was nowhere to hide in the confined passageway; she ducked left as far as she could but the round ripped fiercely into her left arm. Ignoring the searing pain, she saw Finch closing in on her. It was too late to fire again, and lowering her body Oriyanna weaved right and raised her injured arm. Her elbow contacted against his face with a thwack, sending white hot pain through her entire body. At the same time her foot caught his, sending her reeling forward. Desperately, she tried to stay upright, but it was too late and she had built up too much momentum. In horror, she saw the gun slip from her hand as she tripped over the writhing body of the man she'd just shot.

* * *

"Four minutes," said Buer, transfixed by the time on his watch. He felt more alive than he had in centuries; he was about to strike a deadly blow to Arkkadia, something none of his kind had ever managed to do.

"Can you see anything?" asked Finch, as Mitchell glanced down the passage.

"Nothing," he replied nervously, turning his back to the opening. He inclined his head toward the Tabut. "When it happens, will we feel anything?"

"I don't know," Buer replied, his head snapping up as the sound of gunfire punched through the room, drowning out the increasing hum of the Tabut. Horrified, he watched as Mitchell span around as he was shot, only to be met by a second bullet which slammed into his abdomen, sending him to the floor in a cry of pain. "No, no, no!" screamed

Buer, reaching for his weapon and taking cover against the wall. Before Mitchell even hit the floor, Finch was ready. Crossing the room in a few strides, he reached the corridor and squeezed off a round. Whoever was in the narrow passageway didn't have anywhere to go. Feverishly, Finch watched as his shot hit Oriyanna in the arm; a head shot would have been best, but at least he'd found his target. Before he had time to fire again she was on him, and with lightning speed her elbow made contact with his face, snapping his head back. Twisting his body, he watched her reel forward and fall over Mitchell before slamming down into the floor of the chamber. She was Buer's problem now – Finch knew she wouldn't be alone.

* * *

Sam hit the bottom of the lift shaft a second after Adam, and just in time to hear Oriyanna fire off two rounds. "*Go, go!*" he encouraged, but Adam was spent. Sam watched him double over and vomit a mixture of blood and bile onto the stone before collapsing. Another shot echoed down the passage, followed by a cry of pain that could only have come from Oriyanna.

"Leave me," croaked Adam, barely audible above the growing hum. "Just go." Reluctantly, Sam tore himself away; if Adam was going to die down here, it wouldn't be in vain. The person he was most hoping to meet was rushing in on him fast. Neither of them had a chance to fire a shot; instead, they charged into each other like two raging bulls. In a blind hail of fury and adrenaline Sam gained the advantage and pinned Finch to the floor. Letting out a loud, anguished cry he rained a torrent of punches down onto his hateful face, over and over. Not for the first time he felt Finch's bones crunch, but this was far more satisfying than it had been in the motel. He could feel it happening beneath his bare flesh, and this time there was nothing in the way. By the time he slowed down, the sight before him didn't resemble a face any longer, but Finch wasn't dead yet. Painfully, the bloodied pulp still managed to draw a breath, and blood bubbled up around where his nose had once been, each breath bringing with it a sickening wheeze. "Despite everything that you've put us through," growled Sam, staring into his wide, bloodied eyes, "I'm not devoid of mercy."

Somewhere through the pain and confusion the words rang true to Finch; he'd uttered the exact same thing to Euri, just before killing him. It seemed strange being on the receiving end of such a sentence. Helpless to do anything and without the aid of his tiny passengers, Finch could do nothing but watch as Sam Becker raised himself up off the floor, pointed the gun at him and fired.

* * *

Oriyanna was lifted off the floor by her hair. She suspected it was going to tear right out of her scalp.

"I'm not going to kill you, *yet!*" screamed Buer, his hot, rancid breath hitting her face. "First of all, I'm going to make you watch as your precious world burns." Oriyanna's feet were lifted clear of the floor as Buer flung her around like a rag doll, twisting her body so she could see the bomb. Through watering eyes, she could just make out the timer. "That's right," cried Buer, "in just over two minutes this all ends. You were too late." Viciously, he threw her struggling body to the ground, prompting pain to ignite in her wounded arm. Helplessly, she watched as Buer raised his gun and trained it on her head. "I'd think twice if I were you, Becker," she heard Buer say. "The moment you pull that trigger, I'll pull mine."

"We're all pretty fucked anyway," she heard Sam say as he walked into the room, his gun trained on Buer. "Adam's dead, thanks to your fucking virus. As for the rest of the world, well, that's pretty much gone to shit. What exactly do I have to lose?"

Oriyanna felt hot tears welling up in her eyes. Adam had been so close; to have come this far and died – it was almost more than she could bear.

"Well observed and a very good point," said Buer, nodding his head slowly. "It's a pity Finch wasn't as tenacious as you. Despite all you've been through, you still managed to get here. I actually admire that kind of resolve. Unfortunately, for you this is the end, it's time to let the grown-ups play."

Horrified, Oriyanna watched as Buer swung his gun around with lightning fast speed and pulled the trigger. Sam returned fire, but Buer's round had already hit him in the chest, ruining his shot; it hit the wall and ricocheted dangerously back. Sam went down hard, his gun spilling to the floor.

* * *

Adam knew he was dying, he'd known it from the moment he'd seen Oriyanna's face on the plane, right after she'd examined the bloodied mess on his arm. Somehow, it hadn't seemed real, but now it did. Over the vibrations which resonated through the pyramid he could hear Oriyanna screaming, followed by a booming voice which he knew belonged to the man-mountain, Buer, the one who'd tried to kill him back in Colorado. *Where is Sam?* he thought to himself. *Why isn't he helping Oriyanna?*

Summoning what little strength he had left, Adam got to his feet as a single gunshot rang out. Stumbling into the glowing passageway, he looked up in time to see Sam disappear into the chamber, his gun raised. Using the wall for support he staggered as fast as his legs could carry him, his mind not even registering the battered dead body of Finch as he passed it by, kicking the gun from his side. Through the delirium he watched, puzzled, as the pistol went skidding down the smooth floor, before coming to a stop a few feet in front of him. Bending down, he picked up the weapon; it felt as if it weighed a ton. Resting his weight back on the wall he continued his struggle. *I'm going to make it* he thought to himself as the brightly lit opening drew closer. *I'm going to make it.* Two more blasts of gunfire stopped him in his tracks, before he saw Sam's body fall to the floor.

* * *

"That's both of your little companions taken care of," grinned Buer. "Mind you, I have to give them top marks for effort," he added, glancing down at Mitchell who was still writhing around in a pool of blood. "You could have had the decency to hit him with a clean shot." Without pause, Buer raised his leg and stamped on Mitchell's neck, snapping it in one, sickening crack. "It's just you and me now; we can enjoy this together." Buer paced across the chamber and checked his watch. "One minute." He smiled, fixing Oriyanna in his stone cold gaze. "I would throw you through once singularity is achieved, and let you burn with the rest of your people, but I want the pleasure of killing you myself."

Oriyanna watched Buer lean forward, his hand reaching for her throat. As his massive body bent, she saw Adam standing in the passage, a gun raised in his shaky hand. Instinctively, she rolled out of the way as he fired; the single shot slammed into the back of Buer's head, spraying her with warm blood. Had he not been bent forward it would have hit him in the back. Oriyanna caught a momentary look of confusion and bewilderment flashed across his face before he fell forward, dead.

"*Adam!*" she shrieked, as the door began to slowly descend, sealing the room.

He tried to call out to her but his voice was gone, replaced by a fire burning deep in his throat. He couldn't even summon the strength to stumble the last few feet forward and fall into the chamber, which lay so tantalizingly close. As his legs went weak his body slid down the wall. Inch by inch the door dropped; he kept his wide eyes fixed on Oriyanna's for as long as he could, wanting desperately to go to her, wanting badly to help Sam. As the door slowly dropped, her face disappeared from view – it was over. Adam tried to relax against the wall and waited for the inevitable. Suddenly, strong hands were lifting him beneath his arms, pulling him forward, sliding him under the closing door. His weakened body screamed in protest but he went with it, not quite understanding what was happening. Sprawled on the floor of the chamber, Adam managed to roll onto his back and stared up at his saviour.

* * *

Whoever had killed those four guards had done so with military precision. Getting to his feet, Xavier suffered the pain of the two healing wounds stabbing through his body. Pushing the pain to one side, he rushed across the uneven stone ground toward the pyramid. Reaching the entrance, he felt his way along the walls, stumbling and tripping in the dark. He was sure that somehow, Oriyanna was here, she'd told him that one of her companions had seen combat; only a trained soldier or a very talented marksman could have dispatched those men so quickly. The building crescendo of sound which pulsated through the ancient structure only added to his sense of disorientation. Keeping one hand on the cool stone, he arrived at the switching point. Gripping the rope banister, Xavier descended down into the perpetually dark tunnel before arriving in the dim light of the lower chamber. He spotted the rope immediately and scaled the railing, peering down the deep shaft. Somewhere down there, someone was moving. Gazing down and dropping the first few feet, he watched the figure disappear into the passageway. Xavier let the rope slide through his hands, the building friction searing his skin. After what seemed like an eternity, his feet finally found the stone base. Releasing the rope, he hurried into the passage, just in time to see the same figure fire a single shot before slumping helplessly against the wall as the door began to close.

From deep inside the chamber, over the building upsurge of noise, he heard Oriyanna's voice cry, "*Adam!*"

Reaching the stricken body, he jammed his hands up under the man's arms and pushed forward, throwing him under the door as it dropped, before slipping through himself.

* * *

Oriyanna watched in amazement as Adam's limp body lunged into the room, followed by a tall, dark haired man. "Xavier?" she asked in disbelief, her voice all but lost to the noise.

"Where is the device?" he panted, reaching Oriyanna and helping her to her feet.

"On the west side of the room" she shouted, wiping Buer's blood from her face. Xavier rushed over and grabbed it with both hands, feverishly dragging it away from the Tabut. "How long do we have?"

"Forty seconds," he replied as the door sealed shut with a heavy thump. "Can you turn it off?"

Oriyanna ran her eyes over the mess of wires and circuitry. "No," she cried helplessly. "I don't know how to! It's probably booby trapped, too."

"Get them through!" Xavier said urgently, his voice barely audible. Oriyanna stared at him for a few precious seconds, her face showing her bewilderment. "Get them through, save them, save yourself – I've got this!"

"No, no!" she pleaded, realising his intentions.

"Yes!" Xavier replied firmly. "Go!"

Oriyanna knew it was the only way; reluctantly she backed off, warm tears streaming down her face. She reached Adam first; he was still conscious, his eyes wide and feverish. Gripping his shivering arm, she pulled him across the chamber and over the divide, and let go. "Twenty-five seconds," she heard Xavier shout as she reached Sam. Taking hold of him in the same way, she struggled to get his limp body into the west side of the chamber and deposited him next to Adam. She didn't even know if he was still alive. Glancing back at Xavier she fell to the floor and gripped them both tightly.

* * *

The low sound started deep down in the infrasound; quickly it built in volume, resonating through the entire structure. Sound waves travelled through the bowels of the pyramid, bouncing off the walls and seeking a way out. As the frequency intensified, the crescendo of noise spewed forth out of the two ducts on the external walls. For the first time in over three thousand years, the single, solitary musical note of Earth's silent energy echoed out across the plateau and into the night.

* * *

Adam felt the energy of the room flooding through his entire body. Using the last of his strength, he propped himself up on his elbows and gazed upon the Ark. Turning his eyes away from the brightly glowing artifact, he felt Oriyanna's grip, her arms tightly wrapped around his shivering body. *Not long now,* he heard her say inside his head. *Just hold on.*

The noise in the room sounded like the buzzing of a thousand bees, furiously buzzing inside his head. It built and built, and at the point when it felt as if his brain would explode it stopped, bathing the room in a deathly silence. All the hairs on Adam's body stood to attention as small charges of electricity passed over his body in tiny, excitable waves. On the other side of the room was the man who'd saved him. A thin veil seemed to separate them, as if Adam was seeing him through a thick pane of glass. In bewilderment, he watched as the man lunged forward and tore something from the base of the Ark, and in an instant, he was gone. Head spinning and with his body on fire, Adam closed his eyes and thought about the beach.

* * *

Xavier covered his ears when the noise reached fever pitch. Abruptly the sound stopped, as though a switch had been flicked. As the singularity joined the two worlds, the energy expanded all over his skin and deep into his bones. The counter on the bomb ticked under ten seconds. Forcing himself forward, he reached for the Key Tablet. The highly charged air felt thick, making it seem as if he was trying to walk at the bottom of a swimming pool. Xavier reached for the Key Tablet, and grasping the warm metal he tore it away from the Tabut. The shock threw him across the room when the connection was instantly broken, powering the device down. Clasping the Key Tablet tightly, Xavier watched the counter hit zero, and squeezed his eyes shut. The explosion tore through the chamber; the Taribium picked up the energy of the blast and amplified it, but without the power of the Tabut it couldn't reach its full potential. A violent shockwave spread out across the plateau, shaking the ancient structures. The roof of the Tabut chamber collapsed when the Taribium melted into a mercury-like substance. As the roof gave way, so did the lower chamber; and rubble piled into the lift shaft as the ground shook, burying the Ark forever.

Epilogue Part One

Precisely seven days, twenty hours and fifteen minutes after the destruction of the Tabut, a single, solitary Arkkadian craft dropped into orbit around the Earth. Immediately, it dispatched the Sheolian vessel which had been responsible for the destruction of their scout craft, not ten days before. The attack was accurate and swift, and there was no time for the vessel to fire a single shot in return before the craft was engulfed in a massive ball of soundless fire.

Unseen by the sick and diseased world below, the majestic craft then skipped gracefully across the upper atmosphere, its hull glowing bright red. As it sped over the North Pole, a single bright Taribium covered sphere, no bigger than a large weather balloon, fell from its base and hurtled toward the ground. From the craft, they monitored the device as it fell. Reaching an altitude of one hundred thousand feet, the sphere automatically detonated with a thunderous crack which echoed like a sonic boom across the entire globe. From the sphere spread a dark brooding cloud, working its way out from the point of detonation creating circles resembling a stone being thrown into a clear glass-like pool of water. As it spread, bright blue pulses of lightning flickered through it, igniting the oppressive sky in an awe-inspiring light show.

From an orbiting height of two hundred miles, those aboard the craft watched as over the next twelve hours, the dark mass grew in size until it engulfed the entire planet, hiding every last square mile of landmass and ocean. As the last traces of land slipped from their view, the rain began to fall. In every corner of every continent it started slowly, no more than a drizzle, which quickly built into a torrential deluge that would last for seven days. With the flooding and destruction brought on by the downpour also came salvation, for within the falling rain came the cure to the virus, developed from the Earth-Humans who had bridged the six hundred light year gap to the Arkkadian world. Thanks to them, humanity on Earth would prevail.

Epilogue Part Two

"Welcome back to the land of the living," said a familiar voice, as Adam opened his eyes and squinted at the brilliantly white ceiling above. "I didn't think you were ever going to wake up!"

"Sam?" he croaked. It sounded as if he hadn't used his vocal chords in days.

"Yeah, who else would it be?" Sam laughed. "You might want to sit up and take a little look at the view."

Adam lifted his head from the amazingly soft, warm pillow and looked over at Sam, who was propped up in an identical bed next to him, a wide grin creasing his lips. "Check it out," he encouraged, nodding toward the end of the bed. Adam eased himself up onto his elbows. His joints felt stiff and weak, like his voice, he suspected they hadn't been used in days.

"Are we dead?" he gasped. The wall opposite the bed was made of pure, seamless glass. It revealed a magnificent city; Adam suspected they had to be a good ninety stories above ground level. A breathtaking array of buildings rose like glass shards into the crystal clear, reddening sky, before giving way to a vast green forest of mighty trees that stretched into the distance where they met the mountains. The spectacularly lit sky held a large, blood-red sun that dominated the horizon.

"No, but I don't think we're in Kansas anymore." Sam chuckled, shaking his head. "Can you remember what happened?"

"Vaguely," Adam replied, thinking over the events in his head. "I remember seeing you get shot, and I remember shooting Buer to protect Oriyanna." The sound of her name on his lips brought him to a suddenstop. "Have you seen her?"

"No, mate," replied Sam. "I've only been awake for an hour or so. Before that I was well and truly lights out, I don't remember a thing after killing Finch and getting shot." He pulled down the neck of the plain black Tee-Shirt he was wearing. "It's funny that there's no trace of the wound at all," he marveled, studying his unscathed skin. "I guess if you need healthcare, this is a pretty good place to come, even if the rooms are a little sparse."

Adam looked around properly for the first time and realized what he meant. Apart from the awe inspiring view, which was decoration enough in itself, the room housed only their two beds. The floor seemed to be made from some kind of polished grey stone that sparkled in the light, and the walls appeared to be brushed silver. Above their beds hung two white squares which fed back to two monitoring screens via some kind of clear fiber optic cable that glowed neon blue.

"Do you know how long we've been here?" Adam asked, lifting the sheets to find he was dressed in identical clothing to his friend; a plain black soft Tee-Shirt and matching trousers. The material felt as light as air against his skin, and yet it was deliciously warm and comfortable.

"Eleven days," came Oriyanna's voice from the end of the room. "It's nice to see you're both awake," she added, as the door silently slid shut behind her, hiding any trace that it had ever been there.

Adam's heart almost stopped in his chest at the sight of her. The one-piece suit she wore was almost identical to the clothing they'd found her in a few weeks ago, but this time a bright red, silky, full length cape complimented the strange outfit. It began at her shoulders and fell perfectly around her figure, and her long wavy blonde hair shone in the evening sunlight, contrasting against the red material which flickered like flames as she crossed the small room.

"Eleven days?" said Adam puzzled. "Both of us?"

"That's how long the process takes," she smiled, perching on the end of Adam's bed and looking at them both through her wide blue, hypnotic eyes.

"Process, what process?" asked Sam, sounding a little confused.

"The Gift shall be bestowed upon he or she who does a great service or offers a great sacrifice in the service or betterment of our people," she said encouragingly. "Without you," she continued, seeing the shock on both their faces, "not only would I have failed, I wouldn't have survived the night after the crash. Look around." Oriyanna gestured to the vast city that spread out before them. "All of this is still here because of you, and Earth-Humans will endure, because of you."

"You didn't think to ask us first?" said Sam, sounding a little put out. "I mean, that's quite a big thing to just do to a person."

"Oh," she gasped, a little surprised at his tone. "If you decide you don't want it, then it's easily reversible."

"It's… okay," he replied slowly, a sly smile lifting his lips. "I think I'll just see how I get on."

"What happened back on Earth?" Adam exclaimed. He was a little ashamed to think that until Oriyanna had mentioned Earth, he hadn't thought about it, or what might have happened to his sister. Oriyanna reached across the bed and took hold of his hand, her skin as silky as the red cape.

"Your people have suffered greatly, but we have stopped the virus," she reassured him. "The cure came from both of you."

"How so?" asked Sam.

"As you know, before we came through Adam was sick, very sick," she began. "Amazingly, Samuel you were one of the very few who had a natural immunity. Using the virus from Adam and the antibodies from you, we were quickly able to develop the cure."

317

"What were the chances of that?" said Adam in amazement.

"Probably somewhere close to that of two species evolving to look exactly the same," she replied with a smile, remembering their conversation back in the RV. "Sometimes, fate can give us a helping hand."

"That's all very well," cut in Sam, "but just how long will it take to issue that vaccine to near on seven billion people?"

"Don't think so primitively," she almost laughed. "The process took seven days, but the airborne part of the virus was stopped within hours." A serious expression shadowed her pretty features. "We estimate that in the eight and a half days the virus was active, close to a billion will have died."

"That many?" said Adam in dismay, his skin turning white.

"You are a tough race," she reassured him. "You will come through this, maybe even more united than you ever were. It took a great tragedy to bring our world together and make it what you see now. There will be some hard days ahead before you can move forward, but move forward you will – of that we are certain."

"So, is it over?" asked Sam, "Are the ones who did this dead?"

"No, this is far from over" she admitted. "From what I've learned, we now believe there were many more Earth breeds like Robert Finch, all operating in secrecy."

"How many?" he asked, dreading the answer.

"We don't know," she said truthfully. "Hundreds I'd guess. We will be monitoring Earth very closely over the next few years; it is our hope that without leadership, they will choose to melt into obscurity and live out the rest of their lives in the mess they created. We have no real way of tracking them all down and bringing them to justice, at least, not yet. That's not to say we won't try. One thing is certain though, we will make sure that the message is delivered. Those on Sheol have some very tough times ahead, and those directly responsible will be made to pay. The man you killed, Adam, was called Buer. He was a very high ranking Elder on Sheol, one of the people directly responsible for the war. There is only one who is above him, named Asmodeus; ultimately it will be him we will look to bring to justice for this."

"How will you do that?" asked Adam, enjoying the touch of her hand in his.

"That's not something you need to worry about right now, we will do what we need to." Oriyanna released his hand and stood up, the cape falling perfectly around her figure, as if it had a memory all of its own. "Do you mind if I borrow Adam for a while?" she asked, looking at Sam. "There is something I'd dearly love for him to see."

"Knock yourself out," Sam replied. "I mean sure, yeah, of course," he corrected, noticing the confusion on her face from his first statement. "I'm quite happy resting up here."

"Thank you." She smiled, gesturing Adam forward. "Follow me; I think you will want to see this."

Adam got to his feet a little shakily, steadying himself on the side of the bed until his legs seemed as if they could take his weight. "Do I have a pair of shoes?" he asked, noticing the coldness of the floor on his bare skin.

"You won't need shoes," she replied, reaching the door as it magically slid open, creating a break in the perfectly shiny metallic wall. "Trust me." Adam followed her out into a narrow hall. The large window stayed to his left, the glass was so clear it looked as if you could fall right through. "The city you see before you is called Unia," she said proudly, gazing out at the view as they walked. "It is the city of the Elders. The governing council of Arkkadia operate from here."

"It's breathtaking," he observed. The towering glass skyscrapers were colossal when compared to some of the biggest on Earth, and far below, he could see the grid-like city streets. Tiny people were hurrying about like ants. There wasn't a single trace of a car or any other type of motorized vehicle. "Where are we going?" he asked, tearing himself away from the scene.

"You'll see," she teased. The hall opened out into another large, sterile room. Oriyanna paused and placed her palm onto what seemed like a flat metal wall, much the same as the one in their room. To his surprise, a part of the wall slid open, revealing a lift. Shaking his head in wonder, he followed Oriyanna inside, transfixed by the way the material on her cape moved as she walked.

His stomach lunged as they quickly descended down through the building. His ears popped with the change in air pressure before they finally came to a smooth, gentle stop. As the door slid open, he followed Oriyanna out into another large room, almost identical to the one they'd just left. A beautifully inscribed, shining archway stood proudly in the centre. Adam was in no doubt that it was made of the same substance as the Ark and Key Tablet.

"I guess you don't go much on furnishings," he commented, surveying the area.

"We have found over the years that there is no use in material things," she replied, glancing back at him. "This way." She paused and took his hand, not in a comforting way but much more intimately, reminding him of the way she had held his hand back in the airport when she'd used it as part of her ploy to get the tickets. Only this time, it didn't feel like she was acting. Walking half a pace in front, she guided him to the arch and went through.

Adam felt a strangely familiar sensation, for a brief second his hair seemed to stand on end as small, excitable waves of electricity danced over his body. The cold hard floor gave way to sand, and in the blink of an eye, he stood with her on the beach. "How?" he stammered, realizing where he was.

"Not too many days ago, you spanned six hundred light years just as quickly," she coaxed, clearly enjoying the baffled look on his face. "Surely, just a small jump of a few thousand miles can't be that hard for you to believe?" He looked back; the arch seemed somewhat out of place, sitting in the middle of the perfectly white sandy beach. "What

I showed you, back when we were in that lodge, was a real place," she said softly. "I was born not far from here, and this is the one place I can come to that is constant and remains virtually unchanged."

For the briefest of moments, Adam saw a flicker of sadness in her beautiful blue eyes. Reluctantly, he looked away from her and drank in the scene before him, his senses thirsty to experience it all for real. Everything was there; the glass-like blue water, the tiny islands on the horizon, gleaming like jewels under the magnificent large red sun. The mountains looked even more spectacular than he'd remembered; looking around in awe he picked up a faint floral smell which drifted on the light breeze; a new addition to what he'd experienced in his unconscious dream, but welcome nonetheless.

"This is real, isn't it?" he asked a little doubtfully. "I'm not still back in the pyramid, dying at the bottom of that lift shaft?"

"No," she purred, taking hold of his other hand just as she had before, but this time he couldn't feel himself being pulled away from her. Instead, he felt drawn in. "This is quite real," she whispered, leaning forward and kissing him. The kiss enveloped him like a warm blanket; he pulled her in closer, suddenly longing for the physical comfort that came with it. "Stay here with me?" she asked when they finally parted.

"What, on the beach?" he replied, his mind still spinning from her intoxicating touch.

"No," she laughed. "On Arkkadia. Stay with me."

"Y— you m—ean... mean that?" he stuttered, flopping down in the sand and gazing out across the ocean. Oriyanna sat beside him and placed her arm around his waist before resting her head on his shoulder.

"I do," she replied. "But only if you want to?"

"Of course I want to," he said. "But..." he sensed her looking up at him. "But Lucie, my sister. I need to know if she's okay." His heart seemed as if it was being torn in two. "I can't just stay here. And what about Sam?"

"He would be more than welcome. What you have done is known all over the planet , and there is no problem with you both staying, should you choose to do so. You have more than earned it." Adam dug his free hand into the soft sand and screwed it into a fist, releasing the fine grains from between his fingers.

"I can't," he finally said, holding back tears of frustration. "I don't know what kind of world I'll be going back to; I don't even know if she's still alive." He turned his head and gazed down into her eyes. "But I need to know."

"I understand," she replied sadly, sensing his pain.

"Sam can stay if he likes, but I can't. I owe it to my parents to look out for my sister."

"Oh, I doubt very much he will stay if you don't," she said, smiling sadly. "He will be asked, though."

"You could come back with me?" Adam suggested.

"I am afraid I can't," she replied reluctantly. "My place is here; I don't have a choice, and I suspect that soon I will be heading to Sheol to join the war."

"How long do we have?" asked Adam, reaching over and gently brushing her hair back from her face. As he did, she nestled her cheek against his palm.

"Eternity," she replied softly, enjoying the touch of his skin on hers. "You have many years of living to do, Adam Fisher. This goodbye will be nothing more than a blink of an eye. Go and do what you have to do, as will I. When you are ready, I will be here." She leaned in and kissed him again, as they both fell back against the soft, white sand.

Epilogue Part Three

Adam hit the full stop key on the old, antiquated typewriter for the last time and reeled the paper out of the machine while it offered up a series of fast, mechanical clicks. His MacBook Pro sat silent and dead on the other side of the room, a constant reminder of how things used to be.

"Is it done?" asked Lucie, leaning into the study, her hands cupped around a steaming mug of fresh coffee.

"I think so, although I'm still not sure Sam will read it," he replied, smiling at her. "He never was one for literature. Is he downstairs?"

"No, he's in the garage. He sourced a part for his motorbike, thinks he can get it running again." In an almost instant response to her statement, the uncommon sound of a revving engine echoed up from outside. "Sounds like it worked," she smiled, walking into the room and placing her mug on the desk before she picked up the thick manuscript her brother had been working on for the past six months. "I guess things will gradually start returning to normal now."

Adam leaned back in the chair. "Well, when you've seen the things that we have, you have to ask yourself what constitutes 'normal'."

"So it's all in here, then?" she asked, thumbing through the wad of paper as Jinx came slinking into the room and busied himself twisting about her feet.

"Everything," he sighed, thinking of Oriyanna, as he did almost every hour of every day.

" 'Watchers, by Adam Fisher'," she read, studying the front cover. "I like it!" She flicked to the second page. "For my sister Lucie," she read proudly, "Sam, who has become more like a brother than he will ever know, and Oriyanna – even though we are apart, you still fill up my senses. I particularly like the next bit," she said, smiling. "Dear Reader; As hard as this may be for you to accept, this is not a work of fiction." She placed the papers back on his desk and collected up her coffee. "Do you really think people will believe it?"

"I don't know," replied Adam, his voice distant. "Whatever they choose to believe, it makes for one hell of a story."

From The Author

First, let me start by thanking you for not only purchasing Watchers, but also taking the time to read it. The actual story had been in my head for nearly ten years. Thankfully, the independent publishing revolution has allowed me to both write the story and publish it with relative ease.

While the book falls into the Sci-Fi / Thriller genre, I have tried to keep a balance and not make it too heavy on the Sci-Fi part, with the hope that I can span both the Sci-Fi and classic Thriller/Action genres and produce a book that many people can both read and enjoy, without feeling blinded by science and theory.

The subject of the ancient alien theory has fascinated me for quite some time, and while I have used some of these theories and studies to base my book around, I have also used a fair bit of artistic license to adapt it and make both the timeline and the plot fit. Whilst I don't personally believe every aspect of these studies, there is some fascinating evidence to support it. I think we just need to read into it with an open mind and be prepared to ask that ever frustrating question: What if?

If the book has captured your imagination and you would like to read some of the non-fiction based studies, then there is a wealth of information both on the internet and in published books.

I would like to offer my personal thanks to my friend Sarah, who first encouraged me to write Watchers after I explained to her the basic plot line, long before I even put my fingers to keyboard (the modern equivalent of pen to paper). Then, as I began to draft out the first chapters, she took the time to read it in its early form and went on to help me edit the book, helping shape it into the novel that you see before you now.

So, after many months of work and many evenings and early weekend mornings in front on the computer, much to the frustration of my very patient fiancée, Laura, this is where I shall sign off. Maybe now you can go and read a little of the non-fiction based studies that inspired me to write this book. I dare you.

Connect With The Author

Twitter - @Steve_Boston32
Facebook - www.facebook.com/watcherseBook

Watchers Book Two: The Silent Neighbours – Preview

The world has changed. A little over two years ago, the Reaper virus raged across the globe, leaving a billion people dead. As the planet slowly gets itself back on its feet, tensions arise as oil prices soar and Russia puts a stranglehold on supplies, leading to a new nuclear arms race. As the world's superpowers rush to bring their nuclear defence systems back online, there are those who hope to utilise this fragile new world to deadly effect.

Unwillingly thrown into the fight once again, Adam and Sam find themselves in a battle against evil, a fight that will decide the fate of the human race on Earth once and for all.

* * *

The stars hung brightly in the sky, suggestive of a thousand fairy lights connected by an invisible mess of tangled wires. Sam Becker hunched his shoulders down into his Berghaus jacket and pulled the collar up an extra few inches, to try and keep out the biting cold sea breeze, which was like a frozen blade against his skin. Steadying the tiller on the small, four horsepower Honda engine, he gunned the twist grip throttle until it reached the stop. As the small Honda maxed out, he whipped his wrist away from the engine, instantly killing the motor by activating the emergency cut off.

Eyes fixed firmly on the approaching shore, Sam focused on the rhythmic sound of the water lapping at the aluminium hull, and the continuous distant whistle of the biting wind. Fruitlessly, he tried his best to relax. Just as he began to think he'd killed the engine too soon, a breaker picked up the rear of the boat and fired him toward the shore, faster than the feeble outboard could manage at full revs.

As the bow hit the shingle beach with a satisfying *crunch*, Sam was on his feet and jumping ashore, a spiked tie-off rope clenched in his cold, gloved hand. Driving the spike down hard into the shingle he heaved the front of the tender onto the beach, leaving the rear end bobbing in the shallow water. Satisfied the small boat was secure, he hiked his kit bag onto his back and scurried up the shingle bank, his feet making more noise on the loose stones than he would have liked.

The large and looming chateau that was Sam's folly lay in a blanket of ominous darkness at the edge of the beach, surrounded by long grass scrubland to either side. The chilled breeze stirred the unkempt plants, making them swoosh softly and invisibly in the night, a multitude of whispering voices announcing his arrival.

Reaching the edge of the shingle beach, Sam hunkered down by the wire perimeter fence and slid the backpack off his tensed shoulders. Removing his damp thermal gloves he dove an icy hand into the bag and removed a pair of latex ones. They offered nowhere near the same amount of warmth, and the cold sea air blowing in off the English Channel instantly felt as if it were slicing right into his flesh. Satisfied that they were in place, he closed the bag and removed a small pair of wire cutters from a pocket on the side. Starting at the base of the fence, he began snipping deftly at the thick wire, one section at a time. Each time a thick strand of plastic-coated wire gave way, it sent a shockwave of pain through his numb and throbbing fingers.

Satisfied that he'd produced a hole big enough to gain access, he pushed his backpack through and lay down on the coarse grass which had sprung up along the fringes of the beach. With small, wriggling movements he squeezed his way through the self-made breach and emerged on the other side. He was in.

Bending the wire back and disguising the hole as best he could, Sam collected up his bag, dusted himself down and ran in a half hunched position across the grounds and toward the building, his soft-soled shoes almost silent on the grass. An impressive, yet silent fountain lay to his right; it almost seemed as if the concrete gargoyle sitting proudly at the top had his stony gaze on Sam the whole way.

When he reached the back wall of the magnificent, beachfront property Sam breathed freely for the first time in what felt like an age. Back pressed to the masonry, he slipped along the building line silently until he reached the door. It was precisely where he'd estimated it to be when studying the satellite image of the house. Utilising the kit in his pack once again, he removed a small screwdriver from the same pouch and proceeded to pop out the beading from around the bottom UPVC panel. Timing the removal of each bead with a strong gust of sea air, he snapped all four panel retaining beads out of place. Despite the wind helping to disguise the noise, each time one popped out it sounded alarmingly loud in Sam's ears.

Pausing for a second to slip the screwdriver back into his pack, Sam removed a small electronic pass-card reader from his bag and gripped it between his teeth. With hands far too numb and cold to be performing such a delicate operation, he tapped the loose panel with his fingers, right at its base, and it fell in. With a swift and surprisingly accurate movement, he caught the top before it clattered onto the tiled floor on the other side. Allowing himself one more deep breath, he climbed headfirst through the gaping hole he'd just created.

The warmth of the chateau hit him like a deliciously snug blanket, but there was no time to enjoy it. The alarm panel immediately began beeping angrily to itself, as if annoyed by the midnight intrusion. Scanning the kitchen, Sam located the box by its flashing red light. He had precisely twenty seconds. His soft black plimsolls made almost no sound as he briskly padded across the darkened kitchen, which appeared big enough to host a TV cook off competition; camera crew, celebrity chefs and all. However, such shows were a thing of the old world, the world before the Reaper virus.

Reaching the panel, he removed the pass-card reader from his teeth and slid the credit card sized section into a slot at the base of the impatient panel. Holding the LED number pad in his shaking hand Sam watched wide eyed as the small electronic device worked its magic. *Ten seconds,* he thought to himself. The seconds ticked by painfully slowly, as each one of the six-digit deactivation code numbers appeared in bright red on the screen. With no time to spare, the full code finally blinked back at him. Not pausing for a moment, Sam hit the enter key on his control box and instantly relaxed a little, because the main alarm control box stopped its low pitched rhythmic beep and pinged to a welcoming green glow.

Awash with a mixture of relief and temporary elation, he noticed for the first time the smell of freshly ground coffee, mixed with the scent of bread that had no doubt been baked the previous evening. It made him yearn for a mug of the hot drink and something to eat –one, to help him draw some heat back into his cold bones, and two, to take away the salty taste of the spray which had continually assaulted his face on the trip from the cruiser to the shore. But there was no time.

Removing the card reader, he briskly crossed the vast kitchen and hooked his hand through the hole in the door, scooping up his bag. Replacing the card reader, he grabbed two syringes from a netted pouch at the top of the bag and slid them into his jacket pocket. Making his way toward the reception hall, a large clock, big enough to reveal the time in a Victorian railway station, told him it was fast approaching midnight. In less than five minutes the job would be done and with luck, he'd be back in that god-forsaken launch and on his way to the cruiser. Minutes later, he intended for the cruiser to beat full throttle and pointed firmly toward the English coast, which lay out there in a blanket of freezing darkness.

Sam knew the layout of the house well from the plans he'd studied the previous day and without pausing for thought he reached the right hand staircase leading to the first floor. Tiles gave way to a plush carpet which appeared to be grey in color. He was in no doubt that all welcome visitors would be asked to remove their footwear before going near it. He had no time for such etiquette. Taking the stairs two at a time, he was soon on the landing and looking at a line of white painted, Georgian style doors. A mirror image of the layout sat just visible on the opposite wing of the entrance lobby. For a split second, Sam wondered if he'd picked the correct side, but he brushed the thought away in an instant, he was confident he was in the right place. Stopping at the third door, he carefully depressed the handle, the coolness of the brass seeping through the thin latex glove. The large nursery was empty. Bright moonlight streamed in through a grand window on the far wall, casting strange shadows and highlighting the neatly made and empty replica race car bed. The Lighting McQueen duvet cover seemed somewhat out of place in this grand home, but the image of the bright red, grinning race car still smiled enthusiastically back at him all the same. The intelligence had been right, much to his relief; the family were away for the weekend. Although Sam had no compassion for his target, the thought of carrying out his task with a child in the house made his blood run cold.

Leaving the door slightly ajar he continued on down the landing, arriving at an identical door which brought the passage to an end. With the same level of stealth, Sam unlatched the door and slid inside.

The carpet gave way to an impressive wooden floor, which despite the darkness still seemed to shine. At the far end of the room was a king sized bed, this was where Sam's target would be.

One tentative footstep at a time, he drew closer, his breath almost clogged ny his dry throat. This was the tenth such target he'd taken out, then tenth such time he'd been in this kind of situation. It never got any easier.

The rhythmic rise and fall of the mounded bedclothes told him his target was exactly where he wanted him to be. In bed, and fast asleep. Removing one of the syringes from his jacket Sam tore the cap off with his teeth and tucked it away in his trousers. He was close now, he could hear the guy breathing, the slightly laboured sound which came from someone slightly overweight or not quite in the best of physical condition. The sleeping guy's wallet was on the bedside table, carefully, Sam collected it up and thumbed through the cards. His French drivers licence was there; pulling it halfway out Sam looked at the name and the photo – this was his man. Just before he closed the leather Armani wallet something else caught his eye, tugging the three strips of white card free, Sam removed a single airline ticket, destination Lima, Peru; the flight due to leave the following morning. Not a cheap purchase in this recovering world, mind you, his target was a wealthy man. No matter what the cost of the ticket, it was one flight that this sleeping guy would most certainly be missing. Sliding the ticket back, he replaced the wallet carefully onto the night stand.

Standing over the sleeping body, Sam whipped one hand down over the man's mouth, and in the same instant he slid the needle into his exposed neck and depressed the plunger. Instantly, the target's eyes flew open, wide and panicked, a muffled cry of fear reverberating from the underside of Sam's hand; at the same instant he felt warm saliva through the latex.

"Shushhhhh!" Sam said in a soothing and sympathetic tone. "Shushhh." But the sympathy was only evident in his voice; his eyes told a different story.

The Pancuronium took seconds to work, the dose just enough to send Sam's target into a state of complete muscular paralysis. Beneath his gloved hand, Sam felt the man's tensed jawline relax, telling him that the injection had worked its chemical magic. Holding one hand to his lips to emphasise the command to stay quiet, Sam gingerly removed his hand. A long trail of saliva formed a strand between the target's bottom lip and Sam's thumb, it stretched out for a good six inches before finally breaking and falling back onto the man's stubbly chin.

"Mathis Laurett?" Sam questioned in a low voice. "Is your name Mathis Laurett?" Sam knew he had the right man; he'd studied his target's picture more than once and his slightly chubby face had been on the drivers licence. Despite his dishevelled appearance, the man before him was undoubtedly who he was after – still, some small part of him liked them to confirm it.

"Ye— yes," the man croaked, struggling to speak with virtually no control of his throat muscles.

"Do you know who I am?" Sam asked calmly.

"Ye— yes," the man repeated, as if it were the only word he could say.

"Good, then you know why I am here?"

"Ye— yes," Laurett replied, his eyes wide and full of fear. More drool had joined the web-like strand on his chin giving him the appearance of someone who'd just suffered a seizure.

"Mathis Laurett," began Sam. "Under order from the Arkkadian Council you have been sentenced to death for your part in the Reaper Virus outbreak that led to the deaths of almost one billion people, twenty-nine months ago. It has been identified that you are an Earth-Breed. Investigations have shown that you were employed in the staff of Jaques Guillard, an Arkkadian Watcher. During that time, you were responsible for aiding in helping to identify him and ultimately, that

led to his death." Sam paused, he had read charges out like this on
ten previous occasions, however out of all the Earth-Breeds Sam had
executed, the man before him was without doubt the biggest player
he'd killed since shooting Robert Finch back in the bowels of the pyramid, over two years ago. Laurett offered up no comment other than
a gurgled and slightly choked attempt to swallow. "Furthermore, we
have information to suggest that you were travelling out of Heathrow
Airport on the day that the Reaper Virus was released into the population; we believe you are responsible for releasing one of the four
vials of pathogen."

"Please," croaked Laurett. "Please, I ha— have a f— family."

"And what of the millions and millions that virus killed – didn't
they have families?" Sam spat. "Do your family know who you really
are?" He could feel a deep rage burning inside, if he had his way, Sam
would have beaten Laurett to death then and there. But that wasn't
how things were done.

"No," Laurett croaked. "Please, I have information if you s— spare
me my life."

"I'm listening," Sam replied. The retort had taken him off guard, none
of his previous targets had begged for their lives or offered up anything
in trade.

"The one – the one you seek – he is here, and he has plans."

An ice cold hand ran its spidery fingers down the length of Sam's
spine.

For a second, he saw a wicked smile flicker in Laurett's eyes. "Your
silent neighbours are many in number, th— they are everywhere and
they are coming for you!" Despite the Pancuronium coursing through
his body, Laurett managed to spit the last word out with some venom,
beads of sweat starting to form on his wrinkled forehead. They ran
uncomfortably into his eyes and trickled into his messy grey hair.

"Bullshit," Sam replied, his voice slightly louder than he felt comfortable with. He knew they were alone in the house, but he still felt as if the walls could be listening.

"Believe wh— what you want Mr. Becker... you will see." Laurett's eyes were darting around wildly, as if he were searching for something, or someone. It made Sam uneasy. The effects of the drug were slowly wearing off, this time Sam did see him smile, an unmistakable hint of it on the bastard's chubby face. His lips drew back, exposing his yellowing teeth. "E-n-o-l-a," he gurgled.

"Who the hell is Enola?" Sam demanded, as he bit the protective cap off the second syringe.

"You – will see," Laurett croaked, still grinning like a loon.

Sam didn't have time to listen to any more craziness and plunged the needle deep into Laurett's neck. The smile whipped away from Laurett's mouth instantly. The second syringe contained a further dose of the drug – a deadly one. This dose would be enough to paralyse every muscle in Laurett's body, including his heart. A cry of fear spewed out of Laurett's drool-covered mouth as the needle plunged deeply into his fatty tissue. Five seconds after the plunger hit the stopper, his body convulsed violently before falling back into the now sweat-drenched covers, dead.

Stuffing the empty syringes into his pack Sam headed out of the room and swiftly down the lavish stairs. Laurett's final words rang through his mind, turning over and over again. *He is here, he has plans and he is coming for you!* And *Enola*. What the fuck was all that about? He didn't like it, not one bit.

In the kitchen he threw his bag out through the missing panel in the door and hastily followed it. Not bothering to carry out a repair, he hurried to the fence. Sam was always keen to flee the scene of an execution, but on this occasion, the desire was greater than ever. It felt as if he were running from some invisible pursuer, that just when he reached safety they would charge out of the night and grab him.

He knew one thing – he wanted to get as far away from the Laurett Chateau as possible. He was even looking forward to the five-minute ride in the freezing cold launch – every inch he put between himself and the French coast was a good inch. Thinking of the warm coffee with a hit of something a little stronger in it for good measure that he would make once back on the cruiser, and the phone call he would make to Lucie, Sam was relieved when his feet hit the loose shingle beach. He almost slid down the bank to the shoreline, stones avalanching around his shoes.

The small tender was gone. Frantically, Sam scanned left and right, he'd secured it right there, in front of the chateau. "Where the fuck are you?" Sam muttered, his whispered words igniting the cold night air with vapour.

A dazzlingly bright spotlight suddenly forced back the night, lighting the beach up like a stage. "Monsieur, restezoùvousêtes et placezvos mains survotre tête!"

Sam whirled around trying to focus on where the amplified words were coming from, his mind racing. "English!" he shouted, his heart pounding in his chest and through his ears. "I'm English!"

"Monsieur, remain where you are and place your hands on your head," the voice responded in a heavy French accent. "Police," the man added, as if he'd forgotten to include that important piece of information.

"Shit," Sam cursed, blood rushing through his veins at a thousand miles an hour. He heard unseen footsteps crashing on the stones, heading his way. The bright light made it impossible to see where they were coming from. Deciding that some course of action was better than none, Sam dropped his hands and ran, but he was too late. As he took flight he felt a heavy hand grab the back of his jacket, almost lifting him off his feet. A fist connected with his kidneys, and his legs gave way. Sam went down hard, face first into the cold hard shingle; he tasted blood on his lips, mixed with salt. Struggling to focus and ignore the foul eggy smell of the seaweed, he saw a shiny pair of black shoes come to a crunching stop before his eyes. Hands pulled him to his feet, way before his legs were ready to take his weight.

"Monsieur," the man with the very clean shoes began. "You are under arrest on suspicion of burglary."

"Burglary?" Sam croaked, still confused and trying to focus on the guy's face. A mere arrest for burglary would have been fine with him at that point in time, hell, he'd have pleaded guilty to it right then and there if the deal was offered. Sam knew, however, that the pending burglary charge would soon change, once they looked inside the chateau.

Thank you for taking time to read *Watchers*. If you enjoyed it, please consider telling your friends or posting a short review. Word of mouth is an author's best friend and much appreciated.